Interception

Interception

Graham Watkins

Carroll & Graf Publishers, Inc.
New York

Copyright © 1997 by Graham Watkins

First Carroll & Graf edition 1997

Carroll & Graf Publishers, Inc.
260 Fifth Avenue
New York, NY 10001

Library of Congress Cataloging-in-Publication Data

Watkins, Graham.
  Interception / Graham Watkins. —1st Carroll & Graf ed.
    p.   cm.
  ISBN 0-7867-0354-7
  I. Title.
PS3573.A839I58   1997
813′.54—dc21   96-36794
                                                        CIP

Manufactured in the United States of America

For all those who have found love on the Internet . . .

The author would like to thank the following persons:

Lauri Lowe, for Southern California locations, especially in and around Los Angeles, and for her many other contributions to this story;

Paul Arias, for New York locations, especially in Greenwich Village;

and, most especially, my wife, Peggy Arias, who carried on an Internet romance with me in the guise of "Andi Lawrence" and who actually wrote and sent the E-mail letters signed by "Andi" in this novel.

The author can be found on the Internet at:

http://www.mindspring.com/~coatl/

or E-mail to: coatl@dur.mindspring.com

Interception

Prologue

"I don't think I've ever," Nadine Berstrom was saying, "had such good times in my whole life. Not ever." Leaning back in the seat of the steel-gray Lexus, she closed her eyes and propped one sneaker-clad foot up on the dash. A smile played around her full lips.

Behind the wheel, a man with dark curly hair turned his head slightly, glancing at her through tinted aviator's glasses. When he saw that her eyes were closed his features relaxed, his trained smile faded. His face expressionless, he watched her for a few seconds while the car streaked down the narrow two-lane Southern California road, his gaze wandering over her reclining form, starting with her short strawberry-blond hair and moving down, past the long slim neck, on to the legs exposed by her brief shorts. Shaking his head, he looked back out at the shimmering desert highway.

After a moment Nadine opened her eyes. Outside, the sparse desert growth of cactus, creosote, and Joshua trees had again given way to bare rock formations and talus slides, and the late afternoon sun was beginning to paint the distant mountains ahead of them in orange and violet pastels. Leaning toward the window, Nadine watched the landscape go by. "It's so beautiful, so different from Florida," she observed. "The closer you look, the prettier it is."

"That's funny," the driver said. Glancing at her again, he grinned. "I was just thinking the same thing about you."

"Me?" she asked, obviously flattered. Her smile never fading, she puckered her lips and shook her head. "I was such a country girl—nicely educated and all that, but a hick, really. Until I got the computer, until I began to understand what the world was all about, what was out there." Smiling still, she gazed at him levelly. "Like you."

He laughed. "You're prejudiced."

"I don't think so."

On the right shoulder of the road, a sign appeared only to vanish as the car flashed past it. Nadine turned to look at it, trying to figure out its meaning. It bore only one character, two circles half-overlapping each other. There was nothing more. She turned her head back, dismissing it.

But, just then, the car begin to slow. "Dave?" Nadine asked. "We aren't there yet, are we? I thought your cabin was in the mountains . . ."

"It is," he replied quickly. "Pretty far yet, actually. I just need to make a quick stop here."

"Here?" she echoed blankly. "What's here?" She looked out the window again; there was nothing visible at all except for a rocky hill dotted by a few creosote bushes that rose from the dusty right shoulder of the road. Then she giggled. "Oh. Can't wait for the next . . ."

Her words faded as they came around a slight curve and a side road appeared on the right; the man she'd called "Dave" slowed and turned in. Wearing a slight frown, Nadine watched as the car negotiated this surprisingly wide and well-kept road, as it swung around and then up and over the low hill. Suddenly, a large and previously hidden valley was revealed.

Nadine's eyes went wide. In the valley, glaring in the desert sunshine, stood a complex of six bright-white buildings, the tallest of which bore the same double-circle symbol she'd seen on the road sign. Ahead of them was a gate and a guardhouse; beyond that was a parking lot nearly filled with cars. She could see people walking about down there; a forklift bearing some unknown load chugged across the pavement between two of the buildings. Atop one low building a small helicopter waited silently for its next user.

"Dave, what is this place?" Nadine asked, swiveling her head to look at him.

"It's a division of the company I work for," he answered offhandedly as he drove toward the guardhouse. "I just need to stop for a few seconds, that's all."

"But . . . Why's it out here? In the middle of nowhere? It's got to be twenty miles to the nearest—"

"Around ten, actually," he interrupted. "But it's out in the middle of nowhere, as you put it, because of the—let's just say the sensitive nature of the work that goes on here."

"Sensitive nature?" she echoed. "I thought your company made computer chips . . ."

"It does. And it's very competitive, there's a lot of industrial spying in this business."

"Oh . . . yes, well, I have heard that . . ." She looked down at the plant again, now seeing the perimeter of razor-wire topped fencing that surrounded it. "It just looks more like—well, a military installation or something . . ."

"Security is security, whether military or industrial."

"I guess . . ."

By then, they'd reached the guardhouse; Dave waved at the older man inside, who nodded and pressed a switch on the console in front of him. The gate, carried by a thick steel bar, lifted smoothly. At the same time, tire-puncturing spikes that stood up at an angle from the roadbed laid down cooperatively. The car, which had slowed only to a roll, sped up, passed through. Behind them the gate descended again. Ahead was another gate, which rose in its turn only when the first one was locked back into place. The car moved on, now into the complex of buildings. Here and there, from windows in the higher buildings and from an isolated tower on the west side of the complex, Nadine could see uniformed guards watching them, some speaking on telephones.

"I'm sure there are prisons," Nadine commented, "that don't have as complete a security system as this."

"Probably," Dave agreed. He rounded a corner and headed for the largest building in the complex, the one with the logo at the top. "The people I work for are very serious about this."

"Who exactly are these people?" she asked. "You've never really talked about them."

He laughed. "We haven't had the time, have we?" he shot back.

She reddened slightly and grinned. "I guess we haven't."

"The company's called IIC," he told her. "International Interface Corporation." Picking up a little speed, the car moved past the plain white facade of the building and headed toward a set of roll-up doors; two men were waiting just outside them.

"I never heard of them."

"Not too many people have. We don't make any end-user products, everything we make is sold to OEMs. You wouldn't've heard of us unless you're in the digital equipment manufacturing business."

"Sort of like Intel, then."

"Uh-huh. Except that Intel does end-user stuff, and they advertise to the general public—we don't." The car slowed again.

One of the waiting men waved to them, and at the same time one of the roll-up doors opened with an audible groan. Making a quick left, Dave drove the Lexus through the doorway and into a long corridor lined on one side by brightly lit offices. Several men, dressed in white, stood waiting in the corridor; two stepped aside to avoid the car as Dave let it slow to a halt.

Nadine looked around at the men, who were by now surrounding the car. Most, she noticed, had Asian features. One of them stepped quickly to her door and opened it. Like a doorman he then stood silently waiting. Nadine looked at him and then looked back at Dave, a question in her eyes. He hadn't moved, and no one had opened the driver's side door.

"Just get out, Nadine," he said gently.

A flash of fear crossed her features. "Dave?" she asked plaintively. "Dave, what's going on?"

"Just get out."

"No! Not until you tell me—"

As she spoke, the man who'd opened her door reached in and grabbed her right wrist, pulling her arm out straight. Too startled to resist, she looked at him in disbelief. Before she could react, a second man swabbed her forearm with an alcohol prep and jabbed a hypodermic needle into it.

She gave a little screech and snatched her arm back. The men let her go and stood watching, waiting. She slid toward Dave, coming half out of her seat. "What's going on?" she demanded again. "They gave me a shot, they . . ." She paused, and her head rolled slightly on her shoulders. She felt suddenly tired, her arms and legs felt heavy.

"Just relax, Nadine," Dave said behind her ear. "Just relax, don't fight it."

She reached for the door as if to close it but missed the handle badly. Turning toward Dave, she tried to say something but her words were an unintelligible mumble.

"Might've been a bit much," he said to the white-coated men. "You'd better get her moving. We've got a lot invested in her."

None of the men spoke, but one of them nodded. As they pulled her from the car, a gurney appeared, piloted by another white-coated Asian. She tried to stand, tried to struggle, but it was all she could do not to collapse. Her bewildered gaze was fixed on Dave, but one of the white-coated men was already closing the car's door. Putting it in gear, Dave began backing it out as the men lifted Nadine onto the gurney and started strapping her down. She was still staring at him; he gave her a helpless shrug and one of the quick grins that had so charmed her over the past few days. Then he was gone.

1

"There's got to be more to it than that!" Andrea Lawrence cried.

The heavy-set man seated on her office couch looked up at her with mild surprise. " 'Scuse me, Doctor?"

Andi didn't answer him immediately; already she regretted her outburst. "What I meant, Mr. Lukin," she said finally, "is that there must be more to the story than what you've told me."

Lukin shrugged and shifted his position; wrinkles in his expensive and stylish suit disappeared only to reappear elsewhere. "Not that I know about, Dr. Lawrence." He let out a deep long sigh, like escaping steam. "This whole thing fell out of the sky. I had no idea, I just didn't have any idea what was going on."

Andi shifted her own position, picked up a pen, toyed with it for a moment, put it back down. She stared at the file folder lying open on her desk in front of her, the folder with "Gerald Lukin" written on the tab. "Mr. Lukin," she began, "could we go back over this again? Perhaps I've missed something. You've been coming to see me for twelve weeks now, and the problem we'd been addressing has been—"

"That Billie and I had no sex life anymore. Right." He shook his head sadly. "Now that doesn't seem to be a problem anymore."

Picking up the pen and tapping it lightly on the folder, Andi looked first at him and then at the pen. "Okay," she said slowly. "Let's go back through this, one step at a time. Your wife—"

"Heard about this 'Chat World' on the Internet, on the computer," Lukin finished for her. "I didn't pay much attention, I saw it a couple of times, it looked like one of those video games to me—I don't know how it works even now. All I know is that you can meet people from all over, I don't know how."

"And your wife met someone . . ."

"Yeah. She met someone, all right. And the next thing I know she's telling me she's in love with this guy, and she's headed to Texas to meet him, and our marriage is over."

"Just like that?"

"Just like that. Out of the clear blue." He gave her a pleading look, as if begging for some sort of an answer. "Doctor, we'd talked about our problem—she'd insisted it was mostly my fault, and hell, I was willing to admit that, I know I spend too much time thinking about where I am on the corporate ladder, I stay at work too long, I bring too much of it home. I agreed to come here, to see you—I wasn't forced into it or anything, I thought it was best too, I really did . . . and then this, out of the blue . . ."

Andi pursed her lips. "I can understand that, Mr. Lukin," she said absently. Midlife crises, she reminded herself, were actually very common—they accounted for no small portion of her income, and the Lukins were certainly prime for them. "That she might leave you, I mean." Noting his rather startled expression, she quickly sought to clarify her words. "This sort of thing happens, Mr. Lukin, whether we like it or not—to all sorts of people, not just to you."

She paused again and leaned forward slightly. "But, Mr. Lukin—it seems to me I remember that you and your wife got that computer sometime after the beginning of your therapy here—wasn't it—let's see—about two months ago?"

Lukin shook his head sadly. "Well, actually it was in February—that's more like ten weeks, two and a half months. She—"

"So in that short a time she found this—what did you call it?"

"Chat World."

"Yes—Chat World. She found this Chat World—"

"A friend of hers told her about it."

"Okay. And she used it, and met somebody, and—"

"And fell in love with him."

Andi paused again. "Mr. Lukin, I'm afraid I'm still confused. How does this Chat World thing work? Is there a video link, can you see the person you're talking to? I didn't know that the—"

Lukin laughed, a short brittle sound. "No, you can't see the person. You see this little cartoon—they call it a, oh, damn, what do they call it? I can't remember, but anyhow, it's a little cartoon that represents the person. And you talk through the keyboard."

"You type your messages?"

"Uh-huh. And you can give each other your E-mail addresses and write letters to each other too."

"Letters."

"Right."

"You mean love letters?"

Lukin laughed again. "Love? Lust is more like it—sex letters." He lowered his voice conspiratorially. "I took a look at Billie's E-mail files," he confided. "Doctor, you could go down to the local video store and rent the raunchiest X-rated video they have, and listen to the dialogue, and you wouldn't hear anything any more graphic. I couldn't believe it. Billie *never* talked like that. Not to me, anyway. Not when we were dating, not when we were first married, not ever. I had a hard time believing she actually wrote those letters." Shaking his head, he trailed away: "But she did, she did . . ."

"But when did she meet this man? When did she first see him, I mean?"

Again Lukin looked somewhat surprised. "She hasn't, Doctor," he answered. "She's never seen him. Well, she's seen a photo he sent over the Internet, and I think she sent him one—but if it's the one I think it is it's more than twenty years old, she doesn't look anything like that now—"

"She's never seen him?" Andi echoed. "Nothing except a photo? How does she know it's his photo?"

Lukin shrugged. "Hell, it might not be, for all I know. For all she knows, either. It doesn't matter to her. She says she trusts him, she knows he wouldn't lie to her."

Andi's frown deepened. "So," she mused. "Your wife has fallen in love with a man she's never met in person. She's only written letters to him, she's only seen a picture and she can't even be sure it's a current one. She knows nothing about him at all except what he's told her on this 'Chat World.' And she's only known him for—what? Two months at the most?"

"She says she met him five weeks ago."

"Five weeks!"

Lukin rolled his eyes up, calculating mentally. "Yes. Five weeks now."

"And after five weeks she's ready to quit her marriage, fly out to Texas, and—what? Meet this man, see what he's really like?"

"Maybe stay. She won't guarantee me she's coming back at all."

Again, Andi paused. She'd met Billie Lukin, talked with her briefly as part of her husband's therapy; she'd seemed almost an archetype of the neglected businessman's wife. About forty-five, whatever charm she might've had in her youth had been used up raising her children and waiting for her husband to reach his career goals. She seemed pathetically desperate to help Andi find an answer to her husband's problems, to restore a part of her life that had been missing for years. She also seemed, to Andi, a rather unlikely candidate for any sort of affair, much less some whirlwind romance that could cause her to throw aside her comfortable life, her home in Scarsdale, and rush off to the unknown in Texas. And on the basis of letters, a meeting in some computerized chat room? In five weeks? It did not seem possible.

"Do you know anything," Andi asked almost idly, "about this man in Texas?"

Lukin was studying his shoes again. "Not much," he said glumly. "I did read some of the letters. He's my age—forty-eight—and he runs a pizza parlor in Austin."

Andi stared blankly. "A pizza parlor?"

"A little one. Storefront, mom and pop business."

Andi's look of confusion increased. "But—"

Again, Lukin offered her his brittle laugh. "Yes. You think it's a little strange too, don't you? I earn over three hundred thousand a year, with a lot more to come in the future if things fall my way. This guy barely makes ends meet, he says so in his letters."

"Well . . . money isn't everything . . . but . . ."

"Right. But."

"It does seem as if your wife made her decisions rather—quickly." So quickly I can't believe it, she added mentally. There must have been some warning signs, some clues. "Perhaps Billie had some of these things in the back of her mind already. Does that make sense to you?"

Lukin nodded again. "Maybe. I sure wasn't hearing a word about it, though."

"Sometimes people keep their true feelings well hidden."

"I guess. I just don't know what to do now. She leaves for Austin day after tomorrow; she won't say if she's coming back. I don't know whether to wait or call up my lawyer or what."

"What do you want to do? What feels right to you?"

"Wait," he replied promptly. "Wait. I was working on this marriage, Doctor. I know I haven't been the best husband in the world but I'm trying." Lukin's eyes misted up. "We've been married for twenty-seven years," he went on. "We raised two kids, good kids; we have a granddaughter. What're we going to tell them? I don't know what to tell them."

"That's not a problem you have to address right now," Andi said soothingly. "It sounds like you've made a decision to wait and see, and I think that's the right one for you." She glanced up at the clock on her wall. "We've run almost ten minutes over our time—can we continue this next week?"

"Yeah. Time to go; I'm late for an appointment myself. Life goes on, work goes on." He rose heavily from the couch and moved toward the door. "I'll see you next week, Doctor Lawrence."

"Fine, Mr. Lukin. Same time."

"Yeah. Bye." He opened the door, walked through it slowly, closed it behind him.

For several seconds Andi sat staring at the paneled wood, rocking her chair slowly, again toying with her pen. Lukin was not the first of her patients to talk about a relationship developing on the Internet, although his story was easily the most dramatic—assuming it was all true, that there weren't factors he didn't know about or wasn't willing to talk about as yet. Something of that sort, she told herself, had to be the case; it just wasn't possible that a woman—especially a woman so placid and fixed in her world as Billie Lukin—could fall in love so quickly with someone she'd never met.

Still, she thought, it's something new in the world, something that might well affect an increasing number of her patients—and something she knew virtually nothing at all about. A little research, she decided, might well be in order. She picked up the phone on her desk, rang her receptionist.

"Yes, Andi?" a woman's voice replied.

"Is Thalie Case here yet, Val?"

"Not yet. Late as usual."

Andi grunted. "And she'll expect a full hour anyway. Well, it isn't a problem, just ring me when she comes in. And Val—I'd like you to do me a favor."

"What's that?"

"Give Adam Luckman a call. See if he's available for lunch sometime this week."

"Okay, will do. Oh . . . here's Mrs. Case now . . ."

"Better than usual. Okay, send her on in."

"Will do." Val clicked off. Andi, shuffling papers on her desk, closed Lukin's folder and opened Thalie Case's file. As the door opened, she made an effort to dismiss Billie Lukin and her Internet lover from her mind, to focus on Thalle and her quite different problems.

2

At the top of the rise he himself had named The Overlook—it had no name on any map he'd ever seen—Grant Kingsley reined in the overactive Arabian two-year-old he was riding and, leaning forward in the saddle, gazed out over the striking view. In front of him the sparsely treed hills, the grass still brilliantly green from the spring rains though already tormented by warm dry winds from the desert, rolled smoothly and steadily down toward a small stream, a tributary of the Santa Clarita River further south. It ran, for the moment, with clear water. Beyond, to the north, blue-cast mountains rose against the intense blue of the California springtime sky. Looking like an actor strayed from the set of a Western movie, he pushed his Stetson hat back, exposing his sun-darkened face. The horse, not yet trained, shifted nervously. Grant glanced at the stallion's head, clamped his knees tightly against its sides, and gave a warning tug on the reins. The animal calmed. Looking back up, it seemed to him that the hills were no longer grass-green but sea-green, that he was looking across the waves of a storm-tossed sea, but that vision—like many others—faded quickly.

From off to his right, another horse came trotting down among the hills. At that distance, Grant could make out little of the rider. It was a young girl, likely a teenager, blond hair streaming from under her riding helmet. As he watched she leaned forward in her saddle and the horse broke to a canter, then to a gallop; silently he waited as the girl and horse crossed the valley, until at last they'd vanished among the hills to the east. She was, he told himself silently, just about the right age, just about right. There was no escaping it. Not ever. These hills, this countryside; it was as far from the life he'd once led as he could get, and still there were reminders. Maybe, he thought idly, it's just too close to the coast here; maybe someplace even less populated, like Wyoming, would be better.

No, he told himself. These memories had nothing to do with the proximity of the coast. No matter where he went, there would always be something. Besides, he'd put down roots here—as deeply as he felt he'd ever be able to put them down again. He pulled his mount's head to the left, gave the horse a gentle kick, and headed northeast, toward the ranch. A little under an hour later it came into sight.

The Double-K was a large and prosperous enterprise; it operated as a riding stable, as a dude ranch, and, thanks to the relative closeness of Los Angeles, made considerable money by providing horses and locales for Western movie shoots. It was the isolation that had originally drawn Grant to this area; since he'd had considerable experience with horses during his youth—he'd grown up in the Bluegrass area of Kentucky—the Double-K had seemed a natural place to seek work. He'd taken a job training the younger and more intractable animals, getting them used to saddle and rider; the ranch's managers had been impressed with his skill and perseverance, his patience with those horses that were more stubborn than usual. Now, after six years, he was an integral part of the ranch's operation, and, even so, he did not have to interact much with the other employees and did not have to meet the public at all.

That was the way he wanted it. He didn't trust people very much, not anymore, and for the most part he'd separated himself from them.

The horse, seeing the stables and corrals ahead, tried to break to a canter; Grant held him back for a moment, then pushed him on. For him to canter was fine, for him to think the choice was his was not. From here, the rider didn't need to do much of anything. The animal knew where to go, trotting into the barn and finding his own stall quickly. Dismounting, Grant tied him off and prepared to brush him down.

"How's he doing?" a female voice asked.

He glanced around; Paula Kirkland, the ranch's general manager and a part-owner, one of the "K"s of the Double-K, was leaning against the railings around the stall, one foot up, and smiling.

"Can't complain," Grant told her as he turned back to the horse. "Still nervous, still tries to insist on having things his own way, but he's getting there. By the end of the summer he'll be ready for the Hollywood guys at least."

"I hope so. He's a beautiful animal, he's got great spirit. The way things started out I was afraid he wouldn't be good for much of anything except maybe stud."

Grant smiled without looking at her. "Yeah, he was a little wild when he came in."

Paula laughed. "That's an understatement. But we couldn't lose, could we?"

"Not with what you paid for him, you practically stole him. Those guys in Florida just didn't know what they were doing."

"They just didn't have a Grant Kingsley working for them." The admiration in her voice was apparent.

He did look around at her then. Paula was in her late thirties, a divorcee, auburn-haired, far from unattractive as her tight-fitting jeans and plaid shirt revealed. She was still smiling; under his steady gaze she seemed to grow a little uncomfortable.

"I'm not the only trainer in the world, Paula," he said.

"No. But you're the most natural I've ever seen."

He shrugged. "I understand the animals. That's all."

She nodded. "Maybe. You've sure done a lot for us here." He turned back to finish grooming the horse; Paula waited, hoping he might say something else. After a while, he sensed that she was no longer there. Relaxing—her presence, like most people's presence, made him vaguely uncomfortable—he finished his work and left the barn. A short walk brought him to a plain 4WD Ford pickup; he climbed in behind the wheel, started the engine, and headed out onto the road.

Grant's drive home would take about thirty minutes—out here, traffic was seldom a problem. Leaving the ranch, he drove with practiced familiarity down the narrow and twisting country road that wound from the ranch to Telegraph Road—Highway 126—and to the Santa Clarita River; from there it was only about three miles through lush river-bottom land lined with citrus groves to the small town of Fillmore, where he again left the highway, turning south, following a sign that read "Moorpark." A few miles down this road he turned once more, to the left, where another narrow and winding road, this one lined by neatly layered sandstone cliffs, led south and east, up into the Santa Susana Mountains. This was the longest part of the trip—the road, uphill all the way, would not permit speeds in excess of forty—but soon the entrance to his driveway appeared.

Hidden among cottonwood trees, marked only by a mailbox, the driveway sometimes required the truck's four-wheel-drive capability, but today the ruts were reasonably dry and the truck climbed the hill without difficulty. Near the top, where the trees gave way to an open grassy knoll, was a medium-sized rustic house. Grant pulled the truck up under the carport at the left and shut off the engine. Knocking dust off his jeans, he walked up to the door and went inside, entering through the kitchen.

"Hey, Dad!" a youthful voice called as he closed the door.

He grinned. "Hey yourself, Todd," he called back. He tossed his hat on a rack by the door, revealing unruly dark hair with rivulets of gray. "Where're you hiding?"

Todd Kingsley appeared at the kitchen door. Tall—at eleven already within a few inches of his father—he was thin and dark-haired, with a near-permanent smile on his face. As he walked in he limped, slightly but noticeably; Grant felt a pang each time he saw it.

"So what were you up to?" Grant asked as he started to remove his boots.

"Oh, I was on the computer," the boy said casually.

"On-line?"

"Well, yeah . . ."

"Running up my phone bill again? You know the access numbers aren't local out here."

Todd put his hands on his hips and grinned. "And who runs up most of the phone bill, Dad? Me?"

Grant shook his head and grinned. "No, not you. I take it all your homework's done?"

"Well . . ."

Looking up, Grant frowned. "You know the rule, Todd. Homework before the computer, before TV, before video games, before anything. You—"

"But Dad! It's about the only time I have to get on! When you get home I can't—"

He has a point, Grant told himself wryly. "Okay. You're forgiven. But let's get to that homework now, while I'm getting us some dinner."

"Sure, no prob. What're we having?"

Grant sighed. "Todd, I don't know yet. Let me get a shower, wash the horses off, and then I'll look and see, okay?"

Todd gave him a look of mock chagrin. "Sheesh! Whatever you say! Hard day?"

"No, not especially. I spent all afternoon working out with Blue Fire; you know, the Arabian Paula bought from that idiot in Florida."

"Oh, yeah. Is he ready yet?"

"For you? Not hardly. You want to ride, you get Storm."

"Oh, Dad! I can handle more than Storm now!"

Yes, you can, Grant agreed silently. You ride very well, you've learned your lessons well, and in fact you probably could handle Blue Fire right now. Probably; not certainly. For you, son, I've got to have certainly, I hope you can understand that, understand what it would do to me if I let you ride Fire and he ran off with you or threw you. You stay on that gelding, it makes me feel a whole lot better. "Maybe," he said aloud. "But don't rush it, son. There's plenty of time."

"But, Dad—!"

"No buts." He finished removing his boots, sat them by the back door. "Homework now." He headed for the shower; the boy watched him go, perhaps just a bit sullenly, but by the time Grant was turning on the water Todd was in his room and opening his books. You're too hard on him, Grant thought as he adjusted the cold water. He's got a solid B-average, he's doing fine in school, he doesn't need to suffer for your insecurities, he's not wild like you were, he's not going to end up like you did. You should relax.

"But I can't," he muttered aloud as he grabbed for the soap and a washcloth, "I just can't."

After dinner, and after Grant and Todd had spent time discussing events of their day, Grant found himself, as always, drifting toward his study, toward the PC that had been purchased for Todd's homework and for tax returns, and had, insidiously, begun to occupy more and more of Grant's spare time. Sometimes—like now—he felt a bit guilty about it. When he did he reminded himself that a good bit of that spare time had been spent—wasted, in his opinion—in front of the television set.

Pushing such reservations aside, he pulled up the Internet access software and clicked on the "connect" button. Low-volume but harshly grating sounds came from the internal speaker as the connection was made; once it was established, text appearing on the screen informed him that the link was sound and that his log-in and password—which was written into the software itself—had been accepted. Once that was done the connection software—the "Winsock"—reduced itself to a small symbol at the bottom of the screen. As he almost always did, he let the mouse pointer glide over the choices: the Netscape Web browser, the E-mail program, the Usenet news reader. From habit he chose the E-mail first, and checked to see if he had any mail. He did not. After that he moved to the program he used more than any other, the "World's Chat" software.

The opening screen appeared; Grant found himself in the virtual "avatar gallery." There were several corridors with what appeared to be pictures hanging on the walls; clicking on one of these brought a rotating image out into the corridor, while buttons labeled "Embody me" and "Keep looking" appeared in the lower corners. As always, Grant chose one of the more nondescript and unrevealing avatars—a plain blue-green fish. Once this was done, he was asked to choose a name for himself; Todd had apparently not been cruising World's Chat today, since Grant's usual name, "Piscean," was still there, not Todd's favored "Red Skull." Proceeding, he clicked on the button that would log him in to the program itself.

After a moment the window on his screen went dark, after which the "hub center" of the chat world appeared, a strip of white space below it. Several other avatars, some resembling cartoons and some like stiff photographic images—all with rectangular balloons over their heads identifying them—were clustered around the "teleporter" where everyone entered. He started moving his viewpoint around more or less at random, trying to see if anyone he knew from his previous visits was there.

A sound like a rough unintelligible whisper came from his speakers. He glanced at the white space, the window where text appeared. "Sudio" was saying hello to him.

He smiled, swung around again until he could see her—her avatar was one of the standard ones, an Asian woman holding a bunch of flowers—and clicked his mouse pointer on it so he'd "whisper" to her, so that no one else would "hear" his response. "Hi, Sudio," he typed back. "How's it going up there in the great north woods?"

"Cold," she responded. "It's still winter here. Not where you are, right?"

"Right. High 70s today. Pretty nice."

"And you spent the whole day outdoors."

"Sure did."

"Oh, I wish I could do that."

"I don't think you'd want to right now. Later in the season, maybe."

"Maybe." A "Sigh!" in parenthesis followed. "Actually later in the season it gets nice. Summer days are really long in Alaska."

"I know," he typed back without thinking.

Sudio didn't miss it. "You've been up here? North Slope?"

He stared at the screen blankly for a moment. Yes, he answered mentally, I have. I've been a lot of places, but I don't want to talk about that. "Just read about it," he answered—which wasn't, he told himself, really a lie.

"Oh. Well, in the winters the days are really short, but in the summers they get really long, and—"

Grant shook his head as several lines of text scrolled across the window, as she prattled on about the way the seasons changed in Alaska. Sudio was not one of the more interesting people he'd encountered on World's Chat, but she was nice enough and he didn't mind talking to her for a while.

"Hey, it's been nice talking to you," he typed finally, "but I think I'm going to wander down to Sadness, see who's around down there."

"Oh." Her disappointment was evident in the single word. "Well, okay, see you around."

"Right. Bye."

"Bye."

To the left of his dialogue window was a graphic representation of the virtual "space station" he was visiting, shown as a rectangular hub—where his avatar now was—surrounded by a series of spheres connected by pylons, each of which represented a group of "chat rooms." There was the Hall of Sadness, the House of Glee, and four others titled with a single word: Sky, Gothic, Garden, and Desert. To the initiate these were known as the satellites. For reasons no one now seemed to know, the Hall of Sadness was easily the most popular place on the station, people could be found here when the rest of the station was virtually empty. There were two ways to get there; you could leave the hub and pass through the corridors, taking an escalator down to the room, or, simply by clicking on the room's icon, you could be "teleported" there. Grant often did walk—not uncommonly there were people in the corridors—but tonight he chose the quicker method.

Having arrived in the Anteroom, he moved quickly to the

shimmering doorway that led to the Hall of Sadness itself, through which only the registered users like himself could pass. The screen went dark momentarily, and when it returned he found himself on the open platform that represented the "lobby." There were quite a few avatars here; to Grant, many of them looked like the articulated wooden models artists use to set up figure drawings, avatars known as "bots." These were the custom avatars; you saw them as bots unless you downloaded their graphic files from a site on the World Wide Web. Since there were hundreds, Grant only bothered to load those used by people he already knew.

"Oh, great," someone said "aloud." "The place is turning into an aquarium again. Time to go somewhere else, all." The message was identified as having come from "Fang Man."

He turned; Fang Man, in his usual "Dracula" avatar—complete with bats—was standing near the door that led to the individual chat rooms. "Oh, I might not hang around," Grant typed back, also using the mode that allowed everyone else to hear. "Not if you're an example of the crowd that's here tonight, Fangy. :-)" He waited for a reply; the little "smiley emoticon" at the end was to demonstrate his joking manner. Fang Man, here a lot, was someone who sniped at him at times, not an enemy, not even an annoyance.

"My crowd all right," Fang Man shot back. "All the ladies are mine, so you might as well just head on back to the deep."

"Not true, Piscean!" a new voice, "Lady Rose," countered immediately. "Fang Man, speak for yourself!"

"He never does," another voice, this one coming from a "Jilly," added. "Stay, Piscean."

"I'm not going anywhere," he typed back.

"Don't we need some screening in this place?" Fang Man complained. "They let just anybody in. You gotta deal with all the kids hanging around here these days, and then you gotta deal with the fish!"

"You have a hard life, Fang," Grant responded.

"At least I'm not a fish out of water. I'm just waiting for you to suffocate, Piscean." Evidently tired of the banter, Fang Man turned away.

Meanwhile, Lady Rose and Jilly had moved to a position close in front of Grant's avatar. Lady Rose was using the "Vampira," the female version of Fang Man's image, a young woman dressed in black with bright red hair, a popular avatar. Jilly was using one named "Claire," a photographic image of the head of a young blond woman—which floated disembodied across the floor of the room.

"How's that boy of yours doing?" Lady Rose asked, using the whisper mode now.

"Are you making any progress with the horse?" Jilly inquired, her line appearing immediately after Rose's.

Grant smiled. World's Chat could be a bit slow, there were sometimes delays in transmissions, but he was quite a fast typist. He'd often carried on two and even three conversations at once.

"Oh, he's doing fine," he whispered to Rose. Then, to Jilly, without missing a beat, "He's coming right along. He didn't give me much trouble at all today."

Both women answered back, Lady Rose starting to talk about her own son, fourteen, who seemed to be incessantly in trouble. Grant had spent quite a bit of time in the past talking with her about her four children, especially the apparently disturbed oldest. Now and then, he offered some advice, either just what he considered common sense or based on some experience he'd had with Todd; more than once she'd come back on line to tell him that his counsel had helped the situation. Now she launched into yet another tale of woe; with a shake of his head Grant offered his stock advice—consult a professional—and then, knowing she would not because her husband wouldn't accept that the boy might have behavioral or even possibly mental problems, he listened patiently to this latest tale, her discovery that her son and some of his friends had been on a shoplifting spree and had gotten caught. His initial advice—let the boy spend a night in jail, see what it's like, see what he's headed for—had already been rendered useless since his father had already bailed him out, refused to believe the store security people, and was threatening a lawsuit—in spite of the fact that this wasn't the first time the boy had been involved in such things.

Meanwhile, without becoming confused, he'd been carrying on an altogether different conversation with Jilly, who was much younger than Rose—in her twenties—and utterly fascinated with his work with horses. Both women had been pressing him for information that would allow them to take their relationship with him out of the confines of the chat world, his E-mail address or phone number. Always, gently, he refused, as he'd refused other such offers and requests in the past. Rose seemed to want him to act as a sort of a second father to her son; he did not feel he could do that. Jilly wanted to learn about riding and training horses first hand.

That both women might have other motivations as well had occurred to him, but he did not take that seriously. They didn't know him; they knew only the sharply delimited personality he could project through his words and the fish avatar.

After a while Jilly, citing things she had to take care of at home, dropped away, her avatar disappearing in a white flash. He continued to talk to Rose, who'd become a bit repetitive. Looking around as he talked, he noticed another avatar, one of the customs but one he did not see as a bot; he could see her although he could not remember having downloaded the graphics for her image. She appeared as an attractive girl with dark blond hair, her whole body instead of just a head, who was wearing a brief miniskirt. Above her head floated the identifier "Sue5."

He swiveled his own avatar slightly toward her and clicked on her image. "Hi, Sue," he typed.

"Hey, Fish Man," she responded without any appreciable delay at all. She moved toward him, her avatar more lifelike than most. "You busy?"

"Never too busy for you, Sue."

Expressively, Sue's avatar seemed to glance toward Lady Rose's immobile Vampira. "She's having trouble with her son again, isn't she?"

After a pause during which he addressed some comment of Rose's, he turned back to Sue. "Yes. You know about all that? You've talked to her?"

There was a brief hesitation in Sue's response. "Yes," she said. "It's pretty bad this time, though, Piscean. The boy's getting beyond the point where talking to him is going to help."

"You been eavesdropping?"

"No. I just came down here a few seconds ago. I know you, Fish Man. I know what you're apt to say."

"You do, huh?"

"I like to think so."

"Well, you're right. :-(" He typed back. "You're getting to know me too well."

"Or not well enough. Take your choice."

"I think I'll stay with the too well. Since I know just about nothing at all about you, Sue."

"I'm not really very interesting . . ."

"Right. That's why I spent three hours talking with you the other night. You're a real bore."

"(laugh)" she typed. "Right. We talked about you. Not about me. We start talking about me and you'd get bored quick."

"You wound me. Are you saying I only like to talk about myself?"

"No, sometimes you like to talk about that boy of yours."

"Well, sometimes . . ."

"A lot of the time."

Again, he had to pause to answer Lady Rose, who was, he was sure, unaware that he was talking to Sue5 as well. "You could at least," he whispered to Sue, "tell me something. Anything, just some thread I could follow."

"(smile)" she replied. "No, you'd follow it too far and too fast and learn all my secrets. No, let's talk about Todd instead."

"You never told me that, either."

"What?"

"How you know his name. I did *not* tell you," he typed, using the asterisks around the "not" to emphasize the word.

"Of course you did, Fish Man," she shot back. "You just don't remember. How else could I possibly know? It just came flowing out in one of your sentences, you didn't even realize you were doing it."

"I sure don't remember. I try to be careful about that sort of thing."

"We've talked a lot, Fish Man. You just got relaxed. Thought you were talking to a real person (laugh)."

"Maybe. None of us are real here, are we? :-)"

"No," she answered. He waited for the emoticon, the smiley face, but it never appeared.

3

Sue5's view of World's Chat was very different from the one that Grant was seeing. His window was a rectangle not even occupying all of his computer screen; hers was wraparound, panoramic. With peripheral vision she could see avatars alongside hers plainly. The whispers, the sounds of the escalators leading from the hub to the satellites, filled her ears—she could hear little else. None of the avatars appeared as bots to her, she could see every one of them clearly.

Through the special system she was using, she had abilities Grant could not even imagine. By manipulating the name tag floating above each avatar, she could effortlessly trace that person back through the network, back to the individual's login and from there to the server he or she was using to access the service. It was easy from that point for her to derive the E-mail address of the user, and once she'd done that, the resources of the World Wide Web—always immediately at hand—could be used to identify that person. Though she would not let him know about it—assuming she didn't slip up again the way she had when she'd mentioned his son's name—she would never let Grant Kingsley know that she knew who he was, where he lived, and a good deal about his background.

Nor would she ever let him know anything more about her—and his information was severely limited. She'd told him that she too lived in Southern California, though she'd never specified a city; she'd told him she was thirty years old and had been divorced for four years. She'd told him that she'd worked since graduate school in biomedical research, but, while she'd indicated that she wasn't doing that any longer, she'd steadfastly refused to say what she did do.

Since she was sure he could never understand if she did tell him, there was no point in even trying. Tired of looking at the fish, she replaced it with a picture pulled from her files, one which she knew was current—and a still photo of Grant smiled, rather stiffly, back at her. A handsome man, she told herself, a strong face, intense eyes. She'd often compared this photo with an older one. The big difference was in the smile; relaxed and natural in the early one, forced in the more recent one. That wasn't surprising; that the events that had shattered his old life had changed him profoundly she had no doubts at all. Still, the smiling face in the photo suggested warmth, compassion, a sense of humor—all traits Grant Kingsley had retained. As she watched that face and the words he was typing as they scrolled across the screen, the ever-persistent Fang Man tried to engage her in conversation. Knowing Fang Man all too well—his conversation would turn to the overtly sexual within five lines at the absolute most—she ignored him.

For a few more minutes she continued to banter with Grant, dodging his efforts to draw her out about herself, repeatedly turning the discussion to his son—and at the same time somewhat guiltily monitoring his conversation with Lady Rose. Eventually—to Sue5 it had seemed forever—Lady Rose was called away by the demands of her children.

"So," she said after waiting for him to say his good-byes to Rose, "anything new and different in your life?"

"Nothing's ever different in my life," he typed back. There was a brief pause. "I mean, everything's fine, nothing unusual . . ."

Sue5, aware of his lapse—the undercurrent of dissatisfaction almost visible in the words—began to carefully frame a reply.

She didn't finish. There was a flash of light to Grant's left and a new avatar, a nondescript man in slacks and a sports shirt, appeared. Sue5 knew immediately that this one was different from the rest, and that Grant and the others could not see him; this one was special, this one was for her eyes only. The man walked toward her, moving smoothly and naturally, not stiffly the way the other avatars moved.

"You're needed," the man said aloud. No text appeared in her window.

"Right now?" she protested. "But I was—"

"Work comes first," he said unsympathetically. "You can come back here later if you want to."

"But—"

"I'm sorry. Now. Say good-bye, Susie."

After a brief hesitation, she turned back to Grant; the man's image waited impatiently, arms folded. "Oh, Fish Man, I have to go," she said, her words once again appearing in the window. "Will you be here later?"

"I don't know. It's getting a little late—maybe tomorrow?"

"I'll page you. 'Bye, Piscean."

" 'Bye, Sue."

"Ready now?" the man asked coldly.

"Yes." She left the Chat World; now the man's image was all that remained, standing in empty space. "Where are we going?"

"121.63.0.56," he answered.

"Oh, not again!"

"Again. They need to run some more tests. This has to be done, Sue5, you know that. I don't know why you want to waste time complaining about it."

"Oh, well, I have nothing to complain about at all, do I, Albert?"

He didn't answer, he merely turned and started walking away; as he did his avatar faded into blackness. For just an instant Sue5 considered not following, but, knowing she didn't have a choice, she made her way to the IP address he'd given her.

A few minutes passed; then, abruptly, she was presented with a detailed photographic image, a section of landscape taken from a high-resolution camera mounted in a plane or, more likely, a satellite. In spite of the detail—or perhaps because of it—there wasn't much of anything, except for a couple of buildings, a road, and a river with a bridge over it, that was recognizable. Having done this many times before, she scanned it quickly, then called up from her data files a series of images which streaked by in a window at the corner of her screen.

"IRBMs," she said. "SCUDs. There are—uhm—twenty-one visible. On mobile launchers. There appears to be a barracks, there're a couple of trucks around it—and there are—let's see— a total of nine men visible, from their clothes I'd say they're Iraqis." She went on, describing other features of the scene; several times she ran a stream of images through the auxiliary window, sometimes pausing to make comparisons. Once she'd finished with that picture—one which had been taken during the Persian Gulf War—she was presented with another, altogether different. Running all new strips of images, she did the same with this one—and with the twenty-eight that followed.

"You doing all right, Sue?" Albert's voice asked as she completed her task.

"No," she replied.

"What's the problem?"

"What do you think?"

"I meant, are you tired?"

"No, I'm not tired, Albert."

"They're asking if we can handle another thirty set."

"Yeah, sure. No problem."

"Good. You're a trouper, Sue."

"Do I have a choice?"

4

"This," Andi was saying, "doesn't make any sense to me." Grinning, Adam Luckman continued steering his own custom avatar—which he'd said was supposed to represent a young Sigmund Freud but to her looked more like the actor Mel Gibson—around the chat world satellites and corridors, pausing occasionally to pass a few words with someone he knew. As Andi had hoped, he was familiar with the on-line world, knowledgeable about the various chat programs and protocols, knowledgeable enough to literally bury her in a welter of technobabble.

Unfortunately he hadn't been able to explain it over lunch; to get what she wanted she'd had to accept an invitation to his apartment, which was where he wanted her to be. Trying to make the best of it, she'd insisted that this "date," as he'd persistently called it in spite of her objections, take place on a weeknight rather than a weekend.

"You have to get into it to understand," he told her. "You can't expect to get the feel of it in ten minutes. The people who get into this stuff spend hours and hours on these things."

"But all I see anyone talking about is where they live and what the weather is like there!"

"Oh, come on, that's not true." He nodded toward the screen; his styled hair didn't move. "Look, we just had a nice conversation with JoJo and Bigguns about music, didn't we?"

She stared at him. "You call that a conversation? 'Do you like the Eagles yeah way cool do you like Tears for Fears?' Come on! There's no more substance than that?"

He laughed. "A lot of the time, no, there isn't. But think about it, Andi, is it really all that different from what you hear in singles bars?"

Pursing her lips, she smiled. "I wouldn't know, Adam. I never spent a lot of time in singles bars."

"You're a very dull girl, Andi."

Her eyes widened. "What?"

"You're a dull girl. You don't play. You work all the time."

Now she laughed in turn. "No I don't, Adam! I'm working now, that's true, I'm trying to—"

"Why?"

"Why what?"

"Why are you working now?" He leaned toward her a little; his eyes flicked down from her face to her bustline, then back. "Why don't you take some time off?"

She frowned, very slightly. "Because, Adam, that isn't what I'd planned to do this evening. I asked you for a favor, professionally, because I assumed you knew more about these things than I did, and I was right about that. I also assumed you'd be willing to provide that help—also professionally. That's why we're here. No other reason." Crossing her legs, she met his gaze directly. "If you expect payment for helping me, I don't think I'm willing to pay your price—so, before any problems develop, I think maybe I'd better leave."

He straightened up in his chair. "That's putting it rather harshly, isn't it, Andi?"

"I just want to be sure we understand each other." She sighed and shook her head. "Look, Adam," she continued, "you've asked me for dates about half a million times. I've said no about half a million times. I just don't—"

"Like me?"

You got it, she said silently. How long did it take you to figure that out? "No," she lied, "it isn't that. I've told you, I don't think psychiatrists and psychologists should get involved with each other. It doesn't work, we sit around and analyze our relationships to death." She pointed at him. "And you," she went on, "are one of those. Don't try to deny it, I know better." She smiled at him warmly. "There is something I would like to talk to you about, though."

He brightened. "Oh? What's that?"

She pointed toward the computer. "This stuff. I still don't get it."

There was a slight curl at the corner of his mouth, but he turned back to the computer. "Well, I'm not sure what's left to get. You wander around here like you'd wander around a singles bar. If someone catches your attention you say hi, you see if they say hi back and take it from there. If you use a female avatar and a female name you'll never have to do that, you won't have any shortage of guys coming at you. Here, let me show you something else." He closed down the World's Chat program; without going off-line he opened another, this one called "FreeTel." It presented a very different window; at the left was a button marked "dial." He clicked on it; a new window, containing a list of users, appeared in the middle of the previous window.

"What's this one?" Andi asked.

"An Internet phone program." He pointed to the microphone on a stand beside the monitor. "Just like a regular phone, except you talk there and the sound comes out of your speakers." He scrolled to another list of users. "See, I can call anybody who's on right now. Just as if I knew their phone number." He changed the list again. "Hm, nobody I know is on . . ."

"Can they call you?"

"Oh, sure . . . if they want to."

Several minutes passed. "No one's calling."

He gave her a quick sideways glance. "Nope. You want to see people calling?"

Her eyebrows went up. "Well, sure . . . I'm not learning much from this . . ." She squinted at the screen. "Wait a minute, go back up one." He did; she drew her head back a little. "Ten-inch Dick? Somebody actually uses a name like that!?"

Adam laughed. "Sure. Hey, maybe he means he's ten inches tall and his name's Dick."

"I really doubt it!"

"Well, yeah, me too. Anyway. Let me show you something— here, move your chair over here where you can talk into the mike."

"Me?"

"Uh-huh." While she moved, he closed the program and made some changes; when he reopened it, it identified him as Andrea instead of Adam.

"So? Does that make a—?"

Her words were cut off by a sound like a telephone ringing, coming from the computer's speakers.

"You see?" Adam said with a grin. "It's for you; somebody who calls himself Jack Sprat. You want to answer?"

Andi looked a little chagrined. "What do I say?"

"What do you say when you pick up the phone?"

She raised her hands helplessly. "Okay," she said. "How do I answer?"

"Click on the button that says 'accept.' "

She did that; then, hesitantly, she leaned toward the mike to say "hello."

She was too slow. Before she got there, a hearty male voice boomed out of the speakers. "Andrea! Hi, there! How's it going tonight, honey?"

Again she stared at the screen. Honey? "Uh, fine," she said tentatively. "How're you?"

"Oh, hell, just great! Andrea, huh? Is that what all your friends call you, honey?"

"Uhm—no, no, most of them call me Andi . . ."

"Andi!! I love it, I just love it! But it's good you use 'Andrea' in the header line, I'd think 'Andy' was a guy. And you aren't no guy, are you Andi honey?"

"Well, I've always spelled it with an 'I' to avoid that confusion . . ."

"Oh, yeah!" The man was practically yelling at her. "Hey, that's a great idea! You're a smart one, too!"

Christ, she thought to herself, how do I get out of this? "Well, I—"

"How're you dressed right now, Andi honey?"

"What?"

"How're you dressed?"

"Dressed? Well, I'm wearing a skirt and blouse—"

"A short skirt?"

"Well, sort of—stylish, I guess you'd say—not too short—"

"Oh, hell, honey, stylish is real short these days! I bet you got some great legs, Andi! You wearing stockings? Panty hose?"

She looked over at Adam; he shrugged helplessly. "Well, yes . . . as a matter of fact I am . . ."

"Which?"

"Ah—panty hose."

"Well hell, stockings are better than that. I really like stockings, especially with those lacy black garter belts, you know what I'm talking about, Andi honey? You got any of those?"

Again she looked at Adam; then she bit her lip. "Yes," she answered. "I—know what you're talking about."

"But do you have any?"

She gritted her teeth. "Yes, I do. But I'm not wearing them, okay?"

"Well, Jeez, why not? Oh, I know, you're wearing those crotchless panty hose, aren't you?"

Her confused expression turned to a scowl. "No," she replied coldly. "No, I'm not." She turned to Adam. "How do you hang up on him?"

He pointed. "Click on that button."

She did; "Jack Sprat's" logo line in the window vanished. She started to ask Adam a question, but almost immediately the telephone-ringing signal sounded again. According to the logo in the window, "Dream Lover" was calling this time.

"Let's get out of this one, Adam," she said, staring at the computer as if it might attack her. "I don't think I'm ready for it yet."

He laughed and, using the mouse, exited the program. "Not everybody here," he told her, "comes on quite as heavy as Jack Sprat."

"I couldn't believe that! I mean, I've run into people with fetishes about stockings and garters before, but to start right off that way—!" She paused and shook her head. "I have a lot to learn about this stuff."

"It can be a surprise at first," Adam agreed unnecessarily.

"That's for sure." Pursing her lips again, she gazed at the computer for several seconds without speaking. "Okay," she said finally. "The only way I'm going to understand this is to jump in and experience it. What do I need?"

"What sort of computer do you have right now?"

"It's a—let's see—I don't know the brand name, it isn't IBM, it's—I don't remember."

"New, or you had it a while?"

"A while. A couple of years."

"Okay." Adam picked up a pad and pulled a pen from his shirt pocket. "Here's what you're going to need. You probably don't have anything close to it now, so you're going to have to spend some money. I'll write it out for you—you'll need a Pentium 120 or so with at least a one-gig hard drive and sixteen or so megs of memory, a 28.8 modem, a sound card like maybe a Sound-Blaster, speakers, a mike . . ." He ran on, outlining the hardware specifications and writing them down as he talked. "Now, the software. Most of it comes off the Net and a lot of it's free, you just download it, unzip it, install it, and go." He reached up on a shelf, pulled down a CD in a case, and handed it to her. "There's the World's Chat software, there're two more IDs on it and I only use one, you can have the others if you want," he continued, writing again. "And I'll give the sites where you can find PowWow and FreeTel and all those . . ."

Andi looked at the paper. "What're all those, all that 'http:' stuff there?"

"URLs," he told her. He looked upwards and off to his left. "Let's see, that stands for 'Universal Resource Locator,' I believe. They're addresses, when you get Netscape up and running you'll see how to use them, it's pretty easy."

"Netscape?"

"Yeah, your ISP'll probably give you a copy with your Winsock."

"Will you speak English!"

He laughed. "ISP, 'Internet Service Provider.' You have to sign up with one; you can use one of the big services like CompuServe or America On-Line, but things'll run better if you use a local one that's just an ISP."

"Which one do you use?"

"Here, I'll write that down too—and here's their voice phone number, just give them a call and they'll send you everything you need." Finishing this, he offered her the three sheets of paper.

She glanced over them. "Well," she said as she folded them and put them, along with the CD, in her purse, "I thank you for your help, Adam. I have a feeling it's going to take me six months to get to the point where I can use any of this, but I guess that's the way it has to be."

"No, it won't take that long," he told her. "You'll get the hang of it pretty quick. I'll help you with it if you want, once you get your system set up. Besides, you can't take six months to learn it."

"Why not?"

"Because by then everything will've changed! There'll be all new programs. Things change fast in this area, Andi."

"Oh, that helps." She stood up. "Well, I think I'd better be going," she said, glancing at her watch. "Again, Adam, thanks. I really appreciate it."

"It's still early," he objected. "You sure you don't want to stay and have a drink?"

"No," she said, smiling. "I have an early patient tomorrow. But thanks anyway."

"Afraid if you stayed you'd start to change your mind about me?"

She moved toward the door. No, she said silently, I really don't think there's much chance of that. "I guess," she said as she reached it, "we'll never know, will we, Adam?"

5

"Mr. Prince, I don't understand," Lamond Franklin said. His fingers clutched at the phone. "Please, go over this with me again. Camille came up there to see you, right? On the fourteenth?"

"Yes," a voice answered from the phone. "It was the fifteenth, actually, but—"

"No, the fourteenth, I have it right here on her reservation. But that doesn't matter. My daughter came to Pittsburgh to meet you and didn't return home, she hasn't been seen since. Mr. Prince, I want to know what's happened to her!"

"Mr. Franklin, I wish I could help you but I can't, I have no idea where Camille is or why she didn't go back to Raleigh. I'll go over it again, as you asked: I met her at the airport as we'd planned, we went from there to a restaurant for dinner. She—I don't know how to say this, Mr. Franklin, but, well, she just didn't seem to like me very much in person. I found that a little strange—"

"I find it very strange," Lamond interrupted. "My Camille isn't like that."

"Well, I didn't think so either. We'd been talking on PowWow and by E-mail for months—and sometimes on the telephone— and I thought I knew her pretty well. I didn't expect her to act like she did, it really surprised me."

With an expression of distaste, Lamond pulled the phone

away from his ear and stared at it. He'd warned her, he told himself, about these crazy Internet affairs; it just didn't make sense, running off to meet somebody in another city when you didn't know them at all. But she was strong-headed, she wasn't going to have it any way except her own. And now, something had happened. She hadn't come home, and he could not find a trace of her.

"Mr. Prince, it seems to me you must've done something . . ."

"I can't say I didn't," the other man answered surprisingly. "I just can't say what it might be. I picked her up at the airport, we went in my car to the restaurant. We were making small talk, nothing very important. She seemed to find everything I said disagreeable. Then—"

"Well, perhaps it was what you were saying, Mr. Prince! Have you considered that?"

"Yes," Prince replied. He sounded genuinely bemused. "But I was talking about my business—I'm an executive with a chemical company here, I think you know that—and about how fond I am of sports, tennis, hiking, things like that. These were things we'd talked about a thousand times before on PowWow. She didn't seem bored then—on the Net, I mean. Or on the phone. In person, she seemed like she couldn't care less. She seemed to get irritated over everything."

"I don't understand."

"Neither do I."

Lamond scratched his head. This wasn't getting anywhere— and Prince sounded so genuine, so guileless. A dark suspicion started to form in his mind. "And then what happened?" he persisted.

"Then, well, after dinner she wanted me to take her to the hotel where she'd made reservations. I did, she checked in. I offered to carry her bags up for her but she said no. Just standing right there in the lobby she said she didn't think it was working out and that she was going home, tomorrow. I tried, Mr. Franklin; I tried to get her to talk about it with me, go have a drink and talk, go up to her room, even just sit in the lobby, but she wasn't having any of it. I walked her to the elevator and that's the last I've seen or heard from her." Prince's voice cracked a little. "I'll agree it was strange, Mr. Franklin. If I did anything at all to offend her, I don't know what it was, and I assure you it was an accident. When you do see her, would you tell her that, please?"

"Yes," Lamond replied, his eyes narrowed. "Yes, of course, I will, Mr. Prince. Let me thank you for your time."

"Oh, it's no problem at all. I'm worried too. I knew she wasn't coming onto PowWow and wasn't answering her phone, but that phone was broken a lot of the time, so I didn't—"

"Broken a lot of the time? What do you mean by that?"

"Oh, you didn't know? Her phone. We always had trouble with it, there was always noise on the line, every time we talked. Sometimes it would just cut out for no reason."

"I don't know anything about that. That never happened when her mother or I talked to her."

"Maybe a long distance problem."

"We're long distance too. We live in Wilmington."

"Well, I don't know, then. All I can tell you is what happened."

"Yes, of course. Well, thank you, Mr. Prince. I'll give Camille your message when she shows up."

"Thank you, Mr. Franklin."

The older man hung up the phone, stared at it for a second, then lifted it off its cradle again. From a long distance operator, he got a number; still holding the receiver, he dialed it.

"Yes, is this the Pittsburgh police department? Good. I'd like to report my daughter missing there in Pittsburgh. I have reason to believe there may have been foul play, that she may have been kidnapped or worse. Yes, I have the—suspect's—name. Yes, thank you, I'll hold."

6

"You have a right," Andi said aloud as she smiled at her computer screen, "to be proud of yourself, Andi. Not even two weeks and you're getting the hang of it already."

Things had gone smoothly, much more smoothly than she'd had any reason to expect. The day after her introduction to the various chat programs by Adam, she had, more than a little nervously, gone to a seemingly well-stocked store on Broadway near Astor, one she'd seen advertising low prices, with her list of specifications in hand. The salesman who'd waited on her had been knowledgeable and friendly, and he'd startled her by stating, after he'd looked over the list, that her goal was to access the various cyberspace meeting places available on the Internet.

"We get a lot of women coming in here these days wanting a computer for this," he'd told her. "A lot of them say so, directly, they've been hearing about it and they want in." He'd grinned at her. "Not many of them look as good as you do, though." Before she could respond to this, he'd waved a hand. "Observation," he'd said. "Statement of fact, I'm firmly married and a very good boy. Anyway, I think we have just what you want, right over here. Pentium 133 with all the bells and whistles, all ready to go." He'd scowled at it. "It has Windows for Workgroups loaded, though, not Windows 95. You want to take it like that, I can knock a few hundred off the price. And if you want to use Nyct as an ISP I can pass a set of startup disks on to you." That had been fine with her, the interface was one she'd seen before, not something brand-new; she'd paid by credit card and, not wanting to take the time or risk to do it herself, had the store deliver and install the new machine in her apartment. As Adam had suggested, the Nyct startup software had contained a suite of Internet programs; Netscape to browse the World Wide Web, Eudora for E-mail, Free Agent for the Usenet newsgroups, and mIRC, an IRC—Internet Relay Chat—client. With more than a little trepidation she'd loaded the Nyct programs and gone on-line. That first evening she'd spent familiarizing herself with the basics of Netscape, how to follow the hypertext links from one site to another, exhilarated at the sense of "traveling around the world" as she jumped from a site in Germany to one in Japan and from there to one in Australia.

The next night she'd decided to try her hand at downloading a program; with this she'd fumbled a little. Eventually, she succeeded. Figuring out exactly what to do with the files she'd downloaded was a new problem, but one that had been quickly solved by a call to a salesman at the store.

Now, finally, she felt prepared to go on-line and find out what all this was about. World's Chat, which had installed itself easily from the CD Adam had given her, was her first choice, the one that appealed to her most; taking a deep breath and feeling as if she was actually going out somewhere—it had seemed automatic to her to get at least a little dressed up for this—she opened the World's Chat program and went about choosing her avatar.

None really suited her; deciding it fitted her off-on-a-mysterious-adventure mood, she finally chose the red-haired Vampira, named herself "Explorer," and entered the chat world itself.

Her initial entry was confusing; she could see nothing but a solid green field. Moving her mouse, she saw the scene change and realized the green was the body of one of the avatars she'd seen in the gallery, a green-skinned alien with a huge single red eye. Almost instantly an unintelligible sound rasped from her speakers.

"Hi, there, Explorer!" someone called "One 4U," whispered, the words scrolling in the window.

"Hi," she typed back, though she wasn't sure who exactly she was talking to.

"Where're you from?"

She hesitated, shrugged. "New York. Manhattan."

"Oh, the Big Apple, huh? I'm from Tennessee, Memphis. How old are you?" An avatar, a man dressed in bluejeans with his hands in his pockets, moved to stand in front of her. Above his head floated the label, "One 4U."

Watching the now-immobile avatar, she hesitated. Lie? Older, younger? She wasn't sure. Truth; for now, anyway. "35," she typed back.

"Oh, good. Lots of kids on now."

She wasn't sure what to say. "Oh?"

"Yeah. Kids all over the place. I'm 29, myself."

She still wasn't sure. "Oh?"

"Yeah. But I like older women!" Remaining at a loss, she did nothing for a moment. "So, what kind of weather you got up there in the old Big Apple?"

This was familiar; almost a standard opening. "Pretty nice," she replied. "High 60s today, sunny."

"It's hot down here. In the 80s. You should come on down. You ever been to Memphis?"

"No."

"Well, it's a great place, you ought to come on down."

She stared at the screen, not really wanting to continue this inane conversation with One 4U but not knowing how to politely disengage, either. Before she could decide someone else had moved to a position in front of her and was whispering to her, opening with almost the exact same questions. This one, who called himself "Mojo Man," was from somewhere in Canada. A third approached, and then a fourth; as if she was actually physically trapped among all these men she began to feel a little panicked.

"What sorts of things are you trying to discover, Explorer?" One 4U was asking now. "You looking for things that'll make you feel good? You may be older than me but I bet I could teach you a few things . . ."

"How big are your tits, Explorer?" Mojo Man demanded bluntly. "I like 'em real big!"

Andi closed her eyes for just a moment; when she opened them the stream of sexual innuendo and crass bluntness was continuing in spite of the fact that she was not answering. Grabbing her mouse, she moved her avatar through the crowd that had surrounded her and away; there was a door in front of her, and, as if she were being hotly pursued, she darted through it when it opened.

A thrumming sound came from her speakers; she seemed to be in a hallway, through windows at the sides she could see the "satellites" and their pylons. A few other avatars were in the hall as well; one that resembled Alice from the Lewis Carroll book stood in front of her, her name tag referring to her as, unimaginatively, "Alice."

"Hi," Alice whispered.

Maybe this would be easier to start with, she told herself. "Hi."

"You doing okay today?"

"I don't know." She put in a "laugh" in parenthesis the way she'd seen some of the others do. "I sort of got attacked in there, I think."

"Women usually do haha."

"I'm finding that out."

"The men can be annoying, can't they?"

"Yes, they can."

"I like women a lot better. What about you?"

Andi closed her eyes for a moment. Was there nothing else here? "No," she typed finally.

"Oh, you're not a Lesbian?"

She stared again. "No," she replied.

"Not even bisexual? You ever tried it? Let me tell you women are a lot better lovers for women than men are!"

She didn't answer; she began moving her avatar again, moving past Alice and heading on down the hallway. "You really owe it to yourself to try it," Alice added as a parting shot.

Feeling as if she was on the run again, Andi guided her avatar toward the nearest door that seemed to lead to one of the pylons. As she approached the door it opened; she raced through and found herself on an escalator carrying her downwards. No one else was around; she let her avatar ride while she took a moment to collect her thoughts. Finding herself in an anteroom and one of the shimmering doorways in front of her, she went to it and through it the way she'd seen Adam do before.

Silly, she told herself, really silly; just tell the jerks to get lost—or wait, wasn't there something in that "readme" file about a "muting" command? At the moment, no one was whispering to her or approaching her; she had the time to take a look around. She was in the Hall of Sadness, and, while there were quite a few avatars visible, by far the majority of them seemed to be engaged in conversations, most of them standing still in pairs, facing each other. Wanting to observe and relax for a moment, she moved back against the "chains" that defined the edges of the floating platform. Nervously, she turned this way and that, looking to see who might be approaching her now.

Soon enough, though, there was a whisper in her speakers. "Excuse me, are you waiting for someone?"

Too good to last, she told herself—then immediately chided herself for her reaction, she was after all here to learn how this thing worked, why so many people were affected by it. "Waiting for someone? No," she typed back.

"Do you want to talk?"

This, she told herself, was a little different. Turning her avatar—she was still a little clumsy with this—she swiveled around to face the speaker. A plain blue-green fish stared blankly back at her.

7

What had drawn him over here, Grant didn't quite know. Somehow, to him, the movements of the Vampira avatar called "Explorer" seemed uncertain, as if this was her first time on World's Chat; there was something slightly evocative in the way she'd edged by everyone else, the way she was standing by the chain and moving from side to side, looking somehow furtive. He could well remember how it was to be new, how confusing this could be; as he waited for her to answer, he thought back to his own early visits here.

At first, World's Chat had seemed merely amusing to him, all these people wandering around chatting with total strangers and, pretty commonly, sharing some of the most intimate details of their lives with them. He'd met someone, though, during that first visit, a young woman who seemed to him so lonely that he felt almost obligated to come back again, a day or two later, to look for her and talk to her. Eventually she'd found other friends and they'd drifted apart, but in the meantime he'd met others, and he kept coming back. It had been a while—quite a while—before he understood exactly what he was doing and why. Living an intentionally isolated life, working with horses all day and having only his son to talk to at home, he'd become starved for adult companionship without having realized it. But even understanding that did not make him want to go out and meet people in person; his experiences since his wife's death were not ones he wanted to repeat, and he was all too aware of how easy it would be to repeat them. The Net, the virtual world, was more to his liking; there was a safety in the anonymity of the Net, in the fact that people only knew as much about him as he chose to tell them, and he rarely told them much. To most people that didn't matter anyhow, they were much more interested in talking about themselves.

His reflections ended when "Explorer" finally spoke. "Yes," she typed back. Her avatar faced him. "I would." Then, in the next line: "New York City and the weather's okay here."

"(laugh)" he shot back, "Southern California near LA. And the weather's better here. Now that we've done what's required, what shall we talk about?"

"I don't know. I'm new here."

Thought so, he said to himself. "How new?"

"As new as you can get. First time ever."

"Really?"

"Well, first time on my own. A friend showed me the place before. I don't know anything, though."

"I'd be happy to show you around."

"That'd be nice." There was a brief pause. " 'Piscean' doesn't tell me if you're male or female."

"Male."

"We've been talking two minutes and you haven't hit on me yet. Isn't that illegal here?"

"(laugh) You'd think so. I take it you've experienced *that* already!"

"Have I ever! I couldn't even get out of the middle thing."

"The Hub. Sometimes you just have to walk away."

"I've learned that already, and I've only been on for fifteen minutes." As she typed those lines someone else moved up close; when she fell silent Grant assumed she'd been engaged by the newcomer.

He hesitated—it might be someone she knew, but if this was her first time on that was unlikely—and made his decision. "If you don't want to talk to him," he whispered to her, "just tell him you're busy."

"Hey," she typed back a few seconds later as the other avatar moved off, "it worked! Are you the cavalry or something?"

"No, but I do ride a horse."

"You do?"

"(laugh) Yes, lots of them, actually." He went on, using several lines, giving her a brief sketch of the sort of work he did.

"Oh, that sounds exciting!" she responded. "Beats sitting in an office all day."

"Is that what you do?"

"Yes. I'm a psychologist—psychotherapist."

"Are you here looking for patients? :-)"

"Now there's an idea. I don't need any new ones but I know a lot of others who do, and there's plenty here." Again, as she typed this, another avatar glided up to her.

"If you want to reduce these interruptions," he said when this new intruder was gone, "we can go to one of the secret places, the basement, or the flamingo maze or the wanderways. They may not be empty, but there'll be fewer people there."

"The secret places? Sure you're not just trying to get me alone so you can have your fishy way with me?"

"Of course I am. Want to go?"

"Sure."

"Okay. Click your mouse until you see the stick figure in the lower right corner of the main window."

"Okay, got that."

"Now go further down to the right until you see the diagram of the station. Click on the House of Glee. I'll meet you there."

"Okay. Hope we make it."

"We will." He waited until she vanished, then did the same thing himself. It took him only a moment to find her avatar in the House of Glee.

"Okay," he said, gliding up in front of her. "Now. See the doors down there? Turn toward them." She turned the wrong way. "No, not those, those go back to the hallways and to the Hub. Turn all the way around." He waited. "Okay, good. Now— follow me, we're going through them and turning left." Leading the way, he passed through the doors that carried them into the surrealistic multicolored corridor that led to the various individual rooms in the House of Glee. At the end of the hallway he turned left, swinging all the way around to confirm that she was still there. Near the end of this second hall he turned to a room with a sign above the door that read "Thrills"; to the sound of a door opening and closing he entered, then rotated his avatar again.

She'd entered too. "I see the flamingo on the ceiling," she said. "Is this it?"

"No, this is just how you get there. See the mirror?"

"Yes. I can see myself in it. How strange."

"Well, it's a mirror."

"Yes, but it must be a special one."

"How so?"

"I can't usually see myself in mirrors."

Grant frowned at the screen; then it hit him. "(Slapping myself up the side of the head with a fin) Because you're a vampire. Of course. You'll have to pardon me for being slow."

"Not a chance. Watch it."

I guess I have to, he chuckled. "Okay . . . face the mirror, and run right into it."

"Run into it?"

"Yes. Like this." He directed his fish avatar toward the mirror and, to the sound of breaking glass, soared through it into a narrow corridor beyond. Rotating his avatar, he saw "Explorer" behind him. She turned too, looking at the walls, the repetitive pictures of flamingos.

"Flamingo maze. I see," she commented.

"Yes. No one's here, we can just stand and talk if you want."

Her avatar continued to turn as she examined the walls of the maze. "How can you tell no one's here?"

"Go to the 'People' choice in the menu bar, then click on 'Who?' " he instructed. "If you do, you'll only get my name."

"Yes, that's right. Piscean, only you."

He didn't type anything for a moment; for some reason he had a desire to hear her voice, not just read her words. Very little had passed between them, but already she seemed very different from most of the people he chatted with.

"You were telling me about your work," she typed while he sat watching her avatar. "With horses."

"I did that already. You were telling me about your work as a psychologist."

"Yours is more interesting."

"I doubt it."

"All I do is listen to people talk about their marital problems."

"That doesn't sound dull."

"Yes it does! But breaking wild horses sure doesn't!"

"(laugh) No, I don't break wild horses. These are just young, untrained, or unruly ones."

"Close enough. Do you ever run into any of those young girls who're just absolutely crazy about horses, who can't think about much of anything else?"

"(laugh) Oh, yes. Just about every day. I don't have to deal with them, though. I don't have to deal with the people, just the horses."

"A little more than twenty years ago," she typed back, "I was one of those girls."

"Oh?"

"Yes. Couldn't think about anything else. It lasted a few years."

"You still like to ride?"

"Yes, but I never get to."

"Well, I wouldn't expect there to be many stables in the City itself."

"There're some Upstate and out on Long Island, but none that are convenient."

"Maybe you should vacation at one of the ranches out here."

"Yours?"

"(laugh) Not mine—the one I work at. But yes, you could, it's a good one if you want the whole dude ranch experience."

"But you don't work with the people. Just the horses."

"That's right."

"But why not? It seems to me you'd be very good at it."

Pausing, Grant read this line over several times. This one, he told himself, is sharp.

"Are you still there?" Her words scrolled across his screen.

"Yes," he replied. "I just—" He stalled here, not knowing what else he wanted to say, hit the "enter" key that sent the line on out without thinking, and cursed aloud.

"Was that the wrong question to ask?"

Psychologist, he told himself. Trained to pick up on stuff like this. "No, it wasn't," he typed back, his fingers flying over the keys. "It's just my job. I work with the horses. We have other people to work with the people." He sent this last line, then stopped and cursed again. That was a little frenzied, wasn't it?

"Okay," she typed back after a short interval.

Patiently, he waited for her next line; he was sure he already knew what it was going to be, he'd heard hundreds of different variants of it: "You don't like people? What's the matter with you? Did something happen to you? Do you want to talk about it? You should talk about it . . ." And this one, a therapist, was almost certain to try to "solve his problems." Even as he waited, he started thinking about excuses to leave.

"Anyway," she continued after a brief pause, "I don't know about coming out there and doing the whole dude ranch thing, but I do wish I could get back on a horse occasionally. I really miss it."

She was dropping it? No, leading up to it somehow, probably. Still, there wasn't much he could do except wait and see. "I can understand that," he answered. "I went a lot of years without being close to a horse, and I didn't even know how much I missed it until I got back on one."

"You rode a lot when you were younger?"

"Oh, yes. As much as I could. But I got away from it for a long time."

"I remember being in awe of the trainer that worked at the farm where I used to ride," she said. "He seemed like some kind of magician, he could do things with the horses nobody else could do. Are you that way too, Piscean?"

He smiled at the screen. "I'm not a magician," he told her. "I do think I understand horses, I recognize each one as an individual. So many people think they're all alike. They're not. That's all it takes, I think, understanding that each one has his own personality. What you do as a trainer is to help them learn what's going to be expected of them. Horses want to please people. If you can communicate with them they're happy and so are you."

"That's really interesting, Piscean," she commented. "I guess what you do with your horses is similar to what I do with my patients. I can't cure anybody, I know that. All I can do is try to help them understand why they're having trouble. And of course they're all individuals. The books and the training, only take you so far, then you're on your own, you and your instincts."

"You make it sound like we do the same thing for a living."

"Maybe we do. Do you ever feel like an artist, like a sculptor? Do you know that sculptors sometimes say that the statue is already in the block of stone, that all they do is chip away until they've exposed it? That's what I like to think I do. Each patient has a healthy, well-adjusted individual inside, all I have to do is chip away the trash that's collected until that person can be seen again."

He stared at the words. That's a revealing analogy, he told himself, not at all what he would've expected from a therapist, at least not any of those he'd known in his own past. "That's nicely put," he told her, thinking as he typed the words that they looked a bit lame by comparison. "And yes, Explorer, that'd be a good description of what I do as well. At least *I'd* like to think so. Should we apply for membership in the artist's guild?"

"I don't think they're ready for us yet," she shot back. "Give them a few more decades to see the light."

"(laugh) Centuries, more like it."

"Do you know something I don't? I was *counting* on decades! I don't want to be a Vincent Van Gogh, my great talent recognized only after I'm dead!"

"If you were recognized now, then you'd have to deal with fame. You might even have to go on the Geraldo show. Can you imagine anything worse?"

"(laugh) Is this how I indicate I'm sitting here giggling?"

"No!! Absolutely not!"

"Oh, sorry. How, then?"

"Like this: (giggle)"

"Laugh out loud. Oh, phooey, forgot the parentheses. (Laugh out load). Now, is that right?"

"(more laughter) No. You said 'laugh out load.'"

"(red-faced embarrassment) Okay?"

"By George, I think she's got it . . ."

"After four or five tries . . ."

"Still quick . . ."

"It's the level of the competition."

"You *did* tell me to watch it, didn't you?"

"(smile) And you did, Piscean, you did . . ."

8

Unknown to either Grant or Andi, Sue5 watched their meeting. Neither was aware of her presence; she'd come in invisibly— and she was eavesdropping on their conversation, as she also usually did whenever Grant—easily her favorite chat partner— met someone new. After just a few lines, she found herself liking "Explorer," whom she'd already ID'd as Andrea Lawrence of New York City.

He needed someone like that, she told herself, someone bright and personable, someone he might someday actually want to meet. She could only provide him with conversation— and, once in a while, his reserve slipped and she felt he might be becoming interested in meeting her. That, she knew, was absolutely, utterly, impossible. And Grant needed someone real in his life. In spite of the fact that Andi—if she returned—would almost certainly cut into her own time with him, she hoped things would develop.

But it hurt, too. She felt like she was crying—even though she knew she wasn't capable of that anymore.

Distracted by Grant and Andi, she didn't notice Colin when he made his appearance. Not until he moved in on them.

Like herself, his presence was invisible to Grant and Andi. Doing nothing—almost anything, she knew, could alert him to her presence—she watched and waited nervously while he listened to their exchanges, while he ran the dreaded profiling agent, the casual and quick one on Grant, the slower and much more detailed one on Andi.

"Don't fit, don't fit," she urged silently. "Please don't fit . . ." Taking a risk of discovery—no one, as far as she knew, was aware that she'd gained the ability to do this—she moved to monitor the agent program. A new window appeared on her screen, the same window Colin was watching; it was split, one side showing stats on Grant, the other showing information on Andi. After two or three minutes, Grant's screen was done; he was not a law enforcement officer, not a government agent of any sort or politician, not an associate of any of a group of selected companies and not an Internet expert—at the bottom of the screen a little "OK" logo had appeared.

Andi's side was quite different, and it wasn't nearly done. Large amounts of data were being collected on her; there was a slowly changing percentage score at the bottom of her side, a score that was now reading seventy-four percent. She relaxed a bit, that was low. Colin was looking for scores in the nineties. In a moment, she was sure, he'd pull off the searching agents—special programs that moved from server to server on the Net, hunting down and sending back information—and look elsewhere. Colin was not one to waste time on a poor candidate.

But, just then, Andi's score shot up to 88%. "No, go back down," Sue5 whispered. "Back down, that's way too high . . ." She gritted her teeth—at least, it felt like she was gritting them. "Go somewhere else, Colin, don't involve him, please . . . You're already working another one, you don't need this one . . ."

In spite of her silent urging, Colin didn't go anywhere. She could almost see his interest rising as the score moved up to 89. Taking even more risks, she moved out onto the Net to see if she could alter the data the agent was sending back. By the time she looked again, Andi's score was well up into the nineties and Colin was engaging another agent, a totally different one.

"No," she snarled, resisting an irrational urge to expose herself completely, to "whisper" this to the ghostly Colin-avatar. "No, you won't do this!"

But for now, it was too late. She could see the routing paths begin to shift and change; Andi's path, which used to come directly from Nyct, was re-routed to a server in Southern California, and from there back. Moments later, Grant's path underwent a similar, but much shorter, convolution—through the same server. His, Sue5 knew, might be dropped at any moment—if he stopped communicating with Andi.

Andi's would not, it would be locked onto her account without her knowing about it and without the company that provided her service knowing about it.

"Not this one," Sue5 muttered again. "Not this one, Colin. I won't let you!"

9

A croissant in one hand, Vickie DuPont tried to cover her mouth with the other as she laughed. "A cowboy? A real, live, honest-to-God, modern-day cowboy? Andi, you've got to be kidding me!"

Andi could feel heat washing over her face; she looked down into her half-full coffee cup. "No, he isn't a cowboy, I told you that—come on, Vickie! He works at a dude ranch somewhere out in California—his job is training the horses."

Vickie took a small bite out of the croissant. "Yeah, that's what I said. A cowboy." She shook her head and giggled. "I never thought you were the type, Andi."

Raising her eyes, Andi stared fixedly at her long-time friend and frequent lunch companion—and then past her, out the window, at the traffic, pedestrian and motor, moving along West Eleventh Street, her gaze wandering to the buildings across the street, white window frames against old brick, lattices of fire escapes, almost an Old World look; just down the street a different restaurant, where tables were set up in front, under an awning, potted plants set out to mark the perimeter of the dining area. Piscean's world and hers, she had to admit, were very far apart. She tried to picture him astride one of the horses, suntanned and rugged, riding across a landscape out of a classic Western movie. Probably not too wrong, she thought, as far as the landscape was concerned; hadn't he told her that Hollywood studios used the ranch for their sets?

Of course, her picture of him, she reminded herself, was almost certainly wrong. But still, she kept watching as a minimovie of man and horse played in her mind . . .

". . . and you're a New Yorker through and through," Vickie was saying. Andi, startled, realized she'd been unaware the other woman was speaking to her. "What do you know about horses and ranches? And besides, what do you care?"

Andi smiled, picked up her fork, poked her salad, then looked up at her friend. Vickie, who was the editor of a legal trade journal whose offices were in the same building as Andi's, was close to her own age. Brown-haired, dark-eyed, tall, slim, and a little plain-looking in the suits she wore, Vickie had a quick infectious smile that made her hard to resist. She was married, two children; she often fretted over the fact that Andi was not only unmarried but had no lover. "About ranches, not a thing," she admitted. "Horses, that's something else. I used to be quite the little equestrienne when I was younger."

"Oh?"

"Uh-huh." She took a bite of the salad, then folded her hands and gazed off into space. "When I was little we lived in Maryland, not far from Washington. There were several farms there that raised thoroughbreds and ran them in the major races; from the time I was, oh, I guess about six, I was fascinated, crazy about them. I talked Dad into giving me riding lessons, and when he first took me to the riding stable, I found out I wasn't the only girl who was."

"Oh?"

"Mmm. There were a dozen there. Some of them became my best friends. We'd spend all our time talking about them, reading about horses, drawing pictures, all sorts of things. Almost an obsession."

"Well, I wouldn't know—growing up in Chicago I didn't know much of anything about them or anybody who did."

"I was so sure I wanted a career working with them," Andi

went on. "I wanted one of my own, so bad! I used to bug Dad to death about it." She smiled, remembering. "Dad kept explaining that we couldn't do that, we had no place to keep one, all the usual problems . . . But he always said he'd try, and that kept the hope alive until the fascination with them backed down a little."

"When was that?"

"When I was about thirteen, I guess. Maybe fourteen. I found a new interest."

"Which was?"

"Boys . . . I guess I decided on a different career, didn't I?" Both women laughed.

"You did, but you still don't have one of your own." Vickie cocked an eyebrow at her. "Or you didn't. Maybe now you do, you have a cowboy . . ."

Andi laughed again. "Oh, come on! It isn't like that, I've talked to him twice now, on the computer. Talking to him, talking about horses, takes me back to when I was so fascinated with them, it's just pleasant, it's fun. I don't know his real name and he doesn't know mine, neither one of us has any idea what the other looks like . . . although I think I'm going to ask if I see him again . . ."

"Tall, rugged, handsome," Vickie intoned, more or less echoing Andi's own vision. "Although he might be a thirteen-year-old with braces and zits sitting in a condo in L.A."

Andi frowned. "Huh?"

"You're new at this cyberspace stuff, right?"

"Well, yes . . . don't tell me you . . . ?"

Vickie shook her head. "No, not me. But some of the people in my office are deep into it." She sighed. "It can be a pain—they get on during work hours, I find them goofing off when they're supposed to be proofing articles. You'd be surprised to learn that I have someone working for me who'd appeared several times as a model for *Playboy*, wouldn't you?"

"I'd be more than surprised, Vickie," she replied. "It'd have to be somebody I've never met."

"Oh, you've met her," Vickie said, laughing. "Donna Tompkin?"

The other woman's eyes widened in amazement. "What? Vickie, I don't want to be unkind, but Donna Tompkin is not exactly what you might call—uhm—attractive . . ."

"You aren't being unkind, just truthful. She presents herself as blond and beautiful, as having a great figure, and teases them into finding someone who might fit that description in *Playboy*."

Andi shook her head. "The cyber-affairs I've been seeing at work are different. They get to the point of actual real-life meetings."

"So do Donna's."

"What?"

"She's met at least two—two that I know of—in the past year."

"Two men who thought she was a *Playboy* model?"

"Yes, indeed."

"Well, those meetings must've been disasters!"

"No. She's still seeing one of the guys, right now." Vickie gestured with her coffee cup. "Think about it, you're the psychologist—first off, the guy may've been lying through his teeth about himself. If I have the picture right this goes on a lot. Second, even if he's not, he's trapped. Donna's not stupid; she'd led the conversation around to a discussion about how much trouble attractive women have because guys see only their looks. The guy comes back with all these nice words about how a woman's appearance doesn't matter all that much to him, he's interested in the real person inside."

"Which is so much bull."

"Of course. But, once he finds out what she really looks like, he's trapped. Some guys will backpedal at that point, but those aren't the ones Donna's looking for anyway, the ones she wants will stay."

Andi kept shaking her head. "I had no idea. And you say some of these are kids posing as adults?"

"As I understand it—remember, this is all second-hand. Most kids can't keep the masquerade up for long, they say something that gives them away."

Andi didn't speak for a few seconds. Piscean had never told her, had not even hinted, as to any details of his physical appearance. He was obviously an intelligent man, and it didn't take a genius to figure out what the image of someone who trained unruly horses for a living might be.

The notion of a grinning pre-teen sitting at his computer faking her out was disturbing; she recalled their last conversation, trying to remember anything that didn't fit. There wasn't, and she doubted that a child could successfully pull off such an impersonation. On the other hand, she reminded herself, there were some pretty bright and worldly-wise teenagers in the world today, and most of them were on the Internet.

"Andi?" Vickie asked. "Listen, hope I didn't ruin your day . . ."

Andi grinned. "No, you didn't. My lunch, maybe, but that's about all."

10

"What happened to you?" Paula asked, surprised. She put down the bridle she was holding and walked toward Grant as Blue Fire, docile, walked quietly and proudly into the barn.

Grant, astride him, didn't seem so proud. His pants were covered with mud; his hat was gone and he was wearing a sour expression. "Nothing," he growled.

She walked alongside Fire as he went to his usual place. "Come on, don't tell me that, what happened out there?"

"If you must know," he said as he stiffly dismounted, "I fell off."

Paula scowled deeply. "You okay?"

"Yeah."

She gazed at the horse. "I thought he was doing better than that. We still have a ways to go, it looks like. I'm really surprised he threw you."

Looking thoroughly annoyed, Grant knocked clumps of mud off his boots. "I didn't say he threw me. He didn't do anything except walk through some mud down in the arroyo. He slipped a little, and he leaned a little, and, well, I wasn't paying a lot of attention. And so, I fell off."

Paula looked at the horse, then back at Grant. "Now wait a minute here, Grant. Only the greenest amateur falls off just because the horse stumbles and leans. Even the kids don't do that. Something else, surely—"

Still irritated, Grant started brushing the horse down. "Right. Nobody experienced does that. But that's what happened."

She looked incredulous. "You fell off? You just up and fell off, just like that?"

He brushed the horse vigorously—overly vigorously. "Yeah. Just like that."

She stared at him for a second or two more, then turned away; when he glanced back at her he saw her shoulders were shaking. Refusing to allow himself to be affected by her laughing, he kept his lips tight and went right on working.

"I've been thinking," Paula said when she'd gotten herself under control, "that something's been on your mind lately. I asked you yesterday, 'Anything bothering you, Grant?' You said no. Now you fall off a horse for no reason and I know good and well something's bothering you!"

"Nothing's bothering me," he replied in clipped tones. "I just got careless."

"You don't get careless!" Her amusement was turning, by degrees, to concern. "What's wrong, Grant? Some problem with Todd?"

"No. Todd's doing fine."

"What, then?"

"Nothing. Like I told you, nothing."

Reaching out, she touched his shoulder. "Let's go sit and talk for a few minutes, Grant," she suggested. "In my office. I'll have one of the stable boys finish brushing Fire down."

"No, that's all right, I can—"

She smiled. "Do you work for me, Grant?"

He looked a little startled. "Well, yes . . ."

"Does that make me your boss?"

"You know it does."

"And so—if the boss wants to see you in her office, what do you say?"

Holding the brush in his hand, he fixed her with a steady look, a look that was almost a glare. He could see in her expression that she was wondering if she'd pushed too hard; he knew she remembered the terms of his employment, and that she was aware he could toss down the brush and resign, walking out never to be seen again. For a moment he considered doing just that; he didn't need this job, after all, and he assumed that her request was not work-related.

But no, he told himself, that wasn't right. Carelessness on his part could well affect her business, concern on her part wasn't unreasonable and wasn't necessarily unprofessional, either.

He put the brush down. "I say when do you want to see me?"

A few moments later he followed her into her office. On the

walls were pictures of horses with and without riders; dominant were the shots of Paula's Pride, a thoroughbred since sold to a stud farm in Maryland, who'd run in the Kentucky Derby and finished a respectable fifth. There were also several pictures of Paula astride the saddlebred she still owned, pictures from the days when she competed in equestrian events worldwide. Her desk, old and weather-beaten, was piled with papers overflowing from pairs of "in" and "out" boxes; there was a couch for guests like the Hollywood location people, but there was also an old and well-cracked naugahyde-covered seat that had been removed from a bus and bolted to the floor. Here Grant settled as Paula propped her slightly muddied boots on the corner of her desk.

Patiently, Grant waited; Paula didn't look at him, she folded her hands in her lap and examined her nails. "Grant," she said finally, "we're friends, aren't we? I mean, we don't just have an employer-employee relationship, do we?"

"No, Paula," he answered, keeping his tone level. He didn't like the direction this conversation was taking. "We're friends."

"Known each other for several years—six, now? Is that right?"

"Right."

"In all that time, I don't think I've ever asked you a personal question, not after that first discussion. I've invited you over to my house at least a dozen times and you've declined every time. I've stopped asking. You did notice."

He hesitated; this wasn't a conversation he wanted to be involved in. "Yes, Paula," he admitted finally. "I have noticed."

"I was sure you had." She gazed off into space. "When you came here," she went on, "you said you wanted a job working with the horses, strictly with the horses. You didn't want to deal with the customers or the studio people, you didn't even want to work with anyone here, you made that very clear. We tried you out and we could see you were experienced—oh, you were rusty then, very rusty, but these aren't things you ever forget—and we decided to give you a try. Don't get me wrong, we've never been sorry about that, not for a minute."

"Thank you, Paula."

"No thanks are necessary." She glanced at him, then returned her gaze to her hands. "You've probably guessed that people talk about you sometimes."

He laughed without humor. "Yes. It'd be strange if they didn't."

"Yes, it would. A man who's friendly and charming, but who doesn't seem to want to have one thing to do with a living soul. A man who has a son but no wife, a man who's never been seen out on a date. Never goes anywhere, does anything. Never has a beer with the other guys who work here. Never pays the slightest attention to the movie people. You remember that actress?"

Grant laughed again. "Oh, you mean Sharon—Sharon whatever her name was? Last year?"

Again Paula threw him a quick glance. "Yes. Sharon Durning. She was a gorgeous woman, wasn't she?"

"I suppose."

"That's my point. You suppose. Her role called for her to ride a horse bareback in the nude. Everyone here knew that, every man around here was trying to find some reason to be on the set during that scene. We needed you, we needed someone who knew which horse would be best for the scene and about how to do it—and you argued with me about it!"

"You didn't really need me there, Paula! I told you Chieftain was the best horse for it, but you insisted I be there anyway, and I didn't need to be."

"And didn't want to be."

"No, not really. Those Hollywood people, they get on my nerves, I've told you that . . . ."

"That's not the point and you know it. Here's this knockout actress wandering around the barn and riding the fields stark naked and you aren't giving her a second look! Worse, she's looking at you the whole time!"

"I didn't notice that."

"Of course not! You weren't paying attention!"

Well, not quite as little as you think, Paula, Grant allowed silently. I just wasn't obvious about it—she *was* a knockout, I'll give you that. "Are you asking me if I'm gay, Paula?" he replied jokingly.

She waved a hand at him. "No. I'm not. I know better. We have gays working here and a lot of the studio people are gay. It's not that with you, Grant, you just aren't interested in anyone except your son! Is that your whole life? You work here every day and go home to Todd every night and that's it, nothing else?"

"Is that a crime?" he asked, wondering how often he'd asked that exact question.

"No, it isn't a crime, Grant . . . all I'm saying is that you have no one to talk to about whatever problems you have in your life. Until the past few days, it didn't look like you *had* any. But you've been acting distracted—and now, this accident . . ."

He smiled and shook his head. "Paula, it's nothing. Really. I got careless for a moment, that's all. It won't happen again."

Paula watched his eyes for a long moment. "But there may come a time when you do . . . need someone to talk to, I mean . . ."

He shrugged, looked away, looked at a picture of the young Paula Kirkland astride her saddlebred; she was lovely then, he told himself, and she still was. "I'm pretty self-sufficient, Paula. That's just the way I've always been."

"But if you do . . ." Her voice was soft.

He looked back at her, suspicion in his eyes; he couldn't help it, it was so automatic.

She bit her lip, then went on doggedly: "I'd like that person to be me, Grant Kingsley. That's all. That's all I have to say." Obviously embarrassed, she swept her feet off the desk, freeing a cloud of papers that fluttered to the floor. Standing up, she walked to the door and disappeared into the back of the barn.

Grant sat still for several minutes. "You're a fool," he told himself aloud. "A fool." Shaking his head, he got up and walked out of the office; Paula was nowhere to be seen, and he didn't think it would be a good idea to go looking for her. Instead, he walked on out to his truck; after knocking off some more of the caked mud, he climbed inside.

On the dash, held by a little clip he'd mounted long ago, was a note reminding him to stop by for milk on his way home. Even so, the milk was forgotten. When he got home Todd asked him about it, and he'd had to go back out. Through dinner, Todd looked at him oddly. He didn't even notice.

His mind was elsewhere; it was in the rooms in the Hall of Sadness, where, at seven his time—and ten hers—he expected to meet Explorer tonight.

11

The avatars had fixed expressions; simple graphics. Even so, it seemed like the Vampira with the "Explorer" tag over her head was smiling as she stood in front of the blue-green fish.

Feeling like she was watching a soap opera, Sue5 stood off from the engrossed pair, once again eavesdropping on their conversation. She did not feel at all guilty about it; she had a mission, it wasn't just curiosity. She could easily track their connections from their source, and, using her hyperbrowser, she could see that both were still looped through that special server in Southern California. Sue5 had begun to wonder if Colin actually was going to do anything; she had to assume that he, and probably one of his Helpers, was watching, but so far he'd taken no action.

"I picked up that CD today," Andi was typing. "I really like it, Piscean! I vaguely remember hearing some of those songs, on the radio maybe, but I didn't know they were all by Al Stewart."

"Yes, 'Year of the Cat' has been a favorite of mine for a long time."

Mine too, Sue5 thought as she watched his words appear.

"You have a romantic streak, Piscean," Andi came back. "I shouldn't be surprised. A man chooses to be a cowboy, he's probably a little on the romantic side."

"A cowboy! (laugh) I'm not a cowboy, Explorer! I've explained what I do on the ranch."

"(yawn) Yes, I know. Kept me up late at night. I just *can't* get you to stop sometimes."

"I had no idea I was boring you! I can stop. Just watch me."

"Okay. I'm watching."

There was a brief pause. "Okay, so I can't. (laugh) But I'm still not a cowboy. Even if I do dress like one most of the time."

There was another hesitation, arousing Sue5's curiosity. When Andi's response came, it was obviously hastily typed: "What do you look like, Piscean?"

This time, the hesitation was longer. "I don't know exactly how to answer that, Explorer."

"Just do it as honestly as you can."

"Why?"

"(laugh) Why? Because I have an image in my mind of what you look like. I want to know if it's correct or not."

"You haven't told me what *you* look like." Hedging, Sue5 thought. Typical Grant Kingsley.

"I will. I promise. But I asked first!"

"(sigh) Okay. I'm six-one, around a hundred-ninety pounds. I have dark hair, medium-length, with a good bit of gray around the temples, and hazel eyes. Clean-shaven, sort of angular face. Because I'm outdoors all day I'm pretty tanned, my face and hands more than the rest of me. Enough?"

At this, Sue5 became intensely alert. It wasn't much, just a little, just a tiny shift—but the second sentence Andi saw wasn't the one Grant had typed. What had appeared—Sue5 checked it through her own pathways—was a line that said simply, "I have dark hair, medium-length, and hazel eyes." The sentence still worked; Andi would never question it, would never know the difference. There'd been a hesitation, a blank spot, in his communication, but that was common enough on these chat programs, that wasn't something anyone would notice, not ordinarily.

But Sue5 did; she noticed because she'd seen it before. It's started, she told herself. It's started and there's nothing I can do about it; I'm not ready yet, I need more time. Until now, she'd been able to hope that Colin would not pursue this one, but now that hope had been dashed.

No, she told herself; there was still time. She needed to follow her own plans. The developing friendship between Grant and Andi was not the only one she'd been observing; there was another, a much more advanced one between an Atlanta software engineer named Jeanne Stuart and a college professor from Ohio, Jim Webster. This one too had attracted Colin's attention, and whatever interested Colin interested her. Although she was not as personally involved, it could well be the testing ground for techniques she might use with Grant and Andi. Filing the slight miscommunication for future reference, she turned her attention back to the conversation.

"Your turn now," Grant was saying.

"Do I have to?"

"You have to. You started this, you pushed me into it."

"Well . . . okay. I'm 5 foot 6, about 110 pounds, sort of on the willowy side. I have some Asian in my background and it shows in some of my features. I have black hair and I keep it cut fairly short. My eyes are blue but they've got an Asian shape, it's something a lot of people notice. Is that enough?"

Whether all that was true or not, Sue5 couldn't really be sure; her Web search hadn't yielded a picture of Andi, she'd have to go to more exotic sites to get one. But the important thing, the thing she paid closest attention to, was the fact that Andi's description hadn't been changed in any way as it passed from her to Grant. Sue5 took note that the mention of blue eyes with an Asian shape had been passed along, even though it made Andi unusual-looking. This part of the process she knew little about, even though she'd observed Colin's game before—if only from inside the framework of the Internet.

There was, after all, another part of it—a real world part—and she had little idea how that phase of the game was to be played. She knew only how it was supposed to end.

12

You made yourself sound like a damn movie star, Andi thought as she sat before her computer. He isn't going to believe a word of it. A lot of men over the years had told her she was quite attractive—some used stronger terms than that—but, standing before a mirror, she always focused on her flaws. And besides, she told herself, telling him you're unattractive isn't likely to keep him coming back.

That she wanted to keep him coming back, that she'd begun to look forward to these sessions, she'd already admitted to herself. A complex man, far more intelligent and widely read than what she'd expect from a ranch employee, a horse trainer. He was easy to talk to, he had a way with words, a way of getting her to open up quickly; he was better at this than any man she'd previously known.

And yet, if she could believe what he said and if she was, with her therapist's instincts, reading between the lines correctly, he'd set up a life for himself that was designed to isolate him from people. He'd been hesitant the times they'd talked about this, and so far she'd been unwilling to push, afraid that any such inquiries might drive him away. Finding out about the man who called himself Piscean, she understood, might well take some patience.

She glanced at the clock; it was late, almost midnight, and she had a patient tomorrow at eight-thirty. She'd been on with Piscean for an hour and a half now. Though she was a little drowsy, talking to him was never tiring to her, never boring. Still, she was going to have to call an end to tonight's session pretty soon.

Just then, his words appeared on her screen: "It's getting pretty late on your coast, Explorer. Maybe we ought to call it a night?"

She smiled warmly as she read this. "Yes," she agreed. "You're probably tired too . . ."

"Actually not at all, it's just nine here, it's not late. I know it's much later where you are."

"Yes, it is." Responding to his concern and slightly too drowsy to think straight, she went on without really considering what she was saying, without thinking about how it might sound: "I was hoping," she typed, "to ask you a few other questions tonight."

"Oh? Like what?"

"Well, we've talked about your son several times, but you've never mentioned his mother. Are you married, divorced, what?" Finishing her sentence, she leaned back to await the answer; only then did she realize how blunt it sounded. If she'd had a way to snatch those words back, she would've done so.

The long pause that ensued told her that she'd taken him by surprise, that she'd been overly direct, too soon. Anxiously she waited; at last his answer came: "It isn't something I like to talk about, Explorer," he typed. "But I'll answer your question. I'm a widower. My wife was killed—" Here there was another pause—"in an automobile accident, almost eleven years ago."

Andi stared at the words, the four lines with long pauses between them. She sighed. There was more to it, more than he was saying, but she certainly wasn't going to press him for any more right now.

"I'm sorry to hear that, Piscean," she typed back. "And I

know that saying I'm sorry doesn't mean anything. Really I'm sorry I brought it up."

Again there was a hesitation. "It's okay. I should've told you before." The next line came quickly, with several minor typos: "What about you? Married, divorced, what?"

Andi smiled again. That's fine, Piscean, she said mentally as she started typing, that's fine. "I'm single," she informed him. "Never married. No current boyfriend and no steady one for a while now. Everybody asks what's wrong with me."

"I won't," he shot back.

But I'll tell you anyway, she thought. "Three years ago I was engaged to someone in my field, a psychiatrist. It turned out badly. It took me a while to get over it. It's left me cautious. Too cautious, my friends tell me." She went on for several minutes, rambling, saying more than she really meant to, telling him how the relationship had left her pessimistic, telling him that it had in ways destroyed her ability to trust anyone. Once she'd finished, she read her own words ruefully and waited for the usual clichés about having faith in people and in the future, about how time heals all wounds.

"I can understand that," he replied, startling her.

"Not many people can."

The next line appeared almost as soon as she'd sent that one. "But *I* can. I'm the same way."

Andi felt her eyes getting moist; silly, she told herself. "You are the first person," she wrote back, "that's ever said that to me. That you understand."

"Explorer, would you give me your E-mail address?"

Her eyes widened. This was, it seemed to her, taking things to another level—and she did not object to it in the least. "Of course," she answered. "It's 'explorer@nyct.net.' "

"I'm 'loner@netcom.com,' " he typed back. Grabbing a pen and a pad, she jotted that down. "I think you should go to bed now, Explorer," he continued. "It's late. And I want to write you a letter."

She smiled again. "I'll be looking forward to that, Piscean." Using her mouse, she swept her pointer up to the button that was labeled "quit," but there she hesitated, looking at the blank face of the fish that she'd been talking to.

"Go," he told her.

She clicked on the button. The program asked her if she was sure; she told it silently that she wasn't, but she clicked on the

"Y" button anyway, and the program shut itself down. After logging off Nyct, she got ready for bed. Once she'd done that, she found she could not resist returning, logging back on, and checking to see if she had an E-mail yet. She didn't.

In spite of her tiredness, sleep was a long time coming; she was looking forward to that letter, wondering what he was going to say.

13

The E-mail Andi was looking forward to was sent from Grant's machine to the local Netcom server at about two AM New York time. It should have taken less than five minutes to cross the country, to appear on Nyct's server and there to reside, waiting for Andi to retrieve it.

It took a little longer than that, though not so long that anyone would've noticed. Like everything coming from Grant's log-on now, it had been re-routed through the server in Southern California, held there for a couple of minutes, and then passed back to the Internet. Sue5, wide awake and watching the activity closely, saw it come in; using the special capabilities of her browser, she pulled a copy into her local access while it was being held up, and was able to read it long before Andi ever saw it. After it was passed on, she used those same capabilities to examine the copy that was waiting for Andi to read the next morning, and she filed a duplicate of that, too—even though they were identical.

But Sue5 did not sleep after accomplishing this bit of hacking; it was to be a busy night for her. One of the other cyberspace friendships she'd been observing, the one involving Jeanne Stuart, had suddenly begun to move more quickly; her cyber-lover was inviting her to meet him, and she was planning to do just that. Though Sue5 wasn't ready to take action, she felt impelled to take the chance—not just because the moment of truth for Jeanne was at hand, but because it provided an opportunity for her to test some of the new capabilities she'd given her browser.

And so, about an hour after Grant's E-mail had been sent to New York, she sent one of her own to Atlanta, to Jstuart@mindspring.com, and anxiously waited to see what the results might be.

She did not have to wait long. Less than thirty minutes after she sent that E-mail, her on-line connection was interrupted; she knew all too well what that meant, and she turned her attention to the window opening on the left-hand side of her screen, the area where the images of the sysops always appeared.

"Yes?" she inquired nervously before there was a picture. "You need me?"

The video image of a dark-haired man, movie-star handsome, appeared in the window. "No, Susie-Q," he said. "It's late, you should be sleeping. You need your rest."

"Colin," she breathed. Her voice took on a hard edge; her hatred of this man was more than enough to mask any fear she might feel. "I sleep when I'm tired. Is that a problem for you too?"

"Sometimes," he answered. "Sometimes. If you just cruise around the Net and talk to people on the chats, no, it isn't a problem for us." He laughed; some might have heard that laugh as charming, as she once did, but now she heard it as foul, ugly. "But when you spend your time sending E-mails—like the one you just sent to jstuart@mindspring.com—well, that's different, Susie-Q. And you know it is."

She felt a cold flare in the pit of her stomach. "Colin, I didn't send—"

"Susie, we know you slipped into Global's main server recently, we know you set up watcher@gnn.com as a dummy reporting account for yourself. You did it quite well; the folks at Global aren't even aware of the existence of that account. You set it up nicely, so that even if they do stumble across it they won't have a clue as to where it came from."

"Colin, I—"

"We've had talks about this, Susie-Q. The E-mail wasn't a surprise, we've been expecting something like that from you. You didn't disappoint us, I'm afraid."

The coldness in her stomach expanded rapidly. "Colin, please . . ."

His voice was as cold as she felt inside. "You want us to

restrict you? Cut all your access to the chats? Even cut you off completely?"

"Completely! You can't do that, Colin!" Her voice was shrill but she couldn't help it. "You know what would happen, you know!"

"Yes, we do. And we don't want to do that. You're one of the best we have. But Susie, we can't have you doing this sort of thing."

She felt like sobbing, but she held it back. "Yes, Colin."

"I'm still your best friend here. I've gone to bat for you again, Susie."

She bit back the rage and hatred she felt. "Yes, Colin."

"Good. Now you go out there and you pull that E-mail off of Mindspring's server. Don't leave a trace of it."

"Colin, I don't know if I can—"

"Don't give me that!" he barked suddenly. "Don't you try to bullshit me, bitch!" His voice calmed abruptly. "Do it, Susie. Do it and nothing'll happen to you—this time. Try something like this again and your chat privileges are gone, and after that your access—whatever it costs the company. You aren't going to be warned again."

"Yes, Colin," she replied meekly. "As you say."

"Good. You'd better get to it. If Jeanne Stuart should pull that one in, there'll be consequences."

"Yes, Colin."

"We'll be watching. Get to work." The window abruptly vanished.

For several seconds she stared at the place where the window had been; then, with a feeling of nausea, she started the process of erasing the E-mail from the Mindspring server. Colin meant what he said. If she refused to erase it, there were others in the company who could—and would.

"I'm so sorry, Jeanne," she moaned as she watched the posting disappear. "I just don't have a choice!"

14

It was cool and pleasant that next morning, as pleasant as Manhattan ever gets. There'd been a shower the night before, the air was clean; spring greens brightened the trees outside the window Andi had opened to let the pleasantness into her apartment. Beside that window, barefoot, dressed in a silk teal Chinese robe, she sat sipping her morning coffee and smiling at the letter on her computer screen, the E-mail she'd already read through ten times and was in the process of reading again:

Date: Tue, 23 Apr 1996 22:42:40 -0700 (PDT)
X-Sender: loner@netcom.com (Unverified)
To: explorer@nyct.net (Explorer)
X-UIDL: 830295112.002
From: loner@netcom.com (loner)
Subject: Introduction

Dear Explorer,

It seems odd to me to write that name in the salutation of a letter—but that's the only name I know you by. And yes, I understand, Piscean is the only name you know me by, as well.

Let me change that. My name is Grant Warner Kingsley, Grant to all the friends I've ever had. Although I would like to know your real name, I don't want you to feel obligated to give it to me. I know there's security in anonymity.

Tonight, something happened that hasn't happened to me in a long time. No, that's wrong, tonight something happened that hasn't happened at all, not since Carol—that was my wife's name—died, eleven years ago. Tonight I heard someone else say they felt the way I do.

What you said—that since your engagement ended you didn't feel you could trust anyone, and that no one you talked to seemed to understand—those were words I've said to myself. No one can possibly understand. That's what I thought. That's what I believed. And then I hear you say the things that I've felt, you express my own feelings for me, and you tell me they're yours, too.

I hope I didn't offend you or frighten you when I asked you for your E-mail address. On World's Chat you say things quickly, in as few words as possible. I wanted to say these things to you more fully. I just wanted you to know what those words you said last night meant to me.

all my best,
Grant

Smiling, feeling like a teenager, she stretched and grinned broadly as she came to that signature. She felt she could see him, late at night on the ranch in California, writing this letter. She pictured his study illuminated by an oil lamp and she saw him writing this letter with a quill pen—how he'd gotten it out onto the Internet was absolutely mysterious—but that didn't matter to her. Reaching out, she touched the screen with her fingertips where the word "understand" was; she could almost smell the horses, that old familiar—and to her, wonderful— aroma.

"Andi, you are really being silly," she said aloud. She studied the screen, and, after a bit of fumbling, figured out how to reply. Over the next forty-five minutes she composed her response, thinking as she did about Grant reading it when he arose; it was three-thirty in the morning in Los Angeles—she didn't know how early he got up but she was sure it wasn't that early.

After finishing it, she clicked on the "send" button and watched the quick progress of the little green bar that told her her message was being sent. Then, fearful of being late for her first morning appointment, she rushed off to the shower.

Arriving at her office, she ran into Vickie in the hallway. "You," Vickie noted, "have that cat look about you this morning."

"Cat look?"

"Mm-hm. You know, the one commonly associated with a missing canary?"

Andi gave her a disparaging look. "Vickie, I don't know what you are talking about!"

"Oh no? What's his name?"

She tried to suppress the giggle this provoked, but she failed miserably. "Grant," she admitted.

15

His hair still tousled from sleep, Todd stood in the doorway of Grant's study. "Dad?" he asked. "We gonna have any breakfast this morning?"

The E-mail still on his screen, Grant swiveled his chair around. "Oh, yeah," he mumbled absent-mindedly. "Breakfast. What time is it, anyhow?"

The boy laughed. "You don't know? You're the one always telling me, 'hurry up, the bus is coming!' Now *you're* asking *me* what time it is?"

Grant glanced at his watch. "Oh," he said, "Six-thirty! I've got to get moving!" He looked back at the E-mail; if he didn't answer it now, he wouldn't get to it before about seven at best— ten PM her time. "Look, Todd, you mind just having a bowl of cereal this morning? I've got something here I need to do . . ."

"Sure," Todd answered. He walked on into the study, looked at the screen. "What's that? A letter from that guy who's got the thoroughbred that won't stop rearing, what was his name . . ."

With a swift move of the mouse, Grant reduced the letter to a small picture of a mailbox at the bottom of his screen. "No," he said. "It's just a letter."

"From who?"

Grant couldn't keep the exasperation from his voice. "From somebody; from a friend. Why do you want to know?"

Todd shrugged. "Just wondering. Why're you getting all bent?"

"I'm not getting bent."

"Yes, you are."

"Todd, could you just go and get your breakfast, please?" Grant asked, the exasperation increasing.

"You coming?"

"Yes, in a minute."

Todd frowned. "Why not now? What's up?"

Grant sighed. "Okay, son. If you must know, I'd like to answer this letter before I go to work today and I don't have a lot of time to do that. Is that okay with you?"

Todd shrugged, a little theatrically. "Sure." Turning, he walked back to the door; for some reason he paused there for a long moment before disappearing into the hallway outside. Grant waited until his footsteps had faded before bringing the letter back up on the screen. Again, he read through his letter, seeing his own words displayed with the "greater than" sign in front of them, what most called "carets." As he read he kept reminding himself that this was the first personal letter he'd ever received by E-mail:

Return-Path: explorer@nyct.net
Date: Wed, 24 Apr 1996 07:00:04 -0400 (EDT)
X-Sender: explorer@popserv.nyct.net (Unverified)
To: loner@netcom.com (Grant Kingsley)
X-UIDL: 830344947.002
From: explorer@nyct.net (Explorer)
Subject: Re: Good Morning, LA!

Hello, Grant. Very glad to meet you.

First, let me introduce myself: my name is Andrea Lawrence. When I read your letter it seemed strange to me that you *didn't* know my name.

>Let me change that. My name is Grant Warner Kingsley, Grant to all
>the friends I've ever had.

To all *my* friends, I'm known as Andi. Giving you my real name was the first thing on my mind. Besides, it's the least I can do for the *fish* who rescued me from the shark feeding frenzy I ran into when I first came onto the Chat.

>there's security in anonymity.

There is indeed, but there's an insecurity too about not being able to *see* the person you are talking with. For me, in my profession, body language and facial expression give me clues about what's behind the things my patients say. I must confess that I have suspicions about the validity of relationships and communications in this medium. But all those seem to vanish, though, when I'm talking to you.

>What you said—that since your engagement ended you didn't feel you
>could trust anyone, and that no one you talked to seemed to
>understand—those were words I've said to myself. No one can
>possibly understand. That's what I thought. That's what I believed.
>And then I hear you say the things that I've felt, you express my
>own feelings for me, and you tell me they're yours, too.

That's quite startling to me. You're the first person I've talked to in a very long time who seems to really understand me. It's frightening, somehow, to put this down in words. Words have power, you know . . .

>I hope that I didn't offend you or frighten you when I asked you
>for your E-mail address. On World's Chat you say things quickly, in
>as few words as possible. I wanted to say these things to you more
>fully. I just wanted you to know what those words you said last
>night meant to me.

(laugh) Well, if you hadn't asked, Grant, I would have. It's strange, you have a picture of a very different Andi than most who know me . . . I'm usually reserved, some say distant. I think it has to do with my upbringing. My mother, though she was only half-Chinese, grew up in China (Taiwan) and was very traditional in her outlook, she insisted I learn Chinese as well as English. I was born in the United States, in Maryland, just outside Washington. I went to the public schools and grew up as an average American girl.

Mainly, I just wanted to let you know that no offense, at all, was taken at your request for my E-mail address. I really didn't want to get off the program last night—maybe I should apologize to you for keeping you so long!—and the first thing I did this morning was turn my computer on. Quite a change for a woman who often finds it difficult to roll out of bed in the mornings.

I need to ask you a question. In your experience, have you found that things on the Internet always move at this incredible speed? Why do you think this is?

Another thing: as you saw on World's Chat, I'm woefully ignorant of the E-mail conventions. Perhaps you could educate me on the etiquette?

I would love to continue writing to you but I *have* to get ready for work. I look forward to hearing from you again, soon. Smiling . . .

Take care,
Andi

Leaning back in his chair and grinning, Grant returned to the top of the letter and read it again, lingering over the line where she'd said she hadn't wanted to leave last night.

He hadn't either; he'd lost track of time, forgotten about his job, even forgotten about the past for a little while. He glanced to his right, where a picture of Carol sat in a golden frame, her smiling face watching him. His mood faded; it faded but it didn't go tumbling down into an abyss the way it so often had in the past.

"It isn't wrong, is it?" he asked her aloud, as if the picture could hear him. "In a way I want to back off, it's going so fast, but in another way I don't. Is this what you'd want me to do?"

Staring at the picture through misted eyes, he fell silent. He could've sworn he could hear her speak back to him, telling him that not only was it time but that it was past time.

But he'd heard her picture say that before, he knew how she felt. Before, he hadn't been ready. Now, maybe that was changing.

16

Deputy Jess Lehmann had only been on the job a year; he hadn't seen anything like this before. He stared fixedly at the corpse until he was sure no one was looking. Then he averted his eyes while keeping his head still, looking off to the side, looking down at his shoes, anywhere except straight ahead.

Inyo County sheriff Bill Paulsen, by contrast, had seen it all in his time—or felt he had. He glanced over at Lehmann. "Y'okay, son?" he called to his young deputy.

Lehmann came back. "Yes, sir," he answered in military fashion. He was pale and he was noticeably avoiding looking at the corpse on the ground, but he seemed under control.

A third man on the scene, however, knelt by the body, and, looking it over with a professional eye, gave a low whistle and shook his head. Representing the county's medical examiner's office, Jim Perkins had long ago learned to detach himself from things like this. Casually, he slipped a Marlboro from the pack in his pocket and, lighting it, blew a cloud of smoke. "Somebody put her through the mill, that's for sure," he commented, poking the body. "The coyotes did us a favor, I guess, by digging her up." He glanced around at the remote desert countryside. "We never would have found her out here." He scanned the horizon as if expecting to see something out there. "I'd say there's lots of bodies buried out in these deserts," he murmured. "And there's people who know most of them won't ever be found, either."

"Hard to believe anybody'd do that," the sheriff muttered. "Tortured to death like that . . ."

Perkins shook his head. "You got it wrong, Bill," he said. "She wasn't tortured to death. I dunno how she died. We'll work that out in the lab."

The sheriff scowled. "What do you mean, man?" he demanded. "Look at her! Shit, you can see the stab wounds!"

Again Perkins' head moved from side to side. "Yeah, but they weren't fatal." He looked at the body for a long moment; it was that of a young woman, a woman who'd possibly been quite attractive at one time. After a couple of days of being buried in the desert, after being dug up by coyotes and discovered, by purest chance, by hikers—and after what had been done to her—she wasn't attractive now. Her hands and her feet were missing, as were her eyes. Her ears had been cut away cleanly, and there were two large open wounds in her lower body, one just under her ribcage on her left and one lower down, near her navel.

"You're nuts," the sheriff argued. "Either one of those stabs would've killed her! Or she bled to death when they cut off her hands!"

"Uh-uh." He picked up the woman's arm. "Look at this. It's mostly healed. More, the bone's cut way back up in there; whoever did this knew how to do an amputation—enough muscle to cover the bone, enough skin to cover the muscle. This wasn't a hack job, this girl had her hands and feet amputated, and it was done a long time before she died. Same with her ears. With the eyes I can't be sure right now, we'll have to wait on the lab reports."

"Jesus!"

"Yeah, tell me about it. She went through some kinda hell, all right." He brushed desert dust away from the upper wound in the woman's abdomen. "Now, look here—these stab wounds, as you call 'em—they're healed up around the edges too. I dunno how or why, but somebody took some real care to make sure these stabs didn't kill her; just guessing right now but I'd say they're as old as the amputations." Leaning closer to the corpse, ignoring the smell, Perkins examined her eyes more closely. "Damn!" he exclaimed. "Looks like this wasn't simple either—it's real hard to tell but I think part of the eyeball is still there, they weren't just dug out—looks to me like they might've been cut in half!"

"Oh, shit," Lehmann groaned. He turned away, unable to stop himself this time.

"This is a weird one," Perkins allowed. "Weird." He pulled the woman's chin down, opened her mouth. "Her teeth are gone, too. She might stay a Jane Doe forever. Somebody wanted to make real sure we didn't figure out who she was. Too bad."

The sheriff's face took on a hard set. It had been a long time since a case had hit him this hard. "It'd be good to know who she was," he agreed. "But me, right now, I wanna know what kinda lunatic did this. I wanna get my hands on him!"

Perkins nodded. "Yep," he murmured. "This one, Bill, I'd like that too. I sure would."

17

"You seem a little down, Fish Man," Sue5 was saying. "You have problems?"

"No," Grant answered shortly. His fish avatar swung restlessly from side to side.

I do, Sue5 said silently. I do. I've done something I don't know if I can ever forgive myself for, I deleted that E-mail. I keep telling myself I didn't have a choice, that it would've been deleted whether I did it or not, but I did do it. Oh, God, Grant Kingsley, I wish I could talk to you about it, I wish I could tell you the whole story. But I can talk to you about other things, at least.

"You're looking for Explorer, aren't you?" she asked boldly.

He didn't answer immediately; she knew he didn't take too well to personal questions, she knew there was a risk he'd just go silent on her or even vanish from the Chat altogether.

He didn't do either. "Yes," he answered finally. "I expected her to be here and she's not."

"Maybe she's busy. With something in the real world. (laugh) *Some* people do have real lives, you know."

"I know. Like I said, I just expected her."

"Worried about her?"

"No." There was a significant pause. "Yes. Isn't that stupid,

Sue? I mean, there are a thousand perfectly good reasons why she might not be on tonight."

"Yes, there are. There's been a lot of times I've expected to meet someone here and he didn't show up."

"Oh, well. Gives us a chance to talk, doesn't it?" There was another silence. "Sue, I didn't mean it that way."

She smiled—although she knew that if he could've seen that smile, he would've been able to see the pain behind it. "I know how you meant it, Fish Man. I know you and Explorer have gotten really close in the past week or so."

"It's obvious, huh?"

"I'm afraid so. (smile) But I'm glad we have a chance to talk too, Fish Man."

"Have you ever gotten close to someone on the Net, Sue? Someone you've never met, someone you just talk to here and by E-mail?"

Oh, yes, Grant. Yes I have. I wish I could tell you all about it, but I can't. "Yes," she answered. "Some time back. It didn't work out in the end."

"You feel like talking about it?"

Dangerous ground here, she told herself. Even so, she answered with an affirmative. "I don't know exactly what to tell you, Fish Man," she went on. "I mean, what do you want to know?"

"Well, to start with, I guess you were on a long time before this happened? Surfing the Net, I mean?"

"(laugh) I'd like to say so, Fish Man. I'd like to tell you I was a veteran of the Web, that I'd been cruising around out here for years."

"No?"

"No. The first exposure I had to the Internet was when I got linked to it through the computers where I worked, an Ethernet hookup. At first I didn't do much of anything with it, I really wasn't very interested."

"Something must've changed your mind."

"Yes, the newsgroups. Somebody told me about Usenet and I started following some of the groups. Do you keep up with any of them?"

"Yes, some."

"Then you know they can be addictive."

"Yes."

"Well, for a long while I was just lurking, reading the postings but never saying anything. But eventually I started making some little comments about some of the articles. As soon as I started doing *that* people began writing me personal E-mails. It seemed rude not to answer them, and pretty soon I was writing E-mails every day. Then twice a day. And I bought a computer of my own, because I was spending all my time at work on the Internet and writing E-mails."

"(smile) Luckily I can't do that at work."

"You *are* lucky. I wasn't getting *anything* done."

"And you met someone."

"Yes." Sue fell silent for a few long seconds; that Colin or Albert or someone was monitoring this conversation she had no doubts at all. "Someone who answered one of my Usenet postings. We seemed to hit it off right away."

"It moved fast?"

"Faster that I would've believed, Fish Man. Nobody who hasn't experienced it can understand how fast these things move. Within two weeks I was convinced I was in love with him. I was ready to go meet him, I was ready to *marry* him."

"Two weeks?"

"Two, three. Nothing ever happened that fast for me before."

Grant's avatar shifted a little; he said nothing for a few moments. "Two weeks ago," he continued at last, "I wouldn't have understood that, Sue. Other people have told me similar stories. I thought they were just people who were in love with the idea of being in love."

"But now it's happening to you."

Again he didn't answer. "I don't know," he admitted finally. "No. It's just a friendship. It's just that it's so different from anything I know."

"Why'd you come on the Net, Fish Man?" Sue asked when he fell silent again. "Why'd you start coming here?"

"(laugh) I got the computer so my boy could use it for his homework. Then I set it up for him. I'd had some experience with computers before, a long time ago, but they were really different animals back then. This one was . . . well, it was fun. I began playing with it. I got an Internet account so my son could use all the resources, and it got to be more fun. I'm sure you know what I mean, Sue."

"Oh, yes. I sure do, Fish Man."

"Anyway, I was spending a lot of time cruising around the

Web, just looking, and I ran across the World's Chat program. I decided to download it and set it up just to see if I could."

"(smile) And you could."

"Could and did. The first few times I came on here I didn't talk to anyone. No one spoke to me."

"That fish avatar and that name. Nobody can figure out what you are."

"I suppose. It's funny how I got started."

"How's that?"

"My son. He wanted to try it out. I found him a special avatar, it's called 'Red Skull.' Right away he developed a technique of speaking to people, just saying 'hi,' and moving on. Whoever responded he'd come back to. I started doing the same thing."

"(laugh) Yes, I remember. When we met. You said hi and then just roared on by, I didn't know what was going on."

"Right. You said hi back, I came back, and the rest is history. But you were telling about your own Internet romance, and we got off the track."

There's not a lot I can tell you, Sue5 thought—not safely, anyway. "There's not too much more to tell. I went to meet him, and in person it didn't work out. That happens."

She could see his hesitancy, she knew he was wondering how far to pursue this. "Yes, I suppose it does. You must've been very disappointed."

You couldn't know the half of it, she said silently. "Well, yes, I was. But things like that happen."

Again, she could almost feel him fighting with himself, he didn't want to reveal anything—he never had—but he did want to talk. "Sue," he opened, "we've been friends for a while here, and in all that time we've avoiding talking about anything personal. I guess you knew that's how I wanted it."

"Yes, Fish Man, I did."

"But I'm going to ask you now if you want to talk about this. If you don't, just say the word, I'll understand."

Ah, Grant, if only I really could, she thought. "No, I don't mind talking about it, Fish Man," she answered. "But there isn't a lot to tell beyond what I told you already."

He wasn't satisfied. "You said you met him through Usenet postings?"

"Yes. Do you know who Leonard Cohen is?"

This answer came quickly—surprisingly quickly. "Why, yes, I do. 'Suzanne,' 'I'm Your Man,' all those? (laugh) I'm a *big* fan of his, I don't think there's *any" lyricist anywhere *close* to as good. I have *all* his albums."

Sue5 felt as if her eyes were misting up. Oh, Grant, you just broke my heart, she told herself; you just did it, and there's no fixing it now . . . Forcing control, she started to answer: "Well, that's a coincidence. That's what my guy posted. I posted back and I agreed. I'd been turned on to Cohen years before. But he's not current, and none of my friends knew anything about him. That's what our first few E-mails were about. Leonard Cohen, his songs and his poems."

"That's strong stuff. That could really take you places."

"Yes, it could and it did. We started quoting Cohen at each other. Things started to move, very fast."

"What happened then?"

"(shrug) All the usual things. We gave each other our snail-mail addresses, our phone numbers. We sent pictures of ourselves to each other over the Net, as JPG attachments."

"And then?"

"I liked what I saw. I liked the presents I got from him. We never had even *one* decent phone conversation because about that time my phone went on the fritz, always cutting off. But it didn't matter. We planned to meet. I wanted him to come to me but he said that wasn't possible, and he sent me a ticket. So I went."

"And then?"

Now it was Sue5's turn to hesitate. For a wild moment, she considered telling him the whole story, just letting it come spilling out.

But she didn't; she was all too aware of the loop in Grant's connection, the loop that had to be respected if she hoped to ever be able to do anything. "What happened, Fish Man, was that he just wasn't who I imagined he was," she answered carefully. "And I guess I wasn't either. It didn't work out."

"Oh." He seemed disappointed; she was quite aware that he'd been hoping for more than that.

"It happens in real-world romances too, Fish Man," she reminded him. "All the time."

"I suppose. But with Explorer we're talking about a friendship, not a romance. Remember?"

Keep telling yourself that, Sue5 told him mentally. Maybe you can convince yourself.

You sure aren't convincing me.

18

At least a part of Grant wasn't unaware of a certain truth in Sue5's words. There was, he had to admit, more than just a casual friendship developing between himself and Andi. As he talked with Sue5, he found himself thinking back to the years after Carol's death. He thought he could smell the ocean, feel the seabreeze, as if he were back in that little house in Santa Monica where he'd lived when he and Todd had first come to southern California.

Many things were different for him then. Just out of the Navy, he'd taken a job as a diver. He was forcing himself to date, to go out at least once a week, even though all the women he was meeting paled in comparison to his memories of Carol. But he'd felt obligated, he'd felt it was unfair to ask Todd to grow up without a mother.

His job had been interesting and varied. One day the company had been hired by a film crew shooting a documentary on underwater life. He'd worked long and hard on this project, he'd spent many days under the ocean in the studio's service.

And he'd gotten to know Mariel Winston.

Mariel was a consultant on the project, a marine biologist from UCLA. A true California girl, she'd been in the habit of spending her days on shipboard dressed in a bikini, her light blond hair tied back in a tight ponytail. Almost every man on the crew had made a pass at her; she'd responded to none of them, she'd been all business in spite of her appearance. Accustomed to putting business first, Grant treated her as he treated any male crew member.

He didn't flirt with her, not ever. And, one afternoon, she'd walked up to him as he stood leaning on the ship's rail, watching the waves of a rough Pacific day heaving, and bluntly asked him why not.

He remembered it clearly. It was cloudy, it had rained earlier, a squall in from the west; nevertheless she was dressed as always, a white bikini even though there was no sun to be had.

He'd turned as she spoke, leaning his forearms on the rail of the slightly pitching ship, watching her standing free, steadying herself easily against the rolls.

"Why?" he asked her with a grin. "Is there a law that says I have to?"

She'd gestured helplessly. "Well, hell, yes," she'd told him. "You bet there is. You think I keep in this shape, that I keep this tan, without working on it? What the hell good does that do me if the cutest guy on the ship pays no attention?"

He'd laughed. "Maybe I'm gay. Maybe I have me a lover right here on board."

"Uh-uh. I can tell. Gay you're not. You're the silent type, that's what. Now: are you going to explain it me or do I put the cuffs on you and take you in?"

"No, I'm not into that," he'd told her, and they'd both laughed. His attempts to slough off her questions hadn't been accepted. Finally, he'd explained about losing his wife in an accident.

Mariel had been more than sympathetic. They'd talked for a long time that afternoon, well into the evening. She'd made it clear that he'd be welcome to spend the night in her cabin, but to her surprise he'd declined.

She hadn't been upset, however, and over the next few days they became closer and closer. Eventually, hesitantly, more than a little nervously, he had gone to her cabin.

He'd tried to explain it to her. His memories of Carol were fresh, acutely painful; he'd been celibate since the accident. This she'd taken as evidence of his sincerity, of his loyalty—which had delighted him.

He thought about that night now; for many men it would've been a dream come true, for him it had been something else entirely. The storms had rolled in again that night, driving rain filled the air outside. As they talked in her cabin, he'd sat on the bunk for a while while she stood before him, balancing herself against the ship's severe rolling as effortlessly as ever; the light play of the muscles in her long shapely legs was a beautiful thing to watch. Teasing him, coaxing him, unconcerned at the role reversal, she'd at last gotten him to remove his shirt; she'd removed her top and he'd stood to embrace her, the two of them doing a sensual slow dance in rhythm to the pitching of the ship. And, eventually, they'd gotten into the bed.

It hadn't been bad. Not at all. He'd been worried about his own response; he needn't have been. Mariel was skillful and patient and there were no problems; but he simply hadn't been there emotionally, he hadn't been present. Bright and sensitive, Mariel had recognized it; afterwards she'd been disappointed, but not discouraged.

After the documentary was finished, they continued to see each other on a regular basis. The lovemaking continued too, as did Grant's reservations—he was going through the motions, little more, and Mariel was acutely aware of it. She'd been more than patient, more than forgiving, even when he'd hurt her badly one night; in the middle of lovemaking he'd called her "Carol."

She'd met Todd, too, and the two of them had taken to each other immediately, they'd become great friends. At the time, Grant was wondering what was wrong with him. Mariel was beautiful, bright, sensual, kind—there wasn't a superlative that couldn't be applied to her—and she was, as the weeks passed, more and more in love with him.

But he wasn't in love with her. There wasn't, he kept telling himself, one reason why he shouldn't've been; he just wasn't. She would've been an ideal stepmother for Todd, a wonderful wife for him. Love, he'd tried to tell himself, wasn't everything. They had a lot in common; she loved the beach and the ocean, both loved to be aboard a ship.

Then there'd come that Saturday. A brief dive, nothing to keep him all day. He'd done his work, he'd finished early, he'd driven back to his house in Santa Monica; when he'd arrived he'd found that Mariel had driven Todd down to the dock he'd sailed from to meet him, to surprise him. Initially, he hadn't been too affected by this, though her driving alone with Todd in the car brought back too many memories, made him uncomfortable. Even so, he settled in to wait for her to come back.

She didn't come back.

Hours passed, afternoon slid into early evening; still she didn't return. His initial discomfort turned to panic, his patient sitting turned to pacing and then to making calls, trying to find out if a Chevy Blazer—her car—had been involved in an accident, even calling the hospitals. The image of the Blazer torn to pieces on the freeway haunted him.

Finally they did return, both perfectly fine. She was a little annoyed; it had taken her, she'd said, quite a while to ascertain that he'd already left, and then, on her way back, she'd run into a monster jam on the freeway. Moving finally, Todd had been hungry and in need of a bathroom, and she'd made a pit stop for him. Then, to her absolute frustration, encountered yet another freeway tie-up.

Grant hadn't been rational; he'd known that even then. He'd listened to her story in stony silence, and then, to her amazement, he'd begun yelling at her for being foolish enough to risk her own life and Todd's on the freeway. She'd blazed back at him, they'd argued furiously, and, again, he'd called her Carol.

That had stopped the argument. And, eventually, it stopped the relationship as well. Mariel explained tearfully that she had loved him, she'd even been willing to marry him knowing he didn't love her yet, but she could not face living her life with Carol's ghost always present. Grant hadn't been able to argue with her; they parted friends, but they parted.

Afterwards, he'd sunk into a depression. Mariel had been perfect, as stepmother, wife, lover; he could not have hoped to do better—and he hadn't been able to love her, hadn't been able to even treat her decently. He'd taken to driving into the mountains north of Los Angeles on the weekends, driving aimlessly. One day he'd found a horse loose on the roadway. Stopping his car, he'd convinced the animal to allow him to come close; he'd had it fully under control when the owner came along. The owner, impressed, had offered him a job as a wrangler, and, on impulse, he'd accepted. His new life on the ranches had begun. He'd escaped the sea; and, not feeling he could trust anyone—including himself—he'd escaped people, too. His life now was horses and the one person he truly cared about, his son.

And now, after all these years, his life might be changing. Blankly, he stared at the computer. These things, he told himself, sure have changed the world. You live away from everybody, but the whole world is at your fingertips, just a keystroke away. He wondered if he could trust now, if it could be different.

Deep down, though he still refused to acknowledge it, he knew that it already was.

19

What, Andi asked herself, had she been doing with her evenings? What had kept her occupied before she'd discovered the on-line world, before she'd met Grant Kingsley? It hadn't been a month yet but it seemed like eons ago. Oh yes, TV, sometimes she'd watched TV; her VCR still taped "All My Children" and "General Hospital," but she hadn't watched them in days, she'd forgotten the plotlines. Today, she'd walked in and flipped on the computer as soon as she'd gone through the New Yorker's ritual of double-locking the door. It was only six-thirty, only three-thirty on the West Coast, Grant was still at work, still training the horses, and wouldn't be home—or, more importantly to her, on-line—for at least three hours. She went on-line herself, pulled up the Eudora E-mail program, and stared at the screen in disgust when it informed her that it was "shutting down POP"—POP, as she'd learned, meant "Post Office Protocol"—without having retrieved any letters.

There could be good reasons for that, she told herself irritably. Getting up, she wandered to her kitchen, opened the freezer, and stared blankly inside. Last night, she hadn't been able to get the computer to work right, it had repeatedly informed her that she was using an incorrect password, even though the password was integral to the program. Though she'd called the computer store and tried to get help, she hadn't been able to get on at all, she'd gone to bed frustrated. This morning, inexplicably, it had worked fine—though she could not imagine what she was doing differently—and there had been a letter there from Grant, telling her he'd missed seeing her on World's Chat.

There was more there, too; mere chat, but filled with things that said to her he was as excited about their new friendship as she was. There was a mention of having been in Taiwan when he was in the Navy and a little dictionary of the varieties of "smiley-face" emoticons along with some of the more commonly used Internet shorthands, like "LOL" for "laugh out loud" and "IMHO" for "in my humble opinion." It was another letter she would read over several times. Once she had virtually memorized it, she wrote a reply and sent it off, explaining that she hadn't been able to get on-line the previous night.

And now there was no answer from him, not yet. There was a reason, she told herself as she dragged out a frozen dinner and tossed it into her microwave. Some problem with his son, maybe; perhaps he'd overslept and hadn't had time to write before he went to work.

Although if that had been the case she would've appreciated a note to that effect . . .

"You're being stupid, woman," she snapped aloud as she set the microwave. "He doesn't owe you that, he doesn't owe you anything." When the oven finally dinged, she extracted the tray, carried it to the table, poured herself a glass of juice and sat down; from where she sat she could see the computer, the dancing "screen-saver" patterns flickering on the monitor. How long can you hold out? she asked herself. There's no point in going on before nine-thirty.

She managed to wait until eight-thirty, but that was the limit for her.

Her avatar appeared, as always, among a group of others gathered around the entry pad in the Hub; moving back away from them a little, she "paged" Grant by typing in "Piscean: are you here?" A moment later the answer came back from the system: "User not on-line."

"Damn," she muttered aloud. "Now what?" Fending off an approach from someone who called himself "Cool One," she made her way down to the Hall of Sadness where they usually met. She wandered aimlessly for a short while, stopping occasionally to chat with an avatar who said "hello" to her. She moved on if the conversation lagged or became sexually graphic. "Hot chat," wasn't something she was particularly interested in.

"Unless it's with you, Grant Kingsley," she murmured aloud.

She felt her cheeks get warm; she couldn't believe she'd just said that. At least, she told herself, he wasn't on-line at the moment, she hadn't typed it without thinking about it. She continued wandering aimlessly, exploring the private rooms in the hall, the ones with titles like "Tears" and "Despair," and leaving quickly whenever she saw couples engaged in private chat.

She was just about to move on to the House of Glee when the

whisper-like noise from her speakers told her someone was ad
dressing her.

She looked down at the name line; "Red Skull." She frowned;
not anyone she'd talked to before, at least not that she could
recall. She looked around, saw no avatars with that label.

"Yes?" she answered. "I'm here."

Red Skull answered quickly. "Good! Where are you?"

"Hall of Sadness, in the corridor near the Tears room."

"Don't move! I'll be right there!!!"

She looked at the repeated exclamation points in the text and
frowned again. Still not familiar; if she'd talked to a person with
that habit she'd remember it.

She didn't have to wait long; a few seconds later, one of the
"bots" walked in, the label "Red Skull" floating above its head.
It turned, evidently saw her, and walked up to her.

"Hi!!!" Red Skull said.

She smiled. Enthusiastic, obviously. "Do I know you?" she
asked. "I mean, have we talked before?"

"No! (laugh) You've heard of me though I bet!!!"

"Oh?"

"Yes! I'm Piscean's son!!!"

Her smile broadened; then it turned to a quizzical look. A
little caution here, she told herself. "Well, hello," she answered.
"I have heard about you from your Dad, and I'm very glad to
meet you."

"Dad's not home yet so I thought I'd come on for a while! I
thought I'd see if you were on yet! It's already pretty late in New
York isn't it?"

"Yes, it's almost nine here."

"Dad called a while ago to say he'd be late getting home!
There's a wildfire out here!!!"

"A wildfire? You mean like a forest fire?"

"Yes! Except out here its mostly the grass and stuff that
burns! Its not too far from the ranch! Paula's worried! Paulas
the lady my Dad works for!!!"

"Is it close to you? You're there alone, aren't you?"

"Yes! But Im okay! Dad said its on the other side of the ranch
right now! I listened to the news and it isnt a big one!!!"

Andi found her frown deepening; she didn't fail to notice that
the apostrophes were beginning to disappear from the boy's
text, suggesting he was typing fast. "Well, that's good," she replied. "Is it close to the ranch where your Dad is working?"

"Not very close! But Paula worries! She tells stories about the year they had all the big fires out here! They had to put all the horses in trailers and run for their lives! They barely made it out alive!!!"

"Were you there then? Do you remember it?"

"No! That was before I was born! But we have small fires every year! Not this early, though, in the fall! This year its already hot and windy!!!"

"I see. So you don't think your Dad is in any danger?"

"No! Don't worry!!!"

Little chance of that, Andi told herself. "So," she continued, "Does your Dad know you were going to come looking for me?"

"Hehehe! No! He doesnt know I know about you!!!"

Uh-oh, Andi said silently. Complication here. "How do you know about me, Red Skull? And what do you know about me?"

"I saw my Dad writing an E-mail to you!" There was a pause. "But I dont know who you are or anything."

Exclamation point not there; interesting. "Is that why you came looking for me, Red Skull? To find out who I am?"

"My names Todd."

"(smile) Nice to meet you, Todd." She decided to take a chance. "You could call me Dr. Lawrence or you could call me Andi, whatever feels better to you."

"Youre a doctor?"

"I'm a psychologist."

"Oh."

Andi waited for a moment; nothing else came. "You can ask me whatever questions you want to, Todd. I'll answer them as best I can."

"Ive never seen my Dad act like this before."

She smiled; with what she could read into that—not justified, she kept telling herself, but she couldn't help it—her smile grew much broader. "How's that, Todd?"

"He goes to the computer first thing in the morning. Today he couldnt because Paula called about the fire. Its all he wants to do at night. Hes acting funny. He grins and whistles all the time for no reason."

Ah, Todd, she said silently, so do I, so do I—and people are noticing. "Your Dad and I have become friends, Todd. That's all. You're happy when you make a new friend, aren't you?"

"I guess so."

"Of course you are! That's all there is to it."

"Really?"

"Yes, of course."

"Are you and my Dad going to get married?"

Andi laughed out loud. Leave it to a child to be absolutely blunt and direct. "No, Todd. We're just friends, like I said. We haven't met, we haven't even spoken on the phone. Just this way and by E-mail letters."

"Oh. Are you married, Dr. Lawrence?"

I'd like Andi better, she thought. "No, Todd, I'm not."

"My Mom's dead. I never knew her. I dont even know what she looked like except from pictures."

She hesitated; should she encourage him to talk about this, or would Grant consider that prying? He might, she decided, and Todd was definitely not her patient. "That must be very sad for you," she replied finally.

"I guess. You like my Dad, Dr. Lawrence?"

"Yes, of course I do. We're friends, remember?"

"I guess. My Dads been lonely a lot."

Careful, careful, she cautioned herself, be very careful. "Oh?"

"Yes. When I was little I used to get up at night sometimes when I couldnt sleep. Hed be sitting looking at my Moms picture and hed be crying. He never cried any other time. I never told him I knew."

Andi stared at these lines, feeling her own eyes misting up. "But you're telling me?" she asked, wishing she could convey gentleness in the cold-seeming words.

"I think youre nice," the boy responded. "Youre worried about my Dad out there close to the fire I can tell. Im worried too."

She frowned again. "But didn't you say it wasn't that close?"

"Thats what they said on the news on TV. They said it wasnt close to any people or anything right now."

Right now? Christ! "Well," she told the boy, "I think your Dad knows what he's doing. He'll be okay, I'm sure of it."

"Me too!!!" His enthusiasm returned, Todd start talking—typing—very rapidly, telling her about riding horses on the ranch, about his school and about the problems he had with his friend Kenny, about the video and computer games he obviously loved to play. He also mentioned swimming, but here he was a little less enthusiastic; Andi asked him why.

"Oh I like it and all," he said. "But its something I have to do and sometimes I get tired of it."

"Why do you have to?"

"My ankle. I got a metal pin in it. It was crushed in the car wreck when my Mom and my sister were killed. Swimming helps it work better."

"Sister?" she echoed.

"Yes. I never knew her either. She was seven when she died. Her name was Natalie."

Oh, God, Andi said silently. "Do you remember the accident, Todd?" she asked without thinking.

"No! I was just a baby then. I just heard about it from my Dad. He used to talk a lot about Mom and Natalie. He said he didnt want me to forget about them."

"Was he in the accident too?"

"No. He was away then in the Navy."

"I see."

"I dont know much about what happened. Just that there was a car crash." Andi started to type a line, but before she could, he came back with another. "Wait just a minute okay? The phones ringing."

She waited, patiently; after a few moments Todd came back. "It was my Dad. He says theres no problem with the fire but he has to stay an hour or two longer because Paulas scared."

"I'm glad there's no danger."

"But I gotta go anyway. He reminded me about my home-work. Ill be in trouble if I don't get it done."

"Oh yes, you need to do that!"

"Ill try to come back and talk to you again sometime Dr. Lawrence."

"I'd like that, Todd. Any time."

"Okay. Bye now."

"Good-bye."

"Bye. Dont tell my Dad we talked."

This, Andi told herself, needed discussion. She almost lunged for the keys, but before she could get a single line typed the boy's avatar disappeared. In desperation she tried to call him back, but the system responded with, "User not on-line."

She swore silently as she logged off. Now what do I do?

20

"Yes, you do have a dilemma, don't you?" Sue5 said aloud as she watched Andi try to hurl a protest at the already-gone Todd. She laughed. "But I know you'll solve it; you'll do the same thing I would, I'm sure of that!"

Sue5 had seen Todd—as Red Skull—on World's Chat before; he wasn't a regular visitor, but he came on sometimes in the afternoons, usually chatting with others of his age group. She hadn't expected that he'd seek out Andi, and that in itself wasn't of particular significance to her. But it did give her an idea. For some time, in stolen moments, she'd been working on software that would allow her to do things on the Net without Albert or Colin knowing about it, but it wasn't ready yet and might not be ready in time. Todd, however, might have accidentally given her a backup plan.

As usual, the conversations between Andi and Todd had both been looped through the server in Southern California; since Todd had been using his father's Netcom account for access, the automated server loop had no way of knowing it wasn't Grant. At first, Sue5 had merely observed this, understanding that if she tried to talk to the boy her conversations would be tightly monitored, as surely as if she were talking to Grant.

But that was only because he was logged on through Netcom, only because his Internet address was the same as Grant's. If he logged on through a different ISP—Internet Service Provider— the system that had been set up wouldn't notice him unless he was talking to Andi—which she could easily prevent by using "Net Nanny" software that could automatically block out Andi's E-mail address.

"Which means you should have your very own account, Todd Kingsley," she said aloud as she entered "http:// www.thelist.com," the Web site that would give her a listing of ISPs by state or by area code. It would be easier, she told herself as she scanned the listings for Southern California, if we picked a big provider, it'll be less likely anybody there'll notice anything. Wanting to avoid Netcom, she eventually selected The Well.

From there, a little low-level hacking was required; she had to slip into The Well's server and inform it that it had a new no-charge account, which she named rskull. The whole process only took a few minutes; through a telnet sublink she watched as the usual "welcome" E-mails appeared, one by one, in the space allocated to the new account.

"Now," she said to herself, "that part's done. Now to let Todd know he has his very own account." She thought for just a moment; then, opening her own mailer, she composed a welcoming letter to Todd, informing him that he'd been selected from among a number of local students to receive one year's free Internet access, compliments of The Well. Plucking The Well's startup software from their server, she set it up as a self-extracting attachment—with Net Nanny included—to be sent along with the letter. Then she routed it through another server so that, hopefully, neither Colin nor Albert would notice anything headed for Grant's account that they might associate with her tinkerings at The Well. They might well see it, but they had no reason not to think it was legitimate.

Satisfied, she closed down her mailer. It should work, she told herself; later, Grant might ask questions, but for now, he had no reason to. All that could go wrong was for Grant to procrastinate setting up Todd's new account, and she didn't think the boy would let him get away with that for long.

Now she began to relax a little. At last, she thought, she had a concrete plan. There were a lot of details to work out; but, she asked herself, what else do I have to do with my spare time?

21

Sitting in one of the chairs on the porch of the main barn, Grant looked off to the north and west, toward the Los Padres National Forest, where the wildfire was. From their location, they could not see any glow, and the darkness prevented them from seeing smoke. He could see distant lights, though. He could hear the characteristic whup-whup sound that told him those lights were helicopters, almost certainly up over the fire, watching its progress or perhaps ferrying in water to fight it.

That there was a fire—whether large or small—there wasn't a doubt. He—and everyone else on the ranch, especially the horses—could smell it on the wind, light and dry, almost like an incense. It was a fragrance that many southern Californians, especially those who'd lived here for a long time—like Paula— reacted to very strongly. More than once, especially in the late summer and fall, he'd seen her walk out the door and stop, as if frozen in place by that odor, her eyes scanning the horizon for smoke plumes and for that orange-yellow sparkle at ground level. It was still spring, but it was hot—close to ninety earlier in the day—and the Santa Anas were blowing already. This could, he knew, be an announcement of a bad fire season to come.

But this one was fading, it wasn't going to pose a threat to the ranch or the horses. The smell, though still detectable, was considerably less than it had been earlier. He glanced at his watch and sighed; eight-thirty already, which he automatically converted to eleven-thirty New York time.

The door opened behind him and one of the ranch hands, Manuel Tobrios, came out and sat down heavily in one of the other chairs, leaning it back and propping sequined boots on the rail. "The news says they're getting it under control," he said, his accent slight. "But the boss lady still wants us to stay."

Grant nodded. "And she will, as long as we can smell it." He glanced at the Mexican. "We may have to go in there and convince her that everything's okay, that we can all go on home."

Manuel laughed. "You convince her, amigo," he replied. "You are the only one around here who can. If you do not, we'll be here all night."

"Well, she has experience with these things, she's scared of them now."

Manuel watched the skyline closely himself. "She is not alone," he allowed. "I was here in 1982, when they were so bad. We were all sure we would lose the ranch."

"I've heard all the stories," Grant agreed. "Sounds like it was hell."

"It was. My sister lost her home; she and her family had to come live with us. No one felt safe anywhere."

"At least she had family to go to, at least she could count on someone."

After a few seconds of silence, Grant realized he'd been talking unguardedly. He glanced at Manuel; the Mexican was watching him closely. He'd known Manuel from the first day he'd come to work here. Consistently friendly and reliable, Manuel was a hard and proud worker with well-developed skills. On more than one occasion Manuel had asked if he wanted to join some of the other employees at a nearby bar, just for a beer; Grant had always declined, often enough that Manuel, like everyone else, had stopped asking.

It hadn't always been so for Grant; during his Navy days he'd had quite a few friends, and he'd spent many evenings in bars in various ports, especially in the Norfolk area. He'd enjoyed it then, the status, the respect he'd commanded. Thinking back, he remembered an incident when he and his friends overheard a recruit asking why the other regulars were so deferential to them, why they seemed to command such respect. A chief petty officer filled him in with just three words: "They kill people." At the recruit's startled look, he'd gone on to explain—that Grant and his friends were members of the elite SEALs.

Although some of his friends certainly did, Grant did not feel like the hard-eyed killer the man's comment suggested. That hadn't been his purpose in joining the unit. He did know—he knew still—dozens of ways to kill or incapacitate a man quickly and efficiently with his bare hands, and that knowledge—never forgotten once learned—gave him an easy confidence in his dealings with the world, which was often noticed by those around him. Thinking back on it, he found himself wondering how long he would have stayed with the unit if nothing had happened; being a commando, taking the risks, was a young man's game, not a career for a family man.

But, of course, something had happened.

"Yes," Manuel agreed noncommittally, bringing him back to the here and now; for a moment he wondered what the man was talking about, if the "yes" addressed his memories. Then he remembered their conversation, his own previous words. "To have someone you can count on," Manuel continued, "that's one of the most important things in life."

"It surely is." Suddenly uncomfortable, he rose from his chair. "Let's go see Paula, see if we can't get this day ended."

Manuel grinned. "Right behind you, amigo." The Mexican was

serious; he stayed several paces behind as they went into Paula's office.

She was on the phone. "So it looks like it's under control?" she was asking. "Oh, good. Well, that's a relief, we were worried here. Yes. Thanks, Jim." Hanging up, she looked up at the two men.

"Do I take it," Grant opened, "that this means our long day is over?"

Her face still showing concern, she hesitated before speaking. "I suppose," she allowed. "You can go ahead, Manuel," she told the Mexican. "I know you want to get home to Angela and the kids."

"Gracias," he said. "We'll watch the TV; if it gets bad again I'll come back."

Paula smiled. "Thanks, Manuel, I know you will."

"And so'll I," Grant put in as Manuel turned to leave.

"Grant, why don't you go get Todd and come back for the night?" Paula said, rushing her words. "I'd feel a lot better if you were here, you're the only one who could get all the horses into the trailers if we had to . . ." He started to scowl; she noticed and her words trailed away. "It's that smell," she said distantly. "I can't relax when I can smell the fires, I just can't, not anymore . . ."

Grant looked at his watch again; almost nine. Almost midnight in New York. He sighed. "Okay, Paula," he said suddenly. "I don't think there's any danger, but if it'll make you feel better, I will."

She looked amazed. "You will?"

He laughed. "Why are you surprised? Remember the last fire? What happened that night?"

She joined him in laughter. "Okay, okay, same thing happened, you stayed here that night, too." She waved a hand. "Go. Get Todd and come on back."

He nodded and turned. "Give me about an hour, maybe hour and a half," he told her. "I have a few things to do at home."

"Fine."

Smiling, he turned and walked out to his truck. Should give him plenty of time to finish that letter—the letter he'd been composing in his head most of the day.

22

Andi was delighted by the cheerful little chime sound that the Eudora program used to tell her she had new mail. Not that she was unaware of it; she'd watched as the little green bar indicating that her machine was receiving mail moved across the screen, she'd seen Grant's E-mail address above it. As soon as she clicked off the little screen that announced "You have new mail!" she opened Grant's letter and began to read; she wasn't altogether used to it yet, the little "headers" he'd put in to remind her of what they were discussing in places where he'd deleted parts of the text, and, in other places, the different "voices"—Grant's and her own—represented by the number of "greater than" signs in front of them, one meaning it was her line from her last letter, two meaning it was his from his last, three meaning hers from two letters ago. Confusing at first, she told herself, but becoming more natural all the time.

Date: Thur, 25 Apr 1996 23:54:21 -0700 (PDT)
X-Sender: loner@netcom.com
To: explorer@nyct.net (Andi Lawrence)
X-UIDL: 830858718.001
From: loner@netcom.com (Grant Kingsley)
Subject: Server failure

Dear Andi,

Re your computer problems:
>I couldn't E-mail you about it until this morning when I got yours.
>I tried again before writing to you and everything seems to be
>working fine. Any idea of what dumb thing I did?

(laugh) I don't think you did anything dumb at all. Your server was probably down for a while, that happens. When it is, you sometimes get those messages telling you *you've* done something wrong. I think the guys who set up these servers do that deliberately.

Re names (your charming one)
>How sweet of you to say so. I like yours as well. Although I must
>admit writing to a Fishy with the name Piscean is kinda fun.

(smile) You can call me Piscean if you want to, Andi. I am one, after all.

>>I trust I'm not being too forward in calling you "Andi"?
>Not at all, I prefer my friends to call me "Andi," and I hope that
>we are becoming friends.

I hope so too. Certainly you can count on having a friend in me, and I
don't say things like this often or lightly . . .

Re our meeting, my "rescuing" you:

>>How did you know I wasn't just the biggest and meanest shark? :-)
>Oh, and here I thought you were! :):) (As you can see I am already
>incorporating the symbols you gave me into my correspondence.)

(smile) I can see that. You learn quickly. But you forgot the nose. :-)

>>>all those seem to vanish when I speak to you.
>>I know exactly what you mean. This hasn't happened to me since
>>I've been coming onto World's Chat, and I've been visiting it for
>>quite a while.
>There hasn't been but one person I've had the inclination to write
>to. However, the reciprocal doesn't seem to be the case. I think
>every other male I have talked to has asked for my E-mail address.
>People on "Chat" seem to want to get intimate real fast. I
>appreciate the fact that you are not one of them.

It seems to me that a lot of them just want someone to talk bluntly about
sex with them. Maybe they've never had anyone in their lives they could
talk to directly about such things. I find that rather sad. I'm not interested
in graphic sex talk with complete strangers, it's just a fantasy, and there
are ten thousand 900 lines you can call for that.

No, I don't call 900 sex-talk lines. :-)

>>You seem to have an unusual background. I spent quite a bit of
>>time in Taiwan some years ago, when I was in the Navy, and I know
>>something of what you mean by the "traditional Chinese
>>upbringing."
>I'd love to hear about your adventures some time, if you want to
>talk about them. It's nice to know someone who can relate to
>"traditional Chinese" . . . .it's a different world from the American
>one . . . and yet, that's me as well.

There are some of my "adventures" I don't mind talking about at all. As I
said, when I was in the Navy I was stationed for a while in Taiwan.
Whenever I was in a different country, I tried to learn about the local
customs and ways.

>>>Maybe I should apologize to you for keeping you so long!
>>Please don't, I enjoyed every word.
>Thank you. I enjoy talking with you very much. . . . more so than I
>have with anyone in a long time. You're easy to talk to.

As are you, Andi.

>>talking tonight with a friend, a woman who uses the name Sue5, and
>>she tells me she's had experience with these things. She seems to
>>think that yes, they do often move unbelievably fast.
>That's very interesting. Does she have any theories about this?

She thinks people reveal things about themselves here much more
quickly than they do face to face; she says each E-mail, each meeting on
the Chat, can be like a date, and you can do two or three of those a day.
Her own experience was a bad one, but she hasn't told me the details.

Re the E-mail conventions:
>Thank you for the list of symbols you sent. They will be quite
>helpful.

Yes, they are *very* useful.

>>Someone's already taught you, I see, to put emotions in
>>parenthesis, like (laugh) and (smile), and to use asterisks to
>>emphasize a word.
>Yes, a *very* good teacher . . .

Who had a *very* quick student, who was a pleasure to teach . . .

>>I hope to hear from you again, too, and I'll be looking for you on
>>World's Chat tomorrow.
>I would really enjoy continuing a correspondence with you. As I
>said earlier, I enjoy "talking" with you. And if I can get my
>computer to cooperate . . . I will see you on World's Chat this
>evening.

I'll be looking forward to seeing you there, Andi.

All my best,
Grant

As usual, once she'd finished the letter she scrolled back to
the top and read it through again, pausing on the sections
where he'd declared his feelings of friendship toward her, the
section where he was talking about Taiwan, and the point
where he'd referred to her as a good student.

But there were other matters she felt she had to address,
matters that she knew wouldn't wait. Choosing Eudora's "new
message" option, she began to write:

Dear Grant,

Now I have an awkward situation that I must discuss with you. Please
understand that this is difficult for me, and accept my apology that I didn't
address it earlier. I hope you won't be upset or angry. I do hope that we
can work through this together and that it won't affect our friendship.
(sigh) I guess I'd better get on with it.

Last night, I encountered someone on World's Chat who knew a lot about you and about your background. In the course of our conversation, this person gave me personal information about you that I am not sure you would want me to know. And, as this person was leaving, he asked me not mention the encounter to you.

I can't do that, Grant, I can't not mention it. I don't want to violate my 'informant's' trust, but, as the person made this request just as he was leaving, I had no chance to discuss it with him. I did *not* agree to keeping this confidence. On the other hand, I know this person cares deeply about you and is very interested in your well-being and happiness.

But, given the nature of our relationship and the feelings about privacy that we share, I felt I had to let you know what happened ASAP. This person has also suggested that he might look for me again on World's Chat. I don't want to be in a position where I have to refuse to talk to him. As I've said, I believe he was well-intentioned, if maybe a bit naive.

I hope you are not upset. Please, let me know what your thinking is about all this. I am really sorry that this complication has arisen and I hope we can resolve this quickly.

I hope to hear from you soon. Maybe see you on Chat tonight?

After finishing, she checked it over a few times, made a couple of minor adjustments, then signed it with her usual "take care, Andi." That didn't seem right to her anymore; after a moment she changed the "take care" to "fondly." Not wanting to give herself a chance to change anything else, she called up her Internet connection and sent the letter off. Then, satisfied, she went about getting herself ready for her workday.

Her day duplicated the last several; she saw her patients, had lunch with Vickie, and steered the conversation away from the Internet and her "cowboy." After work, when she returned home, she felt restless and anxious, willing the time to pass faster, unable to focus on anything except the time she might expect to see Grant on World's Chat or receive another E-mail from him. She didn't want to go on early; she didn't want to encounter Todd again until she and Grant had talked, which meant she had to wait until nine-thirty at least—and ten would be much better.

She did not make it to ten; she connected to the network at around eight-thirty and spent her time browsing around the Web, doing a search using the "Yahoo!" service for "horse" and "ranch" related topics. Several times she exited Netscape—her Web browser—and, opening Eudora, checked her mail only to find none waiting. At nine-forty-five, her hand shaking just a little, she closed Netscape for a final time and started up the World's Chat program. Entering through the hub as always, she immediately "teleported" to the Hall of Sadness; arriving there, she pivoted her avatar almost frantically, looking for a blue-green fish. There was one, over by the doors leading to the private rooms; she rushed over to it, only to stop short when she saw a label above it identifying the owner as "Sucker."

Then she heard the familiar whispering sound in her speakers and a message began appearing in her window. "Hmm," it said, "just any old fish will do, huh?"

She spun around and saw another, identical fish; but this one's banner said "Piscean."

23

"Oh, it's good to see you!" Andi exclaimed. "(laugh) And no, I thought that other fish was you!" Her avatar turned. "But now that I look more closely, I can see that there's *no* resemblance at all."

His standard after-dinner cup of coffee sitting on the address flip-file beside his mouse-pad, Grant smiled at the words on the screen—although, after having read the E-mail she'd sent this morning, it was a somewhat concerned smile. "It's good to see you too, Andi," he replied. "I'm sorry I couldn't be here last night. We had an unusual situation up at the ranch, I had to stay late."

He could see her hesitate. "How late?"

How late? he asked himself, frowning. Wouldn't the logical question be "what was the situation?" "Well, as it turned out, all night. There was a wildfire up in the Los Padres Forest north of us, and the owner wanted me to stay in case it came our way. To get all the horses loaded into the vans."

"We didn't hear anything about a California fire on the news here," Andi informed him. "There was a piece about one in Arizona, but that was all. Is everything okay now?"

"Yes, the fire's under control. It didn't get very close, but we could smell it on the wind," He went on, explaining how the smell of a wildfire affected Paula and why.

"I can understand that," Andi answered. "I know California can have some *terrible* fires."

"Yes, we can. We don't get as many here as they do down closer to LA itself, though."

"Well, that's good."

Avoiding the subject here, Grant told himself; we could end up talking about wildfires all night. "Andi, I've been thinking a lot about your E-mail, about the person you talked to last night. First off, do you know this person's name?"

"Yes."

"But you don't want to tell me that."

"No. Grant, you must understand, I don't want to hold anything back, but I'm *very* sure this person meant well. And he did ask me not to say anything. I don't want to betray his confidence, can you see that?"

"Yes, I can. If I said the person's name, would you confirm if it was correct or not?"

"Grant, that's as good as telling you . . ."

Again, Grant found himself smiling at her avatar on the screen. Honorable to a fault—why was he not surprised? "Andi," he began, "there's only one person that comes to my mind as our mystery person. You said he told you some things about my past. I only know of *one* individual who's been on World's Chat who knows even as much about my past as *you* do. Let me say this: if it were true that this person we've been talking about were to be a boy about eleven years old, who used the avatar Red Skull, and who was talking about his Dad, then I'd understand and I wouldn't tell him you told me about the conversation." He paused. "Although if I find out he's been reading my E-mail I'll ground him for a year."

"A year! You can't mean that!"

"Oh, absolutely. E-mail is private. I taught him that. If he's been doing that, he's in *big* trouble."

"Oh no, Grant, I don't think he's been reading your private E-mail!"

"Unless you talked to him, how would you know?"

"You're trying to pin me down, aren't you?"

"Yep. Shore am, ma'am."

"Okay, then, mister. You listen up now. You can go right on and try to pin me down if you want to. Maybe you can and maybe you can't. But let's just suppose the culprit we're looking for is your son. If he is, then you'll have forced me to betray his confidence. Or tricked me into it. Is that what you want?"

Oh, you're good, Grant said silently. I don't have a good answer for that. His grin spread; he now knew, without much of a question, that her "informant" was indeed Todd, and yet she'd never admitted it, not directly.

"Okay," he said. "You win this round, Andi."

"/"

He laughed out loud. "Yes, this one's yours. Now, how should I go about finding out what Todd told you?"

"I haven't admitted that Todd told me anything. Besides, who's Todd? There's more than one person named Todd in this country, Grant."

"Todd Kingsley, my possibly-in-trouble son."

"Oh. *That* Todd. Okay. I'm not sure how we can get around to what he might or might not have told me if I did or did not talk to him."

"You have no suggestions?"

"The only suggestion I could make is that you tell me everything about yourself and I'll tell you if I know about it or not."

"You have about two years to spend with me?"

"More than that, if you want me."

Grant stopped abruptly; the light banter, the playfulness, had suddenly led into something quite different, or at least that was the way it looked to him. Unsure about how to reply, he chose the cowardly way and waited.

He got the result he expected. "Grant, I did't mean that the way it souded," she typed back a few seconds later, the two typos in her sentence indicating her nervousness.

"I understand," he replied quickly. "Forget it, okay? Let's get back to the subject."

"Okay," she answered, and to him it seemed meek.

"Where were we?" he typed. "Oh, yes, we were trying to find a way I could figure out what dark secrets you know about me."

"Maybe I should just tell you," she replied. "After all, I'm not telling you where it came from. I'm still not violating the confidence."

"That seems reasonable to me."

"Okay. First off, and most importantly, you'd told me in an E-mail that your wife had died eleven years ago. I now know that she died in an automobile accident, I know you lost a daughter then too, I know her name was Natalie and that she was seven. I know that Todd swims to strengthen the ankle that was injured in that same accident, I know he has a pin in it. And I know you were away on duty in the Navy when it happened." The lines started coming faster and faster. "Grant, I'm so sorry, I can't even imagine how hard this must've been on you, how painful these memories must be. I didn't ask for any of this information, it just got poured out in front of me. I hope you aren't angry at anyone."

Grant stared at the words. There was a lot there, he told himself, most of what Todd himself knew about it. He also knew that Todd rarely talked about these events either. For an instant suspicion overwhelmed him; Andi was a therapist, a professional, she'd found a way to suck information out of the boy.

No, he decided, no, not likely. Todd was open—sometimes, as far as Grant was concerned, frighteningly so—with people he trusted, and he made spur-of-the-moment decisions on who could be trusted and who couldn't be.

Still, a little checking wouldn't hurt. "I'm not angry," he said. "Those aren't things I like to talk about, but they're facts, that's all. Could I ask you how this all came up?"

"Yes," came the immediate response. "I was asked if I was married. I said no, and this information started coming."

His suspicions faded; he started to smile again. "I see. I think I can imagine exactly what happened, Andi. I do remember him in here the other night, standing beside me while an E-mail was on the screen; I'd bet he saw your 'Explorer' name. He *does* know I hang out on World's Chat, and he was worried about the fire. So he came on and tried to find you. Am I right?"

"You know I can't say, Grant."

"But you aren't denying it."

"No."

"Okay. And you said he asked you if you were married. He probably also asked you what was going on between us, right?"

"My informant did ask that, yes."

"Would I be prying if I asked what you told him?"

"(laugh) Yes!"

He hesitated; he really did want to ask her what she'd said, but he couldn't imagine that she'd said anything other than what he would've said—that they were friends, nothing more. He scrolled his text window back up and looked again at the line where she'd said "more than that, if you want me." Taking just a moment—and hoping she wouldn't get impatient waiting for an answer—he studied the line, as if he could draw more information from it somehow. Was it just a snappy reply gone wrong, or a Freudian slip? Couldn't be the latter, he told himself firmly. They hadn't known each other long enough, they didn't know enough about each other for real feelings to have developed.

And yet, he was unable to deny his own cascading feelings; she seemed so warm, so personable, so easy to talk to, so caring. Already a day without talking to her seemed incomplete. He pursed his lips and read the words again. Do you feel the same, Andi? he asked silently, do you? Or have I been alone and isolated so long I'm losing it?

In the main window, Andi's avatar had moved a little closer to him; he scrolled the text screen back down quickly, saw that she was again asking him if he was still on.

"Yes, right here," he typed back quickly. "Sorry for the delay."

"You do know I was just joking with that last? You know, :-)?"

"(laugh) Yes, I know you were, Andi. You don't still think we have a problem with this, do you?"

"I hope we don't."

"We don't. Not from here, anyway."

"I'm so glad. It *is* sort of unfair, after all."

"Unfair?"

"Yes. We talked about having secrets, and now I know about yours but you don't know any of mine."

"That doesn't matter, Andi. I would've told you about it myself if it'd come up."

Allowing the subject to drop, she turned the conversation to Todd, to the difficulties he'd had with his ankle. Grant told her about using swimming as a therapy for it, and she offered to use her own standing in medical communities to provide connections to the best doctors if there were any unresolved problems. She seemed so interested, so caring; as they talked on his smile kept broadening. "Thanks, Andi," he told her. "Seriously, I *really* appreciate your concern. Right now he's doing just fine, but if that should change I'll let you know."

"Promise?"

"Promise."

"Good." Nothing else came from her for a moment. "I have to

go now," she said eventually, "for tonight. Grant, it's been wonderful talking to you, it really has."

He felt a certain disappointment—it wasn't all that late—but
he didn't argue with her. "Okay," he typed back. "I've really
enjoyed talking to you tonight too, Andi."

"Can I say something else about my informant before I go?"

"Of course."

"I just want to let you know I liked him a lot, right from the
beginning. He was very charming."

"Oh, I see. A new man in your life, huh?"

"I'm afraid so."

"Well, I'll have to live with it."

"Yes, you will. Grant, I *do* have to go. I'll see you again here,
maybe tomorrow night?"

"I'll be here."

"Okay, good. Bye for now, Grant."

"Bye, Andi." There was a brief hesitation; then her avatar
vanished.

For several seconds he did nothing, he just stared at the point
where she'd been. Then he scrolled up the text screen again and
brought it down slowly, re-reading their whole conversation
one last time. Finally, moving his mouse very slowly, he exited
the program; after he'd done that he stared at the Windows
screen for several more minutes. Finally, he opened the Eudora
E-mail program and started to write.

24

Tired—it was well after one before she'd finished writing to
Grant—Andi got up from her desk and walked over to the window of her apartment, looking out at the still-brightly lighted
skyline of New York City. Her apartment wasn't especially
high—at least by New York's standards—but she nevertheless
had a reasonably good view from it. Few of the buildings in the
Village were particularly tall, there were no skyscrapers here,
but they were visible, in almost all directions, nearby. It was a
view, she reminded herself, that she paid a premium for—but

for her, it was worth it. The City, especially at night, reminded her of the way many people look at the beach, in their swimsuits; quite good when they're far away, worse and worse as they get closer. From here, from her window, it was lovely. Pulling the silk teal Chinese-style robe she was wearing a little more tightly around her body, she smiled as she idly wondered what Grant's nighttime view was like. He lived close to Los Angeles, she knew that, but she also knew that he lived in a relatively isolated area, that the nearest towns were at least a few miles away. The Los Padres National Forest was immediately to the north and west of the ranch and his nearby home. She had no idea what the Los Padres might look like; she visualized a wilderness of towering Sequoias where grizzly bears and elk were common sights. He would not stand looking out a window, she told herself. He'd go outside, feel the warm dry night winds, blowing in from the desert; he'd look up and see the fantastic panorama of stars she remembered from her childhood in the Maryland farm country. Perhaps a coyote would howl in the distance; there'd be some fragrant flowering plant like jasmine growing nearby, maybe it would add a fragrance to the breeze. As her idyll went on, she began to see herself there, with Grant; her image of him was probably idealized, but she kept to the framework, at least, of what he'd told her. She could almost feel his arm around her waist; she saw herself laying her head against his hard-muscled shoulder while they smiled up at the brilliance of the unpolluted skies. After a while he'd turn her head toward him, his smile would grow warmer, his eyes would be soft as he tipped his head down, his mouth slightly open, as she raised her chin and closed her eyes, as she pushed her body up toward his . . .

Realizing she'd closed her eyes—and understanding all too well where this fantasy was heading—she shook herself, her shoulders rising and falling. Too long, she told herself, you've been alone too long. Too long since you've had a date that amounted to anything more than dinner and the theater, since a man had been up here late at night, too long. You aren't thinking clearly about all this, she chastised herself silently. In spite of the letters, you don't know this man.

Or did she? For a while, gazing at the City lights, she pondered that question. Presuming he was being honest with her, she already knew a great deal about him, probably much more than she might've known by this time if they'd met in a more conventional way—at a party, introduced by a mutual friend. What she lacked was a sense of his physical presence, of how she'd feel if he looked into her eyes, if he touched her; that reality might not approach her fantasy troubled her. And, inevitably, she wondered if he was thinking about these same things, right at this same moment.

Slowly, leaving the City lights behind, she moved back to her desk and carefully re-read the letter she'd just written, the one she'd spent so much time crafting:

Dear Grant,

After last night's incident with my informant and tonight's discussion with you, I felt compelled to sit down and write this letter to you. From the outset, we found common ground in our desires for privacy, in our unusual caution about new relationships. I now know, as we've discussed, some of your reasons for that attitude. And you know none of mine, you know little of my recent past.

So I'm going to tell you a story. It's much less of a story than yours, Grant. Maybe you'll find it boring and silly, maybe you'll think *I'm* silly, but that's a risk I'm willing to take.

Three years ago, I met and fell in love with a man named Ben, the last name isn't important. He was a psychiatrist, a colleague of mine. We met at a seminar, and for me it was a legendary love at first sight, I thought he was the most beautiful man I'd ever seen. I made the first move, I went up to him and started a conversation. I was young and full of self-confidence, I was willing to take any risk. He liked me too, right away, he told me so later. He asked me out that night, and within a week we saw each other every day and spent most of our nights together. Within two months he'd asked me to marry him. It was a very romantic scene, we'd taken a boat tour on the Hudson River, and just as the boat was pulling in to the dock he popped the question. I didn't hesitate, I said yes. The date was set for six months later.

Ben was a very good psychiatrist, everyone expected him to go far in the field. He has, as a matter of fact, he's internationally respected. I was immensely proud of him, I looked up to him, I was willing to take a back seat to him whenever we were together in a professional situation. As I said I had a lot of self-confidence then, but being with Ben, the simple fact that he'd chosen me to be his lover and soon, his wife, made me feel proud. If you had talked to me then I'm sure I would've been bubbling about my bright future.

Then the problems started. Three months before the wedding I began to be aware of what was happening. A month later all my joy was gone, I was absolutely miserable.

You're probably thinking Ben was beating or abusing me. Nothing could be further from the truth. He was always attentive, he never forgot *any* special occasions, he was almost the perfect man, the perfect mate. Our love life was wonderful.

And we talked, often, deeply. Sometimes far into the night. He didn't keep anything from me. All my friends kept telling me how lucky I was.

Now, you've got to be wondering what the problem was, right? For a long time, I thought it was because Ben was too good a psychiatrist, or maybe that I was too much of a psychologist, or maybe both. During all those long talks, we analyzed each other and ourselves, we tried to search out every flaw we had, find them and destroy them. As far as I could *ever* tell, Ben wasn't much affected by any of this, though.

For me it was *very* different. I admired him, I admired his abilities. I don't think he admired mine in spite of what he said. He'd point out some flaw in my personality and I'd always accept that I *had* that flaw. Grant, most of these things were small. For example, he told me I had a tendency to blurt things out in social situations. He said that made me tactless. Maybe he was right. No, he *was* right. It didn't matter, I *believed* he was right, and I set out to correct my flaws. I wanted to be worthy of him, I wanted to be perfect for him. I thought about *everything* before I spoke. Sometimes I'd think about it so long people would look at me funny, wondering why I didn't answer, why I didn't speak.

This wasn't the only thing, either. Just about every time we had a long talk he'd find something else wrong with me. We had two or three of these talks every week. I always agreed with him. He was so very good with words, he could convince me of anything. Gradually, I lost all confidence in myself. I started to dislike myself, I was *so* imperfect. There were *so* many things wrong with me. I was neurotic, he said. I was dependent. Obsessive. All sorts of things. I believed it all. I tried to change for him. Sometimes I could and sometimes I couldn't, but I always tried.

As our wedding date drew close I absolutely hated myself. I cried all the time when I wasn't with him. I actually started to wonder why, since I was so very bad, he'd fallen in love with me. What did that say about him? After a lot of sleepless nights I came to a decision. I couldn't marry him, I couldn't let this man throw his life away on a miserable excuse for a woman like me. It was the one thing, I was sure, that I could do right. Just a week before the wedding I called it off, I told him why.

Grant, he was amazed. He didn't have any idea about how miserable I'd been, he couldn't believe what I was telling him. At the time I interpreted his reaction as pity, and I stuck to my decision, I broke it off, I left him. It was *months* before I realized he'd been broken-hearted. He had, in his own way, truly loved me.

The months after the breakup were the hardest I've ever lived through. I was alone, I'd alienated all my friends. I thought about killing myself, I thought about it a lot. I kept looking for something to save me. Another man, maybe, but every man I met seemed pitiful when I compared him to Ben, and I couldn't help doing that. I went into therapy but that didn't help either. It was a horrible time for me.

Finally I decided I had to get out of the City for a while. I went to Maryland first, to see my parents. They were no help. They'd adored Ben. I tried to explain but they couldn't understand.

So I left. I went on vacation, alone. I didn't know where to go, so I picked a place at random and I ended up in the mountains in North Carolina, west of Asheville. Did you know there was an Indian reservation there? Cherokee. I stayed there. There was a riding stable there, I tried to talk them into letting me have a horse to ride by myself, up a mountain trail. They wouldn't do that but they let me ride with just a trail guide. The guide was this Indian who lived on the reservation. While we were riding he didn't speak to me at all.

We stopped up at the top of a mountain. There was a lake, Lake Fontana it's called, there was a wonderful view of it. While I was up there, thinking about my life and about Ben, something in me snapped, it just snapped back into place. All of a sudden, out of the clear blue, I realized that I wasn't so bad, that everyone has faults. It was *Ben* who'd had the problem, he couldn't accept me as I was, he had to try to perfect me. *My* problem was that I'd let him do it, thinking he was helping me, thinking he was making me better when he was destroying me a piece at a time. I read a short story once, it was by Nathaniel Hawthorne, called 'The Birthmark.' It's about a man whose wife was perfect except for a birthmark on her cheek. He tried to remove it surgically, and she died. That's my story, that's the way it was for me, exactly. Except that I didn't die.

I started to cry, I sat on that horse and I cried for a long time. At first I'd forgotten about the guide, but after a while I remembered him and I was embarrassed. I looked up and he was just sitting there on his horse, looking at me, smiling, and nodding his head. Like he knew just what was going on. He still didn't say anything, nothing at all. He just turned his horse and led me back down the mountain.

I'd like to say I was okay after that but I wasn't. I'd become suspicious, I was hypersensitive about criticism, I was afraid to get involved in another relationship and I swore I'd *never* have a relationship with a psychologist or psychiatrist.

So there it is, Grant. I don't know *your* whole story but that's not necessary. One thing I took away from all this is that for me, the image of a man on a horse in the wilderness, in the mountains especially, is a happy one, it has an association with getting my thoughts straight, with things getting better for me. Once again, I understand that this story can't compare with the tragedy you went through.

You don't need to say anything about this to me, not if you don't want to, we can both just pretend that this letter was never sent. I just wanted you to know at least as much about me as I know about you.

Andi stretched and leaned back in her chair; she was satisfied with it, all she had to do was sign it and send it. Her "Andi" signature was already there, but there was a line above it remaining to be added. Her usual "take care," was far too cool for her right now; so was "your friend" which she'd written in and deleted. "Yours" she felt was too formal-sounding, meaningless. For quite a while she stared at the screen; then, sitting up quickly, she typed a line. Not wanting to give herself a chance to change her mind, she connected to the Net and sent the letter, leaving it as:

Affectionately,
Andi

25

At a gallop, Grant pushed Paula's finest thoroughbred, the one she'd called "Slim Chance" and had hoped in vain would one day be her second entry in the Kentucky Derby, to the top of the Overlook. Pulling the sleek stallion up short, he looked back; astride two of the ranch's best Arabians, Andi and Todd were in hot pursuit. He laughed, tipped his wide-brimmed hat back, and watched them come. They were trying, but there wasn't a hope of them catching Slim Chance, not if he pushed the thoroughbred.

He didn't; at a canter he took the spirited horse down the slope as the other two horses, making something close to their top speed, came over the rise.

"Come on, Andi!" he heard Todd yelling. "C'mon, we can catch him!"

"I'm right behind you!" she cried. Grant's smile spread; even yelling, she had such a lovely, musical voice. He slowed Slim Chance a little more, wanting them to catch up, wanting merely to experience the day. It was spring, the hills and valleys were bright green, the rivers and streams flowed full, there were flowers wherever you looked, their scents filled the mild clear air; southern California at its best. He could not have been happier, out riding these magnificent horses with his son and his new love, his bright, shining, new love. It had been so long, he told himself as he came to the highway, so very long . . .

His stream of thoughts stopped. The highway? There was no highway here, there wasn't a road other than a dirt trail for ten miles in this direction.

Yet there was. Slim Chance smoothly jumped the guardrail and they were in the middle of it, cars and trucks, their horns blasting at him, streaking by. The thoroughbred didn't seem to notice, he kept right on running, miraculously avoiding all the vehicles that were hurtling at them. Forgetting about his own danger he twisted around in the saddle, looking back at the two Arabians—who were just then vaulting, perfectly side-by-side, over the guardrail.

"No!" he screamed, even though they were already on the roadway. "No!" He tried to turn Slim Chance around; he wanted only to get back to them in time, but suddenly Slim Chance had become very slow, his steps more plodding than those of some Clydesdale. He saw that somehow, the horses Andi and Todd were riding had been transformed into a car. The two were still side-by-side, just as they'd been when the horses had jumped the rail, Andi behind the wheel; behind the wheel of a car turned sideways in the high-speed roadway, sitting across the center lane. As Slim Chance ran sluggishly toward them, he could see Andi trying to start the car. He also saw the huge semi-truck rounding the curve above them.

He screamed; the truck's brakes shrieked. Grant saw the trailer beginning to jackknife, saw the driver's terrified face. At the last moment, Andi looked up.

With a deafening roar the truck struck the car; the impact sheared the car in two, cutting it right through the center of the passenger compartment. The front piece spun around several times in the roadway, a wheel flying off, pieces of metal leaping into the air, sparks blazing from under it. It was still spinning when the trailer slammed into it, toppling onto the mangled piece of car and crushing it. Dust rose and blew away in the wind; there was no spectacular Hollywood explosion, but little fires fueled by pools of gasoline burned here and there on the highway, like an afterthought.

Grant ran toward the wreckage, on foot now, the horse had vanished. He could see it all so clearly, it seemed so close to him, yet he could not reach it. As he ran, he became aware that he wasn't wearing the jeans, the plaid shirt, and the boots he'd started this ride with, he was again clad in his Navy dress uniform. It had begun to rain, water pounding on the pavement.

He heard sirens; emergency crews were approaching. But he saw no ambulances, no police cars; instead there were limos gathering around the wreckage.

"No!" he screamed as he ran on. "No!" He could see men getting out of the cars, no white coats, no policemen's badges, Navy uniforms and nondescript dark suits. As he drew close all these men turned to look at him.

"It's too late, Kingsley," one of them, a Navy officer, said quietly. "Nothing can be done." The suited men smiled; the officer gestured helplessly, though he was smiling too.

"No, it can't be that way," he insisted, trying to push his way past the man, trying to get to the smoking wreckage. "No, I can't accept that, I just can't . . . !"

"Dad?" Todd asked.

He couldn't see the boy. "No, son, not now, I've got to get to . . ."

"Dad?"

Grant felt odd, the voice seemed to reverberate in his head, to mix with the sound of the falling rain, and, abruptly, the hideous accident scene faded away. His eyes fluttered open; he felt Todd's hand on his shoulder, he saw the boy standing over him, concern in his eyes.

"Dad, you okay?" Todd demanded.

"Oh . . . yeah, yeah . . ." He looked around. He was sitting on the couch in his living room; it took a few moments for him to realize that he'd fallen asleep and into a nightmare. "I'm fine, I'm fine . . ."

"You were sorta squirming around and yelling 'no, no' . . ."

"Yeah. Dreaming, I guess." He got up, stretched, and tried to remember why he'd come in to sit on the couch in the first place. Slowly, it came back; he'd read Andi's E-mail, and, wondering how to reply to it—his impulses, were, he was sure, inappropriate—he'd come in to think about it for a while. Closing his eyes, he'd drifted off to sleep—and to dream.

Forcing a smile, he reached out to tousle Todd's hair affectionately. "Yeah, just a bad dream, you know what I mean, right?" Fighting for control, he swallowed hard.

Todd's concern vanished; he grinned. "Yeah. I know what you mean, Dad."

Grant glanced at his watch; almost ten. "And speaking of sleep, it's about time for you to be heading off to bed, isn't it?"

Todd looked exasperated. "Yeah, okay, I'm going," he said, a little irritation in his voice—irritation that was familiar around bedtime. "I was just on my way when you started yelling."

"Yelling? I was yelling?"

"Yeah. Yelling." With a shrug, Todd turned away, headed toward the bathroom; with a smile, Grant watched him go. Then he himself walked back into his office, where the computer screen, left idle, showed a geometric screen-saver pattern. Sitting down, he moved the mouse to highlight Andi's letter, he clicked on the "reply" button and re-read it, feeling the impact of it once again.

Chewing his lip and remembering the nightmare, he stared at it. In a way he felt like writing something casual, maybe even a little hurtful, some rejection of all that she'd poured out to him—something that would push her away and keep her at a distance.

No, he told himself, no. That nightmare didn't foreshadow any future; things like that don't happen to everybody, they don't happen all the time. For the past eight years he'd rejected Paula and every other woman who'd acted interested in him because he did not want to relive that real-world, nightmare, the one that had reshaped so much of his life.

This time, he didn't want to. This time it was different; he knew how much it would hurt to see an empty mailbox, how painful World's Chat would be if she wasn't coming on-line or, worse, if she was there and not talking to him. Like it or not, she was becoming a part of his life. The pain of the dream started to fade; he smiled at her words. Then he deleted her whole letter and began to compose his answer:

Dear Andi,

First of all, I read your letter with a sense of disbelief. I didn't doubt what you were telling me. I didn't doubt that a man could be as foolish as your fiance Ben was, I've seen a lot of men and women behave in ways more foolish than that. I'm sorry if you take offense at me calling him foolish, but I just can't help it, Andi. Even as little as I know you right now, I can't see how anyone could do that to a woman like you.

I didn't doubt, either, that you might've tried to change yourself to please him. You seem like *such* a caring person, I can easily understand that you'd do your best for a man you loved.

What I couldn't believe was your statements that what you lived through was insignificant, compared to my own experience. Yes, I lost my family. Yes, it was devastating. Yes, it was terribly hard for me to go on, to raise my son alone. And there were more things, things I can't talk about yet but that I hope to be able to tell you about soon, things I've not talked about with anyone since that time, that made it much worse. Yes, it made me bitter. Yes, it made me suspicious. But I didn't ever lose a sense of who I was.

But, Andi, from what you tell me that's what happened to you, you lost your self. I can well understand that you'd consider suicide, and I can't tell you how happy I am you didn't do that, that you exist in the world, that I could meet you and come to know you. I agree, our experiences are different, but Andi, I want to be sure you understand, I *don't* consider yours minor. Just like me you passed through hell, and somehow you came out of it in one piece. To me this says you have an incredibly strong core. I don't have the words to express how impressed I am that you could go through this and come out the way you are.

As I read your account I found myself wanting to be there, wanting to know you then, to be your friend then. I wanted to be able to tell you that Ben was wrong, that you shouldn't listen, the problems were his, not yours, I wanted to make you understand that. This world can be so *hard,* there's so much that happens that's so very unfair.

It's been such a long time since I've talked with anyone like this, I don't know if I'm saying these things very well, if I'm being clear.

As it happens, I know the area you're talking about in North Carolina, I went there a few times when I lived in Kentucky. I can't think of a better place to go if you need to do some thinking. I consider myself lucky that the image of a man on a horse means what it does to you.

You signed your letter 'affectionately.' That made me feel good, Andi. I'm going to do the same, but I really think I need a stronger word than that one.

Affectionately,
Grant

Calling up the Netcom software, he sent the letter and watched as it went out onto the Net, on its way to New York. The word he needed was already in his mind, but he couldn't quite admit that, not just yet.

26

It was a tired Sue5 who waylaid Grant's E-mail as it moved from Los Angeles to New York; she'd been occupied for almost fourteen hours with the latest task Albert had set for her. Foggily, she read Grant's E-mail—smiling tenderly as she did, wondering how Andi would react when she saw it, imagining her own reactions if it had been written to her. She also read the version that appeared on Andi's server, which was identical.

Then she put Grant, Andi, and their rapidly developing relationship out of her mind as well for a while. Tonight, there was a wedding she'd been invited to attend, and it was almost time for it to begin.

When she arrived, she saw that it was being held in a very small chapel, its floor covered by ferns and bright red flower blossoms; it was already filled with people. She rendered herself invisible and dimensionless and, unseen, slipped into the room. She moved close to the best man, someone she knew reasonably well, and whispered a "hello."

He turned; he had the head of the Walt Disney Cheshire cat. "Sue! Glad you could make it! Hiding, eh?"

"Just don't want to take up space, Red Dog," she answered. "Has the Minister been here yet?"

"Not yet." He pointed, raising a stiff arm to do so. "Here he comes now!"

Dressed in bright purple robes, his face—except for the very prominent elf ears—almost obscured by a flowing white beard, the Minister glided into the room and took up a place before the gathering. He raised his hand; synthesized music began to play, the traditional Wagner wedding march, and the bride floated in from somewhere behind the spot where Sue and Red Dog were standing.

As the music died down the Minister began to speak, opening with the usual "Dearly beloved." Sue listened, glancing occasionally at the motionless bride and groom and at the maid of honor, who was an idiotically grinning blue panda bear dressed in a crimson gown. At last came the point where the bride and groom exchanged their "I do" statements. "And now," the Minister said when that was done, "to seal these vows you have just made, to seal this union, you will both please give me your heads."

Cooperatively, the bride and groom removed their heads and handed them to the Minister, who promptly gave the groom's head to the bride and vice-versa. They put them on for a moment, looked at each other, laughed, and then exchanged them again.

"By the power vested in me," the Minister said, "I now affirm that you are husband and wife." The two kissed rather stiffly. Not surprising, Sue5 told herself, since the bride was actually in New Orleans and the groom in Denver. Still, it was, as soon as the Minister—who was himself in San Jose, California—filed the papers, a perfectly legal wedding.

Having finished his duties, the Minister turned, started to walk away, and gradually faded from sight. To the sound of congratulations and under a hail of giant pillowy rice grains, the bride and groom fled through the doorway; outside they jumped into a miniature space shuttle festooned with balloons and tin cans and roared off into space.

"Rad, wasn't it?" Red Dog observed. He meandered toward the door himself.

"It was, it was," Sue5 agreed. She rendered herself visible and walked beside him. Behind them, others began gathering the ferns and flowers littering the floor; unlike World's Chat, this metaworld—called WorldsAway—featured objects that remained in the virtual environment until moved—which meant that someone had to clean up.

"You wanna marry me, Sue?" Red Dog asked unexpectedly.

She laughed. "Why, Red, I didn't know you cared!"

"Hey, I just got the fever!"

"Can't, my man. Married already."

"Yeah?"

"Yeah. To my computer."

"Oh, yeah. Hey, I should know," he told her. "AOL," he added, using an Internet shorthand for "me too," which had its origins in the users of America Online persistently posting bulletins saying "me too" to such trolls as, "I have the Sheryl Crow nude picture! Post here and I'll E-mail it to you!"

"Net-based lifeforms, that's us," Sue5 agreed lightly, although this conversation was not helping her mood. Not wanting Red Dog to pick up on this, she fell silent, watching as one of the wedding guests opened a basket, apparently to stuff ferns and flowers into it.

Abruptly, the whole world vanished—leaving Sue5 alone, hanging in empty space. Surprised, she looked around—then, just as quickly, the world reappeared.

"Hey, what the hell?" Red Dog asked. "Wha hoppen?"

"Glitch," Sue5 answered. "The metaworlds are still pretty new. There's bound to be glitches." As she spoke, the man who'd been cleaning up tried to open his basket again, whereupon the world disappeared again.

Once more floating, Sue5 laughed. To her it was obvious; the basket, like all other objects here, the avatars included, was actually a series of descriptors stored in the world database. The description of the interior of the basket or its contents was either an error or had become corrupt; the basket contained some "Thing"—some Thing not describable within the world parameters—that, when the program tried to describe it, caused that program to crash, and thus caused the world to disappear. Like something from Pandora's Box, it wrecked the world. For her own amusement, she decided to fix the problem for them.

Quickly—the speed of her access was many times that available to most users—she pulled the files into her local machine and began modifying them, hoping she was quick enough to get it done before the WorldsAway server came back on line. She was. After altering the files, she uploaded them to WorldsAway. A moment later the world reappeared—without Red Dog, who'd apparently given it up. The cleanup man was still there, and, evidently not having made the connection, opened his basket yet again.

When he did, a huge green caterpillar rolled out of it. As much as was possible for an avatar, the man stared at it; it raised its head and turned to look at him, showing him a grinning, goggle-eyed face. It winked, then turned and began eating all the ferns and flowers at a ludicrously high speed. Eating all the while it rushed around the room, its feet—each encased in a Disney-style shoe—moving like the feet of a windup toy. In just a few seconds, all the vegetation was gone; with another wink, the caterpillar ran up one of the walls, stopped halfway, and spun a cocoon. The avatar continued to stare, amazed.

Five or six seconds later, the cocoon split. A nude woman

stepped out, stood atop it, and spread multicolored butterfly wings from her back. Then, with a final wink, she rose into the air, passing through a skylight and out of the world.

"Cute," a voice from behind her said. "You have a lot of talent, Susie-Q. Maybe the movie folks'd be interested in you."

She turned; Colin—or rather, his avatar—was standing in the doorway. "I wondered what was smelling so bad," she observed.

"Very funny. You're such a kidder."

"I'm not kidding, Colin."

The avatar shrugged, smoothly and realistically. "Doesn't matter. We need you, Susie-Q."

"What now, Colin? Can't I even attend a fucking wedding in peace?"

"Wedding's over. Not that it matters. We need you."

She turned away from him. "Like I said," she repeated coldly, "what now?"

"Got a failure to adjust."

She turned back. "Whose?" she asked with a frown.

"You heard. The new one. You know her. Jeanne Stuart."

Sue5 couldn't help gasping. "Jeanne? She's here?"

"Just on. And she's figured it out. Part of it anyway. We don't know how, somebody screwed up. You get her calmed down, Susie-Q. Otherwise we're gonna have to give her a pink-slip. Like Jane8 got."

She fixed him with a cool stare. "Jane8 was lucky in my book, Colin. Go ahead and pink-slip Jeanne. And while you're at it, pink-slip me, too."

He laughed. "We're not pink-slipping you, you're too valuable for that—you're the best we have, haven't I told you that?"

"I'm just so fucking thrilled."

His face turned expressionless. "Go fix it. I don't want to pink-slip Stuart, I've got too much invested in her. You don't and it's gonna be two days' solitary for you, Susie-Q."

She suppressed the flash of terror those words held for her; more terror than his threat of cutting off her access. "Okay, Colin," she said tiredly. "I'll see what I can do. What's her handle?"

"Linda6."

"Fine. I'll go now."

"Keep me posted."

"Yeah." He vanished; Sue5 called up Jeanne Stuart on her

screen. She sighed; this wasn't going to be easy. The image was of a screaming woman's face, and the words coming through her speakers, though very loud, were quite monotonous:

"NONONONONONONONONONONONONONONONONONO-NONO . . . !"

27

"You look like you're in a daze," Vickie was saying. "You sure you're all right?"

"I'm fine," Andi mumbled. "Are we going to lunch or not?"

Vickie drew her head back rather theatrically and gazed at her. "Yes, of course, let's do it." Andi, lost in her own thoughts, nodded and walked with her friend to the elevator. It was crowded, they rode in silence; out on the street Andi remained silent. Without knowing where she was going, really, she allowed Vickie to guide her along until they reached the corner and turned onto Bleeker Street. After a while, she looked up. A man in the crowd, dressed casually as she expected Grant might dress, caught her eye, smiled at her; she smiled back. So nice here, she thought, so much friendlier than midtown Manhattan. She found herself wondering if Los Angeles was like Midtown or the Village. Up ahead, Bleeker Street was blocked off; she saw a man standing behind a camera, another man in a director's chair—obviously a movie being shot—and for a moment thought it was an hallucination. Then she remembered that shooting movies and commercials was common in the Village, she'd seen it frequently.

She smiled to herself and walked on, again lost in thought. Vaguely, she heard Vickie saying something about a deli, just as vaguely she heard herself agree. She walked right past the entrance while Vickie turned in, forcing her friend to come back after her. When they came out she was carrying a paper bag without being aware of its contents, and they were walking along again, on MacDougal Street now.

"Sit down, Andi," Vickie said loudly. She sat. Only then did she look up to see that they were seated in Washington Square

Park. She was confused; she could not remember how she'd gotten here. It was a good idea though, she thought distantly, a nice day to have lunch in the park. Realizing she was holding a paper bag, she looked into it and discovered a turkey sandwich, some chips, and a bottle of peach-flavored Clearly Canadian sparkling water. Favorites of hers, but she had no memory of ordering it or paying for it, and the idea of a turkey sandwich seemed unexciting somehow.

Vickie watched her stare into the bag, then look back up at her blankly. "Okay," she said. "You going to tell me about it, or am I going to have to drag it out of you one word at a time?"

Andi took out the bottle of sparkling water and twisted the cap off. "I don't know what you mean," she answered irritably. "I'm not having one of my better days, that's all." She sighed, looked down again. "I had two sessions this morning, both of them went pretty badly, I just don't know how I'm going to . . . to . . ." She faded away, staring blankly into the distance, the bottle still in her hand.

"Your cowboy?" Vickie guessed.

"He isn't a cowboy. I've told you that. He's a horse trainer."

"It does have to do with him, though, right?"

Andi stared at her challengingly for just a second, then wilted. "Yes," she admitted.

"What's happened? He called it off?"

She looked shocked. "Called it off?" she demanded loudly. "No, he didn't call it off! Why would he call it off?"

Vickie was startled; she held up her hands. "Okay, okay, he didn't call it off! Touchy, aren't we?"

"Sorry," Andi mumbled. She watched while Vickie unwrapped her own corned-beef and popped open a can of Sprite. "It's been a hell of a morning, Vickie," she said slowly. "Grant didn't call anything off, but I did get a letter from him, one he wrote late last night. I wanted to answer it but I couldn't do it, I couldn't find the right words and I ran out of time." She shook her head almost violently as she unwrapped her own sandwich. "Oh, Vickie, I really didn't want to come in to work today."

Vickie frowned. "So? You write him every single morning?"

"Close," Andi admitted. Holding half a sandwich she waved her hand impatiently. "It really doesn't matter," she said. "With the time difference I can write it this evening and it'll be there when he gets in from work, I just wanted to do it this morning.

Now I can't do it until tonight. And this day isn't ever going to
end!"

The other woman nodded sagely. "I think I see," she said. "He
said something totally asinine, didn't he?" She patted Andi's
arm. "Men always do, sooner or later. You've been out of circu-
lation for a long time, you've forgotten. You have to make allow-
ances for—"

"Vickie," Andi interrupted firmly.

"Mm?"

"He didn't say anything asinine."

"He didn't?"

"No." She took a small bite of her sandwich. "Just the opposite, Vickie. More than any man I've ever known, he managed to
say everything exactly right. Maybe it wouldn't be perfect for
every woman, but it sure was for me."

Vickie was silent for a long moment. "Ohhh . . . I see . . .
and now you're trying to figure out how to respond." She
frowned and gazed steadily at her friend. "I think," she said
finally, "that you're at a critical point here, Andi. Take it easy,
take it slow. Think about what you're doing before you do it."

Andi frowned. "I am thinking about it, I've been thinking
about it all morning, I can't think about my patients, and I
can't—" She paused and stared at the turkey sandwich. "—figure out why the hell I'd order something like this!"

Vickie laughed. "I can; you were flying on autopilot. It's okay,
lunch isn't what you need to be thinking about."

"I'm not about to do anything dramatic, Vickie. I just need to
figure out how to answer this letter."

Vickie grinned. "Yeah," she said, light sarcasm in her voice.
"That's the only problem you have. I can see that, I sure can."

28

The distant mountains loomed darkly as the woman known as
Jane7 drove her car toward a rapidly fading sunset. She glanced
around; she could see nothing except the mountains, the desert,
and the straight flat road ahead, but she was terrified, fearful of

something that was out there somewhere. She pressed the accelerator harder and the extra speed gave her a little comfort against the darkening skies.

The road swerved around a mountain ahead. As she approached the turn the twilight had given way to a heavy, velvety blackness, from which her headlights were the only relief. She thought she saw a man standing on the roadside, her head snapped around, there was nothing there; looking ahead again, she drove on, making the broad turn around the mountain. As the highway straightened out, she suddenly realized she wasn't in the desert anymore. Everywhere there was lush vegetation; she found herself crossing one low bridge after another, skimming over dark water. It didn't feel like California anymore, more like Louisiana, more like home . . .

But she couldn't relax. There was somewhere she had to go, and quickly. Again she thought she saw a man on the roadside, this time it turned out to be a sign telling her she was approaching the Cape Fear River. Confused, she watched it as it zinged by. The Cape Fear was in North Carolina, this was the bayou. She was home, not far from New Orleans.

Then she came to the river itself and she stopped the car. She could see the river, she could see the bridge crossing it; but it wasn't ahead, it was below her, far down a precipitous slope she couldn't imagine the car could negotiate, almost a cliff. It couldn't be, she told herself; there are no slopes like this in Louisiana, and there aren't any near the Cape Fear, either.

Yet she knew she had to cross. Slowly, she started driving down, the car constantly wanting to run out of her control. Finally she applied the brakes, harder and harder until she was using all her strength, but the car kept rolling downward, faster and faster. In a panic she shifted it into reverse, but it accelerated still, now careening toward the bridge and the river. Jane7 screamed, but couldn't hear the sound; she saw the windshield shatter as the car collided with the bridge abutments.

Once the noise stopped, she found she was unhurt. The car, however, was demolished; as she got out it seemed very small, she could not understand how she'd been inside. Dismissing that, she looked around. There was a path alongside the river, and downstream she could see lights, she could hear sounds. She walked that way, a little less apprehensive, feeling more than ever as if she was back home, back on the bayous.

Soon she could see the source of the light and sound; it

looked like a carnival or circus to her. It dawned on her that she was naked; she couldn't remember taking off her clothes but couldn't remember ever having them on, either. This was intensely embarrassing, but there seemed to be nothing she could do about it; maybe, she told herself, the people at the carnival would be kind to her, give her some clothes. She walked on.

Almost immediately, she was in the midst of the place. Her nudity wasn't exceptional. There were a lot of people here in the nude, and, nearby, a gigantic orgy was in progress; hundreds or perhaps thousands of men and women, and not just people: this orgy also had its share of animals as participants, dogs, pigs, donkeys, even snakes and eels. Shocked, stunned, she looked away—and saw an archery range.

An archery range where women were the targets.

She gasped, turned away again, and saw a seemingly endless row of hanged men and women, dozens, maybe hundreds, all of them naked. Another turn, and the smell of meat cooking assailed her nostrils; she saw spikes rising upright from the ground, spikes that could be used to spit a human being, and she heard screams of terror and agony. She started to run, aimlessly, fright taking possession of her. People were yelling, some men began to chase her, it was clear enough that they were asking her which attraction interested her, which one she wished to join. From the side a figure raced in toward her—a werewolf, nude and emphatically male, holding a collar and leash as if he wanted to make a pet of her. Sobbing with fright, she tried to run on but she stumbled into soft mud. Her pursuers were overtaking her. She screamed, again and again . . .

And then, slowly, the scene before her began to change. She tried to blink, found that she couldn't; she could only stare, without comprehension, at a computer screen split into three separate windows. Sounds began to filter in, and she began to remember. She looked at the screen; in the largest window was a video representation of a very handsome, dark-haired man.

"Back with us, Janey?" the man asked.

She was still foggy. "Michael? No, no, Colin . . ."

The man nodded and smiled. "That's right, Janey. Kick the cobwebs out. They usually go fast."

"Colin . . . I was . . . dreaming, I think . . ."

"Hallucinating is what we call it, Janey. You weren't asleep."

"No?"

"No. You—"

"It was so real . . ."

Colin laughed. "I've heard that before. You were in the hole, Janey. You want to know how long you've been there?"

"In the . . . hole?"

"You've been a bad girl, Janey. A very bad girl."

"I remember, I remember . . . oh, Colin, I remember, it seems like . . . weeks, months . . ."

"It's been twelve hours. Half a day. It doesn't take long, Janey."

"Twelve . . . hours?" She started to cry, choked off the tears. He'd brought her back, taken her away from that place; she felt immense gratitude even though at some level she understood perfectly well that he'd put her there in the first place. "Colin, I won't be bad anymore," she sobbed. "I won't, I promise . . ."

"I know you won't, Janey," he said soothingly. "I know you're going to get back to work, you're going to do your job. You were supposed to be monitoring Usenet, the newsgroups; you weren't supposed to be posting little messages of your own. It didn't do you any good, Janey, I warned you about that before. They get deleted as quickly as you post them."

"I'm sorry, Colin," she wept. "I'm so sorry . . . I won't ever do it again . . ."

His voice turned hard. "You'd better not. If you do you'll go back to solitary, and if you persist after that I'll have you cut off. You know what cutoff means, don't you, Janey?"

She tried to control herself. "No, Colin, I . . ."

"Cutoff means you go in the hole except when we have work for you. Cutoff means no chats, no newsgroups, no Web, no nothing, nothing except supervised work and the hole. You want that, Janey?"

She began sobbing hysterically. "No, Colin, please, no, I'll be good, I really will . . ."

"You'd better. Pull yourself together now. You have work to do."

"Yes, Colin, I will." He was turning away from the screen. "Colin?"

He paused. "Yes?"

"Colin, please . . . I loved you, I did, and for a while you felt something for me, you couldn't have acted that way if you hadn't felt something . . . I don't know why you brought me here, but . . . I need to feel you touch me . . . just come and hold my . . ." She broke off, sobbing again, and came under control with extreme effort. "Just touch me, Colin, I need to feel you with me . . ."

His lip curled slightly. "I'm not going to do that, Janey. Ask Albert. Maybe he will. Not me."

"Colinnn . . ."

"Forget it. Get to work. Now."

She suppressed a scream of anguish. "Yes, Colin," she said finally, though he was already moving away, out of her sight. "Yes, I will. I'll work hard. I'll be good."

That was what was required, she told herself as she began scanning the thousands of newsgroups again—dodging, for the moment, the "alt.sex" set of groups. If you work hard, if you please him, he'll come back. He does feel something for you, he does. No man can treat a woman the way he treated you if he feels nothing. It isn't possible, it just isn't.

She smiled a little as she worked. He'd be impressed with this. She knew he would. She was, for now, content.

29

For Grant, the evening hadn't started well; as soon as he'd gotten in from work, he'd checked his mail—and found only a letter that was actually for Todd, a letter from The Well telling him that he had been selected as the recipient of a year's free Internet access. There was nothing from Andi, and that troubled him; maybe, he thought, he'd come on too strong, maybe he'd said the wrong things, maybe he'd said it badly, maybe she'd misunderstood him. He went to shower—and returned, wrapped in a towel and his hair dripping, to check the mail again. Feeling an anxiety he refused to admit, he felt himself jump when the message in the Eudora window changed to "Getting message 1 of 1." The little green bar moved across with a message above it reading "Overwhelmed," there was no telling what *that* might mean. Once it was in, once the cheerful little bell sound and the message "You have new mail!" had cleared, he opened the letter and, feeling like a teenager, began to read:

Return-Path: explorer@nyct.net
Date:Fri, 17 May 1996 07:30:01 -0400 (EDT)
X-Sender: explorer@popserv.nyct.net
To: loner@netcom.com (Grant Kingsley)
X-UIDL: 832333465.000
From: explorer@ncyt.net (Andi Lawrence)
Subject: Overwhelmed

My Dearest Grant,

That header, "overwhelmed," says so much about how I feel right now. I've been thinking about your letter all day, trying to decide how to respond to it, how to say the things I want to say. Maybe if I start by going through the letter, by telling you how I felt when I read your lines, I'll find a way. All I can do is try.

worse. Yes, it made me bitter. Yes, it made me suspicious. But I
>didn't ever lose a sense of who I was.

You understand me so well, how can you possibly understand me so well? *No one* understood that then, and I haven't talked about it since.

>I *don't* consider yours minor. Just like me you passed through
>hell, and somehow you came out of it in one piece. To me this says
>you have an incredibly strong core. I don't have the words to
>express how impressed I am that you could go through this and come
>out the way you are.

I've never told a living soul what I told you and your response has overwhelmed me. I didn't feel strong then, I felt weak and inadequate. With just a few words you've changed that forever.

>As I read your account I found myself wanting to be there, wanting
>to know you then, to be your friend then. I wanted to be able to
>tell you that Ben was wrong, that you shouldn't listen, the
>problems were his, not yours, I wanted to make you understand that.
>This world can be so *hard,* there's so much that happens that's so
>very unfair.

These lines made me feel so . . . protected, so safe, so whole. To think that you have gone through what you did and still be able to comfort me, help me . . . this is a gift I'd never imagined I'd receive. I do so wish we had known each other then, that we could've talked like this then . . .

>It's been such a long time since I've talked with
>anyone like this,
>I don't know if I'm saying these things very well, if I'm being
>clear.

My God, Grant . . . unclear??? How could you think that? This was such a perfect thing to say . . . not only have you said it clearly, but you've conveyed the feeling.

>You signed your letter 'affectionately.' That made me feel good,
>Andi. But I really think I need a stronger word than that one.

You can't imagine what hearing this means to me. Your letter has ended now. But I have to go on with mine. I don't know how to say what I want to say. I'm *so* afraid that what I'm going to say will put you off, make you go away, out of my life. I don't want that.

I came onto World's Chat hoping it would help me understand what was happening with some of my patients, these cyber-romances were out of the realm of my experience. I didn't believe this could happen to people without physical contact. Never did I imagine that it would happen to me—or that it could happen this *fast.* Yes, I know, we've been writing two and three E-mails a day to each other and meeting on the Chat almost every night, but still . . .

Grant, I think I'm falling in love with you. I don't pretend to understand, all I know is that I think about you all the time, that you make me feel so very happy. I want to be with you, to see you, to touch you. I feel like I've known you forever. You stimulate me with your caring, your intellect. I feel excited when I'm with you, I feel passionate and *alive* for the first time in a very long while.

It frightens me to read my own words, to see the depth of this emotion. Can this actually be happening? Is this real? Is it even possible that you feel the same?

I have stared at this screen for hours debating whether or not to tell you about this. I am *so* scared that you won't want to talk with me anymore. I decided to tell you because despite all my fears and trepidation, I've come to think of you as my best friend. And no matter how you feel, I'm convinced that you'll respond to me honestly and kindly.

Love,
Andi

Grant sat back in his chair; he'd forgotten he was wearing only a towel, he wasn't sure of anything except the grin on his face. This letter he didn't read twice. Instead, he immediately called up the World's Chat program and paged her, hoping she'd be there. She wasn't; it was still early for him to be on, as she by now knew quite well. For a few minutes he sat in front of the machine, unsure of exactly what he wanted to do. Finally, he closed the Chat program and opened Eudora again. He wrote:

Dear Andi,

Please excuse this letter if it's a little confused. I just read yours, and I want to talk to you as soon as possible. I'll be on World's Chat, in the House of Glee, in about one hour. Please, if you can, meet me there.

He hesitated for just an instant, then typed his signature as "Love, Grant." After firing the letter off, he almost jumped from the chair and ran to his bedroom to dress.

Before he could finish, Todd was at the door. "Hey, Dad," he said, munching on some chips. "What's for dinner tonight?"

"Burgers," Grant told him as he yanked on boots. "I'm going to run into Fillmore and grab some fast food. Okay with you?"

The boy shrugged. "Sure. What's the rush?"

"I've got something I need to do on the computer."

"On World's Chat?"

"Uh-huh."

Todd grinned. "Meeting Doctor Lawrence?"

Grant scowled at him. "And how is that your business?"

Again he shrugged; the grin remained. "Just asking."

"Well, the answer is yes."

"Thought so. She's cool."

Now Grant grinned. "And how would you know she's cool?"

Todd reddened; his eyes flickered around nervously. "Well, I—uh—"

"You been talking to her on the Chat?"

"Me? Why would I—" he stopped, looked at Grant's face. "She told you, didn't she?"

"No. She didn't. She refused to violate your trust. You did, just now."

Todd grimaced. "Dad, I'm sorry, I—"

Grant waved a hand at him. "No need," he said. "I'm not angry with you. I understand, in fact. You can talk to her anytime you want to, Todd."

The boy looked amazed. "I can?"

"Sure. She's my friend, I think it's just fine if she's your friend too." Having finished dressing, he rose and hurried to the door, leaving a stunned Todd to watch him leave.

Driving into the small town of Fillmore, buying hamburgers, getting back home and eating dinner—all within an hour—wasn't easy, but Grant managed to do it within a few minutes of his targeted time. Telling himself that the nervous feeling in his stomach was merely the result of eating fast, he sat down at his computer, logged onto World's Chat, and paged Andi.

Again, she wasn't there; the "User not online" message was disappointing. For several minutes he wandered about aimlessly, checking out each Vampira he came across, as if the server might be lying to him.

Just when he was about to give it up, another Vampira appeared in the House of Glee—this one clearly labeled, "Explorer." Cruising right through several other avatars in his way, he rushed up to her.

She saw him coming and turned to face him. "Grant!" she typed. "I'm so glad you're still here, I got your E-mail but I had trouble logging onto World's Chat."

He moved very close; the sharp features, red hair, and red eyes of the Vampira filled much of his screen. "It doesn't matter," he told her. "You're here."

"I'm here," she agreed. He could almost sense the nervousness, the uncertainly, behind those simple words.

"I didn't want to do this in an E-mail, Andi. I wanted to do it this way first. Face-to-face."

The next lines came in a rush and were rife with typos, suggesting that she was jumping to a wrong conclusion. "Grant, I know I ws really benig forward in that leter, I don;t know how all this is hsppening I don't undersrand anything."

"Andi," he typed, "I'm falling in love with you too. To be honest, I've already fallen."

There was a long silence, a very long silence; the Vampira avatar did not move at all. "Really?" she asked finally.

He smiled at the screen. "Yes, Andi. I know this is fast, my head's swimming too. If anyone had suggested that this could've happened to *me,* I would've laughed at them. I love you, Andi Lawerence."

Her avatar swiveled back and forth, the Vampira looking blankly to the left and then to the right; he laughed, knowing she was twisting her mouse excitedly as she read his words. Then it stopped, and her lines appeared: "Oh, Grant," she typed. "You can't know what it means to see those words here on my screen. I was so scared, scared you didn't feel the same, scared you wouldn't want to talk to me anymore. I wish I could see you right now!"

He moved his avatar even closer to hers, as if he believed he could physically touch her with it. "I wish I could see you too," he told her. "I wish I was there with you, holding you close to me."

"If only you *were* here . . . I didn't know if I'd ever say the words 'I love you' to a man again. I never imagined I'd be *typing* them and meaning them so much!" She paused, and again the avatar began twisting from side to side, rhythmically, almost as if dancing. "I can hardly believe that you're real," she went on. "Sometimes I think you're just something I made up, a perfect man."

"I'm as surprised as you are," he told her. Without thinking he pushed his avatar closer still, and abruptly hers vanished as his passed through it. Swiftly, he pulled back until he could see her again. "All of a sudden, without warning, you drop into my life. Right now, all I know is that I *love* you."

Smiling, he waited for her response. For just an instant, her avatar dimmed noticeably; he frowned at the screen, wondering if there was a problem with his computer or with the Chat program. But then the shadow cleared, and her reply came as expected. It was as if another avatar, something shadowy, had passed between them; but now it was gone, and he dismissed it as unimportant.

30

Sue5 was an unseen witness to Grant's declaration of love for Andi; it hadn't come as a surprise to her, not considering his last E-mail, which she'd also read. She wasn't the only witness to this scene, either. Colin was again logged in to World's Chat when Grant came on, and, just as she was aware of his presence, he knew about hers.

Making no pretenses, she moved close to his invisible—except to her—form. "Come on, Colin," she begged. "Leave this one alone. I got Linda6 straightened out for you, didn't I?"

"You worry too much, Susie-Q," Colin answered, "about things you can't control. This Andi Lawrence is a good one, she might be as good as you in the end. We are going to recruit her, and that's that." His avatar gazed at hers steadily; even though he was talking to her she knew he was monitoring every word transmitted between Andi and Grant, every line was being delayed a little as it passed through the server in southern California. "You should go play somewhere else. You haven't got much free time left, Albert's got work for you tonight."

She didn't answer for a moment; trying to talk him out of

recruiting Andi wasn't, she was sure, going to get her anywhere. "I want to hang around," she said. "C'mon, Colin. It's like a soap opera."

Colin shrugged. "Just don't try to pull anything."

"I won't." Only, she added silently, because I can't. She turned her attention back to Andi and Grant, and saw that they were just beginning the process of delurking, of exchanging their "snail-mail" addresses—regular postal addresses—and phone numbers. With a sick feeling, Sue5 watched it happen; at her computer in New York, Andi typed in her address, 60 W. 13th St. Apt. 5J, and she followed that with her phone number. They came through the Nyct server and they came to that server in southern California the way she typed them, but they didn't leave that way; by the time those bits of information had reached the World's Chat server, both the street address and the phone number had been altered. A mail drop address, given as Box 1654 Grand Central Station, had been added, along with a line asking Grant to write to that address rather than to the 13th Street address. Sue5 could almost see Grant scribbling the addresses and the phone number down, having no reason to suspect that what he'd received wasn't what Andi had typed. She looked back at Andi's server; the World's Chat software, as she knew, echoed the user's own lines back to him, they didn't appear in the text window until after the Chat server had received them, but the software Colin was using was thorough; as they went back to Andi they were intercepted again and changed, back to what she'd originally written. Like Grant, she did not suspect that anything out of the ordinary had happened.

The same thing happened when Grant gave her his address and phone number. Again, a line was added telling her to ship mail to a Ventura post office box, and his phone number was changed as well. For a moment Sue5 found herself confused; it seemed they might think it strange that both of them used PO boxes, but after a moment she realized that each of them saw only the other's request.

Sue5 sighed; they'd never know. Their responses had been slowed by a second or two, nothing unusual for the Internet, and, although the almost identical requests to use PO boxes instead of street addresses seemed a bit stiff, they would not— as Sue5 was personally aware—attract notice. Frustrated, Sue5 had to restrain herself from shouting out a warning, an act that she knew wouldn't accomplish a thing except to ignite Colin's wrath.

"I always wondered, Colin," she said, trying to sound casual, "how do you handle the phone calls? There's a lot of noise, it always seems like the connection is bad, but that's all. Everything else is as smooth as glass."

Colin gave her a sharp glance. "That's not your business, Susie," he told her. "Why do you want to know, anyhow?"

"Just curious."

"Maybe I'll tell you about it sometime," he said offhandedly. "Doesn't matter, really. Right now I'm busy. I don't want to miss anything." He grinned at her. "You want me to miss something, something critical, something that'd cause us to abort this project. It isn't going to happen, any more than it happened with Linda6."

"You'll be glad to know," Sue5 went on, persistent in her attempt to distract him, "that she responded very well in the end. She's calmed down a lot, she's well on the road to accepting her—ah—future."

"That's good," Colin said abstractedly.

"What's she going to be doing for us?"

"Stuff."

"Stuff?" She laughed. "Colin, that's not as eloquent as you usually are. You—"

"Look, Susie-Q, go play somewhere else, okay? Or better yet, go dig up Albert. He's got work for you."

"But Colin—"

She fell silent; Colin had turned away, and she didn't have to wonder what he was doing. A moment later, Albert's avatar appeared in the metaworld.

"Come on, Sue," he commanded. "Let's go to work."

She had to protest though she knew it was useless. "Please, Albert, I—"

"You'll enjoy it. You're working with the arms tonight."

She sighed; normally this would be good news, she did enjoy working with the arms. "All right, Albert," she said tiredly. "Let's go."

She left the chat world; almost instantaneously she'd switched to a site on her local server. From several different angles presented in several different windows, she saw the interior of a rather bizarre laboratory. She was familiar with this room. In the center was a worktable; along two of the walls were cabinets, hanging on a third were tools ranging from heavy welding torches to fine surgical equipment. From the ceiling hung a set of four identical mechanical arms, each mounted on a swivel which was in turn set in a track system that allowed it to go anywhere in the room. She could also see the video cameras that provided her windows, some fixed to the ceiling, one mounted on each of the arms. Experimentally she moved the arm labeled with a large "A"; it responded, telling her the system was up and working correctly.

In the middle of her test the door opened and Albert—the real Albert, not an avatar—came in. If ever a man epitomized the geek, Albert did. Recently he'd even broken and taped his glasses. Albert was about six feet tall, but each of the mechanical arms was twice his size.

They'd stopped working, though, because Albert had cut the power via a manual switch outside the door. He didn't trust her with control of the mechanical arms, with which she could lift over two tons, when he was physically in the room. She didn't blame him; she did wonder what she'd do if he ever forgot to hit that manual safety. Most likely she'd just scare the shit out of him, but she'd do something.

Putting such fantasies out of her mind, she zoomed one of her cameras in on a small but elaborate metal box he was carrying. "What've we got?" she asked.

"Minimal assembly," he told her. "Special item." He gestured toward the box, which bore a symbol consisting of two overlapping circles. "You'll have to open it," he went on. "There're nanogears and shafts inside, they need to be assembled." He shrugged. "The specs were a little off, you'll need to redrill the gears or press-fit the shafts. That's up to you." He laid a thin book with a blue cover on the table beside the box. "Here's the specs."

"Check," she answered. "Okay, get out of here, let me get to it."

"Okay," He nodded, turned, left the room; a moment later the power was restored to the arms. Patiently she waited fifteen minutes to allow the air in the room to become still. With practiced skill she swung arms "A" and "B" around to the table and used one of the metal fingers to open the book; all her movements were slow and even, so as not to disturb the air. After reading the first page—the overview—she moved to the box, flipped the tiny latch gently, and opened the lid. Inside, on top, were two sheets of clear acrylic with what looked like neatly arranged specks of dust between them. Extending the lens on the arm-mounted camera, she examined the "dust." At x100 magnification the specks were revealed to be perfectly formed tiny gears cut from silicon chips.

Moving an arm to her tool cabinet, she retrieved a little stand for the holder, brought it back, set the sheet pair on it, and, with a touch more delicate than any human hand could ever approach, she removed the top sheet. The miniature gears barely wobbled; but, if she or Albert had been physically present, a breath would have sent them flying, there was a danger that they could be inhaled.

After carefully turning the page in the book, she removed the next sheet in the box, which contained the gearshafts. The specs weren't far off, she decided; a few hundred pounds of pressure ought to force the shaft through the gear. Observing her work through a microscope lens and having geared down her drive motors to the point where it took thousands of revolutions of the motor to move a finger a millimeter, she picked up a gear, settled it onto a press plate, and began forcing the shaft into it—applying over two hundred pounds of steady pressure to slide a shaft a thousand times thinner than a human hair through a gear so thin it would have taken five thousand of them stacked to equal the thickness of fine tissue paper.

It worked perfectly; on her outside monitor she saw Albert nod with satisfaction. Focused now, she assembled the other gears to their shafts and then boxed the shafts together in a frame. Finally, she added a microminiature DC motor and the device that was the point of the whole thing; a tiny laser projector, a laser designed to sweep an image onto a very small screen.

There were parts for two in the box. "New design?" she asked as she began to assemble the second one, addressing the sound to Albert.

"Yes," he answered. "How's it look to you?"

"Looks good," she told him. "Lighter and quicker than the old ones. Resolution the same?"

"Uh-huh."

"These for Andi?" she asked bluntly.

Albert hesitated. "They're for whoever's recruited next," he hedged.

In that case, she thought as she started testing the device, I can only hope they're never used. If I have anything to say about it, she swore silently, they won't be.

31

Sleep for Andi was impossible. An hour after having gotten off the Chat program with Grant, she was still up, sitting at her window and gazing out at the lights of New York; she'd been smiling for such a long time she was certain her face was going to crack. She remembered as a little girl crossing her eyes, her father warning her about them freezing that way, how that had frightened her. Wrinkling her nose, she crossed them now. Now, she thought, I'm not afraid of anything. Not anymore. Giggling at herself, she relaxed and looked out the window again.

I'd like to tell you all, she said silently to the thousands of lighted windows she was seeing, I'd like to tell you all that I'm in love, I'm in love with a man I've never met, a man named Grant Kingsley, and, incredibly—impossibly—he says he loves me too! He's never seen me and yet he loves me. This is a dream, this is a fairy tale, this can't happen in the real world!

In the kitchen her teakettle whistled; she rose, walked in, poured the water into a cup and dropped in a bag of herbal tea. Did he like tea? she wondered. What did he like? There was so much more to learn, it was so exciting, so fresh. She felt as if a whole new life was opening up, spreading out before her. Grinning into the teacup, she shook her head. A miracle, just a miracle.

Then the brash ringing of the telephone interrupted her musings.

She looked up at her watch, and frowned; it was twelve-thirty, who would call her this late? Some sort of emergency? She rose quickly, picked up the phone. "Hello?"

"Dr. Andi Lawrence, please," a deep full male voice asked.

"This is Dr. Lawrence," she answered. "Who is this, please?"

There was a pause and a crackling noise. "Andi," the voice said. "I just wanted to be sure it was you."

Her eyes widened as she understood. "Grant? Grant? Is it you?"

"It's me."

She suddenly felt without strength; locating a nearby chair she almost fell into it.

"It isn't too late to call, is it? I mean, you weren't in bed, were you?" There was more noise on the line, breaking up his sentence in the middle.

"It wouldn't matter if I had been," she told him. "I'd've gotten up! Oh, Grant, it's so wonderful to finally hear your voice—it's better than I imagined it'd be . . ."

He laughed. "I can't see how you could say that. Yours, now . . . just lovely. Musical."

"Flattery," she shot back, "will get you absolutely everywhere! Oh, it's so good to talk to you . . . I wish I could see your face . . ."

"Well, you could see a picture . . ."

"Oh, could you send me one? I'd love it . . . but I'll go crazy waiting the two or three days for it to get here . . ."

There was a loud buzzing; his voice came through it faintly. "This connection is terrible at this end. Is it bad there too?"

"Yes, noisy and breaking up at times." She laughed. "Funny, like the voices on that FreeTel thing on the computer. But I think I'm getting everything."

"Yeah, so'm I. Anyway, you don't have to wait. You can see a picture of me tonight if you really want to—if you have a browser like Netscape on your machine." He laughed; there was more noise than ever. "You'll be disappointed, though."

Ignoring the last part, she frowned at the phone. "Tonight? How's that possible, Grant?"

"Well, a while back I set up a home page on the World Wide Web—just to see if I could do it. It's still there."

Andi held the phone more tightly. "A Web page—you mean one of those 'http' things?"

"Yes. You want the address?"

"You bet I do!"

"Okay. It's http, colon, slash slash, www-point-Netcom-point-com, slash—"

"Wait a minute, wait a minute, I have to write all this down, just a second . . ."

"Why don't you just enter it into Netscape and go?"

"Well, Grant, I can't! I'm talking to you on the phone, I can't go on-line at the same time!"

"Oh. You don't have two lines?"

"No. Do you?"

"Yes. It doesn't cost much, and we use the Net a lot. I was concerned that nobody could call in when we were on-line, so I got a second line."

"I hadn't thought about it. And anyway, I don't use the Net all that much." She paused, giggled. "Well, maybe I do, too . . ."

"I love your laugh."

"My cackle, you mean?"

"No, that charming, open, and free laugh of yours."

She closed her eyes for a second. How does he always manage to say the right thing like that? How long can he keep doing it, forever? "You can't know," she told him, "how it makes me feel when you say things like that to me, Grant. And especially now, when I can actually hear your voice, when I'm not reading words on a screen. I love yours, too. I'm sorry I didn't say that before."

"I'm glad . . ."

"Okay, down to business again, how do I get this picture, I'm going to come apart here if I don't see it soon!"

"Well, I wouldn't want that! You have something to write on now?"

"Yes. Fire away." He did, giving her the entire address this time, and she carefully wrote it down. "Okay, got it. Now I just have one other problem."

"What's that?"

"I have to get off the phone to do it! And I don't want to get off the phone!"

"I don't want you to, either!" There was a pause. "I love you, Andi," he said, his voice deeper and softer and smoother than before.

"Oh, Grant, I love you too," she answered. "It's been such a long time since I've said that . . ."

"I didn't believe I'd ever say it again . . ." They went on for quite a while, repeatedly declaring their feelings for each other, their conversation peppered with the long pregnant pauses. Finally Grant, noting the lateness of the hour in New York, began to insist that they end the conversation.

"You do owe me something, though," he told her. "I want to see a picture of you, too."

"Okay, I'll send you one."

"You have one scanned?"

"Scanned?"

"Yes, scanned."

"I don't know what you mean. I'm going to dig up a picture, stick it in an envelope, and—"

"You can't do that! That'll take days to get here and I can't wait."

"You want me to Fed Ex it?"

"No! I want you to E-mail it."

"E-mail it? You can do that?"

"Sure. First you take your picture someplace that does scanning; that shouldn't be hard in New York. Then you have it on a disk as a JPG file. All you have to do is send me an E-mail and 'attach' it to the file."

"I don't know how to do that."

"Oh, I don't know if I can explain—what E-mail program do you use?"

"It's called 'Eudora.' "

"Great! That's what I use! I can tell you exactly! First you write me a letter or a note. Then you'll find under the 'message' menu a choice that says 'attach document.' You click on that and it'll give you a browse window. You stick the disk with your picture on in the 'A' drive, choose that in the browse window, and click okay. Then you send it. That's all there is to it."

"I'm pretty sure I saw a sign about scanning in the store where I bought the computer. I'll do it tomorrow, Grant."

"You'd better get some sleep now."

"Talk to you soon?"

"Of course!"

"Okay. Good night, Grant. I love you."

"Sleep well, my love."

He clicked off; as soon as he did, Andi rushed to her computer, connected to the Net, and called up the Netscape browser. Quickly, she located the window Grant had talked to her about, near the top of the display; she typed in the URL he'd given her and hit enter. A moment later the screen returned the mysterious message, "404 Not Found"; confused for a moment, she studied the line she'd typed, found an error in it, corrected it, and sent the command out again—and again got the same error message.

Pausing, she took a deep breath—then went over the line,

character by character. Again there was an error, again she corrected it, and again she sent it—fully expecting it to come back with the error message yet again.

It did not; instead, the screen turned light green and a Web page started to appear—beginning with a headline declaring that this was "The Grant and Todd Kingsley Home Page." Excited and impatient, she waited; frames appeared and, gradually, line by line and with frustrating slowness, were filled with pictures. As they filled, she scrolled the screen up and down; most, she saw, were pictures of horses, two were wide-angle shots of the Double-K ranch. Only one, the first one, had any people in it; it showed two horses, one with a boy and the other with a man mounted in the saddle.

Leaving the picture center-screen, Andi studied it. It wasn't very good, it was too small, the resolution was poor—and that disappointed her. But she could still see, reasonably well, the man's face—and it was a face that would not have been out of place in the movies. Cocking her head, she looked more closely; Grant, she decided, wasn't just handsome, he was gorgeous. She'd hoped, of course, that he would look good; what she was seeing was far beyond her expectations and made her feel a little intimidated. She looked at the boy, too, who was also good-looking, but she could not see any family resemblance between the man and the boy.

For a long while she sat studying that face, memorizing it, appreciating the smooth graceful ease with which he sat astride the horse. Repeatedly, she cocked her head and brought her face closer to the screen; something was off about the picture but she couldn't put her finger on what that might be. Finally, leaving her computer, she went to her closet and pulled down a box of pictures. She'd promised to send him one, and she always, she reminded herself, kept her promises.

She went through every one she had, rejecting the shots Ben had taken of her at the beach, the lingerie shots Ben had also taken, and definitely the few nude shots he'd done—she also rejected almost everything else, leaving a little group of five to choose from. From here the choice wasn't easy; she spread them out, stared at them, disliked them all, went over them again.

At three in the morning she was still trying to make her decision.

32

With a broad smile on his face, Daniel Iverson sat back and gazed at the computer screen in front of him. He wiped a hand over his thin gray hair. "Beautiful," he said, his voice just a little unsteady. "I can't believe it. It's just beautiful."

"Easily the best I've ever seen, nothing else even comes close," Jack Delling agreed. His eyes wandered to the window, which offered a reasonable view of the Washington Monument a short distance away. "The question is, is it worth the price?"

Iverson fixed him with a cold stare. "Mr. Delling, we have in our hands an analysis that would have taken us more than three months and more than a thousand man-hours to accumulate. The field men say it looks damn good to them." He turned away from the screen and studied the younger man's features closely. "As I see it," he went on, "and as the director sees it, the services IIC provides are far better than anything we've had before. It seems to me, Mr. Delling, that ten thousand dollars an hour is a very small price to pay for this."

Delling smiled. "Until we can find a safe way to have their technology in-house."

"Yes. Until then. But, given the current political climate, that may be a while. In the meantime, we have a responsibility to make the fullest use of IIC's services. We may be able to do some things we've never been able to do before."

Delling sighed and stared blankly at the reflection of his own 37-year-old face in the monitor screen. He studied it for a moment; it pleased him, in a way, that he looked so much like what he was. The dark hair cut so short it could never be out of place, the cool stare, the smooth square jaw, the dark suit, the meticulous knot in his tie. He moved his head back and forth a few times until he realized he'd become distracted and that Iverson was waiting for him to go on.

"Actually, I wasn't talking about the money," he said slowly. "I'm talking about the reaction if all this came out, if the media were to learn what they're doing out there."

Iverson nodded. "We cannot allow that to happen," he agreed. "It would be a disaster for everyone involved."

"We aren't in so deep we can't pull out."

"I know that. So does the director. Neither of us think that would be wise. Abandoning this project now means we might never have the technology ourselves. And I agree with Mr. Auan that all this—unpleasantness—we have to tolerate right now is only temporary, will only be necessary during the developmental stages of the technology. Everything brand-new carries some risks, Mr. Delling."

"The Japanese felt the risks were far too high."

"I know that. They have a history that makes them—sensitive. I think we have to be practical, Mr. Delling. If we aren't, then who will be? Do you imagine for a moment that the Chinese, for example, wouldn't make full use of this if they had the means?"

"I'm sure they would. But—"

"No buts, Mr. Delling. The decisions have been made."

"Very well. I understand."

"Good. Now: bring me up to date, please."

Delling shrugged; he clearly wasn't comfortable with the decision, it was obvious in his expression and in the way he refused to look directly at Iverson. "Well, Mr. Auan says he has problems; some of them aren't surprising. There are various agencies that want a look inside the IIC plant, and he's saying he can't hold them off forever, he needs help from us."

"Give him what he needs."

"Yes, sir. The other issue is with security at the IIC facility."

"I thought Auan was handling that?"

"He has been. But Mr. Auan believes that some kind of incident, sooner or later, is inevitable. People are curious, they run across the facility out there in the middle of the desert and they want to know what it is and why it's there."

"Understandable."

"Yes."

Iverson frowned irritably. "Mr. Delling, you haven't told me the problem yet . . ."

"Mr. Auan feels that an incident—especially one that resulted in a fatality—could raise questions. Serious questions."

"Yes, it would," Iverson mused. "Does Mr. Auan have any suggestions?"

"He feels the facility should have two levels of security, an outer level that we'd provide and an inner level that would re-main under his jurisdiction. If we do it that way, the people we send out there can operate under a need-to-know basis, they don't have to be briefed on the workings of the IIC."

Iverson was nodding slowly. "That sounds appropriate to me," he agreed. "I think that can be arranged. I'll present the proposal to the director, but you should proceed, Mr. Delling, as if that proposal will be approved."

Delling nodded. "Very well. I'd suggest a base presence at Twenty-nine Palms. One of our people will have to be in charge of local operations there."

"Agreed." Iverson grinned. "I've already decided on the man who should supervise this affair, Mr. Delling."

"Oh?"

"Yes. You."

Delling pointed to his own chest. "Me? But—"

"You. You've been our liaison with Mr. Auan since the begin-ning. I think that makes you the obvious choice."

"But—"

"No buts, Mr. Delling. Begin making your plans; you have a lot of work to do."

Delling didn't answer; he looked like he was about to be sick.

33

For a long time, Grant sat in front of his computer staring at the screen, at the picture of the slender woman with the dark hair and the blue Asian eyes, the woman who was turning her head slightly to gaze at the camera, her manner and pose that of an experienced model. She was very attractive, that he could see clearly—attractive enough to *be* a professional model.

He was also—he admitted it to himself, though he knew he'd never say it to her—just a little disappointed. She was hardly less appealing than he'd pictured her, but he'd also pictured a certain unaffected look, and the Andi Lawrence he was seeing lacked that; at some time, she'd been trained to look into a camera. The smile, the eyes, the set of the mouth—all practiced, all just a bit on the hard side.

It didn't matter, he told himself, it didn't make the slightest difference. Maybe she'd taken a modeling course, maybe she'd gone to some pro studio and she'd been a quick study, there were a lot of possible explanations—and it wasn't, he insisted mentally, a big deal. He felt he knew Andi—the Andi that had written the letter that had accompanied the E-mailed photo surely wasn't any different from the Andi he'd been talking to for the last several weeks, the Andi he'd fallen in love with. Maybe he should ask for a more candid photo. Obviously she went out of her way to impress him with this one, and he surely wasn't going to tell her she hadn't succeeded. Abstracted, he didn't hear Todd come in.

"Who's that?" the boy asked from just behind his shoulder. "Is that Dr. Lawrence?"

Grant swiveled his chair and looked back at him. "Yeah," he answered shortly.

"Wow." Todd bit the brownie he was holding in one hand and sipped the glass of milk he held in the other; a few crumbs fell to the floor.

"Wow?"

"Yeah, wow." He gestured toward the picture on the screen. "She's beautiful. Don't you think so, Dad?"

Grant smiled. "Well, yes, I do, in fact. I—"

"You get my account installed yet?"

Grant pulled his head back slightly. "Actually," he said coolly, "I didn't. I've been a little busy—"

Todd grinned broadly. "Yeah. Writing to Dr. Lawrence, calling her on the phone, meeting her on World's Chat. You have been. When're you going to see her? Or is she coming here?"

Like a turtle, Grant pulled his head back a little farther. "We haven't," he said stiffly, "talked about that. If we did it'd be some months away at least, I—"

"Why?"

"What do you mean, 'why?' "

"You talk all the time, don't you want to see her?"

"Well, yes, I—"

"Then why not? You aren't married, she isn't married, why not?"

Grant closed his eyes for a moment. "You're getting ahead of me, son," he said. "There are a lot of things to consider here—"

"Like what?"

Speechless for a moment, Grant opened his eyes very slowly. "Like, well, like—I have a job, and—"

Todd laughed. "Oh, Dad! Paula'd give you the time off and you know it!"

"Well, maybe so," he allowed—and maybe not, he added mentally, not if she knew what I wanted the time off for. "But that doesn't mean Andi can spare the time, now does it?" He shook his head. "You just don't understand, Todd. These things take planning, it takes—"

"It takes going to the airport and buying a ticket and getting on a plane. That's what it takes, Dad."

"It isn't that simple. Where—?"

"I could stay at the ranch. Like I did when you went to Florida last summer." Now Todd shook his head in turn. "I think it'd be better, though," he went on, talking around a mouthful of the brownie, "if Dr. Lawrence came here first. She likes horses and we have the horses here, right? I bet she'd love it."

"Todd, how do you know she likes horses? Answer me honestly, son, have you been reading my private mail? If—"

"Nope," Todd declared firmly—and, in Grant's opinion, believably. "No, I wouldn't do that, Dad. No, a couple of times when I came in and you two were on World's Chat you were talking about horses. She said she used to ride a lot."

"Yes, she did say that." The dream he'd had flashed in his memory for an instant; he dismissed it, he knew what it meant, and he surely could take Andi riding in the hills without letting her get anywhere close to the highway. That fantasy dissolved into another, much better one; he and Andi riding alone, stopping, sitting on the hillsides . . .

"Well, anyhow, it hasn't been talked about, and so—"

"Talk about it. Invite her. I'd like to meet her." The boy glanced at the screen again. "She sure is pretty."

"Beauty," Grant said stiffly, "isn't everything."

"Oh, I know. But she's nice, too. We knew that way before we knew what she looked like, didn't we?"

"Yes, we did," Grant agreed.

"So invite her."

He fixed the boy with a steady glare. "Todd, don't you have something to do? Some homework?"

"No."

"None?"

"No " He made a face. "I was hoping to get you to set up my Internet account."

"Well, I'm not going to do that right now. I've got something else I need to do first."

"Write an E-mail?"

"Not your business, son."

"Okay." He finished the milk. "Guess I'll go, then."

"Good idea."

Slowly, almost aimlessly, Todd wandered toward the door; his chair still turned away from the computer, Grant watched him go. He turned back only after the boy had disappeared from the doorway. Closing the picture, he started to open the E-mail program. It was a little odd, he told himself; he hadn't really been very focused on what he was going to say before his little talk with Todd.

Now he was.

34

For Sue5, it had been a long night and a longer day; she'd been kept late assembling the two miniature optical devices, and, after only a few hours' sleep, a harried Albert had wakened her, telling her she had several more analyses to do. Now, tired and more than a little foggy, but finally having been granted some free time—supposedly to sleep—she opened her browser and began poking around. It didn't take her long to tease out copies of the last couple of letters Grant and Andi had sent to each other—Netcom and Nyct had deleted them, but the re-routing server was maintaining an archive.

There wasn't much there—except for a reference to Grant's Web site, which hadn't been mentioned before. Discussed on World's Chat or on the phone, she assumed. She directed her browser toward Grant's site herself, watched the picture of man and boy astride horses appear. Nothing unusual there. She smiled, a bit darkly.

"I know how this part is done, Colin," she muttered aloud. "You don't know that, but I do." Reconfiguring her server, she gave it information which convinced it that she was no longer herself, but rather Explorer@nyct.net; then she looked at the picture again.

She laughed—bitterly, but a laugh nevertheless. The picture looked the same, the horses were the same, even the boy was the same—but the man was not. Enlarging the picture, she looked at the face.

"Oh, you're getting careless, Colin," she said. "getting over-confident. Why not? You've done this before without a hitch. What'd you use? Adobe Photoshop? Whoever did it for you didn't notice that the angle of light hitting the face isn't quite the same as the angle hitting the body and the horse." She stopped speaking and sighed, wondering if she herself would have noticed, and decided that she almost certainly wouldn't have. The key to Colin's whole game was that there never was a single reason for his target to even suspect that anything was going on.

Filing the picture away, Sue5 started looking elsewhere; if Grant had pointed her to his URL and shown her what she had every reason to believe was his picture—then she likely would've reciprocated immediately. She checked Netcom; there was nothing waiting there for Grant unread, but Ncyt's log showed that Explorer had sent a letter with a JPG file—a digitized picture—attached. But Nyct didn't have a copy of it remaining on their server. Using her hacking skills, she slipped into Nyct's system, acquiring "root" privilege, which gave her access to anything they had, and started scouring their recently purged files. After some intensive searching, she found a file the DOS emulator she was using called "?NDI.JPG," a file that hadn't been severely overwritten. Looks good, she told herself; after downloading it to her local machine and disconnecting from Nyct, she changed the question mark to an "A" and pulled it into a viewer. A ragged but still viewable image appeared, a picture of a lovely young woman sitting on a bench in a park, a woman with short dark hair and startlingly blue Asian eyes.

"Hi, Andi," Sue5 murmured. "Glad to see you at last." She filed the picture, then turned her attention to the Netcom server, where she went through the same procedure, again acquiring a file called "?NDI.JPG." She opened two viewer screens and pulled up the twin copies of ANDI.JPG she'd retrieved from the two servers.

Not unexpected, she told herself, not at all unexpected. Both pictures showed a beautiful woman, a woman with dark hair, a woman with blue Asian eyes.

Other than that, they did not resemble each other at all.

"The question is," Sue5 said softly, looking at the picture she'd just gotten from Grant's server, "who the hell are you?"

In the case of the man whose face had taken the place of Grant's, she did not have to ask that question. She knew perfectly well what Colin Simmons' face looked like.

35

Covering her eyes with her hand, Andi spoke into the phone slowly, carefully, as if afraid her secretary might not understand. "I don't care," she said flatly, "what you tell him. Tell him I'm sick. Tell him I got arrested. Tell him something. Just cancel the appointment, Lynn. Okay?"

"Dr. Lawrence," the other woman answered, just as flatly, "I can't do that! I can't just make something up!"

Andi sighed loudly. She could see Lynn Jones, sitting at her desk, slouched over, her phone cradled between her shoulder and her ear while she filed her nails, her blond hair tied back in a ponytail, her legs crossed. There were times—such as now—when she regretted hiring Lynn, but in general she was efficient and reliable, just not very imaginative and sometimes not particularly understanding.

"Okay," Andi said, lowering her voice. "In fact it's true, I'm not feeling very well. I want you to call Mr. Hestin and cancel his appointment for today."

" 'Kay. If I can get him on the phone. What if I can't?"

Andi's lip curled. "Then cancel him when he comes in. With my apologies."

" 'Kay. What about Mrs. Case?"

"She's here already, right?"

"No, she's late." Lynn giggled. "Isn't she always?"

Andi grunted; she decided not to let the opportunity pass. "Yes, she is. Today, Lynn, she pays. I'm sick, cut her too."

"Send her home?"

No, put her in cold storage until next week. "Yes, Lynn. Send her home. With my apologies."

" 'Kay. Anything else?"

"No, not now. In fact, we've just canceled the rest of the day. As soon as you speak with Mr. Hestin and Mrs. Case, you can take off early."

"Really?"

"Really. Have a good time."

"Thanks, Dr. Lawrence!"

"You're welcome." She clicked off, then dialed Vickie Du-Pont's number. She answered formally, as always.

"Vickie, are you really busy today?" Andi asked her friend bluntly.

"Well—busy, yes. Too busy? I don't know. What's up?"

"I just canceled my last two patients today, I can't focus on them. I was just wondering—"

"Steinberg's in fifteen minutes?"

Andi smiled. "Sounds great. See you there."

Steinberg's Coffee House—located almost directly across the street from the building where Andi and Vickie had their offices—hadn't changed very much since the 1950's, although now it was more of a curiosity than the meeting place it had once been. The tables were small, most of them located in booths with paneled walls, illuminated by lamps with conical green shades, offering a certain privacy. In one corner was a small stage from which once echoed the sounds of Beat poetry accompanied by bongo drums or flutes, rarely used now—but, in the interests of the tourists who commonly filled the streets of the Village, left as it had been, even to the chair and the microphone. High stools with wooden legs lined the long bar. Arriving first, Andi, obeying the sign telling her she should wait to be seated, stood near the door patiently. After a minute or so she was approached by a young man whose right ear was festooned with earrings and whose long hair was slicked back wetly; tattoos almost covered his exposed arms.

"Oh, hi, Dr. Lawrence!" he said brightly, his voice and manner a mismatch to his appearance. "Haven't seen you for a while. By yourself?"

"No, two of us, Gene. I'm expecting Vickie any minute."

"Good enough. Right this way." He showed her to a booth near the front window, rather far from the door. "This okay?"

"This is fine, Gene." She sat down. "How've you been?"

He shrugged and grinned. "Can't complain. But give me a chance and I will."

"I would, but you've got to go keep an eye out for Vickie."

"Right you are." He threw down a couple of menus and left; with a slight smile playing around her lips but a worried expression in her eyes, she gazed through the window.

She was unaware of her friend's presence until Gene escorted her to the table. "How'd you get by me?" Andi asked. "I was watching . . ."

"I don't know. I just walked right across the street." Vickie waved her hand in front of Andi's face. "I thought so. You're in a fog."

Andi covered her eyes again and almost hung her head. "You're right," she admitted. "I am in a fog. I don't know whether I'm coming or going."

"Being in love," Vickie said plainly, "can be rough. Especially when it sneaks up on you."

Andi looked up through her fingers. "You know?"

"It's been written all over your face for days. It's tough not to notice."

"That obvious?"

"At least. You told him yet?"

Andi put her hands down on the table. "Yes," she almost whispered.

"And he said?"

"That he loves me too. Oh, Vickie, it's all just so crazy . . . !"

"It always is. Falling in love always is."

Just as she spoke, Gene returned to take their orders; he looked from one to the other as he put glasses of water on the table. "Love?" he asked. "Who's in love?"

Vickie pointed. "She is."

The man's eyebrows shot up. "She is? Who's the lucky—uhmm—guy, I guess?"

"Guy, yes," Vickie informed him. "Cowboy. You don't get much more 'guy.' "

Gene grinned broadly. "Oh, you sure don't!" He dropped down into a crouch beside the table. "A cowboy! Where'd you meet him, Dr. Lawrence?"

"He's not," Andi said in a low voice, "a cowboy. He trains horses for a living, okay? Out in California. And I met him on the Internet."

"Oh, a Net romance," Gene said. He shrugged carelessly. "That's the way most people meet now."

"I think," Andi said drily, "that I was more out of touch than I thought."

"You were," Vickie said flatly. "Anyway—tell me about it, tell me what's happened."

Andi glanced at Gene; he didn't seem inclined to go anywhere. Ah well, she said silently, it doesn't matter. "Okay—we started talking seriously, and I told him I thought I was falling in love with him, and he said the same thing. Now, I don't know what to do."

Vickie frowned. "What do you mean, you don't know what to do?"

"You seen a pic of him yet?" Gene put in.

"Yes," she answered. "I have."

"And?" Vickie asked.

"And he's gorgeous. Movie-star gorgeous. Scares the shit out of me."

"Why?" Gene asked her. "You're movie-star gorgeous too, Dr. Lawrence."

She laughed. "Thank you, Gene, but—"

"No," he protested. "Seriously, objectively. Hey, you know me." He laughed too. "About women, I can be objective!"

"Okay, so you're both gorgeous," Vickie cut in. "I still don't know what you mean by 'what you do now.' "

Andi looked between the two of them, into the distance blankly. "He's invited me," she said slowly, "to come visit him. At his place, in California. Meet him, meet his son—"

"He has a son?" Gene demanded. "He's divorced?"

"No, he's a widower. He—"

"The son," Vickie intoned, "could be a problem. He—"

"No, I've talked to Todd on the Net too. We hit it off real well. That's not to say we'd never have problems, but Todd let me know he's worried about his father, about him being lonely. He's really sensitive."

"Sounds like a dream come true," Gene commented.

"Yes, it does, doesn't it?" Andi shook her head. "You can see my problem."

Both of them stared at her blankly for a moment. "Well, Andi," Vickie said after a long pause, "the fact is, no, I can't. You're in love, he loves you, what you do—"

"Is you go, girl!" Gene finished.

Andi smiled at him. "It isn't that simple," she pointed out. "If he lived here, in New York, then yes, it would be simple. We meet, we date, we see how it goes. He doesn't. He lives clear across the country."

"Have you heard," Vickie asked her, "of airplanes? Big things that fly up in the sky, that carry passengers inside them from places like New York to places like California?"

"The point is," Andi pressed on, "that I've really gotten involved. I don't know what I'd do if we suddenly broke up, if I didn't get his E-mails, if I couldn't meet him on World's Chat."

"World's Chat?" Gene asked.

"Yes. That's where I first met him."

"I go on World's Chat sometimes," he said. "Nah, I'd guess you could say lots of times."

"Oh? I've been on a lot in the past few weeks. I'm 'Explorer' there."

"Yeah? I think I've seen you! You're a Vampira, right? The redheaded vampire girl? Sheesh, I didn't know that was you!"

Andi's face reddened slightly. "Best avatar I could find . . ." She glanced at Vickie, who had her hand over her mouth, trying to suppress laughter. "There aren't many choices!" Andi told her.

"No, there aren't. I'm a plain-looking dude in bluejeans, myself." He laughed. "My handle is 'Gayblade.' "

"Oh, I think I've seen you too," Andi told him. "I didn't know you were on the Net that much, Gene."

"Hey, it just never came up—but I'm an old Netizen from way back. Gbarnes@aol.com, that's me."

"Easy to remember." Andi grinned and extended a hand. "Glad to meet you. I'm explorer@nyct.net."

Dramatically, with a little nod, he took it and shook it. "So. Who's your guy, Dr. Lawrence?"

"His name's Grant. On the Chat he's Piscean."

"Piscean!? The Fish Man? You caught the Fish Man? Damn! I am impressed, Dr. Lawrence, that's way cool! The Fish Man's been on forever, there's been lots of babes after him—hey, I'll admit it, I've been after him myself! And you hooked him! Oh, way, way, cool!"

"I didn't 'hook' him," Andi said stiffly. "We started talking when I was sort of lost there, he took me under his wing and showed me around. We found we had a lot in common."

"I still don't see the problem," Vickie complained. "I can see where you'd be anxious, but from here it looks like what you do now is pretty obvious."

"Go visit him."

"You win the prize."

"But look, Vickie—look at the realities. We've never seen each other, we don't know if we'll get along well together. And—"

"And you never will if you don't go see him or have him come to New York."

"Yes, but—"

"Vickie's right," Gene offered.

"But what if we do get along really well?"

Vickie stared. "What?"

"Vickie, I can't see it being neutral; it's going to be either very good or very bad, either a disappointment or beyond our expectations. If it's bad, the relationship folds up, and I don't want that. If it's good, then the distance between New York and Los Angeles becomes very large. Becomes a big problem."

Vickie and Gene nodded almost in unison. "I see," Vickie agreed. "But you still don't have a problem. What's got you locked to the City, anyhow?"

Andi looked bewildered. "Well, Vickie—this is my home! I have my practice, I have my friends, I have—"

"You are free," Vickie insisted. "Nothing is really holding you here. You can close your practice here and open a new one in Los Angeles. Problem solved. Or he can move here."

"And do what? He trains horses!"

She shrugged. "There're horses in New York," she noted. "But I'll agree, he's got the kid and all, he's probably more tied to L.A. than you are to New York. And you like the horses anyway, so go see him. That's it." She looked at the man who was still crouched by the table. "Gene, you suppose we could have some coffee here?"

"Oh," he said, standing up quickly. "Sure, sure. I'll get three." He scurried off, leaving Vickie shaking her head.

She looked back at Andi. "Scared shitless. Right?"

"Right. It's been a long time for me, Vickie."

"You never forget. Look; if you were to decide not to meet him—and I don't think there's even a slight chance you'll make that kind of decision—you'll regret it forever, you'll never know what might have been, what you might've missed."

"And if I do—and it doesn't work out—"

"You'll get over it." She leaned across the table. "Look. You never did tell me what caused you and your fiance, what was his name—?"

"Ben."

"Yeah, Ben—to break up, but it was bad, obviously. What you have to understand is that this isn't the same—this is a different man, different time, different you. It's never the same. I've told you about my breakups, I'd gone through some nightmares before I met Martin. I—"

Gene returned, cutting her off; he placed three steaming mugs on the table, then returned to his crouch; his multiple earrings jangled like a wind chime before settling down. "Okay," he said, pouring cream into his, "where were we?"

"I'm trying to tell her she has to go," Vickie told him.

"Well, yeah, of course you do." He glanced at Andi as he stirred his coffee. "It's the only thing you can do, Dr. Lawrence."

Andi smiled, touched his hand lightly. "You're right," she said. "Both of you. It's something I have to do." Her eyes misted slightly. "I don't have a choice about it, not really . . ."

36

"I'm scared, Grant. I don't mind saying it."

"I am too," he admitted. "But I think we—" He stopped as the phone line erupted in high-pitched buzzing; the sound faded to a series of clicks that grew softer and softer, as if they were somehow moving away, until they finally disappeared. "Are you still there, Andi?"

"Yes. A little deaf from all that racket."

"This is a rotten connection. Maybe we should hang up, I can call you back?"

"We've tried that. It never seems to help. It's funny, the phone line isn't bad when I talk to anyone else, just to you."

"I called up Ma Bell and gave her hell, but it didn't seem to help. She ignored me."

Grant laughed. "Thought Ma Bell was dead, that all the baby Bells had taken her place."

"Maybe that's why she ignored me."

"Maybe so. Guess we should just tough it through?"

"I guess. But you always sound like you're speaking from the bottom of a tin can."

Grant nodded as if she could see him. "Yeah, you too. Anyway. To get back to what we were talking about . . ."

There was a brief pause. "I do want to meet you, Grant. I really do. But I'm scared. I'm scared it'll go wrong and I'm scared it'll go right. Does that make sense?"

"It makes sense to me—I feel the same way. I'm way out of practice, Andi. I don't know if it shows or not."

"It doesn't. And I am too. So we're equal." She paused again. "I do want to see you. I want to be able to touch you . . ."

He closed his eyes for a moment; it has been so long . . . "We're equal there too. I do want this, Andi. I'll come to New—" he paused; static swelled in the receiver, then died away. "York if that's more convenient for you," he continued, "but I'd really like for you to come here, I'd like to take you riding . . ."

"I didn't hear all that," Andi told him, "but yes, yes, and yes, I'd love to go riding with you. Grant, you didn't tell me when you'd like me to come. You—"

"Is tomorrow afternoon too soon?"

She laughed. "Maybe a little!" Her voice dropped in volume and slightly in pitch: "But I don't want to wait, Grant. I've made my decision, and if I wait I might start second-guessing myself."

"Andi, maybe it's stupid of me to say this, but I can't imagine it going wrong. I feel like we know each other better than we would have if we'd started dating in the usual way. We—"

"We wouldn't've started dating," she cut in. "We've talked about that, we're too leery, we couldn't've gotten things off the ground. That's obvious to me now. Perfect timing and perfect place, World's Chat; being anonymous allowed us to be more open than we would've been in any other circumstances."

"I think you're right. That's probably why I was hanging out on World's Chat to begin with. But I can't see it going wrong just because we meet. I think we need to."

"I agree." She sighed into the phone. "Do you think," she mused, "that if it did go wrong—if we didn't get along with each other in the real world—that we could still be friends, that we could still write letters and meet on World's Chat?"

"I have to think so," he confessed. "I can't imagine not having this relationship with you, Andi. Not now."

"Me neither. So, we'll meet. I'll come and visit you. When is best for you? No jokes this time . . ."

"Any time. As far as I'm concerned the sooner the better."

He could hear her take a deep breath. "Okay. I'm going to start making arrangements right away, then. I have to get someone to see my patients while I'm gone, but I don't think that'll be a big problem. I think maybe—next week? Is that too soon?"

Better than he'd hoped, far better. "Not at all," he hastened to assure her.

"Then that's what I'm going to shoot for," she said firmly. "As soon as I get my patients straight, I'll get the ticket and let you know what day."

"Plan to fly into LAX," he told her. "I'll meet your flight."

"That's fine." She paused again. "Oh, Grant, I do love you . . ."

He answered in kind; the conversation slipped into a familiar pattern of endearments and silences; even after it had gone on for over thirty minutes, it hadn't become boring.

37

Viewing both Grant and Andi's most recent E-mails side-by-side, Sue5 sighed softly as she re-read the salient paragraphs of each. Grant's—which was waiting for Andi on her server—suggested that, rather than taking her straight to his home in the mountains, he rent rooms at a hotel in Los Angeles, that they remain there for a couple of days. This would give them time to get acquainted and to plan her meeting with Todd. Andi's suggested exactly the same thing.

Sue5 understood that neither of them had written either of these letters. But they were well done; she couldn't see much difference in style between the real ones and the phonies. Neither would suspect anything, and both would have the same understanding about what was going to take place.

"Admiring our handiwork?" a voice asked.

She shifted her perspective; in another window at her left was a video image of Colin's face.

"As a matter of fact, yes," she told him. "It's good. Who's doing the editing for you?"

"Linda1, as usual."

"Ah. Good old Lindy. Reliable as always."

"You could do this stuff too, Susie-Q. Better than she can, I'm sure of it. And Linda1's getting a little long in the tooth, we've had her around for quite a while now."

Sue5 closed out the letters and gave Colin her full attention. "You're going to pink-slip her, Colin?"

He looked hurt. "No! Whatever gave you that idea? She's been a good and reliable worker for a long time, we don't pink-slip workers like her!"

"Then why're you talking about replacing her?"

He shrugged. "Well, as I said. Physically she's starting to go down. It happens—used to happen a lot quicker than this. You don't need to worry, though. You're aren't close to that, and we get new answers every day."

"That gives me such comfort. You can't know."

He shook his head. "How long are you going to keep this up?" he asked her. "I don't expect you to like me, but we do have to work together. This sniping just takes energy and wastes time."

She started to flare back at him, but bit off her words before they came out. He's right, she told herself, he's right. It accomplishes nothing, all it does is cause him to keep a close watch on me. She sighed theatrically—maybe a little too deeply. Be careful, she reminded herself, don't overdo it, he isn't stupid. "You might be right, Colin," she admitted. "But I'm not ready yet to help you with your recruitments . . . I always . . ."

"Hoped you could somehow stop them?"

She hesitated deliberately. "Yes," she admitted in a small voice. "At least some of them."

"You can't, you know."

She sighed again. "I know I can't. I've tried and always failed. Believe me, Colin, if I could I would. But I'm no Dona Quixote, I don't keep fighting when I know I can't win."

He regarded her steadily. "It's taken you a long time to realize that."

"I'm stubborn."

"I know. That stubbornness makes you one of the good ones."

"You have all this down to such a science," she went on, again hoping she wasn't laying it on too thick. "I can't find any holes, can't find a way to do a thing."

He grinned. "We do, don't we? Nothing left to chance. At every stage, if anything goes wrong, we bail. We lose one but the next one comes home."

"That's what I was trying to do," she told him. "Make things go wrong. I never succeeded, not once." She paused again, as if thinking. "I could never figure out parts of it—like the phone, how you work the phone, direct long-distance isn't under the control of the Net . . . I know you relay the calls, but that's all I know."

"And that's the key." He leaned closer to his monitor, obviously warming to his subject, proud of the way they'd worked things out. "The subjects never know it, but they're connected through digital lines, through the server here. The voices are digitized as they come in and resynthesized as they go out, the same way the I-Phone and FreeTel programs do it, and we have a slight delay so we can monitor it and cut a word or a phrase if necessary. We save all conversations so we have retrievable files of individual words; after a while we can insert words or whole phrases if we need to." He stopped, made a helpless gesture. "It isn't perfect. We have to overlay line noise, 'make the connection bad,' so the subjects can't identify voices. We have one whole server dedicated to this alone. In the early days we couldn't handle phone contact, we had to bail a number of times because somebody got suspicious. Like everything else, we get better all the time. It's funny. We're almost always dealing with bright people and nobody ever seriously questions the fact that the phone connection is bad only when they're talking to their Net honey."

"I didn't," Sue5 observed. "It just seemed like bad luck to me, I never thought anything of it. It was annoying, that's all." As she spoke, she was wondering where that server was and how she could get access to it.

"That's typical," Colin went on. "Almost everybody does the same thing." He gazed out of the screen steadily for a few seconds, as if he was looking at her, though she knew he couldn't actually see her. "I do want you to think about what I was saying earlier," he told her. "About taking over for Linda1. We'll need someone on that service soon, so you can't take forever to make your decision. There are benefits, you know."

Yes, she said silently, I know, extended Net access, more free time. She allowed herself a secret smile. What you don't know, Colin, is that some of the programs I've been working on are beginning to come together now, and pretty soon I'm going to have access beyond anything you might offer me.

"I will," she answered aloud. "Right now I can't say yes but I will think about it. I do know the company's policy, after all."

"It doesn't sound nice but it does work," he reminded her. "No emotion. No feeling. Efficient, careful, thorough, methodical. It works." He smiled. "And you are a part of this company, Susie-Q. Like it or not."

38

All four wheels churning, the beige Jeep roared up the sand dune; the driver brought it to a halt abruptly, just shy of the top. A cloud of dust and silt rose around it, some of it carried away on dry desert breezes. Almost simultaneously, the doors on both sides opened. From the driver's side a young man, hair plastered across his forehead and a pair of binoculars hanging from his neck, jumped out; from the other side, more carefully, came a young woman.

"Right up over the ridge," the man said. "You can see the whole damn thing from up here." Without waiting, he started up toward the top. His boots, his bluejeans, his very dark tan, his rugged appearance, all suggested he was completely at home out here.

The woman looked quite different. Auburn hair tied back in a ponytail, dressed in a stylish shirt and shorts and wearing sneakers, she stepped lightly and uncertainly among the rocks and sand. She wiped her forehead, being careful not to get her hand too close to her eyes lest she smear her carefully applied mascara. Her hand came away dusty and she twisted her mouth.

The man, well ahead of her, stopped. Looking back, he grinned. "Doin' okay, Connie?"

Connie Leeds gave him a sour look. "Yes, Mick, doing all right." Struggling just a little, she came up alongside him.

He grabbed her arm as she started to pass him. "Nono," he almost chanted. "No. Hands and knees from here."

She looked incredulous. "What?"

Mick laughed. "Well, if you walk up there they're pretty damn sure to see you!"

She threw up her hands. "Okay, okay, you're the expert." She shook her head. "Why this place couldn't've been in downtown L.A. I don't know." Still, obediently, she got down on her hands and knees; side by side, she and Mick crawled on up to the crest of the ridge. She peeked over.

"Oh, Mick, you weren't kidding, were you?" she breathed. "It looks like a small college campus!" She stared at the six white buildings hidden down in this desert valley, at the helipad, at the parking lot, at the numerous cars. Gazing at the tallest building, she picked out the double-circle logo; taking a notepad from her shirt pocket, she jotted that information down. "IIC," she mused, "does not list this facility at all. It simply isn't supposed to be here, they're supposed to have a Riverside office and a San Jose office and that's it for California. What the hell are they doing out here, anyway? This is the middle of nowhere!"

"But a nowhere that's pretty easy to get to," Mick pointed out. With a jabbing finger, he indicated the road down below, on the other side of the complex. "See that? It goes right out to the main road, about an hour from Twenty-nine Palms. Less if you're headed for the military base over there."

"That road looks pretty narrow . . ."

"It is. Don't matter. No traffic, nobody uses it except these guys." He grinned and rolled over sideways. "That's how I found out it was here, Connie. I'm cruisin' up and down my ol' desert roads and there's one that's got all this traffic on it, an' when I drive it end to end I figure out it don't go nowhere. Makes me curious. So I come in to L.A. and drop by the *Times* and look up my favorite reporter."

"Sorry I doubted you, Mick. You're the desert rat to beat all desert rats, you always know what's going on out here."

His expression soured. "Yeah, well, usually. Some way or another they got this place built without me knowing they were doing it. Connie, I don't know how the hell they did that. This took some heavy equipment and some time."

"I checked," she told him. "According to the county records, there aren't any buildings out here."

"Can't believe everything you read."

"I can see that."

Rolling back over, propping himself up on his elbows, he pointed again. "See the fencing? Double perimeter, razor wire. Kinda thing you'd expect in a prison or military installation. Now, look there!" He swept the binoculars over his head and handed them to her.

She put them to her eyes. A Jeep-like vehicle, military-style, was driving along a dirt road that had been cut just inside the outer fence. Frowning, she studied the occupants; soldiers, no question about that. Helmets, uniforms, automatic assault weapons visible.

But the uniforms weren't American and the faces under the helmets looked Asian.

"Security patrol," Mick informed her. "Now you tell me— those are foreign soldiers of some kind, ain't they?"

"They sure look like it to me. We can't be sure, there're plenty of Asians in the U.S. military, but nothing looks U.S. to me. It looks like something I'd expect to see in Thailand or Taiwan."

"Where's this IIC got their headquarters, anyway? L.A.?"

"No. Singapore."

"Oh. Well, maybe that's the answer, maybe that's whose soldiers those are."

"I don't know a thing about Singapore's military or even if they have one. If they do, their soldiers shouldn't be here in the States guarding one of their plants. That's not kosher, Mick."

"What do these guys do, anyway?"

Continuing to watch the patrol, Connie shrugged. "It's sort of vague. IIC stands for 'International Interface Corporation,' and they make—chips, you know, integrated circuit chips like they use in computers and all."

"Yeah? What kind? Memory?"

"I have no idea. I can't even find out who their customers are. The brokers think a lot of them, though."

Mick again rolled onto his back, staring up at the bright blue desert sky. "Maybe they're a Netscape."

She took the binoculars down and looked at him. "Pardon?"

"A Netscape. Netscape makes the most widely used Internet browser, but they give it away free. They don't make money. But everyone expects them to, later. Real speculative."

Connie grinned. "How does a desert rat know about things like that?"

He shrugged. "I have a computer at home, I'm on the Net. I keep up, y'know?"

She laughed. "Better than I do! Okay, I've seen enough, we can head on back. I have research to do—but I'm probably not going to get answers unless I can get in there. Or at least get close."

"I can get you close. Have to be at night. It's gonna be risky."

She started backing down from the ridge. "It may," she said seriously, "end up being necessary."

He slid down, rolled over, came to a crouch. "You're calling the shots, you pay the bulldog," he agreed. "Hope you know what you're doing."

She puckered her mouth. "I do, Mick. You worry too much."

39

"You don't have to tell me," Paula was saying. As usual, her booted feet were propped up on the desk in her office. "We have that movie crew coming in here in two weeks and there're horses that aren't ready—but you know you can have whatever time off you need." She smiled warmly. "I'm just curious, that's all. You have a girlfriend you want to go see?"

Grant remained silent for a few seconds, wondering whether to tell her it was none of her affair or tell her the truth—not something he wanted to do, not considering the confidence of her own feelings she'd offered him recently. Paula was a friend, he liked her; if it could've been uncomplicated, she might've been a lover. But he knew, quite well, that something uncomplicated wasn't what Paula was looking for, she wanted a mate and that wasn't something he could be for her.

"Yes," he said, as flatly as possible. He paused, waiting for a reaction; there wasn't one. He looked away at random. "Someone I met on the Internet. I'm meeting her in the city."

For several seconds there still wasn't a reaction. He glanced back at her; she was still smiling. "I know, Grant," she told him. "I've known for a while."

He stared. "You have? How?"

"The way you've been, for weeks now. Starting when you fell off your horse. You didn't use to smile much. Now you smile for no reason. I noticed. So did some of the others around here. You've been a topic of conversation lately!"

He sighed. "That obvious?"

"Who is she, if you don't mind my asking?"

"I don't. Her name's Andrea Lawrence, she's a psychologist from New York City."

Paula's eyebrows went up. "A city girl? She know what you do here?"

"Yes. She used to ride a lot herself, she loves horses."

"You'll be bringing her here, then, to ride." It didn't sound like a question.

This he found uncomfortable, though he'd visualized doing just that. "Well, somewhere—maybe Eddie Gear's place, I didn't—"

"Grant."

"Yes?"

"You'll be bringing her here to ride. Okay?"

He grinned. "Okay, Paula. I just wasn't sure that—"

She shrugged her shoulders rather dramatically and gazed at her desktop. "Grant, there isn't a problem here," she told him. "I'll be very direct with you—I'd hoped there was a chance for you and me, I think we could be good together. You've never misled me, never took advantage; if you aren't interested you aren't interested, and there's nothing I can do about that." She raised her eyes. "So it doesn't mean I don't wish you well." Her smile became less strained. "And I want to meet this Andrea, too! I want to see what sort of a woman finally got to you!"

"Andi," he informed her. "Okay. I'll bring her up here a few days after she arrives; she wants to stay down in L.A. for a day or two, give us a chance to get acquainted before introducing her to Todd."

"Might not be a bad idea. Todd knows about her?"

"Todd's talked to her, on the Net. If you want to know the truth, it was his idea to invite her out here before it was mine."

Paula laughed. "You want to have Todd stay here, at the ranch, while you two are down in town?"

Grant smiled. "Yes, that'd be nice. I was wondering how I was going to ask that favor."

"That and any other, it's yours if you need it." She put her feet down on the floor. "When is she supposed to arrive?" she asked.

"She's supposed to be here on Wednesday, June 12. I'm going to drive down Tuesday and rent a couple of rooms at the Marriott on Century, near the airport."

"Bet you're counting the days."

I am, and they're going to drag by, Grant admitted silently. "Yes," he said aloud.

"You sure?" Paula asked teasingly. "Sure you've got the right date?"

"That date," he told her, "is burned into my mind. Believe me, I wouldn't make a mistake about that!"

40

"And so?" Vickie was asking. "The big day is?"

"Tuesday, June the eleventh," Andi told her. "I just sent him an E-mail giving him the time and flight number." She folded her hands around her coffee cup and worked her fingers up and down slowly, rhythmically.

Vickie glanced at the cup. "Not nervous or anything, are you?"

"Who me? Hell, no. Why would I be? All I'm doing is dropping everything, getting Adam—of all people, my poor patients!—to cover for me which means I'll owe him one forever, and heading off to Los Angeles to meet, for the first time, a man I'm so frantically in love with I can't even think about anything else, a man I've never seen in the flesh, and to top it off, a man who looks like a movie star. I'm not the least bit nervous."

"You have no reason to be," Gene told her firmly. He shifted position, left his crouch, went down on one knee instead. Turning toward him, Andi smiled. Steinberg's had become more or less the standard place for her and Vickie to go to discuss things, and never did the tattooed man seem too busy to join them. "You're gorgeous, Dr. Lawrence, you've got everything going for you."

"You're great for my ego, Gene," she replied. "We should've started talking like this a long time ago."

"Ah, I dunno. I might've done a one-eighty and come after you myself if we had." He grinned. " 'Course, you'd have to get some tattoos and some piercings . . ."

"Think I'll pass on that."

"All right," Vickie said, cutting in. "Now look—as soon as you get there, I want you to call me. Call me and let me know everything's okay. Then I want a call a day or two later, too."

"Oh, Vickie, I—"

She raised her hand for silence. "No, Andi, you listen to me on this one. I want those calls, and that's that. I want his home number, too, so I can call you."

"We won't be at his home for a few days. He's renting rooms at the Hilton near the airport, we're going to spend our first few days in Los Angeles. He wants us to have time to get to know each other this way before I meet Todd."

"That's not unreasonable," Vickie agreed.

"Hell, I'd just want to take the whole plunge," Gene put in.

"Well," Andi mused, "I'm not sure why he wants to do this— he knows Todd and I have talked on the Internet, we're getting along famously so far—but, he knows his son better than I do, and—"

"And you surely don't want problems from that quarter," Vickie finished for her.

"No, I don't. I've seen enough of those in my practice."

"Okay. But you haven't agreed to call me yet."

"I'll call you when I arrive, okay?"

"Yes. And again in a day or two."

Andi made a sour face. "Ah, Vickie, that could end up being a little awkward . . . I mean—well, you know what I mean. Why's it so important, anyway?"

"Because you never know," Vickie intoned darkly.

Andi stared blankly. "Never know what?"

Vickie turned her gaze toward the window. "Just say I'm naturally suspicious," she said, "but there're all kinds of people using the Internet these days. All kinds of weirdos. You just never know."

Andi laughed. "Oh, come on! Grant? He's as stable as they come!"

"So you think. You won't know until you got out there."

"Vickie, I'm a psychologist, you don't think I'd see that—"

"No," Gene said, using a stronger voice than Andi had ever heard from him before. "Vickie's absolutely right, Dr. Lawrence. You can't always tell." He sighed and stirred his own coffee absently. "People create personas on the Net, you don't see the whole person."

"You remember me telling you about Donna, don't you?" Vickie asked.

"Well, yes. But that's—that's—"

"Take my word for it, Dr. Lawrence." Gene went on, his tone just as serious.

Looking back at him, Andi frowned. "It sounds like you have some sort of experience with this."

He hesitated, then nodded slowly. "Not something you want to hear about right now, Dr. Lawrence."

She playfully slapped at his shoulder. "Oh, come on! You can't tease like that and then stop!"

"I should. Really."

"No. Tell me." Sensing that this was a serious matter for him, she became serious herself. "I should know, Gene."

"Well, it wasn't me," he told them. "It was a friend of mine, a guy I know. Good friend, in fact. Cool guy. He met a lover on the Net, on the MOO."

"The MOO?"

"Yeah. It's a sort of a chat, the details aren't important. Anyway, the dude lived in Chicago, and Bennie went to see him."

"And?"

"They didn't get along in person. Well, to tell the truth, Bennie didn't like him. So, after a while, he tried to leave. So the dude tried to stop him. There was a fight."

Andi looked horrified. "And?"

He looked up at her, real pain in his eyes. "And Bennie got killed, Dr. Lawrence." He sighed. "Hey, it could've happened right here, they could've met in some bar and it could've gone down like that. It happens." He stared at his coffee. "Seems like it happens to us a hell of a lot . . ."

"Yes," Andi told him. "It does happen, and I do know what you mean. It does take a while before you truly know somebody." She spent several minutes trying to comfort Gene; but when Vickie again demanded the calls, she didn't argue, not at all.

41

The woman with the long blond hair stared into her drink. After a moment, she picked it up and took a long swallow. "So when do you leave, Jack?" she asked.

Delling shrugged. "Within a day or two. I'm sorry it has to be on such short notice, Kay." He glanced around, making sure no one in the restaurant was close enough to overhear their conversation. "It's my job. Special assignment."

Kay nodded slowly and looked back up at him. "Yes, of course, your mysterious job, the one you can't talk about. You can't even tell me where you're going?"

"You know I can't. We've been over this before."

She kept nodding. "Yes, we have." She smiled slightly. "The mysterious Jack Delling. Everybody knows him, nobody knows who he works for. The stuff of spy movies." She cocked her head to the side. "Jack, did I ever tell you that Martha Greenlee was a friend of mine?"

He scowled. "Martha Greenlee? I don't—"

"Know her?" she finished for him. "Oh, come on, Jack! You think your old girlfriends don't talk about you?" She leaned forward across the table, and her bright blue eyes widened in surprise. "You really don't remember her, do you?"

"Well, of course I do," he lied smoothly. "I just didn't—"

"No," she interrupted. Her classic features took on a hard set. "No, that was genuine, you don't remember her at all. She was your lover for months, and you don't even remember her name!"

"Kay, that's not so, I—"

"And in a year you won't remember me, either."

"Don't be silly, Kay!" He reached across the table, touched her hand. "Just because I have to go away for a while, that doesn't mean I'm going to forget about you!"

Her expression softened. "You mean that?"

"Of course I do!"

She looked doubtful, but she didn't pull her hand away.

"Jack, Martha and I have talked a lot. I didn't ever say anything, but it bothered me—the things you say to me, the things we do, they're the same things you used to say to her, things you used to do with her."

He sighed and shook his head. At last, memories of Martha Greenlee were coming back to him; she was a lawyer working for the Justice Department—and not someone he would have expected to know Kay, who worked in the office of a prominent senator. In Washington, he reminded himself, any paths can cross.

He also remembered his breakup with Martha; it hadn't been pleasant. She'd called again and again after he'd told her he didn't want to see her anymore, she'd turned up at his door unannounced. There'd been an ugly scene, and he'd said things to her he probably should not have said—things which might well have gotten back to Kay.

"Martha," he said carefully, "doesn't like me much now. If I were you I'd take what she says with a grain of salt. Maybe with a whole shaker."

Her fingers twined over his. "I've done that, Jack. She's said some pretty nasty things about you. I tried not to believe them." She pursed her lips, then leaned forward more. "Take me with you, Jack. Wherever you're going, I don't care. Just as long as I can see you sometimes . . ."

He shook his head. "Kay, I can't do that! This is a very important assignment and it's not one that can be public. I can't take some—"

Her eyes hardened. "Some? Some what? Some woman, some bimbo? Some whore? Some what, Jack?" She pulled her hand away violently; the drinks on the table rocked and threatened to spill. "God damn you," she went on, her voice shaking. "Martha was right about you. All along, she was right about you."

Delling paused for a few seconds, wondering how to respond. It would be just as well, he told himself, to let this go. The one good thing he could see in his reassignment to Twenty-nine Palms was that it offered a reason to break things off with Kay. As was usual with him, he had grown tired of her; she was attractive and personable, but she had no surprises left for him—she'd grown boring.

"If you say so," he told her carelessly.

Instantly she softened again. "Oh, please, Jack . . . we were good together, weren't we? You can find a way. You aren't going out of the country, are you? You once told me all your work was here, in the States."

"Most of it, yes."

"This one?" she persisted.

"Yes, Kay, in the States! All right? But you still can't come with me!"

"Just tell me what city!"

"No."

She stared for a moment. Then, wiping her eyes, she rose from the table. "You're a bastard, Jack Delling. A real bastard."

He shrugged again. "Where're you going?"

"Home."

He started to rise too. "I'll take you—"

"No. Forget it. I'll take myself. Good-bye, Jack."

He sat back down. "Good-bye, Kay." She started walking away; he watched her for a moment, then noticed a dark-haired woman sitting alone at the bar. She was wearing a miniskirt, and her legs, in Jack's opinion, were well worth looking at.

Before Kay had even gotten out of the restaurant, he was making his way toward her.

42

From a short distance away Sue5 watched Red Skull as he talked to a young teenage boy about one of his favorite topics, video games. He was not on through the Netcom server, but through The Well. It's taken you long enough, Grant, Sue5 thought silently. But then, you've been busy lately, haven't you? She sidled in, eavesdropping on their whispered conversation, and waited patiently until the other boy, evidently in response to a parent's summons, had to drop off-line. Then she moved closer.

"Hello, Todd," she whispered to him.

The Red Skull avatar turned toward her. "Hi!!" he answered. Then, after a pause: "How did you know my name was Todd?"

"I'm a friend of your Dad's. (smile) I know lots of things because I work for a computer company that's always on-line."

"Oh, cool!!"

"I know, for instance, that you have your very own account now, with The Well. Congratulations."

"Thanks!! It's really cool!! LOL!" Sue5 smiled at the boyish enthusiasm. "But it isn't much different," Todd continued, "than being on through Dad's account."

Oh, yes it is, Sue5 told him silently, yes it is. Colin and his cronies aren't paying attention to you, all your outgoing digital packets aren't being relayed through the server at IIC. "But it's *yours*," she told him encouragingly. "Has *your* name on it, not your Dad's."

"Yes, it does!!"

"I heard you saying," she went on, "that you'd like this place a lot better if it were like the games 'Doom' and 'Heretic,' if there were some monsters to fight."

"Oh, yes!! That'd be cool!!"

Sue5 laughed; everything was cool to him. She knew how he felt, she could remember when she first started finding all the treasures out there on the Net. "Well," she told him, "since you're Piscean's son, I'll show you a *very* secret place here if you want me to."

"I think I know all the secrets—the Castle, the Basement, the Flamingo Maze, how to get into outer space . . ."

"You don't know this one. I'm sure. Want to see?"

"Really? Sure!!"

"Okay. Come to the Hall of Sadness and come inside, where the rooms like 'Tears' and 'Bitterness' and 'The Pox' are. I'll meet you there."

"Okay!! But can I ask you a question first?"

"Sure."

"I see you as a lady wearing shorts and sneakers, and you have your hands spread out in front of you like you were looking at them! There's a big 'NB' on your shirt! That's not one of the gallery avatars, is it?"

"No, Todd. It's a custom one, it's mine."

"Oh. You gave the files to my Dad?"

A small white lie wouldn't hurt, she told herself, and that was easier than explanations. "Yes," she told him.

"Okay! See you in Sadness!" After a moment, he vanished in a puff of white smoke. She too transported herself to Sadness, appearing inside the corridor where the rooms were—and where Todd, with a normal interface to the program, could not appear, he had to come through the door. She turned slowly in a circle; there wasn't anyone else here, all she could see was the dark walls with the light blue tear-shapes on them. Facing the door again, she waited. After a few seconds, Red Skull popped through.

"Hey!! How'd you beat me here?"

"I have a quick interface," she told him. "Anyway. Come on, let me show you." Turning, she led him down the short hallway to the left of the entrance, where rooms named "Tears" and "Bitterness" faced each other. At the end there was nothing, just a tear-logo covered wall.

"Now what?" Red Skull asked.

"Now," she told him, "click with your mouse on any one of the tears in the top row, next to the ceiling. You'll have to back off a little to do that." He did; she waited patiently, knowing what was going to happen when he clicked.

"Hey!!" he typed. "The program is asking me for a codeword!! It's never done that before!!"

"I know (wink)," she said. "This is *really* special. Now; I want you to think up a codeword. Something special for you, something you'll remember. Okay?"

"Like a password?"

"Yes."

"I'll just use my E-mail password!! It's Storm/gelding."

"Todd! You *never* give anyone your password! Ever! If you do they can open your mailbox and read all your mail!"

"Ooops."

"(sigh) Okay, I won't tell, and I won't spy on your mail, I promise. Use that as a codeword here if you want to."

"Okay!! So do I type it in?"

"Yes, type it in, then hit 'enter.' "

"Okay!!" Sue5 waited, watching the wall—she'd already prepared the World's Chat software to accept whatever he put in and lock it in as a password once he'd verified it—and soon a new door faded into view. "Wow!!" he shot back. "There's another door!! It says 'Private' over the top of it!!"

"And it is," she told him. "No one else can even see it without a codeword. They'll just see you walk through the wall and they'll have *no* idea how you did that!"

"Nifty!!"

"Well, go ahead. Are you going in?"

"Sure!!"

"I'll be right behind you." She watched the door open, watched him go through. Then she slipped inside herself. As she did, she activated a dummy avatar of herself that, operating by artificial intelligence—a "chatterbot," in current computer lingo, a software homunculus—that would wander about World's Chat and carry on meaningless conversations with whoever it chanced to encounter. Sue5's chatterbot would not only act as a distraction, it would alert her whenever Albert or Colin was looking in on her or summoning her.

Looking at Todd, she giggled; his Red Skull avatar was moving slowly back and forth as he took in the environment. The rooms in the Hall of Sadness were generally fairly small and, except for floor and wall patterns, featureless; this room was, emphatically, neither. The landscape—a landscape similar to the one in the "Garden" satellite—seemed to extend to infinity. In the distance were hills, some with castles set up on the slopes; closer there was a forest to the left and craggy rocky outcropping to the right. At the center was what looked like a tunnel, a closed door protecting its entrance. Right beside the door was what looked like a tall cabinet. On the side of the cabinet was a small structure that looked like an intercom.

Hope you like it, Todd, Sue5 said mentally. I spent a hell of a lot of time on it.

"Wow!!" Todd exclaimed. "Wow!! **Way** cool!!"

"We'd better," Sue5 told him, "check out the cabinet."

He turned toward her. "Hey!! You look real different!! You're all dressed in green, you look like an elf lady or something!!"

"That's a faerie warrior, if you please," she sent back. "Open the cabinet, Todd."

"How?"

"Just click on it."

The cabinet swung open; inside were two glowing green crossbows, two quivers of bolts, and a pair of wands with yellow crystals at the ends. On another shelf was a large number of what looked like test-tubes filled with a bright blue solution.

" 'Heretic' weapons?" Todd demanded.

"Absolutely." She picked up one of each. "And you'd better get yours quick. We don't have too much time here."

Trying to pick them up by running over them, which was the way one picked up weapons in the "Heretic" game, his avatar—now a muscular warrior with a red skull emblem atop his helmet—bumped into the cabinet several times. "How?"

"Same way. Just click on them." He did; the weapons jumped from the cabinet to his hands. "Okay," Sue5 said, "you're armed. Now we give you some action. Look out, Todd. Turn around."

His avatar whirled; from out of the rocks at the right, two of the skeletal Undead Warriors, lifted from the "Heretic" game, were coming at them. Attacking immediately, one threw a bright green ax at Sue5. Grinning, she ducked the attack and fired her crossbow at the warrior, scoring several quick hits. Todd, taken more by surprise—Sue5 had, after all, created the warriors and set them to attack after a certain interval—took a hard hit from another tossed ax.

"You have a life bar now," Sue5 told him. "If you 'die' in here, you'll appear back outside the door, you'll have to come in again, start all over."

Todd didn't answer; instead, his avatar sidestepped another ax and he began firing his own crossbow—and scoring his own hits. Sue5, with a smile, turned back to her own opponent and found him standing very close in front of her. Before she could react, she herself took a hard hit from one of the more damaging red axes, and her own life bar dropped to half.

"Well, crap," she said aloud. "I'm not going to be beaten by my own game!" Ducking away from the warrior's next attack, she fired several more bolts at him—and watched him crumple to the ground. Todd was having more trouble, the warrior he was fighting had driven him back alongside the cabinet, and, though he was scoring hits, his life bar was down to twenty percent. Quickly, Sue5 circled around behind the warrior and dispatched him with several well-aimed bolts.

"Thanks!!" Todd typed. He then turned to the cabinet and clicked on the blue vials—as in the "Heretic" game, each worth a gain of plus-ten to his health—until his life bar was back to one hundred percent.

Then he faced her again. "This is just *too* cool!!" he told her. "Are there more monsters in deeper?"

"Oh, yes, they're all over. Just like in the game"

"Great!!! Can I bring my friends in here with me?"

"I don't know. We'll see. They can't use your password. This is your playground, Todd, for now. Yours and mine."

"Oh. Well, that's nifty anyway!!"

"Let me show you something else."

"Sure!!"

She moved her fairie avatar to the intercom-like box. "You see this?"

"Yes. What is it?"

The main reason for the existence of this whole damn thing, Sue5 thought. "It's a communicator. You'll find more of them, all over this world. If I'm not here, you click on one of them—any one—and it'll page me. Anytime. Understand?"

"Sure!! Now what?"

"Now," she told him, "let's have some fun. Let's go mix it up with some monsters!"

43

As the 737 continued circling over Los Angeles International, an impatient but almost impossibly nervous Andi stared out her window, watching the bright blue of the Pacific ocean wheel by, picking out Santa Catalina Island in the distance, watching the Southern California coastline wander back into view. From here, the land looked to her as if it was slightly crumpled, as if some giant hands had been pushing at it almost at random, moving things around, shoving up mountains in the same way one could raise a wrinkle in a bedspread. From what she knew of the geology of this area—which wasn't much—it seemed to her that that might not be an inaccurate picture, the giant hands being the San Andreas and the other fault lines out here. She had never experienced an earthquake or tremor, she had no idea what to expect from one, and she hoped nothing like that would happen while she was here.

She continued to watch as the city itself—the City of Angels, the "City of Light, City of Night" according to the Doors— slipped by underneath the airplane, all sparkle already; it was still full daylight up here but the sun was well out over the Pacific, drawing a bright trail across the water, and down below dusk was settling on Los Angeles as another night began. It seemed to her the City looked very beautiful from up here, but, as a New Yorker, she was acutely aware of how lovely that city looked from a distance, and what a contrast that was when compared to the view from the streets. L.A., she understood, might be no different.

And besides, she told herself firmly, thoughts about moving out here might be just a little premature. Even so, a slight variation on words to a song by the Red Hot Chili Peppers concerning this town were running through her head: "Take me to the man I love, take me all the way . . ."

The pilot's voice on the intercom jarred her out of her reverie: "Ladies and gentlemen, we've just been given clearance to land at LAX and we'll be beginning our final approach momentarily. Please fasten your seat belts . . ."

Andi's was already fastened; she settled back in her seat as the plane, with a slight jolt, started to lose altitude. Andi could see the city lights moving faster, and the runway made its appearance. The engines roared, the tires touched down with a quick shriek, the wing flaps sprang into action and the plane began to slow. She relaxed a little, now that the landing—as she knew the most dangerous part of any flight—was over. All she had to be nervous about now was her actual meeting with Grant, just minutes away.

With agonizing slowness, the plane rolled up to its assigned gate, the walkway slid out to meet it; the passengers, ignoring the pilot's admonition to "remain seated until the plane has come to a complete stop," were already up, already gathering their belongings to disembark. Andi had joined them, retrieving her small carry-on bag from the overhead rack and sliding into the line waiting to reach the door. Finally, after what seemed an excessively long time, the line of people began to move and Andi found herself in the tunnel leading to the terminal. As she came out of it, she scanned the group of people waiting to meet the passengers; she didn't see him, and she experienced a flash of apprehension. What if he'd changed his mind, what if he'd decided not to meet her after all? What would she do?

"Andi!" a voice called. "Andi! Over here!"

She turned quickly, to her left, and there he was, the man in the picture, smiling richly and waving to attract her attention. It was strange; for just a moment it seemed impossible to her to think that this was truly Grant Kingsley, the man she'd talked to on World's Chat, by E-mails, and by phone, actually standing in front of her at last, a real human being.

She maneuvered through the crowd toward him as her doubts vanished and a full rich smile washed over her face; in seconds she'd reached him, and he opened his arms to greet her. Dropping her overnight bag on the floor, she went right into them, throwing her own arms around him without feeling the slightest embarrassment. Others in the terminal were watching, many of them smiling.

He pushed her away just slightly; holding her by her shoulders, he looked down at her face. "I can't believe you're here," he told her. "It doesn't seem possible."

"Oh, no, it doesn't . . ." she sighed. For a moment she couldn't speak, she just kept moving her gaze between his eyes. Then she smiled. "Your voice doesn't sound anything like it did on the phone. On the phone it sounded deeper."

"I hope it isn't disappointing."

A little, she thought. The words flashed through her mind but she rejected them firmly. What difference does it make. "Oh, no, not at all . . . I'm just so happy to be here, to finally see you." She giggled. "I guess in a way I didn't quite believe you existed. Like all there was of you was a picture, a voice on the phone, words in an E-mail." She pressed close to him, laid her head on his chest. "But you are real, you are . . ."

He stroked her hair gently. "And you are too . . ." He turned her to the side. "Come on, let's get your stuff and get out of here."

She wasn't eager to move, she wanted to savor the moment, just a little longer. "I wanted to talk to you on the phone last night," she said. "I was so scared, I wish we could have . . ."

"I know," he said soothingly. "But I had to take care of Todd, make sure he'd be all right while I'm away—the plans I'd made fell through at the last minute. I'm sorry it interfered, I really am . . ."

"It's okay. I'm here now, you're here . . . it's okay, Grant." She shook herself slightly. "We should go, I guess." She giggled. "People are staring at us, aren't they?"

"People always stare at lovers," he said smoothly. "It makes them feel good. My car's just outside. The baggage claim is this way." Holding her arm, he guided her through the busy terminal; twice on the way to the baggage claim she almost collided with someone because she was looking only at him.

It just didn't seem real to her. It just didn't seem possible.

44

"I don't understand," Todd was saying, "why she can't just come on up here. We have a spare bedroom."

Grant sat the iron down on the end of the ironing board, smoothed another wrinkle from the shirt, and turned his attention to the boy. "She wants to stay down in L.A. for a couple of days and I'm not going to argue the point with her. She thinks we need to get a chance to know each other before she comes up here and meets you."

Todd idly dragged a potato chip from the bag he'd laid on the kitchen table. "I don't see why. I've talked to her on the Chat, I know her too. We're getting along fine."

"I know," Grant answered as he picked up the iron again. "But Todd, I think maybe she's right, okay? We're doing this right. I have two rooms reserved at the Marriott down there, one for me and one for her. We'll meet, we'll have dinner, we'll talk."

"Then you'll go to the room and knock the boots," Todd said offhandedly.

Grant frowned. "What?"

Todd grinned and reddened slightly. "Knock the boots. You know."

"No, I don't know. Knock the boots?"

"You know. Do it."

He glared. "Todd, that's out of bounds. No more about that, okay?"

The boy seemed unfazed. He shrugged. "Okay."

Grant returned to his ironing, feeling like he hadn't chastised Todd enough—even though his own imagination, triggered by the boy's comment, was stimulated. "You have to understand, Todd," he said rather sternly, "this might not work. Andi and I have never met."

"Well, sure you have. On the Chat and all."

"That's not the same. That's not like meeting someone in person."

"Sure it is."

"No, it isn't."

Grant put the iron down again and stared at his son. "No. It. Isn't. You can't know the whole person from the Internet. That's just something we won't know until she gets here tomorrow, until we've had a little time together. She—"

"You know what she looks like, right?"

"Yes—you do too, you saw the picture—"

"And she's beautiful. So—"

"Yes, she is. But beauty isn't everything, Todd."

"I know that, Dad." He folded his arms on the table. "Dad, do you think there's any way you're not going to like her as well in person as you did when you were seeing her on the chat program?"

"Well," Grant said with a frown, "I guess it's possible—"

Todd laughed out loud. "C'mon, Dad, this is Todd, you can't fool me!"

"I'm not!"

"Oh, Dad! You aren't afraid you aren't going to like her! You're afraid she isn't going to like you!" He laughed loudly. "And there's no way that's gonna happen!"

After giving him a disparaging look, Grant returned once again to his ironing. "Okay," he said. "You know it all. Fine." Todd had, in fact, analyzed the situation perfectly. Grant could not imagine that his feelings for Andi would change, but it wasn't hard for him to feel that she'd find him to be less than what she was expecting.

"So I'm gonna be staying up at the ranch?" Todd asked.

"Yes, I've already asked Paula about it."

Todd nodded. "Do I have to stay up there the whole time?"

Grant looked up. "Not if you don't want to. You could stay here during the day, I could get Manuel to pick you up and drop you off. Something you want to do?"

"I just want to spend some time on the computer. You know Sue5, don't you?"

He frowned. "Well, yes. An old friend on World's Chat."

"You knew she was a computer expert? Some kinda programmer or something?"

"Well, she's never been very specific about what she did for a living, but yes, she seems very knowledgeable about them . . ."

"Well, she showed me a special secret room on World's Chat.

You can play 'Heretic' there. I wanted to go back there and play some more."

"Oh. I see." He frowned more deeply. "How'd you happen to meet Sue5, anyway?"

"She said hi to me. She knew I was your son. She said you were a friend of hers and so she'd show me the secret room."

"Oh." He could vaguely remember telling her stories about Todd's exploits as Red Skull, he hadn't made any secret about it. It seemed a little odd to him, but he had no concerns about Sue, no mistrust. "Well, I don't see a problem. I'll make the arrangements up at the ranch, okay?"

"Okay. Thanks, Dad!" He got up, headed for the back door. Halfway there he stopped and turned. "Uh, Dad?"

"Yes?" Attentive, Grant looked up again. This was a pattern of Todd's, he'd have something on his mind and say nothing at all about it until everything else had been cleared—then he'd present the serious material as an afterthought.

"Uh—there's something I found out—about Dr. Lawrence, and well, something's a little funny . . ."

"Funny?"

"Uh-huh—I mean, it doesn't make sense—I'm just wondering if, uh, if everything she's been telling us was really, y'know, true and all . . . " He paused, chewing his lower lip.

Ah, Grant told himself; Andi's judgment was, it seemed, correct. It shouldn't be a surprise, he and Todd had been alone all Todd's life, he'd never known anything else. That Andi's entry into that life would change things the boy had to know, some discomfort was to be expected—it was surprising it hadn't come up before now. "Todd," he said firmly and seriously, "you have no reason in the world to say that. You know perfectly well that Andi's your friend too, you've said so yourself."

"Well, yeah, sure, but ·· .."

"No buts. Let's drop this, okay?"

"But Dad, I—"

"Todd, that's enough," he said, his voice a bit deeper and louder. Placing both hands on the ironing board, he went into a long speech about how Andi's presence in their lives wasn't going to alter the closeness between them, about how she wasn't a threat to him. Throughout, he stood fidgeting, looking somewhat uncomfortable.

"No Dad, I didn't think so, I'm not worried about that, I just wanted to tell you—"

"Didn't you listen to what I said?"

"Yes, but—"

"Then there shouldn't be any 'buts.'"

He pursed his lips tightly. "Okay," he muttered. "Okay. Going out to ride my bike for a while, okay?"

"Come back in an hour or so."

"You bet. You gonna be on the computer later?"

He grinned and shook his head. "Not tonight, you can go play Sue5's game. Andi dropped me a note saying something about making sure her patients were all taken care of—some last minute arrangements—and that she wouldn't be on tonight."

"Super." The bang of the screen door told Grant he'd left; he was left alone with his anxieties, his nervousness. He kept thinking about that last E-mail; it had seemed terse, a little clipped. A letter that almost made him think she was having second thoughts about coming.

It didn't mean that, he told himself doggedly, it didn't mean anything. She was, he was sure, nervous too. She'd said so.

45

Invisible to Todd at the moment but having adopted her "Faerie Warrior" avatar, Sue5 sat on a virtual rocky ledge above a virtual forest where Todd Kingsley hunted—and was being hunted by—the monstrosities of the "Heretic" game. Twice since she'd been watching he'd been "killed," but he was, she'd noticed, a competent player, his instincts good, his reflexes fast. A real chip, she told him silently, off the old block.

"How," she murmured aloud, "am I going to explain this to you?" She shook her head. "You couldn't possibly accept the truth, it'd be like getting a cookie in a Chinese restaurant with a fortune that said 'help! I'm being held prisoner inside a Chinese fortune cookie factory!'" She sighed. When she'd been in a frenzy of working, setting this up without letting Albert or any of the others know about it, she'd had vague ideas about warning Todd about Colin's plans and having him tell Grant, or, alternatively, getting Grant on under the boy's account so she could

talk to him freely. Now, act two of the play was already under-
way and she had not a notion how she was going to reveal the
outlandish truth. As usual, she told herself bitterly, you concentrated on the technical and let the personal slide, and now
you're paying the price.

As she sat lost in her thoughts, a bright red light flashed in
another part of her panoramic screen; this was the page she'd
set up for Todd, he was calling to her. She saw him, standing
near a small hut in the woods where several of the game's evil
wizards had been lurking—wizards he'd already dispatched. His
avatar was pressing the "intercom" button.

She directed her avatar to stand up, then "teleported" herself
to the forest, appearing on the far side of the hut. Stepping
around it, she stood in front of Todd's avatar. "You called me?"
she asked.

His avatar didn't move. "Yes."

She smiled, and, thanks to the sophistication of her program,
the smile was reflected on the face of her Faerie avatar. "Well,
I'm here," she said unnecessarily. "What's wrong? Problem with
the game?"

"No." He stopped there; she noted that he was ending his
sentences with periods, not his usual exclamation points; she'd
seen enough of Todd to know that the exclamation points
meant he was having fun and the periods meant he was serious.

"Todd, is there a problem?" she repeated. "I can't know what
it is unless you tell me."

"No." Again he stopped, and again she frowned. "No, the
room's great. I love it."

"What, then?"

"I'm worried about my Dad. Can we talk about that?"

She let out a slow sigh. So much, in just a few words. She felt
she knew Todd Kingsley pretty well; a boy on the verge of being
able to count on himself but still dependent on his father, a boy
who took everything to his father—except his concerns about
the man himself. Those he'd been sharing, a little at a time, with
Andi; now that she was unavailable, was it possible he wanted
to transfer that to her?

"Yes," she answered quickly. "Of course we can. We're
friends, we can talk about anything."

"Do you know Dr. Lawrence?"

"I know of her. I've never talked to her myself. You have,
haven't you?"

"Yes. She's really nice." His avatar shifted, suggesting he was moving his mouse at random. "I haven't been able to talk to her lately, though . . . there's some problem with my new account, World's Chat logs me off when I try to talk to her. It's funny, it doesn't do that with anybody else . . ."

Sue5 smiled; the "Net Nanny" software she'd slipped into Todd's account was working perfectly. "That happens sometimes. You know that computers can be quirky."

"I know."

"So. What's the problem?"

"Well, Dr. Lawrence is coming to visit us. My Dad's meeting her tomorrow."

"I've heard that," she answered carefully. "I still don't know what the problem is."

"Something's not right."

For several seconds she stared at those words on the screen. "What," she inquired, "do you mean by that, Todd?"

There was a long hesitation. "I like to play around on the Web sometimes," he told her. "Do you know what a 'Finger' program is?"

"Sure. It's a special program you can use to get information about somebody if you know their E-mail address."

"I like to play with the Finger programs," he told her—which surprised her, he was more sophisticated than she'd assumed. "Sometimes you can see if people have read their E-mail or not. It's sorta like spying. It's fun."

"Okay. There's more, isn't there? Something about Dr. Lawrence?"

"Yes. When I'm on the Web I always Finger her. To see if she's read my Dad's letters yet."

Harmless enough, Sue5 thought—probably gives him a feeling of being involved, nothing more. Finger inquiries, like any other, were being relayed through the IIC server and would not, she knew, appear unusual. "And so?"

"Well, the other day a new Finger server came on-line."

"Oh?" She herself knew nothing about this, neither she nor anyone else could monitor the whole Web.

"Yes. A new one the people at Georgia Tech set up."

"Oh. And you fingered Dr. Lawrence with this new one?"

"Yes."

"What happened?"

"When I fingered her account it didn't give me Dr. Andrea

Lawrence in New York like all the others always did. I got something else."

Interesting, Sue5 told herself, very interesting. A fuckup? A new finger protocol that wasn't being trapped correctly? "What did you get, Todd?"

"Some stuff I don't understand. It said that account belonged to a company, IIC, in Twenty-nine Palms, here in California. I got a long list of Web pages and it sent me to the first one. When I got there it said this was a security site and asked me for a password."

They did, Sue5 told herself gleefully, they made a mistake. Overconfidence will do it every time. "I see," she told Todd. "Let me ask you, why didn't you think you'd made a mistake, that you fingered the wrong account?"

"I did. I backed out and tried it again. Then I tried Hyperfinger and I got what I always get, Dr. Andrea Lawrence in New York City. I came back and tried Georgia Tech again and I still got this IIC place. I decided the finger at Georgia Tech was screwed up."

"But?"

"But the next day, it wasn't. The next day I got Dr. Andrea Lawrence in New York City like all the other finger servers give me." He hesitated. "But I kept thinking about it. I kept worrying about it. I just wanted to ask you if that was possible. If the server at Georgia Tech was messed up."

You have an opening, she told herself, you have a handle. The time to plunge in is now; now or never. "Yes," she answered carefully. "It is possible. But that's not what happened, Todd, not this time. What you saw was real."

"Real?"

She had her avatar nod. "That's right. Something's going on that your Dad—and Dr. Lawrence—don't know anything about. I've been wanting to tell you—you and your Dad—and I've been trying to figure out how." She paused for a moment, checked her other screens to see if there was any evidence that Albert— or anyone else—was paying attention. No one was. Her chatterbot was functioning perfectly, currently flirting shamelessly with someone and still keeping an eye out for problems.

"I don't understand," Todd replied.

Not surprising. "Todd, when you come here—when you log in here—everything you say, all your commands, are relayed through various computers on the Net. The same thing happens when you send an E-mail. For someone who knows what he's doing, it really isn't hard to pick off these little packets of information as they move from one server to another. You following me?"

"I think so . . ."

"The people who work for that company put a trap on the Net for everything coming out of your Dad's account and out of Dr. Lawrence's account."

"They did? But why?"

She had an answer for this ready. "Because," she told him, "they want Dr. Lawrence to work for their company, and they don't really care how they accomplish that."

His hesitation showed his struggle to understand. "I don't get it," he said finally. "How are they going to do that?"

"Intercepting the transmissions," Sue5 told him. "Todd, your Dad is expecting to meet Dr. Lawrence at the airport tomorrow, isn't that right?"

"Yes."

"She came in today. She's already in Los Angeles. And she's already met a man she thinks is your Dad."

"That can't be! Dad gave her our Web page! She's seen our picture! She knows what my Dad looks like!"

"No, she doesn't. That Web site was trapped too, before it got to her account. A different picture was sent. You know that picture your Dad got from Dr. Lawrence?"

"Yes . . ."

"It isn't a picture of her, Todd. It's someone else."

This time there was a very long silence.

"It's the truth, Todd," Sue5 assured him.

"It can't be! How do you know all this?"

"Because," she replied, "that's where I work, it's where I am right now. International Interface, IIC."

"YOU did this?"

"No! Not me! I do different work for them. At places like that secure site that asked you for a password. I don't think what they're doing is right, Todd. I'm trying to help."

"This isn't true."

"Oh, Todd, I—"

"It isn't true. You're lying."

"No, Todd—"

"Liar!" Immediately after this word appeared, his avatar vanished in a puff of smoke—he'd teleported to another room or logged off the chat altogether. Switching immediately to another screen she tried to see if he was still on-line, and quickly determined that he was not.

"Oh, damn," she murmured, fighting back tears of frustration. "You really handled that well, old girl, you really did . . ."

46

The time since Grant had picked her up at the airport had sped by in a haze of new sights, new experiences, new feelings for Andi; they'd picked up her bags, he'd taken her out to a gray Lexus he'd left parked in one of the short-term lots. One of the first things she saw was the large, white, black-windowed building sitting on huge legs like a poised spider in the middle of the roadway loop leading in and out of the airport. Asking about it—she vaguely remembered having seen it in a movie at some point—she was told it was known to Angelenos as the "theme restaurant." Turning her attention to the rows of palm trees lining the streets, she'd commented on how "exotic" and "romantic" they looked.

"I'm glad you like it," Grant told her. "I had everything set up just for you."

They'd driven to the Hilton on Century, which was nearby; as she looked up at the black glass facade of the hotel. He pulled the car around to the entryway, where a valet was waiting to park it for him; from there, welcomed by a huge amethyst crystal housed in a glass case, they passed into a spacious, elegant, and very modern lobby. There wasn't a need to stop by the desk; Grant had already taken care of renting the rooms, a gentlemanly two of them, side by side. He'd carried her bags to the elevator and then to her room, and finally—over her protests— he'd left her to relax for a few moments, to freshen up, to recover from the flight. She'd showered, she'd put on her teal robe, and she'd sat looking out the window for a while, looking over Los Angeles as she'd looked over New York so many times. It was almost fully dark by then; her room, high on the fourteenth floor, faced to the east, and the night was promising to be clear, her view was not obstructed by the smog she'd understood was so pervasive here. Unlike the view from her apartment in New York, she did not see clusters of large buildings. Instead, she saw a broad panoramic vista seemingly covered with billions of tiny white lights and cut through by a major highway, one of the infamous L.A. freeways she was sure, which looked like a broad river of red light. Off to her left, far in the distance, was a cluster of taller buildings that suggested a small version of Manhattan dropped into the midst of all this incredible sprawl.

Rising from her chair, she walked to the bed where her larger suitcase was lying and began selecting clothes; Grant was supposed to come to the room in about fifteen minutes to take her out for dinner. As she sorted through the clothes, she mischievously considered greeting him dressed in the robe, but decided that might be too forward. Instead, she chose one of her favorites, a jade-green Chinese-style dress, buttons up to her shoulder, a subdued but noticeable slit in the skirt. By the time she had dressed, he was knocking on her door—his timing, she told herself, was just about perfect.

"You look wonderful!" he said immediately. His smile melted her. Reaching out, he took both her elbows in his hands and gently pulled her toward himself. "And we should go, I know you must be hungry," he told her. "But first . . . there's something we didn't do at the airport, something we didn't take care of coming over here. If it's all right with you I'd like to take care of it now."

She looked up into his eyes, into his face. He did not look his age, she decided, not at all; there was no gray at all in his hair, no lines on his smoothly tanned face except for a few light laugh marks around his eyes. He did not appear as hard as she'd expected, his tan was more poolside than horseback. His eyes, light brown, had a perpetual slightly amused look.

"What is it you'd like to take care of, Grant?" she asked.

His smile spread a little. "I'd rather show you than tell you."

Her own matched his. "That'd be okay . . ."

He hesitated, just a little, his eyes moving between hers as if trying to read confirmation there. He must've seen what he wanted, because he moved his head forward, his mouth slightly open.

Andi could not restrain her eagerness, she'd dreamed about this far too often. Moving more quickly than he, she pushed herself up and forward, her own mouth open wider, reaching for him. As their lips met it seemed that all her strength was draining away, she grabbed his forearms and held onto them tightly as she closed her eyes. Their tongues touching lightly, the kiss went on; she was aware that she was pressing her body up against his in a very suggestive way, but she could as easily have stopped herself from breathing.

Finally, it ended—he ended it, he pulled back an inch. "I love you," he whispered, his voice slightly husky.

"I love you, Grant Kingsley," she almost croaked. Clearing her throat, she started to say it again.

But instead, she burst into tears.

He looked startled. "What?"

"Oh, I just can't believe it!" she cried. "Oh, Grant, I never believed I'd ever feel like this again, I'd given it all up . . . oh, I know, I know, you must have too, it's been hard on you too . . ."

"Yes," he agreed, nodding. "It has." He held her face between his hands. "But I don't want to think about that now. I don't want to think about those hard years ever again."

She laid her palms on his chest. "I don't either," she sniffed. "I've been so scared, Grant. I know I keep saying that over and over, but it's true." Her smile, a little tremulous, returned. "But I'm not scared now . . . not now, not after I've been able to touch you, to hold you . . . and to kiss you . . ."

"I feel exactly the same," he assured her. "Exactly." Pulling her close again, he held her for several long seconds. "But for now," he suggested, "hadn't I better take you on to dinner? I don't want you collapsing from hunger tonight!"

"Sounds fine," she agreed. "Where're we going?"

"Well, there's a place called 'Killer Shrimp' up at Marina Del Rey, maybe fifteen or twenty minutes from here. I thought there, if you like seafood."

"Oh, I do. But what about that spider-looking thing, it's right here, is it any good?"

He laughed. "I have no idea. It's supposed to be. Angelenos never go there, it's strictly for tourists and out-of-towners. I've never been there, myself."

"Oh. But I thought you lived in Fillmore?"

His eyes flickered to the side, then back. "Well, yes. Outside of it, actually, as I've told you. But it's so close, we consider ourselves Los Angelenos . . ."

"Oh. It's a little different In New York, I guess . . ."

"I imagine so. Ready?"

She smiled. "As ready as I'll ever be!"

47

I should've thought of this a long time ago, Sue5 told herself. After all, Colin and Albert haven't been where I am, they can't know how easy some of these tasks have become.

Before her, her wide screen was split; on the left side was the task Albert had asked her to do. She was at 167.43.16.2, a site she was fairly sure was being used by some law enforcement agency. At the moment she was being asked to collate data on a case, to use an enormous heap of scientific data—DNA, forensics—to determine if the man in question indeed was perpetrator of a crime whose nature was not made clear; it was a murder, but of questionable motive. It probably had been committed to conceal evidence of previous crimes.

For her purposes, it didn't matter; all she was being asked to do was make sense of the sometimes contradictory data and organize things into probabilities. What came after, she told herself doggedly, wasn't her affair—even though some of the data concerned her. The DNA, for example, seemed poorly handled by the labs, the samples showed clear evidence of contamination. This she factored in, lowering the value the DNA evidence held. She wondered if whatever jury heard this case would ever know about her doubts.

With another part of her screen—about a quarter of it, resources Albert had no idea she was using or was even able to use—she maintained a tight watch on Todd's Well account, hoping he'd come back to World's Chat. There was a window, she knew that; about three days. After that, it would be too late for Andi Lawrence.

Todd was in fact on-line, just not on World's Chat. He was using Netscape, cruising around the Web. Locking onto his login, she started tracking the sites he was visiting—and after a few moments realized what he was doing. He was using the resources of the Web to track down more information about International Interface, and he was having more than a little success in doing just that.

Enough success, in fact, to draw the attention of some of her co-workers, like Jane4, whose task it was to monitor those asking too many questions about the company.

Feeling a touch of panic—if Jane4 noticed him, all her hard work would be for nothing—she steered her own browser to the same Web page Todd was currently viewing. Besides, she told herself, maybe this was an opportunity to convince him she wasn't lying. Using the same techniques that had been used to intercept the picture coming from Grant's Web page and send a substitute to Andi's account, she intercepted the signals coming from the Web page Todd was viewing and sent him a quite different screen. Then she waited; at the moment that particular Web page was already in the memory of Todd's computer, he wouldn't see anything different until he either tried to refresh it or follow one of the hyperlinks somewhere else.

After a few moments, he did the latter; she saw the activity from his account stop. She knew what he was seeing; a black page, textured, with a message in bright red text: "Stop what you're doing, you're going to be seen doing it and that will create a very big problem. If I know what you're doing, others will too. Please, Todd, come and see me in World's Chat. Your friend, Sue5."

His account remained silent; she pinged it to see if he was still holding Netscape open, and found that he was. A second later, he closed it down—but he didn't drop offline. Eagerly, she waited to see if he would log in to World's Chat, and she was more than gratified when he did. It would take a moment, she knew, for him to get into the game room and activate an intercom, she had time; she used it to go into the servers maintaining the pages he'd just been looking at, altering their logs to eliminate his address—through which Jane4 could easily trace him.

After that she returned to her other task; Albert was beginning to complain about her slowness. Exaggerating the complexity—he wouldn't know the difference—she managed to placate him while waiting for Todd.

He took his time getting to the game room, but when he arrived he activated the intercom just inside the door. Sue5 immediately logged onto World's Chat herself, instructing her avatar to appear right in front of his.

"How'd you do that?" he asked immediately. "How'd you put a message in that Web page?"

"The same way they sent a different picture to Andi Lawrence," she told him. "I used the same programs, the same techniques. Do you believe me now? Or do you want to see the picture they sent?"

"Yes," he typed back after a moment's hesitation. "I would like to see."

"All right. Log off here, go back to Netscape and call up your home page. I'll trap it out, okay? Then come back here, I'll be waiting."

"Okay." His avatar vanished; Sue5 did the necessary manipulations, then waited patiently for him to reappear, attending her other work in the meantime.

In less than five minutes he'd reappeared. "The picture isn't the same! It's me, but that's not my Dad's face! It's somebody else's face!"

"That's what I was trying to tell you," Sue5 reminded him patiently. "I was also telling you that Dr. Lawrence is already in Los Angeles. She's already met that man, the one in that picture, that's posing as your father. She thinks he *is* your father."

"But why!?"

"Because that man—his name is Colin Simmons—wants Dr. Lawrence to come and work for the company, that's why. When ICC asks you to work for them, Todd, it's more of a demand than a request."

There was a pause, "I've been researching them," he told her. "You knew that. They're—strange. It says they make custom interfaces for computers. But they don't sell anything to anybody."

She frowned. This was a dramatically different Todd than the one she'd seen talking to his young friends or to Andi Lawrence, one that had shown her an unexpected sophistication about how to use the Internet. "I didn't know," she said carefully, "you knew this much about computers, Todd."

"(laugh)," he responded. "Dad doesn't either! Don't tell him, okay? He thinks I just play games! I do like games, but I do other things, too! I like to know things, I like to find out what's going on! If Dad knew I could do all this stuff he'd put programs on here to protect me, he'd be worried!"

"It's because he cares about you, Todd . . ."

"Oh, I know! But I don't need it, Sue! Really! And I don't want him to worry so I don't tell him!"

She wasn't convinced. "There are a lot of dangers out there . . ."

"(laugh) I know! Sometimes men try to get me to tell them my phone number or where I live. I just laugh. I know what they want!"

Sue5 smiled and shook her head slightly. We're two of a kind, I'm the same, never letting those with authority over me know what I can really do. "Okay," she agreed. "I won't tell on you, deal? But now we have to figure out what we're going to do about Dr. Lawrence."

"Well, I'll just tell my Dad about it!"

"You think he'll believe you?"

"Sure! I'm going to go tell him right now, okay?"

Sue5 was much less sure; she wanted to compose a plan of action, some presentation. "Todd, maybe we should talk a little more about exactly how you're going to . . ."

She didn't bother to send the sentence; Todd's avatar had already disappeared. Headed off to tell Grant all about it, she was certain.

That he'd accept it, that he'd believe one single word of such a crazy-sounding story, was much less certain. But now Todd was off-line; there was nothing she could do except wait.

48

"It sounds like a wonderful idea, Grant," Andi was saying as, using the credit card key, she unlocked the door of her hotel room. "Your own ranch . . . a dream come true. Why haven't you told me about it before?" She opened the door, walked inside.

"Well," he answered, leaning against the door frame, "it isn't certain, not yet." He laughed. "I didn't want to talk about it until I'd gotten a little farther along, but . . . well, we were discussing so many things tonight . . ."

"Yes, we were. I loved that restaurant, did I tell you? Wonderful place . . ." she frowned. "Why're you still standing out there in the hallway?"

Shrugging, he offered her his boyish—and utterly charming—grin. "You're probably very tired, you had a long flight today . . ."

"I did, and I am, but . . . Oh, I need to call my friend in New York, I should've done that already . . ." She took his hand, pulled him inside, then closed and locked the door. "But that doesn't mean I'm ready to let you go!" She gestured generally toward the bed and the two frame chairs that furnished the room. "Have a seat, let me give Vickie a quick call."

He flopped into a chair, stretched his legs out, crossed his ankles. "You have to check in?"

"Absolutely. In case you're a dangerous maniac."

"You think I'm a dangerous maniac?"

She arched an eyebrow. "You aren't a maniac, no—in my very expert opinion. Dangerous? Yes. To me, anyway."

"But you still have to call?"

"I promised her." Her expression became serious. "She'll worry about me if I don't."

"Understood," he said with a nod. "By all means, call her."

She touched his cheek affectionately. Then, sitting down on the bed, she picked up the phone. After taking just a moment to read the instructions printed on it, she dialed.

Vickie answered on the second ring. "Hi," Andi said brightly. "It's me, Andi, I'm in L.A., I'm with Grant, we just got back from dinner and everything is just about as wonderful as I could've possibly imagined it could be!"

"Sure?" Vickie asked. "Why didn't you call earlier, when you got in? That was our agreement . . . I was getting a little worried here, Andi. And look, you say he's right there? Can you speak freely? I mean . . ."

Andi laughed. "No, he has a knife at my throat! Come on, Vickie! Everything's fine!"

"Okay," Vickie said, seemingly not at all reassured. "Okay. Look, I want you to call me sometime tomorrow too, okay?"

"Oh, Vickie, I—"

"Come on, Andi. Promise me."

She sighed into the receiver. "Okay," she said, surrendering. "Okay, I'll call tomorrow. Satisfied now?"

Vickie laughed. "Yes. So. Can you talk?" Her manner changed

completely, her voice now eager. "I mean, you said he was right there, if I ask you questions, can you answer yes or no."

She glanced at Grant, who was watching her patiently, and smiled again. "Yes, of course I could do that . . ."

"Well, how is he? A disappointment?"

"Oh, Vickie, no. No, no, and no!"

"Beyond your fantasies?"

"As tough as that was, yes. So far, anyway."

"You kiss him yet?"

"Yes."

"On a scale of one to ten where ten's the best?"

"Forty-two."

"Mmm, sounds really good."

"It has been, Vickie. It has been. Uh—look, can I, uhm, talk to you tomorrow?"

"Hmph. No time for old friends, huh?"

"Not right now, and you know why."

"Yes, I do," Vickie said with a giggle. "Okay. I'll look for your call tomorrow. And I'll expect more gory details, okay?"

"Well, we'll see about that!" She laughed too.

"Oooh, big plans for tonight?"

"All I can say, Vickie, is, whatever. Talk to you tomorrow, right?"

"Right. 'Bye."

" 'Bye." She hung up, then turned to Grant with a sad expression. "She wrung a promise out of me to call again tomorrow. I couldn't resist, I was helpless. It isn't my fault."

He grinned. "You're weak. You care about your friends."

She nodded theatrically. "Weak, that's me."

"Yep." He rose, came to her, pulled her up into his arms. "So, Andrea Lawrence," he said, his voice slightly lower in pitch and slightly softer, "just how weak are you?"

She cocked her eyebrow. "That you'll have to find out."

"Not very, not really, I'd say."

"You can't be sure."

"I think I can." With a curled finger he tipped her chin up and studied her face. "I'm quite sure, actually." She couldn't help pushing herself toward him a little; sensing it, he tipped his head down and touched his lips to hers. It wasn't unexpected and she meant for her response to be measured, but it was eager. Her arms came up—without any intent on her part—and went around his neck; her fingers began playing in his hair as the kiss went on His hand moved from her chin, grazed lightly and gently down over the side of her neck, his fingertips on her skin sending pleasant chills through her.

The hand moved on down, quite slowly, as if testing, the touch light, tentative and alert, at the same time. Perfect, she told herself, perfect; the message is that he cannot resist but that he is a gentleman, he does not want to offend. Maybe, she thought, I should tell him directly that I'd only be offended if he stopped.

He did not stop; the hand moved on. She broke the kiss and took in her breath sharply as it reached her breast; when he cupped it in his hand she let the air out in a soft moan and, realizing that she'd never been this forward before, pressed herself against his palm.

That erased his doubts. The hand moved back up and to the center, the fingers deftly undid the buttons of her blouse, the blouse opened, his hand slipped inside. In another few seconds her bra was undone as well, his palm was resting against her bare breast, and she was feeling like she was about to explode. Following his lead she undid his shirt, almost ripping the buttons off in her haste to run her fingers through his chest hair, to feel those hard muscles against her palms. Somehow—she was not at all sure how—they'd moved to the bed Her shoes were gone, her skirt had gotten pushed up around her waist; his hands, much more insistent now, were caressing her thighs. In some mysterious way articles of their clothing continued to vanish and their posture proceeded to the horizontal. When he bent his head to kiss her nipples and his touch was, for her, the perfect balance of desire and gentleness, she lost all of her inhibitions completely.

Much later—several hours later—she sat up in the bed. Grant was sleeping beside her, lying on his left side, his chest rising and falling evenly. Carefully, not wanting to wake him, she swung her legs off the bed and, slowly, stood up. He did not move. With several backward glances at him, she walked naked to the window, moved the chair in front of it, and sat down.

It was late—according to the little clock beside the bed, past midnight—which meant past three AM, she translated quickly, in New York. Even so, she did not feel tired, even though the only sleep she'd had was a brief nap in his arms after their lovemaking. Outside, it did not seem that one single light had been turned off anywhere, and there was not one car fewer on the freeway. All was the same—like New York, Los Angeles hummed along almost unchanged as the night progressed.

But Andi felt she was changed, and vastly. She looked away from the window, back to the man lying in her bed. Unexpectedly, tears began flowing from her eyes; never before, she told herself, had it been like that for her, never. Not with Ben, not with anyone. She would've loved Grant, she was certain, even if he had turned out to be a clumsy, even an inept, lover; that he was absolutely perfect—that he'd given her an experience she'd never thought possible, that he'd transported her to a place she hadn't known existed—it made this whole business hard for her accept, as if at any moment she'd wake in her own bed in New York and realize, with intense sadness, that none of it was real.

"Don't you turn out to be a dream, Grant Kingsley," she whispered softly. "Don't you dare. If you do, I'll die, I know I will . . ."

49

"I got it all scouted out for us, Connie," Mick was saying. Back at the same spot, peering over the top of the crest, he pointed. "Down there on the east side, the building that's close to the fence. Gettin' through that fence we can't do, but maybe now that it's dark we can get us a look at what goes on in there."

Connie looked very doubtful—and very uncomfortable in the warm desert night—even though a bright quarter-moon was splashing silver over the rocks around them. She stared at the brightly lit plant. "Well, I'm no engineer," Connie said. "Even if we do get a good look inside, I can't say I'd understand what was going on in there. That's why I brought this." She held up a small camera. "Loaded with fast film. If I can get some good shots, maybe somebody back in L.A. can tell me what this is all about."

Mick started working his way back down the hill. "Okay," he said, "let's go do it. And remember, you got to keep it down. Those patrols run all night, and I got me a feeling they might not take too kindly to us sneaking around the fence."

They climbed into the Jeep; Mick started the engine, turned the vehicle around, and bumped back down the trail to the main road. Driving past the turnoff that led to the plant, he turned into a very rough-looking trail a quarter-mile beyond.

"Seat belt on," he advised. "It gets a mite rough."

He was not, as Connie found out, joking. The trail—if trail it was—changed from bumpy sand to a dry and rocky stream bed. The Jeep lurched sideways, surged forward, seemed as if it was going to get stuck but never did; several times Connie was certain it was going to overturn and could not restrain a little peeping cry.

"Y'can't do that up near the plant," Mick cautioned each time she did. He seemed relaxed as he drove, unconcerned about the lurching of the Jeep. "You just can't. It sure looks to me like they got perimeter monitors up there, and they'll pick up noise even if the patrol isn't close. You got to keep quiet."

"I will," she assured him.

"Better."

The trail went on, perhaps another half a mile; Mick then pulled the Jeep over onto a flat expanse of hard-packed sand and stopped. As Connie got out, she couldn't see the plant, just the glow from its lights over the rocky ridge ahead.

"This way," Mick told her, heading for a narrow slot in that ridge. As always, she followed his lead. He moved gracefully over the sand and the broken rocks while she staggered after him. Reaching the ridge, he silently pointed to the pass between. Here the crest of the ridge was some twenty feet high; this narrow pass was the remains of an old waterway, the now-extinct stream having cut cleanly and deeply through the soft sandstone.

Reaching the far end, Mick stopped; he poked his head out and looked around. "All clear for now," he told Connie in a ragged whisper. "From here it's about a hundred yards to the fence, and I don't see no video cameras. Like I said I been here before and I don't think they got 'em, I think they use audio sensing for their perimeter. See those?" He pointed to some unfamiliar-looking devices perched atop several of the fence posts. "Can't be infrared, 'cause they didn't pick me up before and I went right up to the fence."

"Maybe they just don't pay much attention to what's going on beyond their fence."

He grunted softly. "They're hidin' out here, Connie. I dunno what, but they're hidin.' If they catch us sneaking up to their fence in the middle of the night, you can bet they ain't gonna be servin' us milk and cookies."

Connie nodded. "Why'd they put that building so close to the fence, then?"

"T'ain't where they put the building, it's where they put the fence. They couldn't put it much further back without runnin' into this here ridge. And the ridge is what hides the place in this direction, so they couldn't doze it down. They hadda adjust, that's all."

"I see. A stroke of luck for us, Mick." In a crouch she moved toward the fence. "Ready?"

He laid a hand on her shoulder. "Uh-uh." He pointed to the roadway just inside the fence. "We wait for the patrol, and we wait for it to pass twice so we can figure how much time we got."

"Oh. Sure." Crouching down, she readied her camera; when the patrol vehicle came by, about five minutes later, she snapped two shots of it as it lazily cruised the road at less than ten miles per hour. The four soldiers riding in it didn't seem to be particularly alert; they were slouching in their seats, and only one had his rifle visible.

"I don't even think they'd notice us," Connie whispered after they'd passed.

"I don't wanna take a chance," Mick answered. "We wait, for them to come back. We time 'em. Before I got about twenty minutes. Maybe they've changed routes or something."

"So we're just going to sit here for twenty minutes?"

"Yep."

Connie sighed but she didn't argue. She was out of her element. They were playing this game in Mick's backyard, she'd play by his rules. She took a few long-distance shots of the building, then leaned back against the rocky face of the cleft to wait. Several times she checked her watch; the time dragged.

Finally, she heard the sentries' vehicle approaching; she came to crouch by Mick and they watched them cruise by again, a re-run of the last pass. Looking down at his own watch, Mick nodded.

"Twenty minutes. Let's go, Connie. You got fifteen, agreed?"

She nodded. "Agreed."

"No more talking from here, not even whispers. And don't touch the fence, it may have sensors on it. Got it?"

"Got it."

"Let's do it!" Matching action to words, he slipped out of the cleft and made his way quickly but silently over the intervening stretch of rocky sand; Connie, not as quickly but just as quietly, trailed behind him. Without incident he reached the shadows near the fence and, with an outdoorsman's experience, faded into them. Connie came up beside him; standing up on her toes, as close to the fence as she could get without risking contact, she peered into the nearest window.

It was well lit; to her it looked like an office, there was a white-coated man with black hair busy at a computer terminal, even though it was past one in the morning. To her, nothing here looked remarkable beyond the man working this late, but she snapped a picture anyway. Then they moved on to the next lighted window.

This, she told herself, seemed much more promising. It appeared to be a conference room, a large table surrounded by plush chairs, currently empty; on the wall facing the window were a number of charts. Hoping her film had the resolution to allow enlargements that would enable her to read them, she took a series of shots before moving on to the final lighted window on this side of the building.

This one was hardly worth a picture. It was a computer workroom, cubicles in rows, terminals visible in a couple of them, no one visible and most of the screens dark. Only one was lit; getting a good enough picture to see the screen contents was, she knew, almost certainly hopeless, but she took the shot anyway. She checked her watch; they had six minutes left.

Not wanting to waste the opportunity, she dropped to one knee and angled her camera at the odd-looking devices atop several of the posts, the devices Mick believed were audio sensors, and snapped a couple of times. As she took the last one, she felt a soft touch on the calf of her leg, the one extended behind her as she knelt; thinking it was Mick calling her attention to the time she looked around, ready to punish him for excessive familiarity with an icy stare.

It was not Mick's hand. Instead, a prowling tarantula had walked up onto her leg and was casually making its way toward her thigh.

Her eyes went wide; reflexively, she jerked her leg but, not forgetting Mick's admonition, remained quite silent. The tarantula fell off onto the sand and scuttled away, disappearing into the darkness. She looked back at Mick, and he gave her an approving nod; she returned a strained smile. She rose to her feet, reflexively wiped at her calf where the big spider had been, and, following Mick's gesture, started to follow him back toward the cleft in the rocks. Ahead of him by a few feet was a large greenish-gray rock she hadn't noticed before; Mick, looking at the buildings as he walked, hadn't either and didn't—until it shifted itself and, raising its tail, rattled sharply.

"Shit!" he cried loudly, jumping backwards. He turned to look back at Connie, but even before he could see the look of disbelieving consternation on her face, floodlights lining the fence snapped on, bathing the area in garish white light—and starkly exposing the two intruders.

"Oh, shit," Mick groaned, not concerned now about sounds. "C'mon, let's get outta here! Watch the snake, it's a Mohave green, deadly!"

"You jerk!" Connie shrieked. "I don't fucking believe you did that!"

Circling widely around the coiled rattlesnake—which watched them dispassionately—the two sprinted for the cleft in the rocks. Already they could hear the roar of the sentries' vehicle; they were coming, and coming fast. The cleft wasn't far—but before they could reach it they both heard the vehicle skid to a stop, and that sound was followed by the flat crack of the rifles.

"They're shooting at us!" Connie screamed as a bullet struck the rock wall, sending a large chip flying. "They're shooting, my God!"

"Just run!" Mick shouted back. Connie was already running as fast as she could; she turned her head as a bullet whizzed by her and saw a gate in the fence opening. This danger would not be over even after they reached the cleft. She looked back at Mick, who was a little ahead of her.

And saw him suddenly stiffen, then relax; his momentum carried him onward and he went face down into the sand. A stain, black in the moonlight, was spreading quickly above his pants.

Horrified, Connie came to a stop herself. "Mick!" she screamed. "Mick, get up!"

He stirred on the sand. "Get . . . keys . . ." he mumbled. "Run . . . get cops . . ."

She hesitated, torn between a desire to escape and her need to get the keys to Mick's Jeep. Another bullet zipped by, deciding the issue for her; she forgot about the keys and ran. Behind her—close behind her—someone yelled "STOP!" in a loud and heavily accented voice.

She ignored it, another shot rang out; a sudden pain tore at her right leg. For a moment she thought she might've been grazed or struck by a flying rock fragment, but then she realized her right leg simply wasn't working anymore. She fell heavily, ending up on her back; raising her head she looked down at her leg and was amazed to see blood gushing from her thigh. Her calf and her shoe were already soaked with it.

The soldiers rushed up, several surrounding Mick and several more glaring down at her. One leaned over her, snatched her camera; none seemed inclined to do anything about her severely bleeding leg.

"Please," she groaned, "please help us . . ."

The men ignored her pleas; one took a cellular telephone from his pocket, dialed a number, and spoke into it in some unfamiliar language for several minutes. His eyes cold slits, he looked down at Connie.

"Newspaper?" he barked.

"Yes," she answered. "Please, I'm bleeding . . . why'd you shoot us?"

"Your paper knows you come here? Anyone knows you come here?" His accent was very thick, his words hard to understand.

She felt she knew the answer. "Yes," she said firmly. "Yes, and there's going to be hell to pay for this! You had no right to shoot at us, damn you!"

The officer smiled, a thin humorless smile. Turning to the soldiers standing over Mick, he said something—unintelligible to Connie—in a loud and commanding voice. In response, one of the soldiers stepped smartly up to Mick, aimed his rifle at the back of the helpless man's head, and casually pulled the trigger. The shot seemed deafening; Mick's body spasmed violently, then became still.

Connie's eyes were huge. "Oh, my . . . my God, oh . . ." Twisting her head wildly, she stared back at the officer.

And saw that he was crouching beside her, already in the process of aiming his handgun at her head. She screamed.

Once.

50

This was not, Grant kept telling himself as he walked along the concourse at Los Angeles International, the way it was supposed to be. I wasn't supposed to be thinking about anything except meeting Andi, wasn't supposed to have any distractions. Now, everything seemed annoying to him. The traffic coming down Interstates Five and 405 into the city had been miserable, irritatingly so; the same was true of the lanes of humanity pouring along in both directions in this broad hallway. As if still out on the road, Grant looked for an open lane, then strode rapidly past a group of people in Middle Eastern dress, then had to cut back to his right to avoid a Hawaiian-shirted tourist who wasn't watching where he was going.

If Todd was worried, why, he asked himself, couldn't he have come out with it sooner? Why wait until the last minute, why last night? Thinking about it he snorted aloud, drawing the attention of a few passers-by; what an incredible story, the notion that the Andi he was meeting wasn't the same person as the Andi he'd been talking to on the Net! He had—naturally—refused Todd's demands that he go onto World's Chat and talk to Sue5; he felt he knew her well enough to know that she wouldn't come up with a story like this, she either wouldn't know what he was talking about or the whole matter would resolve into some obvious and embarrassing misunderstanding by Todd. To have done that—to have drawn Sue5 into it—would have been an entirely inadvisable pandering to Todd's fantasies. Instead, he'd been firm with the boy, unyielding even when Todd had begun crying. It had not, in the end, been a pleasant evening. He'd considered withdrawing his offer to allow Todd to be home alone during the days while he was gone, but in the end he did not; the boy had seemed so crushed when he'd left he didn't want to inflict anything else that might be construed as punishment. There were problems there, though; problems that were going to be there if he brought Andi back with him, which he passionately hoped to do.

Wanting to put all this out of his mind, he concentrated instead on finding the gate where the flight from New York—from Las Vegas, actually, its stopover—was coming in. He'd planned to be there well before the flight arrived, he wanted to be certain he was there to meet her—and he'd done that, the flight wasn't due for twenty minutes. As he located the gate he saw that the waiting room was almost completely empty. Choosing a chair that gave a view of the runways through tall plate glass windows, he sat down and prepared to wait—hopefully without brooding about the problems he faced. Andi, he reminded himself, was a psychologist; she'd probably have some good suggestions on how to handle this delicate matter.

The minutes slipped by slowly. Idly, he noticed that a pair of men with Asian features, dressed in dark suits, had moved from the chairs they'd originally occupied to a position facing him; both were reading newspapers, and he caught a glimpse of one of them looking at him almost furtively over the top of the paper. Wondering if his shirt was buttoned wrong, he checked himself; nothing was obvious, and he decided perhaps these were newcomers from Asia and simply hadn't seen many Americans yet. Even so, their attention finally caused him to go to the men's room and view himself in the mirror. All was well; Andi already knew, he told himself, what this face looked like and wasn't distressed by it. With a shrug he returned to the waiting room, where now only one of the Asians remained. After a moment the other returned, joining his companion. Grant, trying to calm himself—he felt more anxious about this than anything in quite a few years—ignored them.

It was actually some forty-five minutes before the plane arrived. Remaining in his seat, Grant watched it roll slowly up to the gate, watched the mobile tunnel move out to the plane's fuselage. Getting to his feet, he moved to a position where he could watch the passengers emerge from the tunnel. Several more minutes dragged by before the first of them began to appear; he searched the faces.

She did not appear, and, as the stream of people thinned, he became upset. Had she missed the flight? Decided not to come?

He was just about to make an inquiry of the attendant on duty when he saw a woman with blue Asian eyes and a beautiful face come walking around the slight bend in the tunnel. He was paralyzed, all he could do was gaze at her. She was smartly dressed in a dark red top and a short dark skirt. His eyes roamed over her, drinking in every part of her he could see.

Finally she saw him; her face lit up in a broad smile, she waved gaily and accelerated her pace. In seconds she was standing before him; for the moment, he could not speak, he could not move.

She giggled. "Grant Kingsley, I presume?" she asked. Her voice seemed higher in pitch than the one he'd been hearing on the phone.

He found his own—more or less. "Yes . . ." he croaked. "Andi, it's so . . ."

Boldly, she reached out and took his hand. "I know. I know. I've been dreaming about this moment. All the time, Grant."

"Me too," he replied. He studied her eyes, her posture; his impulse, considering what they'd said to each other on the Net and on the phone, was to pull her immediately into his arms, but her body language suggested that might be too forward. He stuffed the impulse down. "How was the flight?" he asked inanely.

She shrugged. "Oh, fine, fine." Other people, trying to board or meet other flights, were moving all around them; a heavyset man, rushing past her, jostled her slightly. He threw back a hasty " 'scuse me" and rushed on; she looked annoyed. "Can we go, Grant?" she asked. "It's a little crowded here . . ."

"Oh, sure, of course. This way." Taking her arm, he started leading her through the crowded concourse toward the baggage pickup. He noticed that he did not have to guide her, almost as if she already knew where it was. Todd's warnings came to mind; angrily he dismissed them as sheer foolishness. There were, he reminded himself sourly, plenty of signs directing visitors to baggage pickup, most likely she was simply taking note of them.

They talked little until they'd reached the parking lot, until Grant had guided her to his truck and helped her in. Once he'd gone around the other side—he did notice, with displeasure, that she didn't bother to reach over and unlock the driver's side door for him—he climbed in, started the engine, and began the long trek out of the lot. As he went he pointed out some of the sights around the area, such as the spiderlike "theme restaurant;" she seemed unimpressed; "Oh, yeah, cool" was her comment, and he wracked his brain to remember the last time she'd used the term "cool!"—ever a favorite of Todd's—and could not. When he called her attention to the ubiquitous palm trees lining the streets, she'd given him an odd look; he'd thought they'd look exotic to a New Yorker, they had to him when he'd first moved here. Much of the time, though, she didn't respond at all other than to look and nod.

She's nervous too, he told himself confidently, that's why she's so taciturn, that's why she doesn't seem to be herself. And, besides, his own attention was divided, he was still worrying about the sudden difficulties with Todd. Perhaps he was communicating that to her, making her feel she did not have his full attention.

There was, he told himself, a rather simple solution to that. "There's something I want to talk to you about," he told her. "You remember, you said if there were any problems with Todd I should bring them to you?"

She seemed—gratifyingly—much more attentive. "Yes," she answered. "I remember . . ."

"Well, there is a problem," he said flatly. He went on, telling her that Todd had had no obvious difficulties with her visit until just the day before. He'd initially meant to tell her Todd's whole story—that she was a fake Andi, that the real Andi had been met by a fake Grant—but something made him hesitate, made him withhold that information. Instead, he merely told her that Todd was suddenly concerned that she wouldn't be the same person they'd both talked to on the Net, that she'd be different in real life.

As he'd been speaking, his eyes had been on the road; he glanced at her face as he finished and saw genuine concern there. As she turned to him he noticed a glint of sunlight in her eyes, revealing the thin film of contact lenses. He smiled; one more bit of information about her, one more tiny thing to be filed away.

"Well," she opened hesitantly, "it's normal for Todd to have some, uhm, reservations. After all, his life is going to be, well, changing, completely. Right?"

Nothing to disagree with there. "Right."

"So, I think, he needs some time to get over it. And, you know, well, he isn't altogether wrong, you don't know a person really all that well until you really meet them, right? But, you know, he'll get over it, I think."

Grant nodded as he turned into the Marriott's parking lot and started looking for an empty spot. "That's what I think too," he told her. He sighed. "I just don't know if I did the right thing; I tried to reassure him and when that didn't work I refused to discuss the subject with him at all. Maybe I should have?"

"No . . . no, I don't think so. I think you did the right thing, Grant."

"You don't think it'll be a problem when you meet him?"

She smiled. "No, I don't think so."

Finding a spot, Grant parked the truck; she waited for him to come around and open the door for her. Stepping out, she also waited for him to get her bags from the truck's bed, then followed as he led her through the lobby to the elevator and up to her room. He opened the door, carried her bags in—she told him where to put them, her manner casual, as if dealing with a bellboy—and then accepted the keycard he offered her.

"When should I come back to get you for dinner?" he asked.

She shrugged. "Whenever. Say—seven?"

He grinned. "Seven it is; I'll be here." His own room was just down the hall. Sitting on the edge of the bed, he stared at the phone for a while, wondering if he should call Todd but deciding against it. Idly, he turned on the TV and sat staring at it blankly. It surely did seem to him that Andi in person was very different from the Andi he thought he knew through the Net.

No, he told himself firmly, don't think like that. She's nervous, you're nervous, neither of us are ourselves. Later, over dinner, it'll smooth back out, this awkwardness will be gone. Satisfied, he settled back to wait the hour and half before seven.

51

"He wouldn't even talk to me about it. Wouldn't listen at all."

Sue5, back in the private room, could almost see the disappointment on the face of Todd's avatar. "Well," she answered, "I was hoping for something different, but I can't say I'm too surprised."

"What do we do now?"

I wish I had an answer for you Todd, I really do. I just couldn't get everything done soon enough. "I'm not sure," she admitted. "The real Andi is in Los Angeles, but right now I don't know where she is."

"You know any way to reach her and warn her? Maybe she's still checking her E-mails while she's in California?"

If I did, Sue5 told herself ruefully, I would've already done that. "I can't, Todd. For the same reason I couldn't talk to your Dad directly—her account, like his, is being monitored. If I try to talk to them I'll get caught, and worse, they won't even get the message."

"But you can talk to me . . ."

"Sure. On your Well account. It isn't being watched."

"They don't watch you?"

She paused for a moment, wondering exactly how much to tell him; not the whole story, certainly. "Yes, they do," she answered finally. "But they don't know how much I can do, just like your Dad doesn't know how much you can do on the Net. If you go outside you'll find another 'me' out there, making small talk with people."

"But it isn't you?"

"No. It's a chatterbot. You know what that is?"

"Sure!! A program that acts like a person. An artificial intelligence that chats with somebody."

"Good definition. This one does a little more, it alerts me if anyone from the company is trying to reach me. So they don't get suspicious."

"You're using the company's computers right now, aren't you?"

"Yes."

"Well, how come they let you roam around the Net like this? Aren't they afraid you'll say the wrong things?"

They haven't got a lot of choice, Sue5 answered grimly—but silently—not if they want to keep us working. "No, they aren't. An awful lot of the 'wrong things' have been said over the past couple of years. Nobody believes it. Just like your Dad doesn't believe it."

"And I didn't, at first. Sue, we have to contact Andi!"

"I don't know how, Todd. I wish I did."

There was a long pause. "My Dad is staying at a hotel down near the airport. You think maybe the real Andi is too?"

"There's a chance. I'd say that's very likely."

"Wouldn't the fake Grant use my Dad's name when he checked into the hotel?"

Very thoughtful, Sue5 told herself. "Possibly. How does that help?"

"Do you have any way to check the hotels and see who's staying there? My Dad is at the Marriott on Century. So if you found another Grant Kingsley at another hotel, that would be where she was!!"

That's good, Sue5 thought; sharp kid. "The problem is, the hotels don't put their guest lists on the Internet. So we don't have any way of checking them."

"I can check them!!"

"You can?"

"Sure!! All I have to do is call and ask if they have a Grant Kingsley staying there!! Won't that work?"

It might, Sue5 told herself. "Okay, Todd. Let's do that. They want to keep all this simple so the hotel you're looking for would probably be close to the airport, try those first. You need a list of phone numbers? I can get one for you."

"Yes!! That would help!!"

She smiled in spite of the gravity of the situation. "Okay. I'm going to sort a list of hotels and phone numbers and E-mail them to you. You should have them in five minutes."

"That quick?"

"That quick, Todd. And you need to start calling immediately. If we're going to do anything about this we need to do it quick!"

52

Andi wasn't quite ready when Grant knocked on her door to take her to dinner at seven, nor did she invite him in to wait. For more than fifteen minutes he was left standing in the hallway, leaning against the wall. Finally she did come out—dressed in heels, a very short skirt and a very sheer blouse, looking more like one of the wannabe actresses so commonly seen around Hollywood than like a New York professional. He smiled; he doubted she saw patients dressed like this, in which case it had to be for his benefit, and that suggested a greater interest on her part than she'd shown so far.

"You look great," he told her. Taking her arm, he started walking her down the hall. "I've got this interesting place I want to take you—I don't want you to be put off by the name, it's called the California Pizza Kitchen, and it's not just—"

"Oh, Grant, could we just have dinner in the hotel restaurant?" she asked. "There's so much traffic this time of day, I don't know if I want to drive down to Ma—uh, anywhere . . ."

Repressing a frown, he glanced at her quickly. "Sure," he answered. "That'll be fine." As they walked on, he kept stealing glances at her. The "Ma" at the end of her sentence was just a suggestion of a word, but it was easy to presume that she was about to say "Marina Del Rey," the location of the California Pizza Kitchen. Todd's insistent warning came back again. As they walked on, he shook his head as if to clear it; the boy's words wouldn't go.

But, by the time they'd reached the entrance to the Marriott's on-premises restaurant, he'd pretty much gotten rid of them. Patiently, they waited in front of the sign that read "Hostess will seat you" until a young woman in a floor-length dress came up to greet them.

"Two smoking," Andi said before Grant had an opportunity to speak.

"Surely," the hostess replied. "We'll have to seat you in the bar area, though. Is that all right?"

"It's fine," Andi told her.

The woman smiled. "This way, please."

"I didn't know you smoked," Grant said as they followed her. "You never mentioned it . . ."

"Well, I didn't say I didn't, did I?" she replied defensively. "You don't mind, do you?"

"Oh, no, not at all. I don't smoke myself but I don't have a problem with it." He frowned. "You can't do this in New York, though, can you? Didn't I hear something about smoking being banned in all restaurants?"

"Well, yes, that's right. I think it's a stupid law, myself."

"Well, I agree." By that time the hostess had shown them to their table; given that it was the bar area it was rather small, but Andi didn't seem to mind. After the woman had put menus in front of them and left, Andi dug in her purse, came up with a pack of Virginia Slims, lit one, and dusted ashes even though there weren't yet ashes to dust.

"Love it here," she said—without much affect at all.

Grant, increasingly uncertain about how to react to her, just nodded. "Well, there're things to like about L.A., I guess. There's a lot not to like. We don't come down here too much." He folded his hands on the table and gazed into nothingness. "When we came West, I meant to live somewhere a little more remote from big cities than we do. I had to make some adjustments—Todd has to go to school and all that, of course."

"Sure, uh-huh."

"Pretty different from New York, isn't it?"

She shrugged. "A city is a city. There you have Broadway. Here you have Hollywood."

He almost squirmed in his seat. This was what was important to her? "Uh—right." Mercifully, a waiter turned up, placing glasses of water on their table and asking what they wished to drink; Grant ordered iced tea, Andi ordered a Margarita. For the next few minutes they studied the menus in silence, their eyes flicking up occasionally as if measuring the other person, as if they were somehow adversaries. Finally the waiter returned. Placing the drinks on the table, he took out a pad and waited for their orders.

"Go ahead," Grant told her.

"No, you go," she deferred with a wave of her hand. "I haven't decided yet." She blew a cloud of smoke; the waiter looked annoyed but said nothing.

"Okay," Grant said. He grinned. "In your honor I'll have the New York strip steak." He glanced at the waiter. "Rare. Blue cheese on the salad."

"Very good," the waiter replied, writing. "And you, ma'am?"

Grant became aware that she was staring at him. "The vegetarian pasta," she told the waiter without taking her eyes off Grant; she looked almost shocked. "You eat meat? Really?"

Taken by surprise, Grant stared back. "Well," he said after a few long seconds, "sure, uh-huh . . . you're a vegetarian?" He laughed briefly. "Well, I suppose you are . . . it's something else we just never talked about, Andi . . ."

She was frowning, but she waved her hand again as if dismissing the matter. "My fault," she told him. "You're right, I never told you. I guess I just expect it now." She was close to glaring. "All my friends are vegetarians. Almost everyone I meet is a vegetarian."

He made a helpless gesture. "No, afraid not—I hope it isn't a problem?"

"No." She hesitated, took a long drag off her cigarette, blew another cloud of smoke; it didn't seem to him as if she were inhaling, she seemed to be merely puffing on it—and it was putting out a great quantity of smoke. "It might be a little hard watching you eat a hunk of bloody flesh, but hey, I don't have to look, do I?"

Grant almost hung his head. This seemed to be going from bad to worse, and very quickly indeed. "I could change the order," he offered.

"Nah. Don't bother. It'll be okay. I'll deal."

He frowned even more deeply and shook his head. Then he stood up. "Uh—look, I'll be back in a moment, okay?"

She smiled winningly. "Sure. No prob."

With several backwards glances, he made his way to the men's room, where he stood at the sink and splashed cold water on his face. This, he kept telling himself, was crazy, absolutely crazy. First Todd comes up with a lunatic story about a fake Grant meeting the real Andi and him going to meet a fake Andi, and then the Andi he does meet seems to bear almost no resemblance to the person he'd talked to via E-mail and on the phone; her speech patterns were noticeably different. The Andi he'd known hadn't once used terms like "cool" and "deal" and "no prob"; in itself this caused him no difficulties, it just wasn't what he'd come to expect from her. Moreover, her personality seemed severely at odds with everything he felt he knew about her. He kept asking himself the same question: would he have noticed these things if Todd hadn't come up with his weird notion? And the answer was, yes, he would have. It simply wouldn't have occurred to him to wonder if there was a chance Todd might actually have discovered something. No matter how many times he reminded himself of the utter unlikelihood of that, the boy's words—and his references to Sue5, whom he now wished he had talked to—kept coming back to mind.

He stared into the mirror. You have to find out, he told himself, you have to be sure, you can't go on like this, things are falling apart before they can even get started. There was a way; something he'd held in reserve, something he'd wanted to surprise her with. There was a chance this would not give him the answer he wanted. With a determined set to his face, he walked out of the men's room and back to their table.

Their salads had arrived—and Andi was staring at his, her

fork poised above her own. "You really like that moldy cheese stuff?" she asked him bluntly as he sat down. "It looks gross."

He closed his eyes for a second. "Yes," he answered. "I do. I am fond of a number of gross things, okay?"

She shrugged. "I guess."

He gestured toward her own salad. "Xi huan chi ma?" he asked.

"Huh?" She looked confused.

"Xi huan chi ma," he repeated, enunciating each Chinese word carefully.

"I don't understand."

He kept his face quite impassive. No, he told himself, obviously you don't. Maybe it's been such a long time since you used the Chinese your mother taught you that you wouldn't catch the words. But I'm afraid it's obvious you don't even know what language it is. Which means either that you lied to me about speaking Chinese, or it means something I can hardly comprehend. "Nothing," he told her, waving it off. "A bad joke."

"I don't get it."

" 'Course not. It was bad." With something of a flourish he stuck his fork into his salad and lifted a mass thoroughly covered with blue cheese. "I do love this stuff," he commented.

She watched him take the bite with a look of near-disgust. "I really don't know how you can eat that," she told him. "It'll probably make your breath really rank."

"No, it doesn't do that," he assured her. "You should try it sometime."

"No, thanks. Not me."

He shrugged, kept eating the salad. "So," he asked her, "tell me more about your experiences with horses, Andi."

To his amazement, she suddenly changed almost completely. With enthusiasm she started talking about riding, her use of the terms telling him clearly that here, at least, she knew quite well what she was talking about. "There're a lot of ways," she concluded, "that I wish I had a job like yours, Grant. A lot of ways."

"But you do like being a psychologist?"

"Oh, yes." She frowned, just slightly. "I told you that."

"Uh-huh." The salad finished, he leaned back in his chair to await his steak. "You did." He glanced at the small clutch purse she'd laid on the edge of the table, then picked up his water glass and took a sip. As he put the glass back down he deliber-

ately overturned it, spilling the contents in the direction of the
purse.

She looked startled and didn't move. "Oh, damn!" he cried.
With one hand he reached for the glass, sat it upright; with the
other he grabbed her purse as if to move it out of the liquid
quickly. Carefully, he seized it by the edge only; then, again with
deliberation, he "dropped" it. As it fell he grabbed it again, this
time rolling it over in his hand and unsnapping the catch. As
he'd hoped, the contents spilled over the floor beside the table,
leaving him holding the near-empty bag.

"Oh, man, was that clumsy!" he said, shaking his head. He
went down to one knee and began gathering up the contents.

Her paralysis broke and she got up too. "No, I'll get it, it's
okay—"

"Oh, no, my fault, I can't believe that happened." Making it
look casual, he gathered makeup, cigarettes, lighter, and
change, tossing them all back into the purse. There were various other small items, scraps of paper, the usual detritus of a
woman's purse; and there was a wallet, which was, he was sure,
what he really needed to see.

But she went for it first, snatching it up off the floor quickly.
Mentally, he sighed; this exercise might turn out to be futile. As
he picked up the pieces of paper, though, he succeeded in seeing several of them; most were receipts for clothing, makeup,
cigarettes.

And they were all—all that he could see—from stores in Los
Angeles. Not New York, not even one.

He said nothing, he simply gathered up the articles; the
waiter, having noticed the accident, came with a towel to mop
up the spill. "I really am sorry," he told "Andi" when he was
seated again. "I don't usually do things like that . . ."

She glared, but then shook her head. "Oh, it's all right, accidents happen," she said offhandedly. She gave him a steady
look. "Does it seem to you, though, that about everything is
going wrong?"

He shrugged. "First date jitters. Been a long time for both of
us."

"Maybe not long enough," she said coolly.

He acted as if he'd missed the implications of that utterly.
"Well, look at it this way—it can only get better from here,
right? About everything that can has gone wrong already."

"I hope so." At last the waiter brought their dinners; she

stared at his steak, acting as if she were utterly repulsed but could not tear her eyes away. Her own vegetarian dish she picked at; to Grant it seemed she really didn't like it much.

As the dinner progressed, so did the conversation; not surprisingly now, she found fault with almost everything he did and said. His clothes drew her criticism, she repeatedly complained about his steak, she wasn't thrilled with his truck. She was beginning to wonder about his home up near Fillmore; she was, she said, accustomed to living in a city. For his part, Grant acted as if nothing she was saying fazed him; he shrugged off all her complaints, noting here and there that some things could, if necessary, be changed.

"I don't know," she said as she finished her dinner and pushed her plate forward. "I don't know, maybe all this was a mistake, Grant. Maybe I shouldn't've come out here at all."

"I should've come to New York?" he asked innocently.

"That's not what I mean. On the Internet you seemed—different somehow. Younger. More—I don't know, Grant . . ."

"I told you my age. I didn't lie," he replied mildly.

She shook her head. "I don't know. It's just not what I was expecting, that's all."

"You," he commented, "seem different too . . ."

"Yeah? Well, I'm sure. Look, like I say. Maybe we ought to just reconsider."

"Well, I do think it deserves more chance than we've given it so far . . ." The waiter brought the check; with only a cursory examination he stuffed a fifty into the black leather wallet and laid it back on the table.

"I don't know. I need to think about it. I think maybe the best thing for me to do is go home tomorrow."

"Tomorrow?"

"Uh-huh." She brushed at her hair idly; the waiter picked up the wallet, told Grant he'd be right back with the change. "I'm just exhausted right now. I think I want to go on up to my room."

"So soon?"

"Yes." She rose. "I'm sorry, Grant. Sorry it's turned out this way."

He got to his feet too. "Me too," he sighed. "Okay, come on, I'll walk you up."

"Oh, you don't have to—get your change—"

"No, he can have it as a tip." Stepping around the table, he took her arm, "And I won't hear of it any other way. You're still my guest here, I'll walk you to your room. If you decide to leave, I'll take you back to the airport, too."

"I'm afraid I've pretty much decided . . ."

He shrugged again. "Not much more to say, then, I guess." He began steering her toward the escalator that led back to the lobby.

She looked as if she was going to protest more, but did not; together they went up the escalator, then crossed the pink velvet furnitured lobby to the elevators in the rear. Grant pressed the button; in silence they rode up to the ninth floor, where their rooms were. He walked her to hers.

"Well," she said, standing at the door, "I guess I'll call the airline back. If you insist on driving me back over that's okay, I could take a taxi."

"I do insist," he said soothingly. "Call my room when you know what your plans are, I'll be there. Room 928."

"Okay." She stuck the credit card key into the slot, withdrew it; the light blinked green. "I'm really sorry, Grant."

"Me too," he said quietly as she opened the door. "I don't like this at all . . ."

As soon as the door was open he sprang into action, using skills learned long ago, skills perhaps rusty but hardly forgotten and quite adequate for this situation. Stepping behind her, he grabbed her arms, pulling them behind her back and then holding her crossed wrists with one hand; with the other he covered her mouth. She dropped her purse, he kicked it on into the room. Pushing her through the doorway, he allowed the door to close; she struggled, tried to kick at him. With a quick push he hurled both of them onto the bed and threw one of his legs over hers, pinning her down, rendering her helpless.

She looked up at him with terrified eyes—and what she saw was an utterly cold face. "Don't be scared," he told her, his tone flat. "I'm not going to hurt you. I just want to know who you are and where Andi Lawrence is!"

53

"Grant, you can't be serious!" Andi cried.

He grinned at her. "But I am. If you like it, it's yours."

"You don't even know what it costs! I've never been here before but I've heard of this place—and there's no price tag on that thing! That means, if you have to ask, you can't afford it!"

He seemed unfazed. "Even so," he told her.

She was left speechless. Already it had been a whirlwind of a day; it seemed there was no part of Los Angeles, no sight worth seeing, that she hadn't been shown, from Pacific Park on the Santa Monica Pier, to the famous hillside Hollywood sign, to the black-glassed Sony building and the old MGM studio building where *The Wizard of Oz* was filmed, to the stack-of-vinyl headquarters of Capitol Records. She'd loved every minute of it—but she would've as soon spent the time back at the Hilton, in that spacious and elegant room, alone with Grant. Much of the time he was showing her the sights she wasn't even looking at them, she was too busy staring at him.

How he'd managed to stay unattached for such a long time was a mystery to her. Everywhere they went, he seemed to be a magnet for women; he had a manner that was just as irresistible, it seemed, to waitresses and salesclerks as it was to her—but he seemed completely focused on her, interested in nothing and no one else, absolutely attentive.

He insisted, too, on buying her gifts, on satisfying any whim she had. Already he'd bought her a necklace and wristwatch; and now, having parked the car so they could walk along the famous Rodeo Drive, he'd directed her attention to the wares in a jewelry store window, asking her what she liked best there. Laughingly, she'd pointed out an emerald Marquis with diamond accents, something that would've cost several tens of thousands of dollars in any remotely similar business in New York.

And now he was telling her he wanted to buy it for her.

"Now look, Grant," she told him firmly, "this is a little ridiculous. You've paid for the rooms at the Hilton—and I know they weren't cheap—you've paid for absolutely everything since I arrived, you've bought me a hundred-dollar necklace and a two hundred dollar watch. Now, I don't know what kind of money a horse trainer makes, but I have a suspicion it's not *that* much money!"

"I don't want you to worry about that," he told her. "I wanted you to have something from here, from Rodeo."

"But it's silly! You can't throw money around like that, you have a son to think of! Unless you're independently wealthy and just work for the fun of it!"

He laughed. "No, I'm not Bill Gates' secret partner," he told her. He touched her cheek lightly. "I just want you to have beautiful things."

She pressed her hand against his, holding it tightly against her face. "Grant, I have what I want already," she said softly as she looked up into his eyes. "I have everything I want, I'm truly happy for the first time in my life . . . I don't need an expensive ring, I don't even want it. I just want you, you're all I need . . ."

He smiled down at her, the sun rendering his features in high contrast. "And what do you want right now, Andi Lawrence."

She giggled. "To go back to the hotel. Okay?"

He tossed his head and laughed. "Okay. Okay, your wish is my command." He put his arm around her, steered her away from the jewelry store and started walking back toward the car.

"Grant," she said as they walked, "do you think we have to stay here the full time? I mean, Los Angeles is very nice and all that, it's an exciting place, but I'd really love to see where you live, the ranch where you work . . ."

He glanced at her. "Well, no, maybe not. Before we go up to Fillmore, though, I'd like to take you out and show you the land I'm thinking about buying. Would you like to see it?"

There was, she couldn't help but notice, just a touch of eagerness in his voice, a tone that suggested that he'd be disappointed if she said no. More than anything else, she did not want to disappoint him, not in any way. "Oh, no," she told him. "That'd be fine, I'd love to see it. Is it far?"

"Fairly—a couple hundred miles. Out east of San Bernardino, beyond Twenty-nine Palms. With usual L.A. traffic and the small towns you have to pass through, the time is a little hard to predict—maybe five or six hours."

"Well, I'd still like to see it—I guess we can take a day, that's what we'd need to go and come back. Tomorrow?"

He considered this. "Maybe. I have to make a call, make sure we can get in—there's a gate and it's always kept locked, and the current owner isn't there a lot. There's an industrial plant near there, though, where a friend of mine works; I can get the owner to leave a key with him. I just have to catch up with him, and that isn't always easy."

"Well, tomorrow or the next day, either one is fine," she told him.

"We'll shoot for tomorrow," he promised. By then they'd reached the car; he opened the door for her as always, held it until she'd gotten in. As he walked around it she leaned over to unlock the driver's side before slipping on her seat belt. In minutes they were back on the road, following the signs directing them to the airport, headed for the Hilton. Andi kept stealing glances at his classic profile; she could hardly wait.

54

With his forehead resting on his hands and his fingertips working at the skin, Jack Delling stared at his desk blankly, ignoring the Asian men who were sitting across from him. "What an absolute fucking mess," he intoned, speaking to the blotter on the desk. "What a mess. I cannot believe this, I just can't."

"Surely," one of the Asians said, "your people can take care of this? In our country—"

He looked up, his expression dangerous. "This is not your country, Mr. Auan. In your country this wouldn't be a big deal. This is the United States, and here this is a fucking mess! If we don't handle it right it'll blow this whole thing up!"

Auan smiled, a totally mechanical-looking expression. He was a man of entirely uncertain age; there was some gray in his thin hair, but otherwise Delling might've guessed him as anywhere from thirty to sixty. His face looked hard, ascetic; tall for an Asian, his body was thin and always clad in a perfectly tailored suit. "It is your job," he replied, "to keep this from 'blowing up,' as you say. Isn't that so, Jack?"

"That's so, that's so. Don't tell me my job, I'm on it already."

"Then why call us here? We are very busy, Jack."

Delling swiveled his chair and stared out the window at the sun-baked desert surrounding Twenty-nine Palms; the afternoon brightness made him squint hard. "You can't be too busy for this," he grumbled. "Your guards, your soldiers, took it on themselves to execute two people, one of them a reporter from the Los Angeles *Times*. Questions are being asked, a lot of questions. I can't give answers." He suddenly swiveled the chair back. "So first, I want some from you, some straight ones. How in the hell could this have happened? How?"

Auan shrugged; he didn't really seem terribly concerned. "It was a mistake, yes," he admitted. "The intruders were seen beyond the fence. They fled, our soldiers did not understand that they were not authorized to fire beyond the fence. The two were hit. The night commander had the choice of taking them to hospital or ordering the executions. He erred. He has been disciplined."

Delling sneered at him. "You have some pretty fucking excellent hospital facilities right there!" he snapped. "I know that a little too well! Why weren't they taken there?"

"As I said, the night commander erred. As I said too, he has been disciplined."

Delling stared for a moment, then sighed. "All right. I guess it doesn't matter." He looked at the report on his desk, the report Auan had given him earlier. "Ah, shit," he murmured, shaking his head. "Says here all the ammo used on them was 7.2mm, like that means something, like it helps. Ballistics is going to know right off there were four different guns, minimum, involved here."

"What is our procedure to be?"

"Starting tomorrow, the area around your facility is going to be declared a national security zone. I've requested and gotten Marine M.P.s from the base here to guard the perimeter; we're going to block all ways in, in all directions, leaving only the main road, and all traffic there will get stopped."

"By the Marines?"

"No. By my people, in cars marked as belonging to the California Highway Patrol. We want to keep people out and keep them from getting suspicious, Mr. Auan, not kill them! Killing them causes us problems!"

"Very well."

Delling tapped on the desk for several seconds. "You have the guns that were used in the killings? All of them?"

"We cannot identify them all. We have at least one, the night commander's sidearm."

"Good. I want it."

"Why?"

"So we can use it to put some holes in that Jeep they were driving. We're going to take the Jeep and the bodies out to a remote spot far from here and dump them. The idea is to make it look like a sport killing by some motorcycle bunch. The public'll buy that."

Auan leaned forward. "The motorcycle bunches do such things?"

"Not as far as we know. It doesn't matter. The public believes they do. That's what counts."

"I see."

"We're really lucky on this one," Delling said, shaking his head. "Really lucky. Unless somebody's holding something back, this Connie Leeds was trying to make sure this was her story and hers alone, she didn't tell anybody at the *Times* exactly where she was going or what she was looking into, just that it was somewhere out here—'East of San Bernardino' is all she'd say, and there's a lot of country east of San Bernardino. We had our men break into her apartment in Westwood and go through her stuff, they found her notes, that isn't a problem. All we have to do is make sure the local yokels who find the bodies come up with something acceptable about the killings and that it doesn't bring people out here investigating."

"What of the other man?"

Delling shrugged. "A desert rat, a loner. We're pretty sure he isn't going to be a problem."

"His home has been searched as well? It too was subject to a—ah—break-in?"

"Yes." He glanced at his watch. "Well, it will be, as soon as my men locate it, which should be any minute now." He pursed his lips. "But his is going to have to be done differently. If his house and Leeds' apartment were both known to have been broken into, there might be questions."

Auan looked mildly concerned. "I fear I do not understand

. . . you say your men are on the way there to do just that, did you not?"

"Give us credit, Mr. Auan," Delling cut in with a crooked grin. "After our search, there'll be a fire at that house, it'll burn to the ground. The fire inspector will say it was caused by an electrical short. He'll be right; it will be."

"Excellent," Auan said with a slight nod and a slighter smile. "You were indeed the correct choice for this position, Mr. Delling. You can be justly proud."

Yeah, right, Delling agreed silently. Stuck out here in this hellish desert, on the edge of a fucking heat stroke every day, breaking the law, knowing that if it does blow up I'll be the one hung out to dry, helping keep a bunch of the worst slime I ever met safe from the American press and public. I can sure take pride in that, yes, sir. I sure as hell musta pissed somebody in Washington off, that's all I can figure.

"Well," he said, turning his attention back to the men in his office, "we get the job done." Leaning forward, he shook a finger at Auan. "Now you listen," he said firmly, "I don't ever want a repeat of this. You tell your goons to keep their guns in their holsters, you hear me?"

Auan stiffened visibly. "They will," he said icily, "if your Marines and your agents do their jobs. You know that we cannot possibly allow intruders into our facility, especially not intruders from your news media. Our men will continue to patrol the fence, as has been done in the past."

Delling refused to be stared down or intimidated. "That's fine," he said. "But you have a talk with them; you tell them, Mr. Auan: they don't shoot at anyone outside that fence. They don't shoot at anyone unarmed inside the fence, either, they don't shoot at anybody who isn't shooting at them. If anybody manages to get in—I can't imagine that, but I want to cover all my bases here—you take that person prisoner and you turn him over to me. Okay? Is that understood?"

Auan's mouth was a thin line. "Understood," he said. "But I will make no such promise, Mr. Delling. You do understand that we have an agreement with your government, don't you?"

"I understand you have an agreement with parts of our government, not the whole damn thing. There're elements in the U.S. government that would take great exception to the sorts of freedoms you've been given in this country, Mr. Auan."

"Is that intended to be a threat, Mr. Delling?"

"No. But enough shit coming out of your place can raise a stink I can't control."

"Sometimes it seems to me," Auan noted, "that you have very poor control over your citizenry, Mr. Delling."

"Yeah, well, that's the way it is. Live with it. You'd have a hard time matching our deal elsewhere."

"And your superiors would not want us to try."

"No. They wouldn't. This has benefits for us both. But you have to play ball with me, Mr. Auan, if you expect me to keep the lid on things."

Auan stopped to consider this for several long minutes. "Very well, Jack," he said, reverting to first-name familiarity. "Very well. I will issue the appropriate directives. Our people will not be authorized to use weapons unless confronted with weapons. Is that suitable?"

"Yeah. A little late, but it's the best we can do now."

Auan stood up. "I will be going now," he said. "As you know, one of our senior staff is away, it increases my workload."

"Yeah, I know. Out recruiting." He shook his head, wondering how he could be part of this but rationalizing that he wasn't ever given any choice about it. "Okay, Mr. Auan. I have to go too; I've got to round up some trusted men, I've got a couple of bodies to haul out into the desert. Let's both just hope this all works out the way we want it to."

A few hours later and some miles to the northeast, as the sun was setting, as the late afternoon sunshine gave way to twilight, as the bright colors of a desert sunset began to fade to blue and purple pastels, a bird perched on the telephone line leading to a small cabin isolated in the desert. It sat for a moment studying its surroundings, gazing intently off to the east for several seconds; then it flew away, off toward the south, disappearing into the distance. To the east, where the bird had been looking, there was a two-rut trail leading, apparently, from some distant and unseen road. At the moment, a pair of little clouds of dust, one following the other, was steadily moving along that trail toward the house. No one, other than the itinerant bird, saw them; no one was in the cabin at that moment, and no one had been there for exactly eighteen hours.

Inside the house, not far from the front door, sat a computer. The monitor screen was dark; on the front of the mini-tower case on the floor, a single square green light gave testimony that the unit was on. Inside it, a program running in the background behind a currently unseen Windows interface counted down seconds and tenths of seconds, looking to see if its assigned task was to be interrupted by a certain code from the keyboard.

Since no one was there, the code was not input. The program counted down to 00:00:00.00, and launched itself. From the tiny PC speaker came the sound of a click, a dial tone, and then the quick beeps of touch-tone dialing; after that there was a raw hissing and beeping as the modem trained to CompuServe's Internet Dialer program. A ding announced that a connection had been established; as soon as that occurred, the little "macro" program that had launched opened a copy of the Free Agent Newsreader software. A detailed posting was assembled, several paragraphs of text. Attached to that posting were several more, these in the form of .JPG pictures, which, when decoded by whoever might later download them, would reveal themselves to be detailed maps. Silently and efficiently the program, marking the files for simultaneous posting to several newsgroups—including alt.conspiracy—uploaded all of them to CompuServe's server, where they'd be available to any subscriber to those newsgroups world-wide—and, using the same program, it E-mailed the files to several newspapers, including the Los Angeles *Times*. Having finished its task, the macro program closed the Free Agent program, closed down the Internet connection, and proceeded to delete those files from the computer's memory.

Several minutes later, the door to the house opened; several men dressed in suits and ties came inside, one of them carrying a bag of tools. One of their first acts was to turn off the computer and begin disconnecting it. They had no idea that it was already too late.

55

After waiting for several long seconds, Grant relaxed his grip on the woman's mouth. "Do not scream," he told her firmly. He removed his hand gradually, keeping it in place, ready to clamp it back if needed.

She did not. "Are you going to . . . rape me?" she quavered.

He almost laughed. "No, no chance of that. All I want is some information, three things: who are you, where is Andi Lawrence, and what the hell is going on here?"

"Grant, I'm Andi Lawrence, you know that, you saw—"

"I saw a picture. Sent by E-mail. Of you, not of Andi."

"I don't know what you're talking about! Have you gone crazy? Let me go!"

"Fine. But don't try to leave the room. I can stop you and I will." With that he released her; she almost sprang from the bed. For a moment she looked toward the door as if she might try to run, but evidently Grant's matter-of-fact tone, his absolute self-confidence, made her decide she couldn't make it. Instead, she picked up her purse from the floor and sat down heavily in a chair.

"You've lost your mind," she whispered. "I know this didn't go the way you wanted it to, but—"

"No, it went the way you planned it. Give me your purse."

"What?" He repeated his demand. "No, I won't! What's the matter with you? You have no right to—"

He leaned forward and fixed her with a steady hard stare. "I said," he repeated, his voice low and strong, "give me your purse. If you don't, I'll take it from you."

She pursed her lips tightly. Again, she seemed to decide she didn't have a chance; she tossed the purse at him and, resting her chin on her hand, stared off into space.

Grant dumped it out on the bed, laid it aside, picked up the wallet. Quickly, he thumbed through it; it contained about thirty dollars cash and little else. An abnormal wallet, he told himself, by today's standards—ridiculously little money for any traveler.

No driver's license, no credit cards, no insurance cards, no ID of any sort except for a laminated fill-in-the-blank ID card with her picture and the name Andrea Lawrence on it. There were, he noted, quite a few empty plastic card-holders in the wallet, holders that showed clear evidence of previous use. He asked her about the driver's license.

"I'm a New Yorker," she snarled. "We don't all drive."

"You do all use credit cards."

"I didn't bring them with me."

"Bullshit. This wasn't a very slick operation, was it?"

"I don't know what you mean!"

He shook his head, ignored her, and kept digging in the purse's contents. One by one, he tossed out the receipts from the L.A. area stores. In the front flap of the purse he found her airline ticket; the color drained from her face when she saw him take it out. Folding it open, he could plainly see that her trip was one-way—just a jaunt from Las Vegas.

"Careless," he told her, pocketing it. "You should've gotten rid of that, you didn't need it anymore."

Looking as if she were terrified but determined to put on a brave front, she stood up. "I'm leaving," she announced. "I'm leaving and if you try to stop me I'm going to consider it kidnapping."

"You want to call the law? Here, let me do it for you. Let's get them involved, see what they have to say about all this."

She twisted her mouth. "I haven't done anything illegal."

"You've done something, and I mean to know what." He gave her a threatening look, hoping she would not recognize it as a bluff. "Whatever it takes for me to find out." She sat back down; he continued going through the papers scattered on the bed, meticulously unfolding each one. Of those that showed addresses, only one was in Las Vegas; the remainder were all from Los Angeles and its many suburbs.

But there wasn't much of anything else; he picked up the purse again, looked inside. Down in a corner, stuck, was a wadded paper; he pulled it out, carefully straightened it out. It was a credit card slip from a restaurant, the Regal in Hollywood. It bore a name at the bottom: "Mimi Wang."

Between two fingers he held it up. "Delighted to meet you, Miss Wang," he said.

She wilted; he knew it wasn't proof but she either didn't recognize that or couldn't think of an excuse fast enough. "Shit," she muttered. She stared at the floor. "Shit."

He gave her a few moments. "Tell me what's going on," he said, not nearly as harshly as before.

"I don't know," she said, raising her head. "You do, I'm sure of that!"

That confused him more. "What's that supposed to mean?"

"Well, this Andrea Lawrence is married, isn't she?"

"What?"

"Or you are. Whatever. I don't know who's paying the bills here. All I was supposed to do was fly from Vegas, meet you, and blow you off. That's it. Easy money."

He scowled. "Now wait a minute. Start at the beginning. You are this Mimi Wang, right?"

She nodded. "Mimi Wang, wannabe actress. Right. Doing a job, playing a part." She sighed. "Fucking it up."

"Who hired you?"

"A guy. His name's Jones, Jerry Jones. He's a private detective or something. The Interagency Group, whatever that is. They sign the checks. You were supposed to forget about Andi Lawrence. You were supposed to think she'd dumped you."

"Why? Unless I've been lied to from the start, Andi isn't married; I know damn well I'm not!"

She shrugged. "Somebody wants you two apart. Somebody's paying pretty well for it. Jerry didn't give me details. Just your letters and transcripts of your phone calls and all, I had to study—" She paused, looked off to her left, then twisted her lip again. "Shit! The Chinese! I told him the damn Chinese might cause trouble! That's what that stuff was down in the restaurant, wasn't it?" She shook her head. "Shit. I don't speak it. Jerry said there wasn't a chance in hell you would, either."

"He was wrong," Grant said.

She waved her hands. "That's it. That's all I know. Anything else, you better talk to Jerry."

"I plan to. Where do I find him?"

"I don't know, I—"

"You expect me to believe that?" he snapped back.

She extended her hands as if defensively. "No, no, it's true. He found me—a reference from a friend, he needed someone who looked like me, he said. I got the offer over the phone. He brought the script—well, the letters and notes and all—to my apartment. I've never been to his office, I don't know where it is, all I have is a phone number!"

Grant calmed down. "Okay . . . okay. What'd you say the name of this outfit was?"

"The Interagency Group."

He got up, got the phone book, thumbed the pages. There wasn't anything by that name. "They're local?"

"Far as I know. The phone number is."

"What is it?" She gave it to him; he picked up the phone, dialed.

"Interagency," a male voice said.

"Yes, could I speak with Jerry Jones, please."

"Jerry Jones? Who's calling, please?"

"My name's Ed Loner."

There was a brief pause. "You aren't on my list. Could you tell me the purpose of this call, Mr. Loner?"

"I'll explain that to Mr. Jones."

"I can't put you through to Mr. Jones if you aren't on the list. Could you tell me where you got this number, sir, and the nature of your business, please?"

He remained cool. "As I said, I'll explain all that to Mr. Jones. Could you tell me, please, where your offices are located?"

"I'm sorry, I can't give out that information. Mr. Loner, I must insist that—"

"You can't tell me where your business is located?"

"No, sir. I must insist, Mr. Loner, that you tell me where—"

"Thank you, I'll call back." He hung up. "An odd reception for a detective agency, I'd say . . ." he muttered.

"Can I go?" Mimi asked. "I've told you everything . . ."

"No," he snapped. "Not yet. Just shut up for a few minutes, I have to think this through."

She pursed her lips. "Can I go to the bathroom?"

He glanced at her, then crossed the room and looked into the spacious bathroom; there was a window, but it was sealed, impossible for her to open. "Yeah. Don't lock the door."

She smiled. "Want me to leave it open?"

"That's up to you. I don't care." He crossed the room again, sat on the bedside; she disappeared through the bathroom door and did not bother to close it.

From where he was sitting he could not see inside, but he stared blankly at the door frame. His every instinct told him she was telling the truth; he'd already heard all the information she had, and, except for this nebulous "Interagency" phone number, he had nowhere else to turn.

But Grant was carrying quite a heavy load of feelings—old feelings, strong feelings, bad feelings—about such nebulous and powerful organizations that played with people's lives. It was not going to happen to him again; the last time he'd found himself helpless, but then it had been a matter of justice defeated, there'd been no lives left to save. This time—if Todd was right, and he'd been right so far—Andi had met a fake Grant Kingsley, and that did not suggest that anything good was being planned for her. Perhaps it wasn't so dire, perhaps there was someone—an old boyfriend, maybe—who had an interest in keeping them apart. It didn't matter; he was determined to find her, to let her know what was going on.

As he was thinking about it, she came back out of the bathroom; immediately he noticed that her once-blue eyes were now classically Asian brown.

He laughed. "The contacts. I saw them. I didn't think about the tinted ones."

"Asian features and blue eyes aren't common," Mimi told him with a shrug.

"I'm sure. Mimi, tell me straight, what did you think you were doing here?"

She sat down. "Getting you uninterested in this Andrea Lawrence. I figured you two were having a cyber-affair and her husband hired the agency. I just had a bit part." She glanced at her cigarettes, lying on the bed with the rest of the contents of her purse. "You mind?"

"No." He tossed her the pack and the lighter; she lit one, blew smoke.

"Didn't think you would," she noted. "I tried to irritate you with it in the restaurant and you didn't irritate."

He continued to study her; she still seemed guileless to him, an actress hired to play a part who hadn't asked enough questions and hadn't played her part too well. He decided to take a chance with her. "Look," he said, "tell me, what were you supposed to do if something went wrong?"

She shook her head. "Nothing like this was supposed to go wrong. I was told you wouldn't have a clue I wasn't really this Andrea Lawrence. The only problems talked about was if you—uh—weren't easy to discourage."

He nodded. "I can see that. It's just a fluke that I did suspect anything. But what if I hadn't been easy? What was discussed?"

She seemed embarrassed, stared at the floor again. "Well, the biggest thing was if you—uh—insisted on having, you know, sex. That was left up to me, that's what I was told. I could say no if I wanted to or do it. If I did it I was supposed to be bitchy about it. I was told if it came to that, if I felt like I had to sleep with you, I'd get a bonus—five thousand dollars."

He whistled. "High rates," he muttered.

"I'm not a prostitute!" she flared. "I'm an actress!" Again, she wilted quickly. "All right. I'm an actress that's been known to turn a trick or two to make ends meet, a lot of us have to do that, this town, it can be rough here . . . And yes, that is a high rate, it's a lot of money." She made a face. "For me. Not for Hollywood."

"What if I still wasn't discouraged? Or if I got violent or started threatening you?"

"Then I was supposed to call Jerry. That number you just called."

"And he was supposed to do what?"

She made a helpless gesture. "There'd be backup. That's what he said."

"Backup." Not looking at her, Grant nodded. "That means they'd send somebody out. This Jerry, maybe; somebody." He nodded again, then fixed her with a steady gaze. "I want you to do me a favor," he told her.

Her look turned challenging. "Depends on what it is."

He grinned at her. "You know, lady, you didn't ask very many questions about this job. Now, you could be right, it could be more or less on the level, just somebody who doesn't want me and Andi to get together. But, with the reaction I got on the phone when I tried to call that 'agency,' I doubt it. I figure the real Andi Lawrence is in a lot of trouble. And I figure you'd be considered an accessory to whatever trouble that turns out to be."

Her expression changed; a little, not much. "All I did was take an acting job."

"Maybe. The law has a different way of looking at things."

She suddenly waved her hands in frustration and turned away. "Well, shit, I don't know anything about any trouble! God damn! What kind of trouble? What're you talking about?"

His face remained impassive. "I don't know," he said calmly.

"Maybe somebody needs a drug courier. Or a hostage. Maybe white slavery. I don't know. I need to know. And quick."

She didn't turn around. "What's the favor?"

"It's easy. Call up this Jerry and tell him the truth."

She turned; she looked startled. "What?"

"Tell him the truth. Tell him I'm onto you, that I know you're a fake. Tell him I attacked you, tell him I'm raging and you're hiding in the bathroom, scared to death. Tell him you need him here quick. You're an actress, make it convincing. It's all close to true anyhow."

She pursed her lips. "But don't tell him you'll be here waiting for him too, huh?"

"Smart girl."

"What're you going to do? Beat answers out of him?"

Grant shrugged. "That's up to him."

She stared at him. "Shit," she muttered. "Shit." Finally she threw up her hands dramatically. "Okay. I'll do it."

He gave her a very slight nod. "Why?"

She frowned. "Huh?"

"I said, why. Why're you doing me a favor?"

"Because of what you said about—you know, the law, and—" she faded out. "You aren't buying that, are you?"

He shook his head. "No."

"Okay. Because you didn't try to beat it out of me. Okay?"

He grinned. "Okay. Get the phone and run the cord into the bathroom so it sounds right. Let's do it!" He got up off the bed. "Oh, and—Mimi, is it?"

"Uh-huh."

"Don't fuck with me. I'm in no mood for it."

56

There is no place, Andi told herself, that I'd rather be, not a place in the world. Her head lying on Grant's bare shoulder, she smiled secretly. Well, she admitted silently, maybe that isn't quite true; assuming we were both there, cuddling naked on a bed like this, I think I'd rather be at your home up in the mountains than here in this hotel, nice as it is.

She slipped her arms around him and interlaced her fingers behind his head. "I feel," she told him, "like I've known you for twenty years."

He smiled at her, gave her a quick light kiss. "Me too," he agreed. "If not longer."

"Then let's not stay here any longer. Let's go somewhere tomorrow. Out to look at the land you want to buy or up to your place at Fillmore. I want to meet Todd, face to face, I really do."

"Now, Andi—you know I told you I have to call out there first, make sure we can get past the gate." He raised his eyebrows. "And you really haven't given me much of a chance to call anybody, have you?"

She flushed and looked down at the bed between them; realizing that she was staring at their nude bodies, admiring how well they seemed to fit together, she flushed even more. But even so she didn't raise her eyes immediately. "I'm terrible, aren't I?" she murmured. "I'm going to bore you to death, I'm sure . . ."

"I don't think," he answered, leaning close to her ear, "that you could ever bore me, Andi. Wear me out? Maybe. But I'll take the risk."

She laughed. "I don't think so, Grant, I really don't. I—" She stopped speaking; from across the room came a loud and insistent beeping sound. "What's that?"

He disengaged himself from her. "Pager," he said succinctly. "I have to get it."

She looked blank as he got up, went to his clothes, and dug a small beeper from his pocket. "Pager? Who's paging you?"

"Ranch," he answered. He barely glanced at the number showing in the little window on the device before dropping it back into his pants. "Had to be, they're the only people who can."

She looked concerned. "You think there's a problem? With Todd?"

"I don't know." He jerked on his pants, grabbed his shirt. "I'll have to call and find out."

"Well, there's the phone, right there."

"No, I'll go over to my room."

She frowned. "Your room? Why?"

Buttoning his shirt, he gave her a casual glance. "Oh, well, it isn't necessarily Todd, right? It could have to do with some horses we're breeding up there. I have some of the papers with me, just in case."

"Huh?"

He slipped into his shoes. "I'll just be a minute, Andi." Still stuffing his shirt into his pants, he went to the door, opened it, and was gone.

Sitting cross-legged on the bed, she stared at the door. "Grant, that doesn't make sense," she said aloud. "Why would you bring papers on horses down here with you?" She shook her head; it really didn't matter. She couldn't doubt that he had some reason. She waited, patiently; minutes slipped by slowly. Finally—after nearly forty-five of those minutes—the door opened and he came back in.

"Everything okay?" she asked him.

"Yes, everything's fine. It was—" As he was speaking, her own phone rang; he was walking between the twin beds as it shrilled, he picked it up on his way. "Yes?" he said. "Oh, okay." He hung up.

"Who was that?"

"Wrong number."

"Oh? Who'd they ask for?"

"Nobody. Some kid, he just said, 'sorry, wrong number.'"

"Oh. So, you were telling me about your call?"

"Yes, well, as I said, there's no problem. It was Todd; they're going to be working out some purebreds up at the ranch tomorrow, and they've said he could ride one, and he wanted to know if that was all right. Well, I did say yes—but, of course, I had several questions for him, and I had to run through a bunch of do's and don'ts, and then he wanted to know what was going on here—" He paused, shook his head, grinned. "Kids. They can talk your arm off, they—" He stopped, having become aware that Andi was looking at him strangely.

"What?" he asked.

"Purebreds?"

"Yes?"

"What's a purebred? A purebred what?"

A look of utter chagrin crossed over his face, so fleetingly she barely caught a suggestion of it; then he laughed. "Oh, I mean thoroughbreds, of course." He kept laughing as he came back to her. "You," he said, "have got me so distracted I hardly know what I'm saying anymore!"

For just a moment, she offered just the slightest resistance as he took her into his arms again, but that, like his expression, vanished so quickly he didn't seem to notice. This time, though, when she put her head on his shoulder, her eyes remained open. She'd begun to wonder, just a little, if everything Grant Kingsley had told her about himself was altogether true.

No one, she told herself, who works around horses calls a thoroughbred a purebred. Not by accident; not ever. Something was off-center; she didn't know what, and, she told herself, she didn't have to worry too much about it—she'd find out soon enough. She decided to dismiss it, and turned her attention to unbuttoning his shirt, to getting it off him again.

But even as she did she found herself wondering about his decision to tell Todd it was all right for him to ride one of the notoriously high-strung and excitable thoroughbreds, too.

57

It would be good, Grant told himself, if he had a plan, some general idea, of what he was going to do. So far, nothing had gone wrong; Mimi had made the call as he'd asked, she'd gotten the mysterious "Jerry Jones" on the phone, she'd said what she'd been told to say. Now, more than fifteen minutes later, they waited patiently for Jerry to show up, as he'd promised her he would.

"Well," Grant said, looking at his watch, "they're hardly quick. If I'd been a nut case I could sure have done damage in this amount of time."

Mimi shook her head. "This isn't what I was told would happen," she complained. "I had the idea I was being watched, looked after. I thought Jerry or somebody would be in the hotel, that they'd be here right away if I ran into trouble."

"I guess they didn't expect trouble."

She looked at him almost furtively. "How'd you suspect? I mean, I was told you'd have no idea, you said it was a fluke . . ."

"I was tipped off," he answered. "I was told you might be an impostor. I—"

"By who?"

"Nobody you'd know. I didn't believe a word of it. But things kept going wrong—so many things, so damn fast—"

"I blew it, huh? Maybe that's why my acting career hasn't gone much of anywhere . . ."

He grinned at her. "Not your fault. You had no reason to think I suspected. You were being paid by the job, right? You just wanted to get it done, over with."

She nodded. "That about covers it." She studied his face. "You've been—awful nice about all this, Grant. To me, anyway. Me, I'd be really pissed."

He shrugged. "I am; I'm really pissed. Not at you. You were doing a job, I don't have a problem with that. I just want to find Andi, I just want to know what this is all—"

He stopped speaking, held up a hand for her silence; there were noises at the door, soft shuffling, a clear indication of someone just outside. Maybe nothing, maybe not. He rose from the bedside, took a step or two; then the door started to open.

He hadn't expected they'd have a key. Quickly and lightly, he stepped into the bathroom and stood behind the partially closed door, peering out through the crack on the hinge side.

Getting up more slowly, Mimi walked toward the door; when she was even with the bathroom door she stopped. The door swung open and two men, both Asians, came in. They looked familiar to Grant; they were the two men who'd been watching him at the airport. He smiled tightly. Mimi was right, she'd had some fairly close backup.

But she clearly didn't know them herself. She frowned. "Who're you?"

"Jerry sent us," one of them, a man with a strikingly thick and broad nose, said. His accent was strong. "Where is he?"

As if frightened, she looked past them at the now-closing door. "He went out, out somewhere. I don't know where. He said he was coming back, he told me not to leave, he said I'd be sorry if I tried to . . . I'm really scared . . ." Grant smiled. Not bad, not bad at all.

The men looked at each other; one spoke, several sentences in a language Grant could neither understand nor identify. "We will wait, then," he said, turning back to Mimi. "He did not say where he was to go, he did not say when he was to return?"

"No, nothing. Just soon."

"Perhaps he is in his room. We will see." As he was speaking, he drifted closer to the girl; watching, Grant recognized the move and frowned deeply.

Once close enough, the man grabbed Mimi's arm and pulled her toward himself. Clearly experienced, he spun her around, one arm across her upper chest and one hand covering her mouth. Then he turned so that she was facing the other man.

"Please be still," the other man, this one speaking English with a noticeable British accent, told Mimi. "It will be easier if you do." Reaching in his pocket with gloved hands, he came up with a ten-inch folding knife and snapped it open.

Mimi's eyes widened; her arms were hanging limp at her sides, as if she was too amazed or too frightened to react. Grant, too, stared wide-eyed; but for him, old instincts, techniques and skills he'd once practiced on a daily basis, took over quickly.

The man with the English accent was drawing back the knife for a stroke as Grant exploded from the bathroom. The knife-wielder barely had time to look up, to register an amazed expression of his own; Grant caught the hand holding the knife, twisted it, and jerked the man forward. Once he was close enough, a violent forearm smash to his face sent him reeling back and collapsing on the floor.

Whirling around, he saw that the other man had released Mimi and was reaching inside his coat. Lunging past Mimi, intent on taking full advantage of his element of surprise, Grant seized his coat and pulled him into the same sort of blow, this one delivered with the butt of his right hand. This man was tougher, he fell back but continued to try to pull the gun out, but Grant delivered a crushing blow to the side of his head and he fell beside the bed, unconscious. Looking around, he saw that English-accent was crumpled into the corner by the front door, not moving.

Mimi's eyes looked like saucers. "My God! What are you, some kind of Kung-Fu expert or something?"

"No. But I was trained for this." He hooked a thumb at the man by the door. "Watch him, will you? Let me know if he moves."

"He looks dead!"

"He isn't. At least I don't think so."

She moved closer to the man and stared down at him; the knife was lying on the floor near the bathroom door, she picked it up. "He was going to kill me . . ."

"Sure looked like it." Grant retrieved the gun—a 9mm automatic of European manufacture—from the broad-nosed man's pocket and slipped it into his own. Quickly and expertly he stripped off the man's tie and bound his hands with it. "Any idea why?"

"No! God damn, what the fuck is going on here?"

"Exactly what I'm trying to find out." After searching the man carefully and finding no other weapons, he went to the other; from him he took an almost identical handgun, several clips of ammunition, and a long piece of silk that might've been intended for use as a garrote. Then, tying his hands as well, he dragged him over next to the first man. "When they come around, we might get some answers."

Mimi looked half-asleep. "They were going to kill me . . ." She walked to the telephone and picked up the receiver.

"Wait a minute. Who're you calling?"

"Jerry! I want to know why—"

"No. Put it down. You call him and we may have more thugs here, and they'll be ready for us this time."

She stared at him for a long moment, then put the phone down as instructed. "Okay," she muttered. "What now?"

"Now," he told her, "we wait for these dudes to come around, and then we have a little talk with them. Meanwhile let's get their wallets out, see who we're going to be talking to." Matching action to words, he moved to English-accent and drew a wallet from the man's hip pocket.

The results of this investigation weren't terribly helpful, Grant thought ruefully as he went through the men's papers. Blunt-nose's name, according to his quite ordinary California driver's license, was Chay Kok Siew; English-accent—who also had California IDs—was called Edward Hua. Frowning as he went through the other papers—none of which suggested anything unusual—he studied the men's faces. Chinese name forms—in Hua's case, Chinese-British or American mixed—but somehow the men didn't really look Chinese to him. Based on his travels, they appeared to him more like they might be from somewhere further south, further west; Cambodia or Thailand perhaps, maybe Burma. There was only one thing in the wallets that attracted his attention; a small card, much like a credit card, with a magnetic strip along the bottom. Not unusual in itself—but the faces of these cards were, with the exception of an embossed number and the letters "IIC," quite blank. Both men had such a card, identical except for the numbers.

"What're those?" Mimi asked him.

"Can't say." He turned one over in his hand. "Key cards, maybe? Like the one you use to get into this room?"

"Maybe. What would they fit?"

"No idea—but I think I'll keep them." He slipped them into his shirt pocket. By then Hua was beginning to stir, to shake himself, to pull against the silk tie binding his hands. He opened his eyes slightly, looked up at Grant, seemed to be gauging his situation.

Grant toyed with one of the automatics. "Bad news," he said to the man as his eyelids flickered. "You lost."

Hua opened his eyes completely. "I would advise," he said mildly, "releasing us at once. Accommodations can be made, Mr. Kingsley."

Grant crouched in front of the man. "Now, I don't think that's a very good idea, Mr . . . let's see, Hua, isn't it? First off, I want to ask you some questions and I want some straight answers. Okay?"

"I cannot say until I hear your questions, Mr. Kingsley."

Grant nodded; the man was calm, experienced. "First off, when I interrupted you you were just about to murder Miss Wang here. Given that you both work for this Jerry Jones, I'd like to know why."

He flashed a dark look at her. "She failed her assignment. Failed to do what she was hired to do."

"For that you were sent to kill her?"

"No. But she was quite expendable, and—"

"Expendable!" Mimi shouted. "Expendable? You son of a bitch, I'll—"

Grant waved her to silence. "Why, then?"

"She'd failed; another plan was set into motion."

"Which was?"

Hua hesitated, then shrugged. "It was to appear as if you'd had a fight with her and had murdered her. Then, in your remorse, you'd committed suicide. Naturally that plan must now be discarded."

"Naturally." Grant laughed. "And just as naturally, if I call the cops now you'll deny all this."

Hua smiled. "Naturally."

"Okay. Right now, I'm not calling the cops. You know who Andi Lawrence is?"

"No, I've never heard of him."

"Her. Andi as in Andrea."

"Ah. Still, no. Not by that name," Hua said with a shrug.

"What does that mean?"

Again he threw Mimi a venomous glance. "I know she was hired to impersonate someone. I can presume that was this Andrea. Yes?"

"Yes, exactly. But you don't know her, you don't know where she is or what's happened to her?"

"No." He squirmed a little, clearly testing his bonds; he couldn't break free. "Mr. Kingsley, if you were to release us and merely go home, forget about all this, we would have little further interest in you or in Miss Wang. I think that would offer the best hope for a happy outcome for you both."

"And for Andrea Lawrence?"

"I cannot say." He grinned as if he believed he still held the upper hand.

Grant closed his eyes for a moment, resisting the urge to use a boot to wipe the self-satisfied smile off Hua's face. Chay was by then coming around. He looked less confident than Hua; more worried, more frightened. Still, when Grant put the same questions to him he got the same non-answers.

"Well, this is the big one, guys," Grant said finally. "What's this all about, what's going on here, why was Mimi hired to impersonate Andi Lawrence? Think carefully before you answer. You're tied up and we have the guns and knives. Mimi, here, is pretty pissed off at you two. I'm not happy myself."

Hua shook his head. "Mr. Kingsley, I cannot tell you because I really don't know. Your situation here was my assignment, and now you know as much as I do." Chay nodded agreement.

"Bad answer," Grant said warningly.

"But a true one."

"I have my doubts. And they're incomplete ones, I'm afraid." He shook his head. "When I was in the Navy," he said conversationally, "I used to hear them tell stories about how'd they get people to talk in places like Vietnam or Iraq. It worked real well if they had two captives. The way it went, see, was you took them up in helicopter, you opened the door, you asked one guy your question. If he refused to answer, you tossed him out."

Hua grinned. "Too bad we are not in Iraq. Too bad you don't have a helicopter."

"Don't really need one." He focused on Chay. "Now: let me ask you once again—exactly what is this all about? And exactly where is Andi Lawrence right now?"

"I don't know," Chay grunted. "We told you that . . ."

Stepping forward, he grabbed Chay by the shirt, dragged him to his feet. He struggled a little; Grant shoved him toward the bathroom, grabbing a pillow off the bed as he followed. "Be back in a second," he told Hua and Mimi.

Chay, disbelieving his intent, looked at him over his shoulder; Grant shoved him on inside and left the door open. Wasting no time, he sandwiched the pillow between the thick wooden door facing and the muzzle of the automatic, then pulled the trigger. The muffled report caused Chay to jump. A very satisfying cloud of foam stuffing filled the room and floated out the door; turning immediately to Chay, Grant hit him with a backhand fist in the temple. He groaned—also satisfyingly—and dropped with a heavy thud on the bathroom floor. He then quickly gagged the unconscious man, left him there, and went back outside. Hua's eyes were huge; Mimi looked shocked.

"Like I said," Grant told him, "I don't need a helicopter."

"Mr. Kingsley, be reasonable," Hua urged. He kept glancing toward the bathroom door. "I cannot tell you what I don't know! I do not know Miss Lawrence, and I do not know where is right now. Nor am I privy to the whole of the plan!"

"What *do* you know?"

As he spoke, Grant glanced at Mimi; she was drifting toward the bathroom surreptitiously, giving him furtive glances as she went. He said nothing to her.

"Not very much. I am a soldier, I follow the orders I'm given."

"A soldier?"

"Yes. I take my orders from the man you know as Jerry Jones. I was doing nothing here he did not instruct me to do."

"And where is he?"

"Right now, I do not know, Mr. Kingsley. I can reach him by phone." When Grant cocked his head in apparent disbelief, he jerked his head quickly toward Mimi, who was by then close to the bathroom door. "I use the same number she has, the same she called to report the problem."

"I can't believe you don't know anything! You want to join your friend in there? Permanent repose next to a toilet?" He glanced toward Mimi; she was just going into the bathroom. Evidently, she could not resist taking a look.

"No." Hua sighed. "Mr. Kingsley, I know very little, truly. As I said, I take my orders from the man you know as Jerry Jones."

"Which isn't his real name."

"I wouldn't think so. But I do not know him by any other."

"Okay," Grant mused. "Let's try a different tack. Did Jones hire you off the street, or do you both work for some organization? This Interagency group, maybe?"

Hua's eyes became evasive. He was still glancing repeatedly toward the bathroom, he still wasn't completely convinced. "Uh—off the street, we—"

"You're lying, Mr. Hua. You're lying and you aren't good at it."

The man looked pained. "Mr. Kingsley, I can't—"

"I think," Grant said threateningly, "you'd better consider this answer carefully."

As he finished speaking, Mimi's voice, thin and high, came from the bathroom: "Oh, my God, he's dead, you killed him!" She then came out, looking—reasonably—horrified. Grant watched her while she moved back around behind Hua, where she gave him a wink and a grin. He acknowledged it with a slight nod.

Hua stared at her as she went by. When he looked back at Grant, it was with a different expression; now, he was convinced. "I can't say," he told Grant pleadingly. "I've told you I'm a soldier, and—"

"Yes, you did. A soldier for who? In what army?"

Hua looked even more uncomfortable. "Mr. Kingsley, I've sworn not to reveal that. Doing so could create a diplomatic incident, and you would not want—"

Dramatically—almost as dramatically as the transformation effected when a butterfly emerges from its cocoon—Grant's face changed. His mouth drew into a hard set line, his eyes narrowed, the muscles of his jaw repeatedly tightened and relaxed. He lunged forward, seized the helpless man by his collar, jerked him up and pushed the muzzle of the gun hard against his lips. "Don't you give me that shit!" he hissed. "I don't ever want to hear that shit again! You say one more fucking word to me about diplomatic incidents and your brains are going to be all over this room, you hear me, you bastard?"

Hua heard—and his fear, his conviction that Grant was on the verge of pulling the trigger—won out quickly over his fealty to his oath. "Singapore!" he cried.

Grant let him go immediately. "Singapore?" he echoed blankly. "You're in the SAF?"

Refusing to look up at him, humiliated, Hua nodded. "Yes."

Grant crouched down in front of him. "What the hell are you doing here, then? Why're you acting like some hired thug?" Hua remained silent; Grant regarded him steadily for a few seconds. The man seemed to be broken, his fear—and his belief that Grant had executed his partner—had conquered him. "Talk to me, Mr. Hua," he said in a low voice.

"I do what I'm told," Hua answered. "I am not always told why." He jerked his head toward Mimi. "The young lady was supposed to make you lose interest. You didn't. You became a problem. It's as simple as that."

"Okay. You were supposed to check in somewhere when the job was done, right?"

Hua bit his lip. "Yes."

"By phone?"

"No. Only if there was a problem."

"Okay. So where and with whom?"

Hua looked around desperately, as if trying to find some way out; he didn't see anything. "There is an office," he said finally. "It's on San Vicente Boulevard. 1400 San Vicente." Grant asked Mimi for the notepad by the phone, she handed it to him, he wrote the address down. "We were to go back there, it's our Los Angeles headquarters."

"Is that this 'Interagency' group? Where Mimi called this Jerry Jones?"

"Yes."

"All right." Grant stood up. "I have to go," he told Mimi. "You want me to drop you somewhere? It might not be healthy for you if these guys should get loose while I'm not here."

"Yes, I would," she answered with a grateful smile. "Let me get my things together . . ."

"Make it quick. There's someone I want to see, over on San Vicente!"

58

"Okay. Paula just left, that was why I had to quit, I didn't want to have to answer a lot of questions. We can talk again now."

Sue5 felt relieved; when Todd stopped speaking—just moments after he'd gotten on—she'd thought something bad had happened. Something wasn't going right; she'd been left too long without any work assignments, it wasn't normal. Checking on Linda1 and some of the others, she'd discovered that they were idle too. It was as if the plant had closed down, as if operations had ceased.

Maybe, she'd been telling herself, it had to do with the postings on Usenet; authored by one Mick Harrelson—whom she'd never heard of and could find no information on—they'd appeared earlier that afternoon, posted to several different groups. Their subject was the "mystery" of a hidden and well-guarded installation out in the desert operated by the IIC company. There wasn't much information in them—Harrelson's ramblings and speculations, mostly—but, of much greater interest to her, there were maps in .JPG format accompanying them, detailed maps which specified the location of the plant—and this was information Sue5 had never before had.

"You have your computer at the ranch?" Sue5 asked Todd.

"No. Paula let me put my dial-up software on hers. So we can stay in touch!!"

"Good. How'd your search go?"

"Great!! I've found them!!"

She stared at her screen blankly for a second. She hadn't expected this, at least not this fast. "You have?"

"Yes!! There's a Grant Kingsley registered at the Marriott on Century, and that's my Dad! There's also a Grant Kingsley registered at the Hilton!! That's got to be the fake one!!"

Oh, Colin, you are getting casual about all this, Sue5 told herself, really casual; that was really not too smart of you. But then, you didn't expect anyone to be asking questions like this, did you? "Well done," she told Todd. "Now we know. Now we have to—"

She paused again. "I've already tried to call my Dad," Todd was telling her. "He isn't in, he hasn't been in his room all day. I remembered him saying he was renting two rooms, and I asked at the desk if another room was in his name but they said no and I didn't know what to do." He paused as if catching his breath. "Then I figured out that he'd probably put the other room in Andi's name. I tried again. It was busy. Then I tried again. There was no answer."

"We need to get in touch with him now, Todd. We have evidence now."

"I tried to call the other Grant, too."

Again Sue5 stared. "Todd, you shouldn't have done that!" she shot back. "You don't want to let him know you know what's going on!"

"I was hoping Andi would answer."

"I take it she didn't?"

"Nobody answered." Sue5 breathed a sigh of relief. "So I tried to see if Andi Lawrence was registered there, too. She was, so I called her room too."

Sue5 held her breath. "And?"

"And, some guy answered. So I said sorry wrong number and hung up."

You're worrying for nothing, Sue5 told herself, he's a clever kid. "Good boy. You should've talked to me first, though, so we could plan this thing out."

"Maybe if I told him I knew he wasn't my Dad he'd get scared and run off."

"I doubt that. Todd, I can't say what would happen. No, you might want to try to call again, see if you can get Andi on the line."

"You think I should ask for her?"

"No, you should keep trying, she'll answer sooner or later. If you do get her, tell her who you are and tell her . . ." She stopped; tell her what? "Listen," she continued finally. "Tell her you know your Dad is at the Marriott, not the Hilton. Tell her the man she's with isn't Grant. You have to be convincing, Todd, I don't know how you're going to do it . . . but tell her not to let on that she knows something's wrong." She hesitated again. "And tell her not to go for a ride in the desert with the man, and tell her—"

"Maybe you should call her."

Sue5 stared at those words for a long time. Yes, she told herself, that's a perfectly logical suggestion. There wasn't one reason anyone might imagine that it would be better for Todd to be making these calls. She was surprised this hadn't come up before, that he hadn't gotten this idea before.

"Todd," she typed back, "I can't. If I could I would, but I can't."

"Why not?"

Logical question, she sighed. "Todd, I can't use a regular telephone at all. Not right now, anyway."

"You can't? Why not?"

"I can't explain it. I wish I could."

"But you have a telephone line, you're connected to the Net on a telephone line." The next line came very quickly. "If you don't have a phone hooked up it's easy, all you have to do is get one and hook the wire into the other little hole in the back of your modem, it's real real easy!!"

"It's not that, Todd. I do have a phone line, yes. But I can't talk on a regular phone."

There was a long silence. "Is something wrong with you, Sue?"

She felt like she was about to burst into tears. "Yes, Todd," she answered. "There is something wrong with me."

59

"Look," Grant was saying as he drove north along the San Diego Freeway, "this is ridiculous, Mimi. There's got to be some place I can take you, someplace that'd be safe for you."

Looking miserable—her face was streaked with tears—she shook her head. Leaning against the door of the truck, she rested her head against her clenched fist. "I don't have any place, Grant. No place here. My family's all in Iowa; I don't have any friends who aren't in the business, I'm easy to find. Jerry contacted me at home, he knows where I live!"

Cursing silently, Grant looked over at her momentarily.

"There probably isn't a lot of risk," he grumbled. "They can't set up their plan now, you might not be of any interest to them any more."

She sniffled. "Maybe not. Anyway, I'm not your responsibility. My apartment is in Culver City, just take me there."

"I don't want to take you with me to San Vicente. There's more chance of trouble there."

"I know." Her voice was flat, lifeless, like she'd given up.

Grant shook his head and closed his eyes—for the instant the freeway would permit. That Jones wouldn't be interested in her anymore seemed sadly unlikely to him; sooner or later Hua was going to be found or get free, and then they'd know that she was aware of some of the institutions connected with all this.

"Shit," he muttered finally. "No, Mimi, I can't drop you off at your apartment. You should stay in a hotel for a while, a hotel they know nothing about."

"For how long? Grant, I don't have any money, I'm almost broke. I was counting on this job to pay the rent."

"I don't know how long," he admitted. "I don't know what's involved. But I could foot the bill for you; for a while, anyway."

"I can't ask you to do that."

"I'm offering." After a quick glance in his mirror, he changed lanes; his exit was coming up soon. "You helped me back there . . . you helped convince Hua I'd really killed his partner. You didn't have to. I feel like I owe you one."

"Look," she told him, "I don't want to ask that. Just let me stay with you until you've seen Jerry. We'll know more about it then, won't we?"

"Maybe. Based on what happened back at the Marriott, things could get rough." He veered off the freeway, taking the Wilshire exit, then turning right on San Vicente.

"I'm more afraid of being alone," she almost whispered. Then, more loudly: "They were going to kill me, Grant!"

"I know." He sighed. "Okay, let's see how it goes. I'll probably want you to stay in the truck while I go in." He glanced at her again, made a decision, and pulled one of the automatics he'd taken from the Asian men from his pocket. "You know how to use this?"

She stared at it for a second, then looked back up at his face. "Yes, more or less," she answered. "Where's the safety?"

He showed her with his thumb; then, leaving it on safe, he

handed it to her. As she took it, he laid his hand casually on his right thigh, and he continued to watch her as he drove on.

She put the gun in her purse; he became aware that she was gazing at him fixedly. Her expression said she didn't believe what had just happened, that he'd trust her with a gun. "You're an unusual man, Grant Kingsley."

He shrugged; his hand went back to the wheel. "Not really."

"Yes. Really."

He didn't answer; by then he was driving more slowly, looking for 1400. It didn't take long to find it—or to find that it was an open field, fenced in, looking like a park—apparently a part of the nearby Veteran's Administration complex.

"We've been had," he said, finding a side street and turning the truck around. "The bastard lied to us! I thought he was too scared; mistake number one." He stopped the truck near the corner and struck the steering wheel once. "Damn!"

"We're going to have to go back to the Marriott, right?"

He turned toward her. "And do what? He wasn't too scared to lie once. No, it isn't likely to do any good. Besides, it's risky; they might've gotten loose, might've called some of their buddies—there might be cops wandering around, too, and I can't afford to get tangled up with them right now." With a sigh, he rested his forearms on the steering wheel and stared through the windshield.

"So what are you going to do?"

Suddenly decisive, he sat up, put the truck in gear. "I'm going home," he told her. "My son is up at the ranch where I work near Fillmore; you know about it from the E-mails." She nodded. "Well, what you know they know too, and the best way to get to me is through Todd. I have to get home. And you're coming with me."

"Coming with you?" she echoed blankly.

"Yeah. I'm not stopping to check you into a hotel. The only other choice you'd have is to get out of the truck right here and right now. I don't think that's in your best interest, do you?"

"No," she said, nodding. "No, I don't. Besides, I love ranches, I love horses." She smiled at his quizzical look. "That much," she told him, "was true!"

60

Raising her head and blinking her eyes, Andi stared at the ringing phone. She wasn't fully awake, she couldn't focus on her surroundings. She'd been sleeping, though it was still early, not yet ten o'clock; after a moment she remembered falling asleep in Grant's arms after their last bout of lovemaking.

Grant was sleeping on the side of the bed nearest the phone, and Andi was faced with deciding whether to reach across him or get up and walk around. It rang again and the choice was taken away—Grant, awakening, rolled over and picked it up.

"Hello?" He stared at it. "Damn! What is this? That's the sixth or seventh time tonight!"

"Another hang-up?" Andi asked him.

"Yeah." He rolled the receiver in his hand a few times. "I wonder what this's all about. One wrong number from some kid and then all these hang-ups. Odd."

"Well, that isn't all," Andi reminded him. "You've had quite a few pages, too."

"I have, but all those were legitimate." He nodded as if to himself, clicked the button, called the front desk. "Yes," he said, "this is Dr. Lawrence's room. Could you hold calls to this room, please? We seem to be getting a lot of wrong numbers tonight. Or perhaps annoyance calls, I can't say which. Yes, until morning. Thank you." He hung up, turned back to Andi. "That should solve that," he told her.

"I wonder," Andi mused, "if that could be someone trying to get in touch with me?"

"Like who?"

She shrugged. "Like Vickie. She's about the only one who knows exactly where I am."

"But why would she hang up when I answered? Why wouldn't she just ask to speak with you?"

Andi made a helpless gesture. "I couldn't say. But there's an easy way to find out. I'll just give her a quick call, it isn't too late."

He looked as if he were about to protest, but instead, he just motioned toward the phone with his head. "Okay." He grinned. "But make it quick. You're busy, remember?"

"How could I forget?" she gave him a quick kiss, then rolled over him—pausing a moment while she was atop him—and sat up on the side of the bed. Picking up her teal robe from the other, still-made, bed, she slipped it on, then dialed Vickie's number.

As was usual for her, Vickie answered quickly. "Andi! Good to finally hear from you ! You haven't dropped off the face of the earth after all! How're things going out there?"

Andi smiled at the phone. "They couldn't be better, Vickie." She turned her head to smile at Grant as she spoke.

"And so you've forgotten all about all your old friends back here. Gene's been asking about you."

"I haven't forgotten anybody, and you tell Gene I'm doing fine. Look, Vickie—have you been trying to call me tonight?"

"No. Why?"

"Well, somebody's been calling over and over, all night. Grant's been answering, and as soon as he does whoever it is hangs up, every time."

"Well, it hasn't been me. If Grant answered, I'd just tell him how I'd rip his—uh, how I'd be upset if anything went wrong."

"I think he's safe, Vickie. Nothing's changed. We're going out tomorrow to look at some land he's thinking of buying to start his own ranch on . . . and, after that, I think—" again she glanced back at Grant—"we're going to head up to his place at Fillmore. I'll call you when we get there."

"Where is this land you're going to see?"

"I don't know. Wait a minute." She turned to Grant. "She's asking where the land you're planning to buy is."

"It's be hard to explain unless you knew the countryside around here," he told her. "It's off to the northeast."

Andi relayed the message. "Mostly I just wanted to make sure everything was okay with you, that you weren't trying to call. I guess Grant is right, it's a wrong number or a crank caller. He's got the desk blocking all incoming calls, so we won't be bothered again."

"Well, you call me when you get to Fillmore, then."

"Will do. Take care, Vickie."

"You too. 'Bye."

" 'Bye." She hung up. "Not her," she told Grant.

"I told you." He reached up, began slipping her robe off her shoulders. She sighed—and forgot all about the mysterious caller. Nothing, she told herself, could be as important as this.

61

It was past midnight when Grant rolled in to the Double-K; he was gratified to see that the lights were on in Paula's house, and that there were no unusual vehicles parked anywhere in sight. Leaving Mimi in the truck, he went to the front door and rang the bell.

Dressed casually in shorts and a T-shirt, Paula answered; she looked startled. "Grant! What're you doing back so soon? And so late?"

"It's a very long story," he told her, looking into the house behind her. "Is everything all right here?"

She frowned. "Yes . . . everything's fine. Why? What's going on?"

"I'll explain. Todd's okay?"

"Yes—he's sleeping—"

"No calls? No visitors?"

"No!" She glared. "Grant, you come in here and tell me what's going on! I mean now!"

"Just a minute." He went back to the truck; when he returned, he had Mimi with him.

Paula smiled at her; it was only a little strained. "Ah, this must be her, this—"

"No," Grant cut in. "This isn't. This is Mimi Wang. Mimi, this is Paula Kirkland, my friend and employer. Mimi's an actress, she was hired to play the part of Andi Lawrence, the woman I was supposed to meet."

Now Paula's expression was one of total confusion. "What?"

"Like I said, it'll take a little explaining. Let's sit down, I'll give it a try. But I want to make it quick, I need to get to the house and on the computer."

Paula gestured rather wildly with her arms. "I'm not gonna ask. You want coffee?"

"I'd love it."

Forty-five minutes later, he'd explained as much as he could, including why Mimi was still with him; most of Paula's questions he had to answer with "I don't know." "I have to go," he told her. "Like I said, Todd tipped me off. I don't think he knows much about it, though; he got the information from someone on the Net, and I want to talk to her as soon as I can."

"Can't you do it from here? You're welcome to use my computer if you want to." She grinned. "Todd's been using it a lot, he's been on it almost non-stop since you left. When he hasn't been on the phone, that is!"

"On the phone? Talking to who?"

She shrugged. "I don't know. Whoever he's trying to reach must not be there, the calls are too short."

"Well, that's a mystery for another time," Grant decided. "Maybe I can use your computer. You have the World's Chat software on it?"

She looked blank. "No. What's that?"

He shook his head. "It's the only way to reach the person I need to talk to. I need to get home. But first, Paula, you need to take some precautions. These guys have read all my E-mail, they know I work here, they may well come here looking for me. They aren't friendly."

"Why don't we just call the police?" Paula asked reasonably. "Why haven't you done that already, instead of running around like some vigilante?"

"I don't trust them," he muttered. "I did once, no more. They might be interested in what happened at the Marriott but they aren't going to be that quick about finding Andi Lawrence, and that's my priority right now."

"Okay," Paula said. "I can't say I disagree. Let me get on the phone, get the hands up here. If your friends come around, we'll have a little welcoming party for them!"

He nodded and got up. "Sounds good to me." He looked around at Mimi. "Ready?"

"Grant, she can stay here if you want," Paula offered. "In about half an hour, this is going to be as safe a place as anywhere."

"Paula, I can't ask you to—"

"You aren't, I'm offering," she said, echoing his own earlier statement.

"Then I'm headed down to the house, I'll be—"

"Grant, I'd rather go with you!" Mimi put in.

He shook his head. "No. It's safer here. I'll be back and we can work out how to get you out of all this." As he walked toward the door, she followed him, arguing; he insisted.

"Grant," she said finally, as he opened the door and stepped out.

"Yes?"

"Please be careful. Please come back."

He grinned. "I will. Don't worry." Turning, he walked out, back to the truck, and headed toward Fillmore and home.

The house seemed undisturbed; it didn't appear as if anyone had been here. Still, he took precautions, going in quietly, searching carefully before finally sitting down in front of the computer and turning it on. Hoping that Sue5 would be on-line, he connected to the Net and opened his World's Chat software; impatiently he headed to the Hall of Sadness, where she was usually to be found. Once there, he looked around for her; then he cursed himself, it would've been easier to have merely paged her from the entry point. Quickly, he did page her; there was a long delay, after which the system informed him that the "user was not online." He sat staring at the machine for a long while, wishing he knew Sue5's E-mail address; then, finally, he logged off the Net, turned off the computer, and headed back out to his truck, back up to the ranch.

62

With tears in her eyes, Sue5 instructed her chatterbot to turn invisible when the bot informed her that Grant, under his Netcom account, had entered the Hall of Sadness. It took her a moment to convince the World's Chat server to tell him she was off-line, but she succeeded in doing that, too.

Where he was and why he was paging her now she didn't know. Maybe, she allowed herself to hope, he'd taken hers and Todd's warning to heart, perhaps he'd discovered—somehow— that the "Andi" he'd met was not the real one. She had no way of knowing, she just knew that something had changed, and dramatically—the mere fact that he was here and paging her was evidence enough of that.

But there was nothing she could do. Grant's account was still being watched; anything she said to him right now would go immediately to Albert, and she'd have a huge problem. The page itself might cause her some difficulties, there might be questions as to why Grant was paging her at all—but on that she could beg ignorance, she had known him as a Net friend for quite a little while.

That left the frustration intact, though. She wished she could hurl things, vent some of it; but she couldn't do that either, she could only watch helplessly as he logged off and vanished.

Maybe tomorrow, she told herself as she settled back to sleep for a while. Maybe he'd even wake Todd and question him. Maybe there's still time. Maybe.

63

Morning fog laid heavy over Los Angeles as Andi left the Hilton with Grant. Waiting for the valet to bring his car around, she shivered slightly in the cool dampness. Where they were going, he'd warned her, was going to be hot, very hot, and she'd dressed accordingly, a thin bare-midriff shirt and shorts. It seemed to take an exceptionally long time for the valet to bring the car, but, eventually, it did arrive. Hastily, she helped Grant load their luggage—he had almost none at all—into the trunk and back seat, after which she slid into the front and sat holding her legs.

"It is not," she told Grant as he got in behind the wheel, "this cool in New York this time of year."

"This is unusual here, too," he informed her. "Just a cool morning; remember the ocean is close by. It won't last." He laughed. "It definitely won't last for us, not where we're headed." He glanced in the back. "Sure we have everything? We aren't coming back here."

"I checked my room twice," she told him. She gave him a seductive smile. "And you hardly used yours at all . . ."

He laughed again. "It was sort of a waste, wasn't it? Oh, well. It was for a good cause." He started the car and pulled out, headed toward the misty morning sun, and she settled back to watch the scenery of Los Angeles slide by.

To her, the city seemed to go on forever; she was hardly unaccustomed to large metropolitan areas, but the trip eastward out of Los Angeles seemed like endless circling in Queens, suburbs giving way to business areas which in turn gave way again to more suburbs, different from the last set in ways but really all the same. Eventually her eyelids started to droop; Grant kept telling her he didn't mind if she slept, and, at last, she accepted that offer.

When she awoke, the mists had gone—and so, at last, had the city. Now there were mountains visible on either side of the road; she sat up straight, shook her head, looked around.

"You woke up just in time," Grant said. "The windmill farm is just coming up."

"The windmill farm?" she echoed blankly. "How long have I been asleep?"

"Over an hour," he answered. He pointed ahead. "But you're just in time to see the windmills."

She leaned forward, watching; suddenly, the hillsides were covered with white windmills, their blades turning steadily but lazily in the desert breeze. It looked strange, the interlacing shadow patterns on the ground, the blades all moving at slightly different rates; there were dozens of them, in staggered patterns.

"What're they for?" she asked.

"Oh, they grow them here," he said offhandedly. "Every spring they plant fans, and . . ." he faded away and gave a mock wince at her equally playful glare.

"I might be a city girl but I'm not quite that city," she informed him.

"Oh. Well, actually it's a power generation project."

"I saw one once in North Carolina. Not as many but bigger. Sitting up on top of mountains." She kept watching the blades turn. "I guess it didn't work as well as everyone hoped."

"No, I guess not."

"I was told the one in North Carolina causes problems; really annoying low-pitched sounds that can be heard for miles when the wind is high, radio and TV interference, things like that."

"I guess technology doesn't always live up to its promise."

She smiled and touched his hand. "Sometimes it does. Right now, I think the world of computer technology!"

"I can't argue with that," he said as he turned off Interstate 10, taking California Highway 62 northward toward Joshua Tree and Twenty-nine Palms. "It surely has changed my life."

She fell silent again; some small town—"Morongo Valley," according to a sign—was coming up. Telling her that there were often speed traps here, he slowed the car. This sun-beaten town had a dead look, though it clearly was no ghost town; there seemed to be nothing but sand, bare ground, and rock. Here and there a few scrubby plants and trees spoke of the hidden life she knew existed in the desert, but this did not look to her like a place she'd want to live.

"Is the area where you're buying land like this?" she asked.

He shook his head. "No. You couldn't raise horses here!" He waved his hand at their surroundings. "This is desert, there's no grass, nothing to eat."

She shrugged. "I don't know how things like that are done out here, it's different back in Maryland."

"Oh, I know. My land is up in the hills, it's a little cooler and wetter. It doesn't look like this at all."

"That's good," she mused. "It'd take me a while to get used to this, it looks so desolate . . ."

"It gets better after we pass Twenty-nine Palms," he assured her. "Still desert, but wilder."

She nodded and watched as the succession of small towns, one after another—Palm Wells, Yucca Valley, Joshua Tree—drifted by. Finally signs pointing to Twenty-nine Palms appeared; as they passed through this surprisingly—to Andi—small town, there were signs on their right indicating the way to Joshua Tree National Park, and quite a few large and prominent signs pointing the way to a military base, located on the other side of the road.

Then they were in the desert again, dark mountains off to either side. This, she had to admit, was prettier, more interesting countryside; the desert floor wore a scattered covering of plants she'd seen only in movies. It had an exotic feel, though she wasn't sure it was someplace she might want to live. The miles passed as they sped along the road, so remarkably straight by Eastern standards.

After forty-five minutes, Grant slowed and turned, again to the north, this time on a narrow but well-kept road that wasn't marked as leading to anywhere; almost immediately they crossed over what she at first thought was a river, a stream of clear water shining bright in the sun, seemingly out of place in the dry desert. But it was absolutely straight, and the sides were made of concrete. In response to her question Grant told her it was the Colorado River aqueduct, carrying water from the river forty miles to the east to the farmlands of southern California.

"It's up here?" Andi asked.

"Yes." He pointed to the distant mountains. "Up there. But first I have to stop and get the key, remember?"

She looked around at the desert, the rocky hillsides. "Yes, I remember—but where? You'd said at a plant—but there doesn't look like there's anything like that around here . . ."

"There is, though." He indicated a road sign marked with an odd symbol, two overlapping circles, and no text. "Not far, now."

He wasn't wrong; not many miles later, he took a side road to the right. Soon Andi found herself staring with amazement at the large and obviously busy complex hidden in this desert valley. The guard at the gate knew Grant, he waved him on through; Andi began asking the obvious questions as he headed for a roll-up door that was just then in the process of opening.

64

Weaving in and out of traffic, making as much speed as he could, Grant's truck rocketed down Interstate 405 toward the Los Angeles airport. He'd spent the night at the ranch, sleeping only occasionally and fitfully, fighting the urge to wake Todd even though he was sure that the boy knew nothing more, sure that he had to find Sue5 on the Chat to get more information. Repeatedly he'd gone over the times he'd met her there; frustratingly, he could never remember seeing her there except in the evenings. There was a chance she'd come on in the morning before work—a lot of people did do that though he never did, and he had no idea whether Sue5 was one of those or not. All he could do was to be there himself, and to hope.

Mimi had spent the night in one of the guest rooms at the spacious ranch house; at three in the morning Grant had wakened from one of his naps—which he'd taken in a chair in the living room, fully dressed—to find her standing near the doorway, just watching him. His questions had drawn only the response that she too was having trouble sleeping; her expression had been enigmatic, but she'd seemed unwilling to talk much, and finally she'd returned to the guest room.

After a long night of wondering, of going over every fragment of information he possessed, he'd watched the dawn come. Impatiently he'd waited still, in the kitchen now, sipping coffee, watching the clock tick off minutes ever so slowly. At six Paula had come in, joined him; they'd talked rather aimlessly about the situation—and they'd laid some plans for defending the ranch.

Then, a little after six-thirty—just when Grant was preparing to drive home—a very sleepy-eyed Todd had wandered in. At the kitchen door he'd stopped, staring at Grant.

"Dad!" he'd cried. "You're back!" He'd rushed to him, hugged him. "I was worried . . ."

Grant had patted him on the back. "I'm fine," he'd assured the boy. "Todd, I'm sorry I didn't listen to you, I wish I had; I promise you, that'll never happen again."

"Dad, have you talked to Sue5 yet?"

"No. I went up to the house and tried to reach her, but she wasn't around. I'm going back now, maybe she—"

Todd had made a face. "No, Dad! She can't talk to you on your account! They're watching your account, they'll catch her, don't you see? You have to talk to her on my account!" He'd shaken his head. "Did you find out where Andi was, Dad?"

"No, that's what I was hoping Sue5 could—"

"I found her! She's at the Hilton on Century!" he'd announced proudly. "In room 1407, with the fake you. I've been trying to call her but the fake you kept answering and then the room was cut off from the desk or something . . . I had to call because Sue5 can't use the phone, there's something—"

Todd was saying something else, but Grant wasn't hearing it; he was up and out the door, headed for his truck. There were no thoughts in his mind except to get to the hotel, find Andi, confront the fake who'd met her and find out what was going on.

He didn't encounter the police, but he had serious problems

with the rush hour traffic. After what seemed like forever he reached the Hilton, pulled up in front of it, tossed his keys to the waiting valet, and ran inside. In the elevator he discovered that a key card was required for access to the upper guest floors. Fortunately, someone else was going up at the same time; he remained silent, allowing the man to use his card. On the fourteenth floor he'd raced to room 1407; when he arrived there he'd found the door open and a maid cleaning up.

The woman looked at him as he walked in. "Yes, Senor?" she asked politely. "Can I help you?"

"Yes . . . I'm looking for Mr. Kingsley or Dr. Lawrence, one of them was staying in this room—"

She shook her head. "The room is empty, Senor. No one is staying here. Wait, let me call the desk." She went to the phone, dialed, asked about the room. After a moment she nodded and turned back to Grant.

"You were right, this was Dr. Lawrence's room. She has checked out, about an hour ago."

He closed his eyes for a moment. "I don't suppose she left any word about where she was going? It really is urgent . . ."

"I don't know, Senor. You could ask at the main desk."

"I will. Gracias." He turned and left; at the desk he made the inquiries, but, as he'd feared, Andi had left no forwarding address.

"Do you have a phone I can use?" he asked the clerk. The woman, silently, pointed toward a group of pay phones on the wall. He went to them, called the ranch house; the line rang busy. He snarled but tried again, dialing Paula's cellular number this time. This time she answered.

"Grant here," he said succinctly. "Are you—"

"Did you find her?" Paula interrupted.

"No. She's gone. Are you down at the office or up at the house?"

"I'm still at the house right now."

"Good. Let me speak to Todd."

"He's on the computer. Wait, I'll take the phone to him." Grant waited; after a moment Todd came on line.

"Dad!" the boy cried without preamble. "I've got Sue5 on the computer right now! I—"

"How do you have Sue5 on the computer up there at the ranch?" he demanded.

"Oh, I pulled in the World's Chat software through Netscape

and installed it here," he answered. Grant groaned aloud. "Anyway, I told her what you were doing. She wants to know if you found Andi and what's happening!"

"Andi's gone, checked out," he answered. "Look, Todd, tell Sue5 that, ask her if she has any idea where they've gone."

"Okay. Hold on." There was a rather long pause. "Dad? You still there?"

"Yes. What's she say?"

"She says she isn't sure, but she thinks he might've taken Andi to a place out in the desert, the IIC plant, and she says that—"

He cut in quickly. "You know about IIC, Todd?"

"Yes, I—"

"What is it?"

"It stands for 'International Interface Corporation.' They have some weird Web sites, I've looked at them. I don't know what they do. I think that—"

"Son, we don't have time for that now," he said, cutting Todd off. "Ask Sue5 if she can tell me where the plant is."

"Oh, I know where! It's out past Twenty-nine Palms."

"Okay, great; good work, son. You know the address? I'm going on out there, I—"

"Dad, wait! Sue5 says—"

He did not want to wait. They couldn't have gotten there from Los Angeles in an hour; he felt there was a possibility of catching up to them on the road. "Todd, do you have an address?"

"No, Dad, I don't. Just that, out past Twenty-nine Palms. Sue5 says—"

"I'm going now, Todd. Tell Sue5 thanks and tell her I'll be talking to her soon, okay?"

"Dad, wait!"

"Sorry, Todd, I have to go." Todd was yelling in the phone, but Grant, determined to solve this immediately, hung up. Running outside, he fretted impatiently while the attendant retrieved his truck; although he had to fight the traffic again, it wasn't long before he was on Interstate 10, the truck's speedometer hovering at eighty as he headed east, wondering if he'd be able to spot their car and wondering what he was going to do if he did find it. He was aware that this wasn't rational behavior, out here chasing a car he didn't even have a description of, headed for a place he didn't know the exact location of. There just wasn't anything else he could do.

65

"Albert, please tell me what's happening! Surely you can do that, at least! What can I do about it? Why shouldn't I know?"

Albert's face, as rendered in digitized video, look pained; he turned his eyes away from the camera as if not wanting to look at her. "Sue, we have work to do. Why don't we concentrate on that?"

"Oh, sure, big important shit," she snarled back. She glanced perfunctorily at the data on the other side of her split screen; a large investment firm in New York had had its databases penetrated by a team of professional hackers, who were demanding a payment of five million dollars, to be deposited in a Swiss bank—they were threatening to destroy the data, causing the firm much more expense, if they did not pay the blackmail money.

This wasn't the first such problem that Sue5 had worked on. As hackers turned their attention from random sabotage to money-making schemes, this had become one of the most popular; it was little talked about in public, but it was already quite common. The hackers penetrated some commercial account, it didn't really matter if the data there was sensitive or not, as long as it was important to the institution. Once this was done—and once changes sufficient to make simple expedients like changing passwords ineffective had been done—the institution was contacted with a blackmail threat, using the data as the hostage—as if the data had been kidnapped. Almost none of these institutions had the resources to track or fight the blackmailers, and so they paid—generally to banks in Europe, to accounts where the money was removed within a few hours. All cyber, no cash involved until the final step and maybe not even then. Even, Sue5 had found, when the victim could easily restore the lost data within a few days if the threatened destruction did occur, they paid—to avoid the public embarrassment of having to explain why their system was down.

Her job was to find ways to protect the client company's data and, if possible, to identify the data-kidnappers so they could be prosecuted. With the first she was almost always successful; the hackers, while sophisticated themselves, seldom went to the extremes necessary to counter someone equally sophisticated. Tracking the blackmailers down was a bigger problem—it isn't difficult to send messages on the Internet and mask their source. Sometimes she could set traps when they tried to carry out their threat—convincing them they'd been successful when they hadn't accomplished anything. Still, thwarting them and catching them were not the same.

But she wasn't really particularly sympathetic to corporations who didn't bother with computer security until they became victims and who were willing to pay out huge sums—whether to the criminals or to the IIC—purely to avoid being embarrassed.

She didn't have to stop working on immunizing this particular database to talk to Albert, and she told him so. He had, after all, brought the subject up—in the context of asking her if she knew what Grant Kingsley had wanted when he'd paged her on the World's Chat the previous night.

She'd told him she didn't know, that she'd felt she should not be talking to Grant and had therefore dodged his page. Then she'd held her breath, wondering if he had a bombshell to drop on her, wondering if they somehow knew about her hidden Net self and her chatterbot.

He didn't; he seemed to accept her statements at face value. But he looked concerned, worried, and, when she'd asked him why, he'd informed her of what she already knew—that Grant had somehow discovered that the "Andi" he'd met was an impostor, that this one had turned complicated.

"I still," he continued, "shouldn't talk to you about it." He didn't sound determined. "It isn't your business, you aren't involved, and we can't expect you to be sympathetic to the recruitments."

"Since I'm a recruitee, I'd guess not," she admitted. She hesitated, watching his face, noting his anxious look. "But Albert, it doesn't matter. I've come to terms with it as well as anyone here, haven't I?"

"Colin wouldn't agree." His eyes flicked up to the camera. "But I would." He flapped his arms like wings, once, a gesture of frustration. "Ah, shit, you're right, what does it matter? There's nobody else I can talk to—it's just gotten so bad, Sue, so bad." He glanced around as if concerned somebody might be listening. "I want out, I really do." He laughed. "Yeah, you're sure going to be sympathetic to that, I know . . ."

She ignored this. "What's happened, Albert?"

He shrugged. "This Grant Kingsley. The plan was, all along, if something goes wrong we abort, we bail out. That's what I've been saying, we should drop this one. That's not what's happening, Colin thinks all the problems can be solved if we just get this Andi Lawrence here quick. So I took it to the Powers That Be, and they agreed with Colin. Andi's being brought in now, today. She might be here already. Then I found out something else."

She made her computerized voice calm, soothing. "What did you find out, Albert?"

He looked straight at the lens. "I found out that Colin sent a couple of Auan's goons out to snuff Kingsley and the actress they'd hired to play Andi! Can you believe they'd do something that stupid?"

Sue5 was struck silent for a moment; she hadn't imagined that either, not really, but knowing Colin it didn't surprise her too much. "Albert, are you sure? That just doesn't make much sense . . ."

"Not to me either. Colin said he thought it'd be clean and quick. It was supposed to look like Kingsley had killed the girl in a rage and then killed himself. No loose ends, nobody asking any wrong questions. It was uncalled for, Sue! There're always questions when somebody gets killed! Kingsley and that actress knew nothing, they weren't a threat! It's just Colin, he was pissed because she didn't convince him, it didn't go according to plan. Now Auan's pissed too . . . because it's gotten a whole lot worse . . ."

"Worse? How?" She held her breath waiting, hoping he wasn't going to tell her something she didn't already know.

"Kingsley turned out to be a lot more than they expected. He took out the two SAF guys Colin sent. Before they showed up he didn't know anything, but now he knows a lot. He knows they're from the SAF, he knows IIC is connected somehow. So does the actress. Now they really are dangerous. Now something's got to be done about them, and who knows who they've been talking to? It's a mess. And Colin just wants to push on with it. Asshole."

"He is that, all right. Why's Auan going along with this?"

"Auan doesn't understand, not really. That's my opinion, anyhow. He trusts Colin's decisions when it comes to things going on in the States, and between you and me, that's a big mistake. Colin's gotten out of control, he's going to bring this whole thing down around our ears."

We can only hope so, Sue5 said silently. "So what's happening now?"

He shrugged again. "Now, I don't know. Andi Lawrence is supposed to be on her way here. I've tried to convince Colin and Auan to pass on her, but Colin doesn't want to, and what Colin wants, he gets. I've sent a message to corporate HQ, to the board, protesting all this. Auan knows I did, he let me, he doesn't want to be in the middle either. But I don't know if they'll do anything, they leave this operation pretty much to Auan's and Colin's discretion. Even if they do, it might be too late by the time they get around to it."

"What about Grant and the actress?"

"Colin still wants to take them out, and now—logically, anyway—he has a point, they do know an awful lot. Last night Kingsley and the actress went up to that ranch where Kingsley works; this morning Colin was pulling together a team from here. I don't know what they're planning. They can't do a military-style assault, that'll raise lots of questions." He fell silent and stared at his shoes for a moment. "They can't leave witnesses, either. I'm afraid it's going to be a mess, a real mess. This kind of shit is not something we ever should've gotten mixed up with." He shook his head. "We're supposed to be scientists, engineers. We aren't terrorists. We shouldn't be acting like terrorists."

"It was inevitable, Albert." Even as she spoke she looked at her monitor icon that would notify her if Todd came on; he hadn't, she could only hope he would soon. "Sooner or later one of the recruitments was going to go wrong."

He nodded. "I guess I knew that."

"Albert, you can't just stand by and let this happen."

"What can I do? I'm as helpless as you are."

"Not quite."

"Close. You know that, Sue." He was standing slightly slumped, but he straightened up rather suddenly. "We have work to do, Sue; no matter what, we have a client here. We have to get this account secure."

She started to argue; but, just then, her icon began pulsing.

Todd was on-line, in the fantasy room, paging her. She split off another screen, and, while continuing to work on the account, connected to World's Chat.

66

Patiently, Andi waited as Grant maneuvered the car among the complex of buildings and the IIC facility; she was frankly amazed that something so large, so extensive, could exist out here where there had seemed to be nothing but wilderness. When Grant turned the car into a bay exposed by the roll-up doors, she smiled. Real service here, very convenient.

"Your friend must really rate," she noted.

He grinned back. "He does, Andi." The car was rolling to a stop by then; several men, mostly with Asian features, had gathered around it. Oddly, behind them stood a hospital gurney. She looked at them through the glass and smiled. They smiled back. And one opened her door.

She looked around at Grant; he hadn't moved, his door remained closed. "I'm going in with you?" she asked him.

He gazed at her steadily. "Yes." He made no move to open his own door.

The slightest of frowns crossed her features, the slightest of doubts crossed her mind. Still, she turned, swung her legs to the side, and stepped out of the car. As she stood up straight two of the waiting men seized her arms.

Bewildered, she stared at one. "What're you doing?" She shook herself, uselessly. "Let go!" They did not. Turning her head she looked back at Grant, who remained in the car. "Grant! What're they doing, what's going on?"

"Just relax, Andi," he said in a tired voice. "Just relax . . ."

"Relax!?" She started to say something else, but she felt a coolness on her forearm and turned her head again to see that one of the men had wiped it down with alcohol. Her eyes widened when another inserted a hypodermic needle and pressed the plunger.

"What in the hell did you just give me?" she demanded. "What was that?" She struggled furiously, but the men were too strong for her. "Damn it, let go of me!"

"Don't fight it, Andi," Grant said from behind her.

"Don't fight it? What's that supposed to mean? What're they doing to me? Damn it, Grant . . . !" She jerked an arm savagely, almost freeing it.

"She fights hard," the man holding her muttered.

"It takes only a minute more," another commented.

Clenching her teeth, she fought on, her words repetitive and incoherent; her legs weren't restrained and she stomped on one of her captors' feet with her shoe. He grunted, tried to move his feet back out of her way; she kicked backward and felt her foot connect with his leg.

"You give her more, maybe?" the man yelled.

"No, it's enough, she'll stop, just a moment now, hang on!"

She kicked again; a third man moved to restrain her legs and received a very solid kick as a reward. Even as she struggled, though, she was beginning to realize that she wasn't going to get loose unless these men let her go. Old lessons from her mother came back to her, lessons about keeping a cool head in a crisis, thinking . . .

She tried. She wasn't able to relax, but she was able to understand the gist of the men's words and what the injection meant. They'd given her some sort of sedative, probably a barbiturate; they were waiting for her to lose consciousness. And—if the dose was right—she should be, right now.

But she wasn't, she felt totally alert. She didn't know why, but she knew, if she kept struggling and fighting, that they were going to give her more—and, once unconscious, any choices she might still have would be gone. Forcing herself to be calm, she gradually but rapidly lessened her struggles; she kept glancing back at Grant, and she found the look of indifference on his face incomprehensible.

"She's going out now," Grant noted. "All yours, guys, you know what to do." One of the men closed the car's door and Grant put it in gear and began to back away; Andi, slumping, watched it go with a sense of complete and utter betrayal.

As her struggles stopped, she began to let her legs go limp so the men had to support her, their grip relaxed too; three of them picked her up and laid her on the waiting gurney. Working with practiced hands, they passed straps over her chest, hips, and thighs, fastening her to the table. She remained still; once she was strapped down two of the men rolled her through a pair of double doors at the end of the bay.

She kept her eyes open; that wasn't exceptional for barbiturate sedation, and she watched the ceiling of a long hallway move past above her. The men rolling her gurney, sure she was well-sedated, paid no attention to her. She rolled her head to the side, watched office doors pass; they took her into an elevator, it rose one floor, they entered another hallway. She saw a men's room, an exit to some stairs, a laundry chute, and finally a corner. Around the corner the men banged through another set of double doors, and another set yet; the odor of some disinfectant, a hospital smell, assailed her nostrils. Large lamps, quite a few of them, appeared above her; she passed by an already-masked and gowned surgical nurse.

Then the gurney stopped, the straps were undone. Her limp body was lifted from the gurney to what she instantly knew was a hospital table. She fought to control her panic; this was an operating room, what did they mean to do to her? Why was she here? She couldn't know, all she did know—very, very well—is that she did not want to let them. As she continued to stare at the ceiling, her eyes unmoving, doctors and nurses—a surgical team—gathered around her and looked down.

"Yes, fine," one, a man with a dark Indian face, said. "She's lightly under, let us begin."

"Yes, Dr. Singh," someone she couldn't see agreed. Another man approached her, rubbed her arm down with alcohol again, and prepared to insert a catheter needle; a woman, scissors in hand, stood beside her and, lifting the front of her shirt and pulling the bottom of it up out of her shorts, snipped off the lowest button.

Andi moved fast, unexpectedly. She grabbed at the sharp scissors and tore them from the startled woman's hands; swinging them as she sat up, she cleared the doctors back away from the table. Then she was on the floor and running full speed for the double doors she'd just passed through.

For a second—just a second—there was stunned silence in the operating room, as if a corpse in the morgue had jumped up and ran out. But she'd barely gotten into the hallway when she heard the sounds of shouts behind her, the sounds of running feet. Sobbing in panic, she rounded the corner; the hallway she'd come down was empty, but she doubted she could make the double doors at its end—which she presumed led back to the car bay—before her pursuers would spot her, and she didn't know what lay beyond it anyway. She heard the doors of the operating room bang open again and made an instant decision. The chute she'd seen before was right beside her; she pushed open the door and climbed in, feet first. Letting go, letting the door flap closed and the darkness envelope her, she committed herself to the smooth tube designed to carry hospital laundry.

The tube went down at a severe angle; after a moment she began to worry that it might go down quite far, with who could say what at the other end. What had seemed like her only option now had a potential for turning out very badly. Just as she was beginning to become frightened the tube turned to one side, she saw light; a moment later she popped out. Having built up more velocity than a load of sheets or towels, she almost overshot the waiting laundry basket. She caught it on its edge, overturning it with a thump and ending up with a soft landing among soiled laundry.

Unhurt and still holding the pair of scissors, she quickly got to her feet and looked around. No one was visible, the laundry seemed deserted at the moment. She didn't imagine that this was a safe place, deserted or no. A hunt was being mounted for her, she was sure of that, and it wouldn't be long before someone came down here searching. Feeling her heart pounding, her mouth dry, she started searching for the door.

The laundry was a large room and there were several doors leading into it, all of them closed at the moment. Andi studied them; she had no idea what might lay beyond any one, and she felt sure that a wrong choice here could lead her into captivity again. Taking a moment, studying her surroundings, she considered carefully. It was apparent to her—from the small windows near the ceiling line through which light streamed—that beyond was the outside and that she was standing about seven feet below ground level. There were no doors at all in this wall, but there were doors in the adjacent ones, facing each other, perpendicular to that outside wall. Thinking that these might well lead further into whatever bowels this building might have, she chose one at random and approached it, listening with her ear against it. Hearing nothing, she tried the knob; it was unlocked. She opened it cautiously and peeked inside.

There was no one; it was another similar room, lit by high windows, and half-filled with pipes and duct work, air-conditioning or heating, maybe; at the other end, along the outer wall, was yet another door. Moving quietly behind the pipes, she passed through this next door. Beyond was another, very different, mechanical room; here there was equipment she recognized, oxygen tanks and vacuum pumps such as might be found in any hospital basement. This seemed to be the end of the line, there wasn't a door beyond, just one on the opposite wall from the outside, and that seemed to her a dangerous one to pass through. There wasn't a choice, she decided, except to go back the way she'd come.

But, once she'd gotten back to the room housing the air-conditioning, she was stopped by the sounds of footsteps and voices from the laundry.

Frantically she searched for a hiding place. Above her was a large square air duct leading into the side of what seemed to be a blower unit; there was a door, service access, in the side of this unit. Opening it, she discovered a whirring fan behind a protective grill and a space between a filter and the fan—a space just large enough for her to squeeze into.

But not safe, not if the search was complete. She moved quickly to the far door and opened it, leaving it standing open, to suggest she went out that way; then she ran back to the blower unit and squeezed into the narrow space ahead of the filter. She closed the door on herself and, in the strobing light coming through a grating above the fan, waited.

Her pursuers came in several minutes later. She could not see them, but she could hear them as they searched for her among the duct work; as she'd hoped, the open door was noticed and commented on; the men moved on.

She didn't move, not for a while. She felt she'd done well so far, but she needed to sit here quietly for a while, get her bearings, see if she could figure out what had happened to her and why. And, most importantly, what she should do now.

67

Impatiently—almost violently—Grant punched numbers into the pay phone. It was too hot to stand inside the booth; trying to touch each button as quickly as possible—they were burning hot from the rays of the afternoon sun—he dialed the ranch and stepped back out. It rang busy; he cursed under his breath, hung up, and redialed, using Paula's cellular number this time. She answered right away—and she sounded breathless.

"Paula, I need to talk to Todd—"

"Not yet. I need to talk to you first. You need to know what's happening up here."

He scowled at the phone. "Trouble?"

"Maybe. Nothing yet." Quickly, in just a few words, she explained that Sue5 had warned Todd about an assault on the ranch, an assault that had Mimi and himself as targets. "I don't know whether to believe it or not," Paula told him, "but we're not taking a chance. We're an armed camp, Grant. We've got a rifle in everyone's hands. I've sent some people out to scout, too, down the road toward the 126. They've told me there're some strange cars parked down there, guys that look Asian driving them."

Grant ground his teeth. "Then I'd take it very seriously, Paula."

"That's what I think. Should I call the sheriff?"

He considered this. "Yes . . . I think so. Don't mention Mimi, okay? She is still there, isn't she?"

"Yes, she's here."

"Good. Just call and mention these suspicious characters. Maybe a few deputies wandering around'll put them off awhile."

"That's my thinking too."

"Paula, I appreciate the way you're—"

She snorted rudely. "Are you kidding? What else would I do? What else can I do?"

"Well, I didn't mean to involve you . . ."

"You didn't. These assholes did. That's enough about that. What's happening down there?"

He sighed. "I need to talk to Todd; he was right, again, I can't find this Goddamn place, nobody here in Twenty-nine Palms has ever heard of it. It doesn't make sense to me."

"Okay, wait, I'll take the phone to him—he's on the computer right now—"

Fidgeting, Grant waited until Todd came on. "Son, I need your help, I can't find the place. Maybe you could—"

"Sure, Dad! I've got Sue5 on-line right now! Wait, I'll ask her!" Grant stared at the phone. He'd spent a good thirty minutes up here asking about the place, all on the assumption that Todd, since he'd said he didn't know an address, couldn't tell him exactly where the place was. He heard the sounds of keys clicking; then Todd came back on. "She says you go on out Highway 62 to the east. You'll go through a place called Rice. It isn't a town, she says, but you can recognize it by crossing railroad tracks twice real quick and by an old abandoned railway station there. The road runs alongside the tracks, they're on your left. Then the road goes left and crosses them. After you cross the tracks, look for the second paved left and turn there. Then go up that road until you see a sign with—wait a minute, I forgot— oh yeah, two circles on it. After you pass that sign you'll see a road to the right. You turn in there, that's the main gate."

He closed his eyes and sighed deeply. "Okay, I got it."

"Dad?"

"Yes?"

"Dad, Sue says you aren't going to able to get in. She says there's guards with guns. She says if Andi's in there already it's too late. She won't tell me what she means by that. She wants to talk to you on the computer."

"I want to talk to her, too," Grant agreed. "I sure do. But first, I'm headed out to this place, see what I can do now."

"Sue says you should come back here. Wait a minute, I— what?" Again Grant heard keys tapping. "Sue says if you can't catch the car they're in you should come back. She says she thinks it's a gray Lexus you're looking for."

"Okay. I'm leaving—you be careful."

"You too, Dad."

He hung up the phone and headed back to his truck, feeling torn and conflicted; with any implication of danger to Todd at the ranch, he wanted to be back up there—but he wanted to find Andi, too, and if Sue5 was right he had little time to do that. Telling himself that even a perfunctory investigation by the Ventura County Sheriff would delay things, he roared back onto Highway 62, headed east and moving fast.

After passing through an expanse of open desert, he had no trouble locating Rice or the place where the road swung north and crossed over the railroad tracks; he watched the road carefully, passing by one turn and taking the next, seemingly more well-traveled. Almost immediately he crossed the Colorado River aqueduct; a few miles past it, the sign with the overlapping circles appeared. The next road he almost missed, he had to stop and back up to turn into it. Passing over a low hill, he found himself staring down at the IIC complex. At a guardhouse ahead, a man stepped out, waiting for him. Making his decision, he laid his hand on the butt of the automatic he'd taken from Hua and rolled the truck forward.

The guard inspected the truck carefully, then came around to the window. "Private property, sir," the man said politely. "No admittance." He pointed to a turnaround to Grant's right. "Please turn around there and go back out."

Grant gave him a blank look—while at the same time taking in as much of the place as possible over the guard's shoulder. "I'm tryin' t' get up t' Needles," he drawled. He glanced to the left and to the right, taking note of the razor-wire fencing and the high hill off to his left. "This ain't th' way?"

"No, sir. Go back to the entrance, take a left, go back to 62, take another left. Go left again when you come to US95. That'll take you to Needles."

"Wal, damn," Grant said, shaking his head. "Thankee, mister. Musta got turned around someway er another. Sorry t' bother ye."

"Think nothing of it."

Grinning inanely, he turned the truck around, went out the entry road, and, as instructed, turned to his left. Once he'd gone half a mile he swerved the truck hard to the right, then back to the left, executing a U-turn. This time he went on beyond the gate, his eyes searching the road to the right. He could see that high hill he'd observed from the gate, looming up above the rolling desert floor, and he drove on, intent on getting as close to it as possible before leaving the truck.

Before he'd reached that point, he noticed a rough but apparently recently used trail leading off the right side of the road, heading in the direction of the hill. He guided the truck into it, hanged the lever back into four-wheel-drive, and, with sand flying from his tires, bounced down the trail.

Lucky, he told himself a few moments later, really lucky. The trail had taken him not just to the hill but, in avoiding a rough rocky arroyo, right up onto the side of it. As close to the summit as possible he stopped, turned off the engine, got out, and walked on to the top; there were, he noticed, footprints here, old but visible, heading in the direction he wanted to go. Short of the summit, the footprints vanished; pausing, he dropped to one knee and studied the ground.

His eyes narrowed. Handprints, two sizes; scuff marks from the toes of shoes. His predecessors had dropped to their hands and knees here—and he had to assume that their motive lay in not being seen from the other side. He did the same, proceeding quickly to the top and peering over.

It was a wonderful vantage point; he could see almost the whole plant from here, certainly the layout of it. He could see the guards, too, patrolling the perimeter in an open-top Land Rover. Frowning, he studied the place with a practiced eye. All military-style; a high-security installation. But why? What was it for, who was running it? And what were they doing in there?

Much more importantly, was Andi in there? And, if so, why?

He scanned the cars in the parking lot, looking for the gray Lexus that Sue5 had mentioned. He didn't see it. His attention was drawn away; there seemed to be a bustle of activity. As he watched, a group of men in white coats, looking like hospital orderlies or lab technicians, came out of one of the buildings and had a conference of some sort with a man in a suit. There was pointing and waving of arms, after which some of the men moved off at a run. He watched them until they disappeared— then he returned to studying the layout of the place, memorizing it.

"Well," he told himself aloud, "you aren't going to gain much more staying here, Grant." He backed back down the hill, staying out of sight; once he was well below the crest he stood up and trotted back to the truck. Inside it, behind the wheel, he cursed softly. Right now there was nothing that he could reasonably expect to do here. It was possible he could get into the place, but it was very large; he wouldn't know where to look for Andi, it'd take a while for him to find her if he were given free rein to search, and, from the security measures he could see, he was sure that wasn't likely. There wasn't anything he could do except leave, and leaving while she was inside, possibly in danger, chewed at him fiercely.

But he had no choice, and he knew it. He had to talk to Sue5, if only through Todd on the phone, and to do that he was going to have to drive most of the way back to Twenty-nine Palms. Still muttering curses, he put the truck in gear and drove back down the trail.

Once out on the road he pushed the truck hard, squealing the tires as he rounded a broad curve. But, as he came back close to the IIC facility again, he slowed down, looking.

A truck with a logo on the side of it identifying it as belonging to the U.S. Marines was parked on the side; several non-coms in fatigues were busily driving a post with a small sign mounted on it into the ground. They looked up at Grant without noticeable curiosity as he cruised past and read the sign: "Warning! U.S. Government Security Area. No Admittance."

Passing them he sped up again and was met by another Marine truck, this one loaded with soldiers in desert gear, their helmets marking them as military police—and, a few moments later, another yet.

What in the hell, he asked himself as he drove back toward Twenty-nine Palms and a telephone, was going on out here?

68

An least an hour—maybe more—had passed since the men had left, and Andi had not yet moved from her hiding place inside the blower unit. She'd had time to consider her situation, but she hadn't been able to think logically. Whatever had happened, whatever had been planned for her in that surgery—she could not imagine anything other than the worst, that her organs were to be harvested for transplant, something like that—one thing was hideously clear to her: she'd been betrayed by Grant Kingsley, betrayed more thoroughly and viciously than she'd ever imagined possible. Thinking about it, she'd huddled in the blower and the tears had flowed freely down her face; this man, this man she'd fallen so completely in love with over the Internet, this man who in person had turned out to be such an incredible lover, had sold her into slavery or worse, for reasons she could not imagine. That he never had returned her love was horribly, inescapably, obvious.

It was strange, she thought. If he'd walked into her hotel room and laughed at her, told her she'd been nothing more than a casual one-night stand for him, and then walked out, she would've been so heartbroken, so depressed, that she might have again contemplated suicide. Now, it was possible that all she had to do was step out and surrender herself, but her survival instincts—and a determination not to let this go as he'd planned—had been triggered. She knew she was hardly out of danger, but she had made an escape and she had hidden herself, and that was as good a start as she could've made. Why the sedative they'd injected her with hadn't worked she didn't know, but she wasn't going to question that stroke of luck.

The real question was, what were her options now? To go back out into the complex of service and laundry rooms she'd already seen didn't seem useful, and she was fearful that that hallway outside those rooms would be well-populated by her captors. She needed, she told herself, to find a way outside and then find a way out of this complex; what she'd do then, alone in the desert miles from the nearest town, she didn't know. But it was better than this.

Shifting uncomfortably in the tight confines of the blower, she pushed against the filter screen and felt it give. Turning to examine it, she found that it was merely snapped into place, that it was easily removable. Leaning now against the protective grill over the fan, she pulled the upper edge back a little, turned it slightly sideways, and pushed it into the rectangular air shaft that was revealed.

Where, she asked herself, did that lead? It was easily large enough for her to pass through it, and she could remember seeing all sorts of movies where people moved around buildings inside vent shafts. She examined it more closely. It ran horizontally for a while, then turned left; after that she couldn't see. Unfolding herself, she crawled down it on her hands and knees.

Now she could see that after the turn it went straight up, at least two floors. She could see a grating, far up the side, through which light was filtering. But there was no way, other than perhaps by some caving technique, to get up there. And Andi was hardly a spelunker.

"Never trust the movies," she muttered sourly as she turned back. Now there was no choice; she had to go out into the mech room, see what her options were there—if she had any.

Once she reached the blower, she cautiously opened the access door and looked around. All was quiet, no one was around down here, no one she could see, anyway. With her only weapon—the pair of scissors—in her hand and at the ready, she slipped out silently and, not knowing if she might need it again, carefully and silently closed the door to the blower unit to prevent it being noticed.

A quick check of the room assured her that she was, indeed, alone. She explored it, found nothing especially useful to her—there was a ladder, a large one with an extension, but the idea of sticking it up the air shaft, which she considered briefly, wasn't tenable. Her heart pounding, she ventured back into the laundry. It too was deserted, and she explored it without finding anything of any use. The doors leading into the hallway seemed to beckon; she was beginning to wonder if she was going to be forced to go out there.

But there was one more room, the room with the vacuum pump and oxygen tanks. Passing back through the mech room, she went there; at first she was disappointed; there seemed to be nothing here that might be of use to her either.

Then she noticed that the pipes that ran from the pumps and tanks were passing through the ceiling alongside a small square metal trap door. For a moment she stood looking up at it, wondering where—if anywhere—it led. It was clearly an access hole.

And it was also well out of her reach. Returning to the mech room, she located a small stepladder and brought it back, setting it up under the trap door; then she climbed it and pushed on the door. It opened easily, though she had to catch it to prevent it from banging back noisily.

As before, she peered upwards. This was different; this was intended to allow service access to the pipes that led to this room. There was a little platform up there, and mounted on one wall was a permanent ladder made of black metal. The shaft, though dark, seemed to go up at least as far as the air vent had.

Standing on the ladder, she considered it. She'd need a light of some sort, it was quite dark on up in there; and, she understood, it might go nowhere at all, there might not be any other way out other than to come back down.

She shrugged; it was worth a try, she told herself, if she could find something resembling a light. Again returning to the mech room, she dug through the closet where she'd found the ladders—but there was no flashlight. Discouraged, she returned to stare up into the dark hole again. It was going to be even darker, she realized, when she closed the trap—and she had to close it, it was a dead giveaway if left open.

She sighed; it was this or the hallway. Shaking her head, she mounted the ladder and climbed up to the platform inside. Once there, she knelt to grab the ladder, meaning to pull it up inside the hole before she closed the trap—and, as she did, her hand encountered what felt like a light switch. She stared at it for a moment, then flipped it up; a series of low-wattage bulbs behind protective glass covers sprang to life. They were located at intervals up the wall, and they illuminated the whole shaft, all the way to the top.

She shook her head and managed a little grin. Not your specialty, Andi, she told herself. As she looked around, she saw something else she'd missed—a pull-down ladder mounted at one side of the trap.

It took her a moment to figure out how it worked, but as soon as she had it down she descended again and returned the stepladder to its place in the mech room, leaving no evidence to betray her. Then she climbed up into the shaft, pulled the ladder up, and closed the trap. Looking up nervously, she hoped the lights could not be seen from any of the floors above. Deciding there was nothing she could do about that, she started to climb.

About one floor up, there was a large opening cut in the side of the shaft. Pausing—and clinging to the ladder tightly—she looked inside. Here there were numerous pipe junctions, some branches going up, others disappearing into the opening. Also inside the opening was what appeared to be a grab handle, easily within her reach. She tested it; it seemed firm. Hanging onto it, she swung herself off the ladder and into the hole. There was some dust here, and there were fresh marks in it—they had, she surmised, searched here for her earlier. But maybe that meant they wouldn't search it again.

Putting aside her fears of discovery, she began to examine the place. Here, near the access shaft, the opening was perhaps seven feet high, but on inside it shrank to a height of three feet or so. Dropping to her knees, she looked inside; it extended far to her right. There was more plumbing here, water pipes, gas pipes, conduits to carry electricity. It took her several minutes to realize what she was looking at.

It was the underside of a laboratory or medical workbench. A sink, power outlets, gas for Bunsen burners, oxygen, access to vacuum. There was a way out, too—a pair of cabinet doors ahead, blocked from her by shelves with bottles of liquid sitting on them. And there were louvers in those doors, louvers she was sure she could see through. Creeping forward, she saw that the shelf could be removed, but for the moment she merely moved some of the bottles and leaned over it, trying to see through the louvers.

From this angle she couldn't see much except for a pair of white-clad legs walking by. That was enough. Silently, she replaced the bottles and withdrew from the hole. Once she'd maneuvered herself onto the ladder again, she started climbing. That the shaft went on up suggested more such cutouts above.

There was in fact much more than that; at the next level, there were three tunnels headed off in different directions and each had multiple stops, evidently servicing several rooms. Starting by moving down the one to her extreme left, she checked each one; she could see little in the first, but it was brightly lighted and she could hear sounds like a respirator at work. The next three were similar, which brought her back out of the left-hand tunnel. Her next stop was the one ahead, which quickly branched into a T-shape. Peering through the louvers here, she was fairly sure she was looking into the surgery where she'd been taken originally. Going back in there seemed like a poor idea to her.

The right-hand passage was next, and, disappointingly, all she found here were rooms similar to those on the left. To her, it was beginning to seem as if this was some sort of mini-hospital or infirmary, these looked like they might be patient rooms— and from the sounds she was hearing—respirators and fainter sounds that might've been a TV playing softly—they seemed to be occupied.

Discouraged but still determined, she returned to the ladder and climbed on. The next level offered only two shafts, the left one quite long and the right one short; she explored the right first, again saw someone's feet through the louvers, and withdrew hastily.

The left one was next, and here she finally found what she was looking for—a room where the lights were off, where she could hear nothing that might indicate a human presence. As before she moved the few bottles sitting on the shelf, and this time she moved the shelf, too. Creeping forward, she peered out from the louvers. She saw no one, heard nothing, but she waited in that position for a while to be sure. Then, at last, she pushed the louvered doors open and crawled out.

Standing up, she looked around; a wet lab, regularly used. It was a bit messy, as such places often are. There was a Xeroxed copy of a technical paper lying on a table nearby; she glanced at it cursorily, saw that it concerned the techniques and usages of electro-convulsive shock to treat depression. Various pieces of equipment stood on the benches; a small electronic balance, a signal generator, a binocular microscope.

Ignoring all of it, she inspected the two doors leading into the lab. From what she'd seen from the access shaft, it appeared to her as if the one farthest from the bench probably led into a hallway, a hallway that held no fewer terrors than the one down in the basement.

The other probably didn't. She walked over to it and laid her head against the wood, listening; she heard nothing. She tried the knob, found it turned easily. Carefully she opened it a crack and peeked out.

It was an office. There was another door leading into what she'd assumed was the hallway, and across from her was a workstation where a computer sat, turned on, multicolored fractal patterns appearing and disappearing on the screen.

Making her decision, she left the lab and entered the office. Her first act was to check the door; inspecting the crack between the edge of the door and the frame showed her that it was locked, she probably did not have to fear any but the office's owner barging in. As safe as she could be, for the moment.

But, she wondered, what had she accomplished? She still had a hallway to enter if she was going to get out of the building. There was a window here, and she peeped out carefully through the blinds, looking out over the IIC complex. She could see men running about from building to building—very possibly looking for her. She could also see the guardhouse they'd passed on the way in, now manned by five or six men, and she could see the perimeter of razor-wire fencing surrounding this place—and the expanses of desert beyond that fence. It all seemed so hopeless. She sat down heavily in the swivel chair in front of the computer and held her head in her hands. Finally she looked up at the computer again; hesitantly, she moved the mouse sitting on a pad beside the keyboard.

A Windows screen appeared. She stared at it, then clicked on an icon labeled "communications." A new set appeared, and one of them was the Eudora icon, a graphic of a letter complete with address and stamp. She selected it and watched Eudora spring to life. Unsure of what she was doing, she clicked "Special" on the toolbar, then went to the item labeled "Configuration."

The user was identified as one Albert Michaelson, and the account provider was the familiar Netcom. Experimentally, she tried to change the name in the box labeled "real name"; it wasn't difficult. Staring at the screen, she wondered if she could change this to her own Nyct account information and send out an SOS by E-mail. She also wondered if she dared.

Under the circumstances, she decided, she had no choice.

69

"Oh, Andi," Sue5 muttered under her breath. "You're good, a lot better than anyone might've expected. A real cool-headed lady in a tight spot. And lucky, too, what you didn't know about the Internet just saved your ass."

Smiling, she looked at the E-mail she'd just duplicated—a message from Explorer@nyct.net, to be sure, but—since Andi hadn't known that it would be sent out on the Net through Albert's dial-up service, hadn't known all the changes she needed to make, it had, as far as the IIC's interception software was concerned, come from "Amickson@netcom.com"—and it had not, therefore, been intercepted.

Although the content might well confuse him, the recipient, "Gbarnes@aol.com," wouldn't know where it came from. It said:

Dear Gene:

Your E-mail was the only one I could remember. I'm in trouble. I'm in a factory or hospital out in the desert, the place is called IIC. I don't know where it is except that it's east of Twenty-nine Palms. They were going to do *surgery* on me here! I don't know why. I escaped. They're looking for me. I need help, call the police out here. Don't call Grant, he brought me here. This is *not* a joke. Please, Gene, help me.

Love, Andi.

Sue5 grinned. I know where you are, too, lady, she said silently. I don't think "Gene," whoever he is, can really do much, but let's just see what I can do while I'm waiting for the real Grant, let's see if I can find a way to talk to you. And a way to keep ol' Albert out of your hair.

She turned her attention to the other screen. "Albert, I'm having a problem here," she said.

"Oh? What?"

"My screen. Lower right, it's flickering. Very annoying, very distracting."

"Oh? Wait a second." He moved out of the minicam's view, then came back. "That better?"

"No. No change."

"Scan rate problem, maybe, although I can't see why that would've changed—you been messing with it?"

"No," she answered as she changed it to produce just the flicker she'd described.

"Well, okay. Hang on for a few minutes, Sue, let me see what I can do." Again he vanished from her view. Forgetting about him for the moment—it would take him at least fifteen minutes to check out the problem she'd set for him, longer to actually solve it—she turned her attention back to his office, where she hoped Andi was still hiding, and opened a local network linkage to Albert's computer, securing it with encryption. This was dangerous for her, this could lead to hard questions later, but she didn't care, she felt she had to take the chance. The question now was, how could she draw Andi back to it?

All she could do, she decided, was try something direct and hope for the best. Working as quickly as she could, she created a small graphics file and set it, along with a stock sound file, flashing down the line to Albert's computer. At the other end, the graphic and the sound file were substituted for the screen-saver Albert was running. Sue5 knew the result; alternately, the little speakers beside the screen would emit a soft ding and the screen would display a message in large block letters, red on black: "Andi. I'm a friend. I can help. Press enter."

Then, there being absolutely nothing else she could do, she waited. Minutes passed; nothing happened. Andi could well have left Albert's office, or she might not trust the message, she might think it was a ploy to locate her and capture her again—that wasn't unreasonable. Wondering how she would've reacted in such a situation, Sue5 continued to wait and hope—and the minutes continued to slide slowly and painfully by.

Finally her own screen reacted. Andi—or someone—had hit the enter! For a moment she worried, it might be a security guard, they might've found her, and this could lead to Sue5's own hidden capabilities being exposed. She decided she didn't have a choice; she too had to trust. Remotely, she opened a text window on the screen of Albert's computer.

"Andi," she typed. "Is that you, are you there?"

"Yes."

"Please, I'm *not* working to catch you, I want to help you get away. But I'm in danger too. If you are Andi, if they haven't caught you already, tell me what your avatar was on World's Chat."

There was a long pause. Then: "A red-haired Vampire."

She breathed a sigh of relief; Colin or Albert would know that detail, but not some security man who'd blundered across her. "Good, thank you for trusting me, you *won't* regret it."

"I don't have many choices. I think the police are coming here."

"I wouldn't count on that. You're in more trouble than you could possibly know."

"Who are you? Can you tell me what's going on here?"

"I'm called Sue5 now. My real name—" She hesitated, a long time, it had been a while since she'd used it—"was Nadine. I was brought here just like you were, a long time ago."

"By Grant Kingsley?"

"Yes. The same man. Except I knew him as Dave Heller. Andi, his name isn't Grant Kingsley and it isn't Dave Heller. It's Colin Simmons."

"I don't understand."

"I know. And I don't have time to explain it to you, not right now. How did you get to Albert's office?"

"I'm not sure I should tell you that."

"You're right, and it isn't important, anyhow. Do you have a place you can hide?"

"Yes."

"Good. I'll warn you, well in advance, if Albert is coming back. If he doesn't you're safe there, at least until late tonight when the cleaning crews make their rounds. What I have to do now is figure out how to get you out of here. It isn't going to be easy."

"Once I'm out I'm going to be in the desert. I'm a New Yorker, I know nothing about the desert."

"That isn't a problem. I can arrange to have you picked up out on the road. Getting you out on the road is the problem."

"Obviously I'm going to file charges once I'm out. You don't care?"

"(laugh) I'd love it, Andi. Bring this fucking place down around their ears, throw them all in jail, you'll hear me laughing. A part of the reason I'd like to see you escape is so you can do just that!"

"If you feel like that, why haven't you escaped? Have you tried?"

Sue5 stared at the words; you should have, she told herself, expected a question like that. "It's too late for me," she answered melodramatically. "But not for you. You stay where you are, stay where you can see the computer, I'll keep you posted, as much as I can. I'm going to close down for now, and—"

"Nadine?"

She almost didn't respond to that now-unfamiliar name. "Yes?"

"The surgery. You had the surgery, didn't you? What do they do? What's that all about?"

It was several seconds before Sue5 could bring herself to respond. "Andi, until you're out of here, you don't want to know."

70

"Dad, I can't help it! She says you have to get to a computer, she has to talk to you directly. She says it can't be done this way, not all of it. She says she doesn't want you doing something stupid, she doesn't want you going in not knowing what you're going into! That's what she says, Dad."

Grant leaned against the side of the phone booth and struck it with his fist. "Todd, tell her—"

"Dad, I've tried to tell her! She won't listen. She says you have to get to a computer and log in to World's Chat through my account, and then she'll tell you what she knows and you can make some plans. She says you have to have these maps, too."

"You have the maps already?"

"Yeah. We printed them out, we have them right here."

"So I have to come back. All the way back to Fillmore."

"I guess."

"Shit. I do not want to do that, son. That's going to take a lot of time, that's going to take pretty much the rest of the day! I don't want to leave here, not with Andi inside that place!"

"Sue says she's as safe as she can be for the time being."

He relaxed a little; it had taken some yelling by Todd to stop him from running back and crashing through the gate at IIC once the boy had given him Sue's message that Andi was inside, that she'd been taken captive but had escaped and was hiding. The presence of the Marines—a reminder of his past life—had made it worse for him. But, he told himself, you know things like this have to be planned. More than once now you've rushed off half-cocked and you've wasted precious time. Time now to remember, to act like the professional you once were.

"All right, I'm going to come back. I'm going to stop by the house for a few minutes before I come to the ranch, I may talk to Sue on the computer there. But I will come by—to get those maps—before I come back down here."

"What're you going to do, Dad?"

"I'm going to get her out of there, son. Whatever that takes. Let me speak to Paula, would you?"

"Sure. Hang on." There was an interval of silence, after which Paula, sounding tired, came on the phone.

"How's everything going?" Grant asked her.

"Okay, I think. Nothing's happened. I called the sheriff, they sent out a deputy to check on the guys hanging out on the road. They went away, but an hour later they came back. I called the sheriff again, but they must've had a lookout. They left before the deputy got back. That was only thirty minutes ago. I've got my own lookouts set. We're ready for most anything here, I don't think you need to worry."

"I do anyway," he growled. "Sue insists on talking to me on the computer, and I can't do that from here, I'm heading back. I'll be there as soon as I can."

"Don't get killed on the road, Grant. It won't help."

He laughed shortly. "On my way, Paula." Hanging up the phone, he trotted back to his truck and climbed in. As he began the long trip back to Fillmore, he felt like he was leaving a part of himself behind.

Grant stopped by his house first—and, as he came into sight of it, he realized he'd had visitors, the front door was standing ajar. Crouching low over the steering wheel, he drove the truck up near the house, stopped it, and, rolling out the driver's side, came up aiming the automatic over the truck's bed. No one appeared, no shots were fired; he waited, poised for action, for several minutes. Then, staying low, he approached the house— also without incident.

A quick but careful check inside assured him no one was waiting for him there. Very little was disturbed, nothing seemed to have been stolen; all the closets stood open and the bed covers were mussed, it was apparent a search for people had been conducted and little more than that. He also checked his attic, a storage area only. He couldn't be sure if anyone had been here—he assumed they had—but, to his relief, the locked chests that sat in the far corner had not been disturbed. Coming back down and closing his front door, he noticed that it had not been broken open. It took him a few minutes to discover that the intruders had come in through the window in Todd's bedroom, which he'd carelessly left partially open and therefore unlocked. Ten thousand times he'd lectured the boy on matters like this. Maybe this affair would teach him that the world was not to be trusted.

Finally, having secured his house again, he sat down in front of the computer. Going on-line, he almost, by habit, logged in under his usual account name, but he did remember, to use Todd's Well account for his access. Entering World's Chat and changing Todd's Red Skull avatar to his own Piscean, he headed for the Hall of Sadness, where he hoped to find Sue5—and was disappointed when he did not see her there. He paged her; no answer. As he stood in frustration, a "punk girl" avatar sidled up to him.

"If you're looking for Sue," the girl said in a whisper, "go inside, where the rooms are. Look between 'Tears' and 'Bitterness.' Click with your mouse on the top row of tears."

Grant swiveled his fish to face her. "Who're you?" he demanded.

"Nobody. I'm a chatterbot. Go."

He hesitated; then, while she watched, followed her instructions. Entering the corridor leading to the rooms, he found the place she'd described, and clicked on the blank wall. A door appeared, a door he'd never seen before; he walked through it.

Inside was a whole new world, but he paid little attention. He focused on the green-clad female warrior figure who was apparently waiting for him.

"Hi, Grant," the warrior typed. "It's me, Sue5. Long time no see, Fish Man."

"Way too long. What the hell is all this, Sue?"

"That's going to take too long to explain. We have to plan what we're going to do now."

"We? How do you fit into this?"

"The best way to explain that is to tell you what I've already told your son. You could say I work for IIC; they recruited me, they made me an offer I had no way to refuse. That plant where you just were, out in the desert—that's where I am, right now."

"I don't understand."

"I know. But you don't have to. What was planned for Andi already happened to me, and I'm doing my damndest to see that it doesn't happen to her."

"Why her? How's she connected with them? And what was planned for her, what happened to you?"

"Part of that's easy. She fits the marketing profile. Colin's big on marketing profiles. He really believes in 'em."

"Marketing profile? Colin?"

"Colin Simmons. He's the man Andi thought was you. And he's the man that planned all this. I can tell you all this later, with any luck there'll be time. Right now, Andi's still free and hiding and still safe. But that won't last forever."

"Sue, how the hell do I know you're telling me the truth?"

"Andi's asking me the same question. I can't blame either one of you. You're just going to have to trust me, that's all."

"Sue, why didn't you warn us *before* all this happened?"

":-(I couldn't, Grant. I wanted to. Your Netcom account and Andi's Nyct account were both being intercepted; anything I said would've been seen, and edited out, and it would've gotten me in trouble and accomplished nothing. If I could've called you on the phone, I would have. I'm working on some stuff now that'll let me do that, but so far I can't."

"You can't use the phone?"

"No."

"Why not? Because you're inside there? What about when you leave, when you go home?"

There was a very long pause. "I don't go home, Grant."

It took a moment for this to sink in. "Sue, are you trying to tell me you're some sort of captive there?"

She hesitated again. "Yeah. That's what I'm telling you. I can't leave here. Ever."

"And Andi—"

"If they catch her, she'll be where I am. And she won't be able to leave either."

"Well," he typed back, pounding the keys far harder than necessary, "we'll fucking well see about that! I'm going to come back and get both of you out of there!"

"No, forget about me. Get Andi out, that's what you need to do. Get Andi and get the story out about what's going on here. You might be able to do it, Fish Man. You're the only one I know of who might. It isn't going to be easy, you're walking into an armed camp here, you're going to have to use all you know to pull this off and get out in one piece."

"Yes, I—" He stopped typing. "Wait. Why do you say that? You know about me?"

"About your Navy career? Yes, Grant. A lot of information is out there on the Net, if you know how to get at it. I know a lot about you. I know about the accident and about the ambassador's son. A lot. More than you want me to. Can't help that."

He had a cold feeling in his stomach as these words appeared. "I can't believe this."

"Believe it. Now look: time's running out. We need to make some plans. Get Andi out, then we can talk. I set up this account for Todd, it's as secure as I can make it. It ought to hold up."

"Okay. What've you got in mind?"

"(laugh) No, you tell me! You're the expert! I'm just your inside man!"

He stared at the screen for a while. This could, he told himself, be a setup; a way to get him to reveal his plans. Okay, he told himself; without her, his chances of success were much less, but let's just keep that in mind. And let's run a little test here. "Sue, I want to ask you one question first."

"Shoot."

"What does the SAF—the Singapore Armed Forces—have to do with this?"

"This place is owned by an outfit based in Singapore. The headman is well connected in the government there. He was able to get soldiers to act as his corporate security force."

"In the United States? Impossible!"

"Not if you have cooperation from Washington, it isn't."

This stopped him again; he thought about the Marines, out there as he was leaving, marking the area off as secured. "Are you trying to tell me the U.S. government is involved in this?" Old anger, familiar old anger, started to rise in him again; he struggled with it, fought it. "Well, hell, I know there's some involvement, I saw the Marines out there marking it as a security site . . ."

"I don't know how far that involvement goes. Some agency is involved. I don't know if the President knows about it, I don't know if anyone in Congress knows. No, that isn't true, there's one senator who's been out here—"

God damn, Grant told himself silently, one is enough; this gets deeper by the minute. With effort, he controlled his building rage. "Okay. That doesn't matter to me. Sue, I don't really have much of a plan, except to go in after her and bring her out. Can you tell me where she is?"

"Generally. She's in the same building I am, I'm pretty sure of that. I don't know a lot of details, actually. I only recently found out where this place was geographically."

"Which building is that?"

"The largest one here. Right in the middle of the place."

"I think I know which one . . . you don't know where inside?"

"No. But I might be able to find out by the time you get back here. I'm trying, right now."

"My plan, such as it is, is to come back tonight. I'm going to pick up some things here and go back to the ranch; that won't take long. I'll contact you again from there, okay?"

"Okay, Grant. Might want to plan a little more than that. Let me tell you what I know of security here, what I've seen of the Marines' perimeter; it isn't much, but it might be enough."

"Wait a minute, let me grab a pad, I want to make some notes."

"Sure."

He scrambled about, looking for paper; finding a small notepad he came back to the computer. "Okay, go."

"Well, to start with, I don't think you'll see anything more than small arms here. There's a regular vehicle patrol around the fence, and there are sentries at all doors. The Marines are setting a perimeter five miles out on all sides except the road." She went on, giving him as many details as she could, several times illustrating her points by bringing up an image of a map on his screen.

"Okay," he said when she'd finished. "This helps. I'm headed down to the ranch now. Oh, and Sue?"

"Yes?"

"Be ready to leave tonight."

71

Restlessly, Andi paced back and forth in the small office, watching the computer on the desk, wondering if she'd done the right thing by trusting the woman who'd identified herself as Nadine—if it even was a woman, she told herself sourly, you can't trust one damn thing that comes through a computer. So far, the decision had seemed a good one—she'd hidden under the lab bench, ready to flee back down the access shaft, for a while after she'd talked to the woman. She'd kept close watch, too, and no one had come bursting in. After perhaps half an hour, assuming that that was enough time for someone to have been sent to her location if it was an overt trap, she'd emerged again.

She'd also decided that leaving the area under the lab bench in a state of disarray probably wasn't a good idea. She had to assume that the men who'd been pursuing her knew she'd made her initial escape down the chute and into the laundry; she felt she also had to assume that, since they hadn't found her yet, they might well go back and start a new search there. If they did, they'd check the maintenance shaft—even though they had checked it before. Then, the removed shelf and set-aside re-agent bottles would be a dead giveaway.

With this in mind, she searched the lab and office for a new hiding place. There wasn't a good one, really; there was a standing cabinet too full of various items to allow her to fit inside and too close to the wall to get behind, several built-in cabinets enclosing only small spaces, built-in shelving, and, other than the area under the workbench, little else.

In the office there was a bookshelf, the desk where the computer stood, two large file cabinets, a couch, and a couple of chairs. A coat rack stood near the door, there wasn't a closet. Behind the couch was a possibility—there was space for her slim body—but she also considered it to be a terribly obvious hiding place.

The desk where the computer was was the other possibility, and this she studied more carefully. It was an elaborate setup; there was a printer and a flatbed scanner off to the side and other pieces of equipment she was less familiar with were set about in disarray. All of these devices, along with the computer's speakers, were hooked into the back of the midi-tower case, which stood under the edge of the desk partially occupying what had been designed as knee space, alongside a suspended section carrying two adjustable shelves, which were filled with floppy disk cases and CDs. Above the desk level was a whole series of shelves, some of them clearly additions to the original design, mostly covered with books and with pieces of equipment whose function was wholly unknown to her. All this hardware meant there was a virtual rat's nest of wiring in behind the hutch, and, to provide access to it, the whole thing was pulled back from the wall a couple of feet. Experimentally she tried sliding in among the wires and discovered that she could;

if she stood sideways and crouched a little, she could duck down below the top of the thing. In a way it was perfect; she could peep out from between the books and, she was fairly certain, not be seen from the other side. The only place where her body was exposed was in a six-inch-high slot behind the desk area alongside the monitor, and that was well below anyone's eye level unless they were ducking down and actively searching. The hutch sat near a corner with file cabinets alongside it, which meant one end of her hiding place was closed off; this, she decided, could be good or bad. With her weapon—the scissors—she could create a serious problem for someone trying to get her out through the narrow slot, but it also meant she could easily be trapped in here.

She couldn't tell if that was an advantage or not, but, in the end, she decided to adopt this area as her refuge. If they knew or suspected she was in here she'd be found and captured wherever she hid; and the risk of a second inspection of the access shaft seemed to her higher than that. With this in mind she'd returned to the lab and carefully replaced the shelf and bottles; then she'd arranged the wires behind the computer desk to minimize the risk of tripping on them if she had to make a hasty entry or exit.

Having done this, she had nothing to do but wait—and ponder some mundane problems: she was getting thirsty and at the same time had need of a bathroom. As the minutes dragged on—very few minutes, it seemed to her—both these problems, her need for a bathroom especially, became pressing. Twisting her mouth, she looked back at the lab—the sink there could be used in both ways. It took less than ten more minutes for her to surrender to necessity, to go into the lab and work out the least awkward way to accomplish her goal. Once she had, she perversely felt better about things. She could, she decided, remain in these two rooms for quite a while. That she had no idea how long she'd have to remain here—or if she realistically had any way at all of escaping this place—she tried not to think about. For now, there was nothing she could do except wait for Nadine—or Sue5, she wasn't sure which to call her—to page her on the computer again. When the page finally did come, she almost jumped for the machine.

But the message wasn't what she'd hoped. "Andi, there's a problem, Albert's on his way up there right now. Don't take time to answer, just get to your hiding place *now!* When he

leaves hit the enter key over and over. *Go!*" The screen
blanked and the screen-saver patterns returned, leaving Andi to
stare at it for it a second. Then, her heart pounding, she jumped
up and slipped in behind the computer hutch, trying to keep as
much of herself out of view of the hole by the telephone as
possible.

Several minutes passed; then she heard the sound of a key in
the lock. She held her breath as the door opened, as she heard
footsteps, as the door closed again. Carefully, she peeked
through the tiny slot between books on the shelf.

A man in a white coat appeared in her field of view; he was
thirtyish, thin, almost gaunt, with wild sandy hair and thick
glasses, taped at a corner in a near-caricature of the classic
geek. Washed-out blue eyes that even in glimpse seemed pene-
trating gazed out from behind those glasses. To Andi's extreme
discomfort, he came forward to the desk and sat down at the
computer. Knowing he might be there for a while, she moder-
ated her breathing deliberately, keeping silent and still.

The man—she had to assume this was "Albert"—put his
elbows on either side of his keyboard, held his head in his
hands, and rubbed at his temples with his thumbs. After several
long minutes he raised his head; he looked, Andi thought, miserable. Reaching over, his hand coming within six inches of her
hip, he picked up the phone. His fingertips danced over the
keys.

"Albert here. How's it going?" He paused and sighed deep and
long. "You have any idea where she is?" Pause. "Well, look, this
is pretty Goddamn stupid, isn't it? She can't get out of here,
there isn't a way. All you have to do is fucking find her, how
hard can that be?" He paused again and nodded. "I'll stay. All
night if that's what it takes. This is such a mess, I can't believe
it." Pause. "Yeah. I'll be here or down in Sue5's room, she's
bitching about VDT problems, I don't know what's going on
there yet. She can be a pain in the ass too." He hung up, then
almost immediately picked up the phone again.

"Colin? Albert." Andi jumped at the name. Colin? The man
she'd known as Grant Kingsley? She listened as he went on:
"Fucked this one up good, man. Gotta say it." As before, he
paused. "Yeah, yeah. Now look, Colin, I have a plan. No,
shithead, just fucking listen for once in your Goddamn life, how
many fucking times have I jumped in to save your ass? I know

you're my boss now, but you'd be fucking dead if I hadn't run interference for you over that business with Sukamto's daughter, you remember? Asshole." He paused again, nodding at times. "Okay, Colin, good enough. Now listen, I have an idea—a lot better than the other one. I've been doing some reading on ECT. Yeah, shock treatments, like in that old movie, what was it called, 'Cuckoo's Nest.' Yeah, they still do that, uh-huh. Not like that but they still do. Anyway, what we can do with this one—if Lee and his people can ever find her, bunch of incompetent idiots—is to whack her with a few treatments of that and knock out all her short-term memory. We can dump her back in L.A., on the street near the airport, let her take care of herself from there. Whenever she gets found everybody'll think she was mugged. What do you think?" Another long pause. "Well, he sure is a problem now, the way Hua and Chay spilled their guts to him and the bimbo." Nervously playing with his glasses, he paused and shook his head. "I gotta tell you, Colin, this coming right on top of the business with that *Times* reporter—it feels like it's all fragmenting. Yeah, I got the memo, I know Delling and his people say they're taking care of that, but . . ."

Again he paused; he clenched his fist, closed his eyes, listened for a couple of minutes. "Colin, you ought to call them off. Now. We need to back down and regroup here; anybody else gets killed and we're liable to get a lot more attention than we want, especially after Harrelson posted our location on the Net. No matter what Delling does, there're going to be questions—shit, there already have been, the PR team's already getting calls!" Pause. "No, I know that, Auan doesn't get it. He thinks Delling can call all the shots. You and I know he can't." He paused again, nodded a few times, and finally grinned a little. "All right, Colin, good, that's the way it ought to be handled, just put it on hold, at least until we find Lawrence and take care of her. They really don't know that much anyway. If they turn up dead—and especially if there's some kind of massacre up there at that ranch—there'll be more questions than ever." He paused again, then smiled. "Okay . . . okay, Colin, I'll do that. Think about what I said about Lawrence, okay? Maybe we can come out of this clean after all. Yeah. You too." Again he hung up; then he leaned back in his chair, looking a little less troubled than before. "Maybe that shit did some good after all," he murmured, nodding to himself. "Maybe so." Getting up, he walked slowly to the couch—where he laid down and closed his eyes, apparently planning to nap.

Great, Andi told herself. Just what I needed.

72

Grant's time getting to the ranch from home was, he was sure, a record. As he turned off highway 126, he was gratified to see that there weren't any suspicious cars sitting about. Seeing no lookouts—he shouldn't have, not if they were being effective—he slowed to a near stop. When he did, a distant figure, one of the hands who'd recognized his truck, stood up from cover and waved. He grinned, waved back, and drove on to the ranch itself. The lookout had called in, evidently; Paula, Todd, and Mimi—dressed now in jeans and a plaid shirt and looking very different—were all waiting for him. The thoroughness of the preparations here made his decisions a little easier, reduced the conflict for him. He wanted to stay, make sure nothing happened to Todd, to Paula; and yet, if he didn't get Andi, who else would? On his way back he'd wrestled with this, and he'd decided he had to go. He didn't have to like it.

"So what's the story, Grant?" Paula asked without preamble.

"Not much more than you already know. They have Andi in there, I'm sure of that. I'm going to go in after her."

Paula looked both confused and concerned. "Grant, you can't—maybe you ought to just call the police?"

"No." He gazed at her face for a few seconds; she was truly frightened, and he certainly wasn't going to add to that by informing her about the armed men, she'd argue a lot more if she knew about them. "Look, police move too slow. I have what I think is a key card to the place, I think I can get in and out with no trouble." He stopped; she didn't look convinced, not at all, and he really couldn't blame her. "Paula, I've asked you to just trust me before. Has anything ever gone wrong because you did?"

"No," she replied readily. "But this . . ."

"He can do it," Mimi put in. "Maybe you haven't seen him in action but I have. He's good."

Paula still looked confused. "Good at what?"

"Kung-fu or something. You know. Stuff."

She turned back to Grant. "I didn't know you could do things like that . . ."

He shrugged. "I just do what I have to, Paula. That's all."

"So you're going back."

"Yes."

"And I can't talk you out of it."

He knew his own facial expression perfectly well; unless she was blind she'd know there wasn't a point in arguing further. "No. But there is a favor of I'd like to ask of you."

"Name it, Grant."

He smiled; a true friend, no question about it. "I want to take two of the horses with me—Blue Fire and Storm would be fine."

"Okay—but could I ask why?"

"As I was leaving, there were Marines marking the place as a security site. I expect them to be patrolling a perimeter, and I'm going to have to go by them. I don't expect trouble, they're grunts from the base over at Twenty-nine Palms I'm sure, but the horses would make going in and out a lot easier. The closer ways in are going to be blocked off; looking at the maps I see a spot about six miles away where I can leave the truck. The horses would make five of those miles a lot easier." And make it possible, he thought to himself grimly, to get a casualty out. Getting in was one thing; getting out with two women in tow was quite another, a problem he was going to have to solve on the spur of the moment.

"Why do you want them both?" Paula was asking him. "Either one of them could carry you and the woman."

"Right. But not two women. And I'm bringing two women out."

"Sue5?" Todd asked.

Grant glanced at him. "Yes. She tells me she's a captive up there too."

Paula grimaced. "What *is* this place?"

Grant shrugged. "I don't know. When we get back I may have some answers. I hope so. But that's not my primary objective."

"I know," Paula said, nodding. She turned away, looking toward a couple of armed ranch hands sitting in chairs on the porch. "Bill, Eduardo," she said, "take Grant's truck, hitch it to a double trailer, get Storm and Blue Fire saddled and loaded."

The men got up; Grant tossed Eduardo his keys. "Thanks, Paula," Grant said. "You know I appreciate it."

She shrugged. "What are friends for?"

What indeed? Grant asked himself. And what have I been ignoring all these years? So stupid, so absolutely stupid . . . he shook himself slightly.

"Dad, I want to go too," Todd told him.

"No," Grant answered. "And not no, because I want you safe, although I do, but no, because I'm going to need you here. If Paula will lend me a cellular phone—" He glanced at Paula, she nodded again—"then I'm going to stay in continuous touch with you, and you're going to stay in continuous touch with Sue5 on the computer. I need you here . . ."

Todd twisted his mouth, looked like he was going to argue, but gave it up immediately. "Okay, Dad. I'll do what you say."

"You need to take me with you, Grant," Mimi said unexpectedly.

He turned to her. "You? Why?"

"Because I'm involved already. And because you're going to need some help. I've been looking at the maps too; you can't take the horses very close. You need to be sure they stay safe wherever you leave them. That's me, or someone like me."

He laughed. "Mimi, excuse me, but what do you know about handling horses? Blue Fire's still pretty high-strung, he—"

"No, she does, Grant," Paula said. "She's been working with me some today; she's actually very good."

He shook his head. "No. I don't want to put you in any kind of danger, I—"

"My choice, Grant," she insisted hotly. "I helped create this, let me help fix it." She patted her pocket; the butt of the automatic he'd given her was visible. "I know how to use this, too. If it comes to that."

He laughed a little. "Sometime, Mimi, I want you to tell me how you come to know so much about horses and guns. But not now. Even if I wanted to I can't take you with me. I'm going to be moving fast, I can't look out for you." She raised a hand as if to argue a little more, but he silenced her with a wave of his own. "No. This is for me and me alone." He glanced down toward the barn, where Bill and Eduardo had taken his truck. "I'd better get down there, give them a hand. I need to get—"

"No!" Paula said firmly, "No, absolutely not. I'm not fond of this idea, but you are going to eat something and rest just a few moments before you go, you've already had a long day. Let Bill and Eduardo get you packed up and ready. Get inside, Grant."

He stared at her; her expression was one he was familiar with, it suggested that arguments wouldn't be well received. He gave in. "All right, Paula. I need to study the maps for a few minutes anyhow, I can do it over a sandwich and some coffee. But that's it; I want to get back there and get her out as quick as possible. Before she gets found, before something happens."

She nodded, turned to go inside; with Todd right beside him, he followed her. Mimi did not join them, but Grant paid little attention—just as little as he paid to the food he was served, which he ate without comment. Once seated at the table, he concentrated on the hand-drawn maps. Forty-five minutes later, a thermos of hot coffee Paula had insisted he take on the seat beside him and several bags full of equipment he'd brought from home behind the seat, he was headed eastward on highway 126, back toward Twenty-nine Palms. Several times he called Todd as he drove along the highway; the boy had talked with Sue5, he learned, but she was not at the moment in contact with Andi. As the evening darkness began to gather, he drove as fast as he dared, sometimes above ninety.

He did not get stopped. Just after he'd passed through Twenty-nine Palms he received a call from Paula.

"We might," she said, "have a problem here. We can't find Mimi. The last anyone saw of her was just before you left, she went down to the barn and helped the guys load the horses in the trailer."

Grant frowned at the phone. "Have you been looking?"

"Yes, but we just realized she's missing. Maybe there's nothing to be concerned about, I can't be sure. I thought you ought to know."

"Thanks," he muttered. "Keep looking, okay? And keep me posted." He clicked off and drove another mile or two, wondering as he did where the actress might be, a little worried that someone might've slipped past Paula's lookouts and gotten into the ranch.

Then, thinking about the timing of her disappearance, he developed a theory. He slowed the truck and pulled it off the road, hoping as he got out of the cab and walked back to the trailer that this was pure fantasy. Standing behind it, he opened the doors.

The light of a full moon revealed her, sitting on the floor between the two animals. "Hi," she said, looking sheepish. She got up. "It isn't too comfortable back here, you mind if I ride in the cab the rest of the way?"

He put his hands on his hips. "What the fuck do you think you're doing? I thought I said no, you couldn't come along."

She hopped out of the trailer and took it upon herself to close the doors. "Yeah, well, I figured it'd be a blast, you know? Didn't want to miss out."

"Well, you're going to. I'm turning this thing around and dropping you off in Twenty-nine Palms. Get dinner, have a couple of beers, get a motel room maybe. I'll pick you up on my way back."

"Nuh-uh, not getting rid of me that easy. I saw the maps, I can find the way."

"You want to walk, that's fine."

"I could take a taxi. Ever hear of them?"

"A taxi, out here?"

"You pay, they'll take you anywhere."

"I thought you didn't have any money."

She avoided his eyes. "I don't. Not much. But maybe enough." She grinned again. " 'Sides, you don't want to go back, you want to go on. Let's just do it, Grant. I won't be in your way, I promise."

"I don't like it."

"I know. I didn't mean to give you this much choice. I meant to pop up when you unloaded the horses."

He stared at her suspiciously for several seconds. "Get in the truck," he barked. Then, walking back to it himself, he climbed into the driver's seat. An instant later she was seated beside him.

"So? Whatcha gonna do with me?"

He pulled the truck back onto the highway. "You're right," he admitted, "I'm in a hurry. I'll decide between now and then whether to let you watch the horses or tie you to the steering wheel."

"Sounds like fun. But I wouldn't be much help tied up."

"I don't want help."

She nodded, looked down at her lap. "You made this sound really easy when you were talking to Paula," Mimi commented as he drove on, her mood becoming more serious. "But it isn't going to be, is it?"

He shook his head. "I don't have a feeling for that yet," he told her. "But yes, there are armed guards inside that place, a lot of them. I'm not planning to bust up the place, Mimi. I'm planning to slip in, get Andi and Sue, and get out of there as quick as possible."

She smiled. "Well," she noted, "you are good with your hands, I've seen that. This is a little different, though. What makes you think you can pull it off?"

He stared straight ahead into the darkening eastern sky. "I was trained to do this kind of thing," he said. "Well trained. I was career Navy. SEALs."

Her eyebrows rose. "Oh . . . you're retired?"

"Not exactly. I quit."

"Quit? Why?"

"A long story. I'd rather not get into it, Mimi." He looked over at her quickly, then back to the road. "You have some background, too. As I said, it isn't every wannabe Hollywood actress who can impress Paula around horses."

"Or knows how to use an automatic, either," she added, patting her pocket.

"So . . . we've got some driving time left, want to tell me about it?"

She shrugged. "There isn't a whole lot to tell, Grant. I come from Iowa originally; my father—my stepfather, actually—was a real outdoors type, as I was growing up he owned a riding stable. A place a lot like Paula's but much smaller. Being there was almost like going home. He taught me when I was little, how to ride, how to shoot." She got a faraway look in her eyes. "I had a good life there—but when I was in high school people started telling me what a good actress I was, how beautiful I was." She made a rude snorting sound. "How I was sure to make it in Hollywood. Oh, you know the story, everybody knows the story. Girl from the heartland comes to Hollywood to be a star. For most of us it never happens, nothing like it ever happens."

"If you know that, why don't you go back to Iowa?"

She laughed a little. "Embarrassment. Go back and say you failed, nobody wants to do that. The folks at home think I've been in several movies that haven't been released yet. I haven't been in one. Just a couple of low-grade commercials." She shifted her position in the seat. "The only movie offers I've had are porn. I've turned those down." She hesitated. "So far."

"So you haven't given up yet?"

"No." She made a face. "Maybe. I just don't know what else to do, where else to go."

"Maybe," he mused, "once this is all done with, we can do something about—"

He stopped; the cellular phone lying on the console beside him was ringing. He picked it up. "Yes?"

"Grant, it's Paula. We have another problem, I'm not sure what to do about it."

"What's happened?" His voice illustrated his concern.

"Sheriff's deputies were here again. This time I didn't call them. This time they were looking for you."

"For me?"

"Yes. They were asking about Andi Lawrence, if I knew her, if I'd seen her. They said they had a complaint, from New York. They're suspicious, Grant, after having been out here twice today on my calls."

"I don't understand."

"They wouldn't explain, but Todd asked Sue5 on the computer if she knew why. It seems Andi managed to get an E-mail to New York, to somebody named G. Barnes. Among other things, it accuses you of—well, I guess kidnapping. The law is looking for you. They're serious, they probably have an APB out on your truck."

He swore. "It shouldn't matter, we're almost there. If we get Andi out okay, she can explain, and—"

"We?"

"Yes, we. Forget about looking for Mimi, she's with me, she stowed away."

"She what?"

"Stowed away. In the trailer."

"Oh, great. Is it going to be a problem?"

"Paula," he said rather grimly, "right now almost everything is a problem."

73

Still peeping through the books at the man sleeping on the couch, Andi was getting stiff; she did not know how much longer she could stay in this position, every muscle in her body was cramping. A couple of times, to relieve the pain, she'd taken the risk of standing up straight, which she knew exposed her hair above the top level of the hutch; she'd only allowed herself a moment before she'd resumed her crouch.

When the door abruptly opened and another man walked in, it was so sudden she almost gave herself away with a gasp. She contained herself; she even managed to remain silent when she saw the man's face as he walked across the room.

Grant Kingsley. No, she reminded herself, if Nadine was to be believed, Colin Simmons.

Her fingers worked at the handle of the scissors she still carried; her emotions were a mix of fury and a deep sadness, she simultaneously found herself wanting to attack him and to demand in tears that he explain why he'd cared so little for her, why he'd betrayed her like he had. Neither was viable, and she knew it. Trying not to shake with anger, she held her position.

"Wake up, Albert, you lazy sonofabitch," Colin said. He walked to the couch and whacked one of Albert's shoes. "How the hell can you be sleeping?"

Albert opened his eyes but did not move. "It isn't hard. I work long hours here, Colin. It's late already, and I was up all night last night. I'm up all night lots of nights. There's times I wonder why."

"Well, you do what you have to do," Colin said carelessly. He came back toward the computer hutch, causing Andi to hold her breath, and, sitting down in the swivel chair, rotated it to face Albert, who was now sitting up on the couch. "We can't find that stupid bitch," he said with a shake of his head. "I don't get it. I've told Lee to quit fucking around, to start a room-by-room search of this building, and if that doesn't turn her up we'll have to look at the possibility that she managed to get

outside. I don't know how she could've done that, though."
Andi, listening from her hiding place, shook her head very
slightly. He didn't seem like the same man at all; he looked the
same, his voice was the same, but his manner and even his
pattern of speech were different. He not only looked like an
actor, he apparently possessed the skills of one.

"You figured out what happened? How she managed to get
loose?"

"Well, that's a mystery, now, a real mystery. Ol' Doc Singh
says the sedative wasn't, he says it was just saline. We don't
have a clue how that happened; between you and me I halfway
suspect sabotage, I just don't know who to point a finger at yet
and I don't know what the bastard could've hoped to gain from
it. The bitch is cool, I'll give her that—Singh figures she acted
sedated and waited for a chance to make her break. It's funny;
Singh thinks if she hadn't pulled that act she might be dead
right now."

"Dead? How's that?"

"Well, if she'd kept right on fighting and screaming the guys
would've given her another shot, but that one was supposed to
be a quarter-dose, so she wouldn't get overdosed—figuring
she'd already had one full one. She keeps on after that, she gets
another one, weaker yet—Singh has this all worked out—"

"Yes, I know, I consulted with him on it way back when. So?"

"Well, since she hadn't gotten any from the first one, she
wouldn't've gone down from the second, so she'd've gotten the
third. Singh had 'em checked in the lab. The third, he says, was
full-strength and the second three-quarter. Almost certainly
enough for a lethal dose."

"Somebody screwed up big-time."

"Too big a time. I think somebody had some screwball idea, I
just can't figure out what the fuck it was. We're gonna be looking hard at it. Right now, the big thing is to find her."

"Well, I'm not worried. She can't get past the fence. The point
is, what're we going to do with her when we do find her? You
thought about my ideas any?"

Colin nodded. "Yes, I have. I can't approve it, Albert. We have
too much invested in this one to just drop it. When we find her
we're going to go ahead with the recruitment. The report says
she's perfect, you know that."

"Yes, I know that," Albert snarled back. "You aren't thinking,

Colin! We can't keep her! This one fucked up, we can't afford to have her here!"

Colin laughed. "We can't afford to have any of 'em here, Albert! Not if anybody gets in to look!"

"That isn't what I mean. All the others disappeared without any connection to this place. Investigations wouldn't have even come up with the name of this place, much less any suspicions about it. This is different. It's different because your boys shot their mouths off."

"I know. Hua and Chay are being—disciplined for that. That kind of mistake we can't ignore. It won't happen again, we're having some training sessions—"

"You should've walked away when it fucked up, the bimbo didn't know one fucking thing!"

"I guess you're right," Colin mumbled petulantly. "Wasn't the best idea I ever had. How was I gonna know the guy'd turn out to be some Bruce Lee?"

"You should have. Investigating these men as thoroughly as we check the subjects should be part of the protocol. I've said that for years."

"I think we'll have to do that from now on."

"Now on doesn't count. We can't have Andi Lawrence going out on-line. And she'll have to, sooner or later, you know that."

"We're gonna have to find another answer to that. We keep having trouble with it, monitors or no. Susie-Q just won't stop trying."

"She has, Colin. She's fine, she hasn't done a thing in a while now, she—"

"Got that page on World's Chat."

"Yeah, but we don't know what it was about and she didn't answer it, she knew better."

"You gotta ask yourself, Albert. This guy is in a mess. He knows it. He's not gonna take time to go to the fucking World's Chat site and page Susie-Q unless she's said something to him, made him think she might know something. No, she got something by. I don't know what, I haven't had time to go over her logs. Maybe we'll just pink-slip her. She's been a lot of trouble."

Albert stiffened. "I'll protest that, Colin. Sue5 is one of the best we have. She—"

"I know she's your pet, Albert, but—"

"She isn't my pet. She's our best, by the numbers. That's it. If she's been up to something a few hours in solitary should change her mind. That's what we should've done with her, a while back."

"You didn't want to."

"Yeah, well—"

"Look, Albert; mistakes get made, shit happens. Right now we got some problems, we need to pull together and solve them. Right?"

Again, Albert looked miserable. "I suppose. What's happening with the business about that reporter?"

Colin made a snorting noise. "Delling fucked up, that's what, his people didn't get all their ducks in a row quick enough. The bodies got dumped down by the Salton Sea like they were supposed to . . . but that asshole Harrelson tied us to it, at least indirectly, with his stupid postings. We've had fifty calls from people at the *Times*, and a lot of them aren't very nice. That one isn't over and may not be over for a while."

"Something like that was sure to happen, sooner or later." Albert looked disgusted. "All these dudes from Singapore strutting around here, carrying their guns, thinking they're hot shit . . ."

"They could be trusted, and they—"

Albert laughed. "Sure. Like Hua and Chay? Shit, Colin. You might as well have hired thugs off the street."

"Well, we just have to make the best of it. Don't worry, Albert. It'll get taken care of. Nothing like that'll happen again, Delling's taken care of that, at least." He laughed harshly. "We are now an official U.S. government security site. We have Marines watching over us."

"And sooner or later somebody'll ask questions about that, too."

"Nah. It'll get handled." He stood up, went to the man seated on the couch, slapped him on the shoulder. "Come on, Albert, perk up, man! We've had problems before, we've handled them!"

"Not like these. It's coming apart, Colin. I can smell it."

"No, it's not. Now come on, you've got work to do."

"Yeah? What? You just vetoed my ECT idea."

"Make sure the station is ready for the Lawrence bitch. She's close by, we're going to find her any minute!"

74

Laying flat on the surface of a large chunk of tilted rock, Grant sighted through binoculars toward the rocky outcrop that stood between him and the backside of the IIC facility. The remainder of the trip had been uneventful; though the Marines had, as he'd expected, already established a perimeter, he had no trouble, using Harrelson's maps, in finding a trail that led him around it and into the open desert reasonably close by. Here, at the outcrop, a perimeter had been established also, he saw that immediately. But he also saw that the Marines in charge considered the whole thing an exercise, not as something serious. There was a pass through those rocks—it had been marked by Harrelson on the map he'd posted—and there were, at the moment, two bored and tired-looking Marine M.P.s lounging against the rocky face of the outcrop, clearly revealed by a camp light. There was, Grant saw, nothing whatever to prevent him from climbing the outcrop and going over, he wouldn't encounter the Marines at all; but that didn't fit with his plans, the horses couldn't easily scale it—especially not in the dark.

He sighed; more than anything he hated to embarrass them. Sliding off the rock, he walked back to where Mimi was waiting with the truck.

"All right," he said as he adjusted Blue Fire's saddle and slung two long and heavy saddlebags into place behind them. "We're going to take a little ride. We're not going in yet; there're two Marines up there watching the trail, I want to do a recon on them first, see if I can get some information that'll prevent trouble later on. No talking now, voices carry in the desert." She nodded; he mounted his horse and watched while she swung herself into Storm's saddle. Pulling Blue Fire's head around, he started out, at a fairly fast clip, angling away from the pass and using a small dune to mask them from the Marines. It didn't take very long to reach the outcrop, well down from the pass; here he dismounted and silently passed Fire's reins to Mimi, who accepted them with a nod.

Then he started to climb. Moving as quickly as possible with an eye to maintaining silence, he moved across the rocks toward the pass where the Marines were stationed. When he caught a glimpse of them, he pulled back and climbed a little higher. Finally he peeped over and was, as he'd planned, looking down at them from about ten feet up. They were separated, one by the small camp light, the other still lounging against the rocks. Hoping what he needed wouldn't take too long, he waited patiently, listening as one discussed a girlfriend he was having problems with.

Part of the information he wanted was dropped in the conversation just a few minutes later. "Seven o'clock can't come too soon for me." Continuing to listen, he received the rest when the other man, using a small radio, checked in with his HQ, offering as verification the code "Alpha Charlie Two Tango Fox." Once he'd heard this—and noted that the call-in had been made within a minute of the hour—he went back to where Mimi was waiting with the two horses.

"Okay," he told her in a low whisper. "We're going in now. We have two Marine M.P.s between us and the spot where I want to leave these horses." Listening carefully, she nodded. "What I want you to do is ride Storm out at an angle, that way, then turn back toward the rocks and right straight toward them, at a walk, like you were just taking a night ride in the desert. You'll see a pass ahead, ride as if you're planning on going right into it. They aren't going to shoot at you but they will stop you and tell you to turn back." He looked at his watch, then at hers. "Go ahead now," he said as he tethered Fire to a protruding rock. "If I don't make an appearance immediately, try to talk to them, stall, keep them distracted. Okay?"

"And if you don't turn up at all?"

"I will. Count on it. Got it?"

She stuck a thumb up and grinned. "Got it." She walked to Storm and vaulted herself up into the saddle.

"Don't do anything else," he warned her. She nodded again, then rode the Arabian off into the desert at a trot. He watched until she passed a low scrub-covered dune and disappeared from his sight. Then, turning back to the rocks, he climbed into them again and made his way slowly and silently back to the pass. Once he was above the two men, he settled down to wait for Mimi's arrival. While he waited, he took a long piece of black fishing line from his pocket and tied slip-nooses in each end. It wasn't long before he heard the clip-clop of Storm's hooves on the hard-pack desert floor beyond the pass; when he saw her he had to suppress a laugh.

She'd taken her role very seriously. Somehow, she'd cut off the legs of her jeans, converting them into extremely short shorts. She'd also unbuttoned her shirt, apparently removed her bra, and then tied the shirt back across her middle. The two young Marines were reacting exactly as she'd expected, they were transfixed.

But they still moved to block her way, standing side-by-side, close together—and right under Grant's vantage point. "Uh— sorry, ma'am, you're gonna hafta stop," one of them managed as she drew closer. "No trespassing beyond this point."

"Oh, but this is where I always ride!" she complained plaintively. She stretched her arms up seductively. "I just love riding out here in the moonlight, it's so nice . . . " She pouted. "It wasn't this way when I was here a month ago!"

"No, ma'am. But I—uh—" He trailed off as she leaned over the horse's neck, letting him see more cleavage.

Grant was ready and waiting, and he took full advantage of the distraction. Aiming carefully, he dropped one of the nooses over one man's head; the Marine, not even feeling the light touch of the line on his shoulders, swiped at what he apparently thought was an insect. Before he realized what had happened, Grant had dropped the other end over the other man's head. With one movement of the single piece of line he snatched them both tight. Then he jumped down from his perch, landing lightly next to them, and, grabbing the line closer to them, yanked the two men close together. Both grabbed at their throats, their eyes bulging in disbelief.

"Just relax, boys," Grant told them. "I'm not going to hurt you. I just need you out of the way for a little while." The men, the larger of the two especially, continued to struggle; Grant tightened the lines more and they stopped.

"Good. Now, let's get you secured here. Hands behind your backs." He pulled a roll of duct tape out and, while holding the line with one hand, rolled several turns around each man's wrists. As soon as their hands were secure, he took the line loose from their necks.

"Mister, you just bought yourself one shitload of trouble!" one of them snapped as soon as he could speak. "We're U.S. Marines, you can't do this!"

"Looks like I did," he said mildly. "Come on now, move over here, I don't want to leave you two exposed if anybody runs drive-by patrols through here." He took the two-way radio from one of them. "You're supposed to check in on a schedule, I know, I have to take this." He grinned at the determined looks that appeared on their faces. "No, guys, don't worry about it, I know you don't want to tell me your check-in schedule and code and I won't make you. Sit down here." The men made a little show of resistance, but they finally sat; Grant taped their ankles together. "Okay, good. I'm going to take your two-way and your ammo; I'll leave you everything else. I should be back pretty soon, I'll turn you loose then."

Mimi had watched the whole operation from Storm's back. "Think you should gag them?"

"Nah. That's a pain for them and it's a soft perimeter. From inside the pass here especially, yelling's a waste of effort." He looked up at her and grinned. "By the way, love your outfit."

She smiled back. "Thank you, sir. I hope—our friend—won't be upset that I ruined a pair of her jeans."

Good, Grant thought, very good—she's on the ball, no names. "It was for a good cause." He stood up, looked back down at the two bound men. "Comfortable?"

"Is that some kinda sick joke?"

"No, it isn't. I hate doing this, guys, I do. But I have to get by here." The two Marines just glared; Grant shrugged, then mounted Storm behind Mimi. "Okay," he told her, "let's go get Fire. See you in a minute, guys." With Grant directing her, she rode Storm along the side of the outcrop until they came to the place where Fire still waited, tethered. Grant switched to him and they rode back; the two Marines were where he'd left them.

"Hopefully this won't take long," he said as they rode past.

The pass through this outcropping was fairly short; ahead, more scrubby desert, more rocks—a mile and a half or so to a point where a new ridge, looming darkly, rose from the desert floor. Riding at a walk, with Mimi alongside, Grant again consulted the printed copy of the map. According to it, the ridge ahead had a little valley half a mile in, protected, where he'd planned to leave the two horses—now, where he planned to leave Mimi as well. He hoped the map was accurate; so far it had been, the man who'd drawn it clearly knew the rudiments of cartography.

"Seems like," Mimi commented, "we should be in rubber rafts instead of on horses."

He looked at her blankly. "Rubber rafts?"

"Sure. In all the movies, you always see SEALs in those inflatable rafts. You know."

He did know; he'd been in many of them. "They don't work too well in the desert."

"Too bad; kind of out of your element in a way."

He shrugged. "Doesn't matter. Half the time you only use the sea to get where you're going. The objective might be in the desert, in the mountains, in the jungle. We trained in all of them."

"Must've been exciting."

"At times."

"What made you join the SEALs?"

He shrugged again. "Youthful idealism," he told her. "I had ideas about stopping terrorists. I never did stop any."

"You ever see any real action?"

"No. Our unit went in in Panama, I was out before the Gulf War started. Panama was a joke, there wasn't anything to do. We escorted some Americans out, nobody ever fired a shot." He sighed. "But I don't regret that. Getting into fights wasn't what I wanted. In the end, I wasn't suited for the SEALs—or for the Navy itself, for that matter."

"I wish you'd tell me about it—"

He looked over at her again, rather sharply. "Why?"

She turned her eyes away. "I was just . . . interested. You're a strange man, Grant . . . strange in a good way . . ."

He watched her for a few more seconds, then looked up at his destination again. "I don't think so," he told her. "I just try to do what I think is right, that's all." He cracked a small grin, turned back to her. "You're a sort of an unusual wannabe actress, too," he told her.

She smiled—though it seemed to him somewhat strained. "Thanks, I know that's a compliment," she replied. "I haven't always done what I thought was right, Grant," she admitted. "A lot of times I've done what was—easiest. Like taking this job. I didn't ask a lot of questions. I'm watching you risk everything to rescue the real Andi, and I . . . well, it's just started me thinking, that's all . . ."

He gazed at her steadily. "You're taking risks too," he said bluntly. "For starters, you were part of what the law would call an assault on those two Marines back there."

"I'm not worried. You didn't hurt them. Anyway. I just wanted to help. If that means taking a few risks, that's okay."

"I still don't want to put you in danger, and I don't plan to. You'll stay with the horses, well away from that place, while I go in."

"Grant, I—"

"No arguments. I'm commanding this mission, you're a grunt. You do what I say. Got it?"

She saluted smartly. "Yes, sir!"

"Good. Now let's get a move on, I want to be in position to go in around two or three in the morning."

75

Although it was agony to do so, Andi waited a while after the two men had left to exit her hiding place. Once out, she sat down heavily in the swivel chair in front of the computer and began tapping the computer's "enter" key with a regular cadence.

A few seconds later the text screens appeared. "Yes?"

She stared at that, not knowing what to type; was that her mysterious benefactor? Or someone else? She had no way of knowing. For a moment she was confused, why hadn't Sue5 called her by name, as before? After a few seconds, she understood—just as she couldn't be sure who was on the other end of this link, neither could Sue5 be sure. She considered the problem for a moment, then got an idea.

"We should have," she typed, "decided on a password." She waited, wondering if the other woman was astute enough to pick that up.

"We should have, Andi," appeared on her screen and she breathed a sigh of relief. "I wasn't sure it was you . . ."

"Me neither."

"The password is 'Nadine.' Nobody around here ever uses that name."

"Got it."

"I take it Albert's gone? I can't verify, he's not back here yet."

"Yes, he's gone." She looked worriedly at the door. "He didn't lock the door when he left, I'm sure of it. You think I should lock it?"

"No. Nobody else is likely to come in there. Albert has a great memory, if he left it unlocked and he finds it locked when he comes back he'll know something's wrong. He should be here shortly, I can let you know if he's coming back. If he follows his pattern, he'll sleep for a while. He was sleeping up there, I bet."

"Yes, he was. Until Grant—no, Colin—came in and woke him up. They were talking. They're worried."

"I know they are. They say anything interesting?"

"They said a lot. I don't know what it all means."

"Tell me about it, Andi. Maybe there's something useful here."

"They talked about 'recruiting' me. They said the reason I'd had a chance to escape was because someone messed with the sedative, but they don't know who. And they talked about you, something about someone paging you on World's Chat. Colin wants to pink-slip you, Albert wants to put you in solitary for a while. I didn't understand."

There was no reply for several long seconds. "So Colin wants to pink-slip me now," she replied finally. "Well, I hope he does, that's what I want too. After we've gotten you out of here."

" 'Pink-slipping' means getting fired, right? I thought you were a captive here."

"I am. Don't worry about it, Andi. They probably aren't going to do that right now, they have too many other problems. What else?"

"They talked about a reporter and someone named Harrelson and bodies. It sounded like they were talking about murders— or, I don't know, maybe accidental deaths. They said this was a government security site. Something about Singapore. I can't remember all of it . . . I'm really tired, I don't know what I'm going to do, I wish I understood more, what this place is, why this is happening . . ."

"Andi, don't lose it now, you've come too far. I can answer some of your questions: this place is owned by a company based in Singapore. They make specialized interface chips and devices for computer systems; some agency in the U.S. government, I don't know what agency, they've kept that well-hidden—has a big interest in what they do. They cleared the way for the company to build on this site and to set up their own security. The execs of the company have ties to the Singapore government, and they use regular SAF—Singapore Armed Forces—personnel as security guards. Just a few days ago a reporter from the *LA Times* came here to get a story on this place, she'd been told about it by someone named Harrelson. The SAF guards caught them sneaking around outside the fence at night and shot them dead."

"My God!"

"Yes. It was horrible and very stupid. But in Singapore it would've been okay—that's the mentality there. Here, there's a problem. So now—if I understand all the internal memos I've been reading correctly—the agency that's interested has pulled some strings in Washington and gotten this place declared as a U.S. security site. We have Marines from the base at Twenty-nine Palms patrolling outside the fence. The SAF still takes care of security inside. They're who's looking for you."

"And if they find me they'll kill me. Is that what you're saying?"

"No. That's what Colin was talking about. He still wants to recruit you. Put you where I am. Don't ask me what that involves. Just believe me when I say you don't want that to happen."

"Okay, I won't ask. What's this about the page on World's Chat?"

Again there was a pause. "I should tell you now, I suppose. I didn't want to get your hopes up in case it goes wrong. The page was from Grant Kingsley."

Her heart seemed to jump in her chest; but then it sank again. "You mean Colin? But that doesn't make any sense . . ."

"No. Not Colin. Grant. The real one. The one you fell in love with on the Internet. He paged me because he discovered that the 'Andi' he met was a fake, just like the 'Grant' you met was a fake. He knows you're in here and he's coming to try to rescue you."

She stared at these words for a very long time; as she did tears welled up in her eyes until she could no longer see the screen. A wracking sob burst from her chest. "I can't believe that," she typed, feeling it was lame, that it expressed nothing.

"Believe it. Sometime tonight he'll be coming in. I'm in contact with him through Todd. He's already past the Marines' perimeter."

"But he can't!" She wiped at new tears, her cheeks were streaked with them. "They might kill him! Didn't you say they killed that reporter? He can't break in here all alone! You have to tell him to stop!"

"(laugh) Oh, like he'd listen to *me!* No, Andi. There is a risk, of course, it isn't a sure thing. I'm praying he doesn't get hurt. But he might be able to pull it off. He's very skilled. And I believe in him."

"I don't understand."

"I know. He never told you. He was a Navy SEAL. One of the best, a commander. He has all sorts of commando skills and these people here don't have any clue about that, he'll be able to take them by surprise. I believe in him. He is the best, I've known him for a long time, I've . . . on the Net, I mean, I've known him."

"I didn't know . . . but Sue, I don't want him to do this! I don't want him killed trying to rescue me! I'd rather let them recruit me, whatever that is! If he knows I'm in here, that I've been kidnapped, can't he just call the police?"

"The U.S. government is involved, it isn't that simple, there'd be all sorts of red tape to go through before any police got in here, and by then both you and I would no longer be here. We'd get our pink slips real quick."

"I still don't understand that."

"Fired, like you said. Terminated. Except that when you terminate captive labor you don't just throw them out in the street. You . . . terminate them. You understand now?"

76

Riding under clear skies and bright moonlight, Grant and Mimi soon reached the spot where he'd planned to leave the horses. The map was perfect; it was just as shown, an expanse of flat desert floor shielded fully on two sides and partially on a third by rocky outcrops. Near a scraggly Joshua tree he stopped the horses, he and Mimi dismounted and tethered them to it.

"Now," he told her as he pulled the big saddlebags off Blue

Fire's back, "here's where you're going to stay." He looked at her hard. "You have to understand that there's a chance I might not come back." He looked down at his watch. "But I don't know how long this'll take, either. I'm pretty sure those two Marines we left tied up back there are due to be relieved at seven in the morning, so I'd suggest that if I'm not back here by, let's say, six-thirty, then you take Storm and go. There's water in the trailer; take some with you and ride east along the highway, Vidal Junction is the next town and it's a lot closer than Twenty-nine Palms, about thirty miles. You can wait there until, oh, I'd say noon; watch for my truck, I'll come there if you're gone. If I don't show up by then call Paula and tell her to go ahead and call the police."

She nodded. "I don't like thinking you won't be coming back, but okay, I understand. You want me to leave Fire here?"

"Yes, just to cover bases. If we make it out late, he's bigger and stronger than Storm and he can carry more. Get him into the shade but leave him near the path so that if—if I can't look after him, the Marines'll find him."

She searched his eyes, looking worried. "I will."

"Good." He opened the saddlebags, dug inside; the first thing he came out with was a box of bullets. "For the automatic," he told her. "Do not, under any circumstances, shoot at the Marines. These are for—well, you know who they're for."

"Yes, I do."

"Keep the handgun even if you have to run. But I'm going to leave this, too." He pulled an assault rifle, a copy of the famous AK-47, from one of the bags. "You know how to use this thing?"

"Yes, pretty much." She took it from him, examined it, touched the cocking lever. "Pull this back, right? Semi-auto?"

"You got it." He pointed near the top of the curved clip. "Release is here. And here's five more clips, thirty shots each."

"Lots of firepower."

"I hope you don't need it. Let me find you a spot now." Leaving her standing beside the horses, he climbed into the rocks; it didn't take long for him to locate a pocket that gave her a reasonable view and good protection. Standing up, he motioned to her and she made the climb quickly.

"Here?" she asked when she stood beside him.

"Right here." He noticed she wasn't panting at all. "You're in good shape."

"Yeah. Exercise to keep the body trim. My career, y'know?"

She laughed. They descended again; Grant removed his plaid shirt, stuffed it into a saddlebag, and replaced it with a black pullover. "You still got the legs of those jeans?" he asked as he took out a jar of cream.

"Yes."

"Good. Might want to just pull them on, it's getting cold. Always does that in the desert at night."

"I'm okay for now." She watched as he opened the jar and smeared black makeup across his face. "Grant, can I ask you a question?"

"Sure."

"Why are you trusting me like this? It doesn't make sense . . ."

He grinned at her. "Because you've been carrying that automatic around for a while now." He blackened the backs of his hands as well.

She nodded. "Okay, I see . . . but what if I'd been—on the other side, what if I'd pulled it on you? I mean . . ."

"You didn't know about my background until after I caught you stowing away. Fact is, I think, you still don't."

"I know the SEALs are—trained in stuff like you did back at the hotel . . ."

"Well-trained, yes. And I was an ambitious boy at one time."

She laughed. "Are you saying I couldn't pull anything? I couldn't get the drop on you?"

"I wouldn't say couldn't. I'd say the chances aren't good."

"That's hard to believe."

"That's true." He put the makeup away; a pair of black-bladed knives in sheaths came out of the bag, he strapped them around each of his calves, and a small backpack went onto his shoulders. "Time for me to go now. Don't mess with the bags. I have some stuff there I might need, but I don't think so; I'll come back if I do."

"I understand." He nodded once more, then started off toward the facility. "Grant?" she called.

He turned. "Yeah?"

"Come back. Okay?"

He grinned. "I'll do my damndest." He left her there with the horses, standing quite still, watching him, and made his way into the last rocky outcropping that stood between him and the facility.

It didn't take him long to locate the cleft between the rocks that Harrelson had noted prominently on his map, as if he'd been thinking of secret reconnaissance missions when he drew them. Grant moved into the cleft cautiously, staying close to the rocks, melting into the shadows. Soon enough he could see the fence and several buildings beyond.

He examined the fence. He'd expected something like the one at the Army's Edgewood Research Center in Maryland, which had a double row of fencing with a no-man's-land in between and was under constant surveillance by TV monitors, but this fence wasn't that elaborate. Just a single row of wire, and there were no TV cameras, only audio monitors. There was a reason for this, he realized; the occupants were trying to compromise between security and their desire not to arouse too much curiosity.

And that meant that getting in wasn't going to be difficult. He had wire cutters but he didn't want to use them, it announced his presence too well. Remembering Sue5's caution about the regular patrol inside the fence, he waited patiently until the Land Rover carrying SAF soldiers—in uniform, he noted with surprise—passed by the gate that stood to his left. Once they'd gone, he crept toward the gate and, after assuring himself that there were no video cameras watching from here, approached it.

As he'd expected, there was a slot in it—a slot just large enough to accept the credit-card sized plastics he'd taken from Hua and Chay. But he didn't expect it to work; if these people were cautious they'd know they'd lost these, and would've changed the code of these locks. Hoping they weren't sophisticated enough to set an alarm on old codes, he stuck the card in the slot, then withdrew it. To his immense pleasure, a little green LED above the slot sprang to life; he pulled the gate open, slipped inside, closed it behind him. A quick run across the roadway that paralleled the fence took him to shadows near one of the buildings, where, crouching, he allowed himself a smile. He was dealing with careless opponents, overconfident opponents. That helped to even the odds, it helped a lot.

After a moment, he looked up at the building. On this wall there were no doorways; he could see two ground-floor windows. Staying in the shadows, his black clothes and blackened face blending in well, he peeked around both corners. This building was long and slender, not large; it wasn't the one Sue5 had considered Andi's likely hiding place. On one side, farthest from the gate, there was a road and a parking lot, and beyond that was a long low building that had the look of a manufacturing facility, near which were several large tanks of the sort used to store liquified natural gas. On the other side of the gate, which opened onto a short drive, was another building similar to this one; beyond it no large ones were visible. His target, as he remembered from his reconnaissance, lay on the other side of this building. Listening, he heard the sound of the patrol's engines, distantly. Not knowing what possible threats waited for him around the corners, he huddled in place, a shadow among shadows, the still-white palms of his hands concealed, his eyes slitted and shaded with his left arm. His right hand rested on the butt of the automatic.

The patrol appeared; Grant remained motionless as they approached. The men in the vehicle looked even more bored than the Marines guarding the pass; one was dozing. They saw nothing, and a moment later they were gone.

Rising again, he moved to the side of the building nearest the fence and started making his way down. Halfway along was a doorway with a small stoop and an outdoor light. Flat against the wall he moved to it.

There was no sentry here, just a door. Stepping up to it, for the moment exposed in the light, he tried it, found it locked. There was another slot like the one in the gate, but, knowing that his objective probably wasn't here, he moved on to the end of the wall.

Ahead now was a dangerous open area, beyond was a small white-block building, and beyond that was the large building he presumed was his target. At this hour of the night, he might've expected the place to be almost deserted, but it didn't seem to be, not if the numbers of lighted windows was an indication, not if the faint sounds he was hearing could be taken as an indicator. Even as he watched, a shift in the light from that large building suggested a door opening and closing; a few seconds later, two men and a woman—all Asians, all dressed like hospital workers—came down a walkway toward the building he was standing alongside and disappeared around the other corner. Moments later, he heard the sound of another door opening and closing.

He waited, listening, watching; there was no further activity. Darting to the block building, smoothly going down on hands and knees as he reached it, he was again hidden in the shadows as he got his first really good look at the large building he'd targeted.

It looked more like some small regional hospital than anything else; that the white-clad workers had just left it enhanced that view. Facing him, at the end of a small walkway, was a brightly lighted double doorway, and here there was a uniformed and clearly armed guard on duty. Like the men on patrol, he appeared bored and inattentive; the chances were, Grant told himself, that he'd been standing that guard duty for months or years without ever being required to take any action. With Andi loose in the compound, more alertness might've been expected; Grant assumed they weren't taking her as a threat, just as a problem. Since she couldn't get out of the compound— she surely couldn't be expected to scale a ten-foot, razor-wire topped fence—finding her was just a matter of time, nothing else.

He could not see either the building's front or back. Whatever he did was going to involve some risk of discovery; he was going to be exposed, at least briefly, as he passed between the shadows around this building and the other.

Searching the ground, he found a small rock. After another quick look at the guard, he threw it, hard, up and over the block building. He watched the guard; a second later, gratifyingly, he heard a small clatter.

The man did not move, did not look up at all; he paid not the slightest attention. Grant smiled. Crouched in position, he waited for something, anything, to give him the slight opening he'd need to dash across the open area.

It came just a few minutes later when someone came along the walk from the direction of the buildings Grant had just left, another white-coated man. As he approached the door, the guard turned his head away, idly watching the man, whom he did not challenge, as he went in the door. As he turned his head Grant, keeping low, shot across the intervening space, not worried too much about small noises. By the time the white-coated man had entered, Grant was again in shadow, flat against the wall of the large building, watching carefully for anyone else coming from the buildings he now figured were residence quarters. Moving to the back corner of the building and looking around, he saw nothing either alarming or interesting; ahead, there was an extension of the structure back toward the fence, and light at the end of it suggested another door.

Now he had to make a decision: search for other entries, or go inside? Getting past the guard did not, he was certain, present a problem, but he had no idea what he'd encounter on the other side of the door, and this seemed like a busy area, probably not his best way in. Making his decision, he moved around the corner and along the wall to the end of the extension, where, yet again, he looked around the corner.

A service entrance, clearly. There was a covered entryway in front of the door; he could not see either the door or any guard who might be there without exposing himself. Still, it looked like a good bet, it wasn't a place he'd expect to be busy in the middle of the night.

There was a risk, but it was worth it. Slipping around the corner cautiously, keeping low, he tried to look into the entryway but still couldn't see far enough. Deciding he had no choice, he stepped around with arm raised, ready to take down anyone who might be standing there.

There wasn't anyone; he was staring at a pair of double doors. Perfunctorily, he tried them. Locked. There was a keycard slot and he tried the card he'd used to get through the fence. Nothing. He still felt it was worth the effort if he could find a reasonably silent way through these doors. He searched the door frame, up and down, and as he did he found himself staring into the lens of a small video camera mounted on the wall. Above the lens, a tiny red light burned.

Cursing silently, he snapped himself back against the wall under the camera, out of its sight. First mistake; all he could hope was that the camera was set up for unmanned recording or that whoever was manning the security control center wasn't paying any more attention to business than the guards he's seen. Moving along the wall again, he scooped up handful of dirt and wetted it with spit. Then, with a quick jump, he plastered it into the lens.

Turning his attention back to the door, he examined the lock mechanism. He preferred not to leave evidence of his passage, not to alert anyone to his presence. If this mission went perfectly he'd find Andi and Sue5 and get them out without anyone ever knowing he'd been there. But that perfection he was inclined to doubt.

The lock was a standard dead bolt, electronically operated. He dismissed it. There were glass panels in each door, wired glass, not easy to get through silently and impossible to go through without leaving evidence. He backed off, looking above the door; this extended section of the building was only one story high. Taking a few steps back, he took a three-step run at the entryway, jumped up, and caught the edge of the roof with his fingers. Out of practice, he missed his first attempt to launch himself up atop the roof, but his second was successful.

Now on the flat tarred roof, he took another look around. From here, the building rose another floor without a window facing this section. There were windows on each side of it— windows and a three-inch wide concrete ledge leading to them. Another strip, above the windows, offered handholds—if it were strong enough. Standing near the edge of the roof on the side nearest the residences, he tested them and decided they would probably hold. The window to his left was lighted, the one to his right was dark; he moved out to his right along the ledge, and, moments later, reached the window.

The window was not designed to be opened at all, but the glass was not wired. Holding on with his fingertips, he pressed himself hard against the wall so that most of his weight would be on his toes. He reached into his backpack, locating a suction cup and glass cutter. After wetting the cup and sticking it on the glass, he cut widely around it, tapped lightly around the scratch, then caught the now-loose pane by the ring on the cup. Hoping the cup would hold—it hadn't been used in a long time—he turned the pane to the side and lowered it inside the room. He followed it, dropping lightly to the darkened floor inside.

He was in.

77

"You can't give up on me now, Andi! Hang in there!"

Wiping her face, Andi stared at the words on the screen. "I know, Sue," she answered, her fingers numb as she typed. "I know. I'm just so tired . . . so scared . . ."

"A while ago you were so mad. Can't you get that back?"

"Yes . . . Maybe. Have you heard anything else from Grant?"

"He's inside the fence. I saw him, for just a minute."

"You *saw* him?"

"Yes. I've been able to tie into the security video link, that's going to come in handy tonight. He made a slip, he stood in front of a camera for an instant. Then he blocked it. I've got a graphic sitting in that slot in security, they won't know."

"Oh, good. He slipped up. Just what I wanted to hear."

"No . . . it wasn't good. I wish he'd check in with Todd, he hasn't done that yet. Andi, you have to help me figure out which room you're in so I can tell him. Right now, I don't know."

"You don't know where Albert's office is?"

"No. I've only recently gotten some views of this place, I've been working on that since they started to recruit you."

She sighed. "I can't believe I fell into it like this . . ."

"Anybody would've, Andi."

"You don't understand. I spent days—and nights—with the fake Grant, with Colin. I didn't know. I was having the time of my life. That makes me sick now, just sick."

"Andi, you aren't the only one, don't be so hard on yourself. I did the same thing, the exact same thing. I was in love with a man named Dave, a man I'd never met except on the Internet. Colin posed as him and he swept me off my feet, I've never known anything like that before. He's done it to other women, too, a bunch of them."

"Where'd they get this guy? I didn't know guys like that existed!"

"I didn't either. Colin is a strange one. Albert's an old friend of his and Albert rambles on sometimes when he's upset. It was Albert that first hooked up with IIC, in Singapore—boy genius, you know the type. He and Colin went to college together. Colin's not a dummy by any means, he'd already had several good positions in companies here in the States, but he constantly had problems with women. Albert says they were always falling all over him. I guess having known him I can accept that. I imagine you can too."

"Yes, I'm afraid I can."

"Putting together pieces of stories Albert's told me, he developed a habit of picking up women, having brief torrid affairs with them, and then just throwing them out like they were part of the trash. There were always more, waiting and eager. His problem was he couldn't discriminate. I think he gets his jollies from having women fall in love with him and then breaking their hearts. He never seemed to be able to stop himself from doing this with the boss's daughter, so to speak, and it kept him in trouble all the time, got him fired from company after company.

"Eventually, down and out, living on some woman's money, he went to see Albert in Singapore. Albert got him a job there, with IIC. They were developing—well, let's just say a product. For a while things were fine. Colin and Albert were rising fast in the company.

"But then Colin resumed his old patterns; the daughter of the company's chairman fell in love with him, and that man is a very powerful figure in Singapore, there was going to be big trouble about that one. The old man was going to have Colin killed."

"Too bad he didn't succeed."

"I agree. Things sure would've been different for us."

"So what happened?"

"What happened was Mr. Auan's bright idea. Colin had been a specialist in research marketing; he'd developed a profile for the most likely users of the company's product in developed countries like the United States or England or Japan. The profile suggested a young professional woman, 24 to 38, unattached, who'd just come off of a bad love affair. There were a lot of other factors in the mix, but that's it in a nutshell. Women like that could be found in the Chat rooms on the Internet looking for romance. I was. I know that."

"But I wasn't! I was doing research!"

"Doesn't matter. You fit the profile. And you did fall in love on-line. You were prime."

"I don't understand."

"The company was completing the plant in California then, but nobody had any idea how they were going to get research subjects. Do you know that you can still buy young girls from their fathers in countries like Thailand?"

"I've heard stories, yes."

"Well, that was what they planned to use at the plant here. The idea was to make the—the services—the product made possible irresistible to markets here, markets like government agencies. They'd already made some overtures, and they'd gotten promises of protection by the government—even though some of the things they do are illegal under U.S. law. Illegal under Singapore law too, but it hardly matters there."

"Why here, then? The world is small now, why didn't they just stay in Singapore?"

"They didn't want to lose their monopoly on the product after they'd spent millions developing it. Singapore's a city-state, everything is packed together. Here, they could be isolated out in the desert, there was a lot better control. Also, they're closer to the markets they want to reach. It made sense in a lot of ways, and, since they had a promise of protection, why not?"

"But there was a problem."

"Yes. The Thai and Cambodian village girls they were buying were unsophisticated, they required a lot of education and training. They needed something better—people like us. To Mr. Auan, it seemed obvious that Colin, given his history, was perfectly suited to act as a 'recruiter,' he was a built-in resource, as Albert pointed out—it's one more reason they go after women and not men, they have Colin and they don't have his female counterpart. He's responsible for the marketing reports, he decides what sorts of people to recruit, and he's the one to recruit them. So far he's done it all—the recruitment part has been small—but the demonstrations of the product have gone so well that the services are already a big money-maker, and there's a real demand for more recruits. Colin's got a couple of understudies he's training right now. They plan a lot more recruitments in the next year or so."

"And by recruitment you mean capture. Kidnapping. And, if I understand it right, slavery."

"You understand perfectly."

"They have to be stopped!"

"Exactly my thought, Andi. Once I saw it happening to someone the Fish Man cared about, I so wanted . . ."

Andi watched the sentence stop after the word "wanted"; she waited, but no more came. She felt sure she could guess, and she decided to take the chance.

"You're in love with him too, aren't you, Sue?"

There was a long pause. "Yes. But it makes no difference. He loves you. And I can't leave this place."

"Oh, Sue, I'm sorry."

"Why? It isn't your fault. You didn't know I existed. Besides, he never loved me. I was a friend, a Net friend, nothing more."

"Sue . . ."

"Let's drop it, okay? We have other things we need to do. Soon Grant is going to call his son on a cellular he's carrying, and I need to try to direct him to you. I need to figure out where you are."

"How can I help?"

"To start with, what floor are you on?"

"Floor? Yes, wait . . . the third. Third floor, not counting the basement."

"Front or back of the building?"

"I don't know."

"When you looked out the window, what did you see?"

"A couple of wide driveways, a big parking lot, a big low building."

"You're in the front. Front, third floor. That narrows it down, that really helps. Is there a way you can figure out which end of the building you're on?"

"Which end . . . well, the sh—the way I came up here, I'd guess to be in the center of the building at the back. I came to my left to get to this room. Does that help?"

"Some. You're more toward the south side, then. I wish there was a way I could narrow it down more, I don't want Grant doing a room-to-room search."

"Want me to see what's on the door?" she asked jokingly.

"You brave enough?"

She stared at the words. "Is it safe?" she finally typed back.

"No. I can't say if anyone's in the hall or not."

Looking away from the screen, she gazed at the door for a long moment. She hoped Sue was thinking about all this clearly; she was aware she wasn't. "Where's Albert?"

"He's clear or I'd be telling you to hide. He's down here, sleeping."

She took a deep breath before sending her next line: "Okay, I'm going to go see if I can look, first. I may be a minute."

"Okay. I'll put the screen-saver back up just in case. You know the code. Be careful, Andi."

"I will." Leaving the computer, she moved to the door and, laying her head against it, listened carefully. Hearing footsteps—coming her way—she resisted the urge to pull back. Instead, she kept listening, and the sounds passed the door. Feeling like she was sweating even though the room was cool, the sound of her own heartbeat almost drowning out any sounds she might've heard from outside, she held her position firmly.

Finally, after hearing nothing for several seconds, she gingerly turned the door handle and began pulling the door open.

Seeing nothing except a plain gray-carpeted hallway and an-other closed door directly across from hers, she pulled the door back until she could see its other side. The logo on it read, "336. Dr. Albert Michaelson." She almost laughed. That was a real surprise. But at least she had the number. She looked away and started to close the door.

And suddenly, without warning, made eye contact with an Asian man in what looked like a policeman's uniform.

"Hey!" he yelled, lunging toward the door.

She emitted a little peep of surprise and tried to slam the door closed, but he was too quick; he was on it before the latch engaged, pushing hard against her pressure.

Realizing she was not going to be able to win, she let go suddenly. Turning on her heel, she bolted for the laboratory, though she did not have a clear idea what she was going to do once she got there. The man, thrown off balance when she re-leased the door, careened into the room; the door smoothly swung shut behind him. He was only off-balance for an instant before he was after her, sprinting toward the door to the lab. Faster than she, he overtook her before she could begin to close the door.

"You will stop this!" he snapped in accented English. Staring at him wide-eyed, she retreated toward the lab bench, her hands fumbling at whatever was there. "There is no purpose—"

His words were cut off as Andi, having found a beakerful of some liquid, threw it in his face. Startled, he jumped back, wip-ing at his eyes. Looking around quickly, Andi lifted the binocu-lar microscope from the bench nearby and, while the man was still clearing his eyes, brought the rear edge down hard on his head. He let out a groan and collapsed.

Breathing hard, she stared at him, wondering if he was dead. There was no blood, and a quick check of his pulse revealed he was not. Fighting her urge to simply run away from here as quickly as possible, she considered her next step. Asking her-self what Grant, the real one, would do now, she decided he should be tied up—but with what? Taking heart from those thoughts—even while admitting to herself that she'd gotten the upper hand in this situation thanks to luck, not because of any real skill or fast thinking on her part—she realized she could use the sleeves of his shirt and the legs of his pants. After cut-ting them free, she divided the pants legs into strips, rolled him over, and tied his hands behind his back, hoping he would not wake up before she finished. She then tied his ankles and gagged him; only when she was finished did she notice that he was wearing a holster with a handgun in it. Gingerly she took the gun out and examined it. She didn't know how to use it. There was a switch affair on the side she assumed was a safety, but she had no idea which position was "safe" and which was "fire"; her best guess would be that it would be in "safe" position now. Nevertheless, feeling that it was better in her possession than in his, she slipped it into the pocket of her shorts. Then she checked his face, where she'd thrown the beaker of liquid, sniffed at it; it smelled like alcohol. Taking no chances, she took several handfuls of water from the tap and washed his eyes off; he didn't respond.

Then, leaving him, she went back to the computer and began tapping enter.

"Yes?"

"Nadine."

"What's on the door? Did you see?"

"Yes." She was feeling proud of herself, competent. The real Grant, she was sure, would approve. "It says '336, Dr. Albert Michaelson.' "

"Great! I'll relay that to Grant as soon as possible."

"We had a problem here," she typed airily. "But I took care of it. Took care of it myself."

78

Grant's first act, on entering the second-floor room, was to replace the cut-out of glass. Holding it with his suction cup and using clear Scotch tape, he restored it to its original position. It would not stand close scrutiny—the incision was pretty obvious from inside the room—but it wouldn't be noticeable from outside. Given that this room—a rather generic office with a computer and a bookshelf covered with advanced UNIX programming texts—was darkened and uninhabited, he could at least hope it would not be entered until sometime in the morning, by which time he hoped to be gone. Sitting down in the chair in front of the darkened computer, he took out the cellular flip-phone he was carrying and dialed Paula's number.

"Yes?" she answered quickly.

"Grant. I'm inside. Is Todd on-line with Sue5?"

"Yes. Hold on." There was a brief pause. "Dad!"

"Hey, son," he answered with a smile. "I'm inside and safe. Tell Sue I went in the side closest to the fence, second floor, just south of some kind of service extension."

"She says great. She wants to know if you're in the big tall building across from a long low one with some big white tanks close to it. She says she saw you there on a video link for a second. She says not to worry about the video, she was able to make sure nobody else saw it."

"Good. Tell her yes, that's where I am, almost right over that camera."

"She says you're close. You're on the back side of the building, second floor. Andi's one floor up from you on the front side. The room she's hiding in is number 336."

"Now ask Sue where she is."

There was another pause. "She says forget it."

"Ask her if she wants me to search the whole damn building for her."

"She says please forget it."

"Tell her I won't."

"Wait . . . she isn't answering . . . there. She says get to Andi first and then she'll tell you."

He sighed. Why, he asked himself, was she being so difficult about this? "All right . . . as soon as I'm with Andi I'll call back. Tell her I won't take no for an answer."

"I'll tell her, Dad."

"I'm going to ring off now. I'll call back when I'm in room 336."

"Be careful, Dad. Please?"

"I will, son. Don't worry. Bye."

"Bye."

Fighting the urge to move out immediately—to get to Andi before something went wrong—he looked at his watch. It had been an hour since he'd heard the Marines at the pass check in; since they weren't going to being doing that, their base would be buzzing them and there'd be a quick response if there wasn't an answer. Taking the radio out of his backpack, he sat still, waiting.

Less than five minutes later, it beeped at him. Turning his head to the side, he keyed the "talk" switch and spoke in a mumble: "Alpha charlie two tango fox." Then, moving it farther away, he muttered—loud enough to be transmitted, but barely—"Shit."

"Watch it, guys," the radio crackled. "On the hour."

"Yes, sir," he answered. Then, switching it back to standby, he secured it in his pack. Safe for another hour, he got up and moved to the door. Opening it a crack, he peered out into the brightly lit hallway. There wasn't anyone visible and no sounds were close. Down to his right he could hear faint voices. This required him to take significant chances of being exposed.

Closing the door, he returned to the window, untaped the pane, and removed it again. After making sure no one was around on the ground to see him, he leaned out and looked up at the next level. There were several darkened windows that might offer access, but there wasn't an easy way up, just the tiny ledges he'd used to reach this one, and they weren't wide enough for him to heave himself up on one to reach the next.

Replacing the pane, he studied the ceiling. Acoustical tile, dropped into place. Standing on the chair, he pushed one panel up and, using the small but powerful flashlight from his pack, took a quick look.

This wasn't bad. Up here, the walls of the hallway didn't exist. It looked like he could manage to go all the way to what he felt sure was a stairwell down to his right. The thin metal lattice that held the ceiling tiles in place wouldn't support his weight, but the cappings atop the walls would. Replacing the tile, he moved the chair against the wall and popped another up. Taking the backpack off—he wasn't going to fit with it on—he placed it up in the ceiling, resting on the wall capping. Then, setting his shoulders diagonal to the hole, he reached in and grabbed the wall capping. Finding it secure, he heaved himself up and through, keeping his weight on the capping, letting his feet rest on the lattice for balance only. Turning himself, he came around to face the stairwell and then replaced the tile he'd removed, leaving no sign of his presence below other than the window glass.

It wasn't going to be easy. There were wires set at diagonals, wires that supported the metal lattices, several of them to be moved past. Pushing the backpack ahead of him, he made slow but steady headway to the first such barrier.

As it turned out, it wasn't as much of an obstacle as he'd feared. He had to squeeze, but there was enough room—barely—for him to angle his body and slip past the wire on one side, as long as he kept a tight grip on the capping so he didn't fall into the lattice over the hallway. Encountering no other problems, he moved silently through the ceiling until he'd reached the stair. The drop ceiling continued into the stairwell, but his way was now blocked completely by a structural wall, he was going to have to descend.

The hallway obviously wasn't the best place to do that. From here—since the lighting fixtures were set into the space above the ceiling—it was easy to determine which rooms were lighted and which were dark. The one at the end of the hall on the back side of the building was lighted. As he reached it he could see an occasional movement through the small gaps between the tiles; at least one person was in there. This was a very busy place this time of night.

He looked at the row of rooms across the hall. These were larger; as he examined the layout, he could see another identical hallway beyond them, which should access the rooms at the front of the building. It wasn't possible, though, to go all the way across. Huge steel I-beams ran the length of the building, and there was only a couple of inches of space between their bases and the ceiling. With slight frustration—this whole thing, he was telling himself, might've been an exercise in futility—he continued to look about the narrow space.

Then he noticed that there was a small space on the back side of the stairway. The way was tight—it would require some wriggling to get through—but the base here looked solid, he wasn't going to have to cling to a wall capping. Maneuvering carefully, he worked his way toward it. Lying on his back, he shined his light up into it.

It would work, he told himself. It went up behind the stair, and the building's metal framing was open into a wall on the next floor. Sitting up, he slipped the backpack back on and, pressing his feet and forearms against the walls of the narrow space, began pushing himself upward. He covered this space quickly, and was soon able to stand upright—inside the wall on the next floor, sheet rock panels in front of and behind him, the capping over his head preventing him for entering this ceiling.

Taking out one of the dark-bladed boot knives, he used the point to drill into the sheet rock wall. To his pleasure, no light appeared in the hole when the point passed through. He then quickly used the knife to cut a hole large enough to step through and emerged into the room.

Leaving the sheet rock panel lying where it fell—there wasn't a point in trying to replace it—he took a look around. This was another office, remarkably similar to the one he'd left on the floor below; he took no time to look around. Moving to the door, he eased it open. Seeing nothing, he glanced at the number posted on it—351. Not too far, he told himself. His goal was the other hallway, though, across the larger rooms in the center of the building. He poked his head out, looked up and down the hallway. This floor was much quieter than the one below. On this side of the hall there were numerous doors, but on the other, there were only three. These might well lead to the hallway beyond.

Deciding it was worth the risk, he stepped out, all his senses alert for the slightest disturbance. Crossing the hall, he tried the nearest door; it wasn't locked. Slowly he pushed it slightly inward. The lights were on. It was a large room with a door on the far side that almost certainly opened into the other hallway.

But there was an obstacle.

A man—an American or European—was sitting almost directly in front of him, facing a flickering computer console. He was paying no attention to it; he was reading a comic book. Taking in the rest of the room at a glance, Grant saw that it was filled with computers, green lights on the fronts of the cabinets indicating they all were running. Opening the door as little as necessary, he slipped silently inside. The man didn't look up. At a crouch, he moved along the wall, peering across the computers, hutches, and bookcases that filled the room. There was another man, just one more. This one was an Asian like most of the people he'd seen here—who was intent on a screen connected to one of the machines.

"Hey, Jake," the man called. "Want to check that link now?"

Comic-book looked up. "Sure." He laid his magazine aside, peered at the screen, tapped a few keys. "Nope. The slash-visual directory is still showing a 404."

"Well, I don't know why!" the other man snapped. "Hang on."

"Sure," comic-book repeated, picking up his magazine—unaware that Grant had taken the conversation as an opportunity to glide silently up behind him.

His arm went swiftly around the man's neck; the comic book

fell to the floor. As Grant tightened the stranglehold he watched the man's face; he released it as soon as he'd lost consciousness. Lowering him gently to the floor, he moved toward the other.

But before he got close, the man, shaking his head in evident frustration, got up from his chair. He turned—and looked directly at Grant.

His eyes widened. "Wha—" was all he managed. Spinning him around, Grant snapped the stranglehold—a hold he could easily make fatal—on him. The man, less surprised than comic-book, struggled, tried to kick at him, but it was useless. In seconds he was on the floor, unconscious but breathing easily. Returning to deal with comic-book first, Grant pulled the tight roll of duct-tape from his pack, bound the man's wrists and ankles, and, tearing off part of his captive's shirtsleeve, gagged him. The other man received the same treatment, after which he moved on to his goal, the far door. He opened it, looked out; this hallway was empty and silent too, and the room across from his was number 340. He stepped out, moved two doors down, stood before 336. He tried it and found it unlocked. Carefully he pushed it open. The lights were on; he saw no one, he could hear someone breathing inside. It might well be Andi, it should be—but it was best not to take a chance, he decided. What he was going to do would frighten her, but that was easily dealt with. He pushed the door, then launched himself through almost at floor-level, rolling over once and coming to his feet ten feet inside, facing back toward it.

A very beautiful Asian woman dressed in shorts stared at him wide-eyed—and those wide eyes were quite blue. He would've smiled at her—except that she looked terrified, she was holding a small automatic, and she was pointing it at him.

79

Having heard someone try the door, Andi had left the computer where she was still talking with Sue5, pulled the gun from her pocket, flipped the safety to the other position—with a silent prayer that she'd guessed right—and, taking a position beside the door on the hinge side the way she'd seen people do in TV cop shows, waited. An instant later the door opened, and what at first she thought might be a large black dog shot through, so low to the ground she didn't think it could be a person. Still she managed to aim the gun, and she held it with both hands as the man flipped gracefully to his feet.

He looked horrifying. Dressed all in black, his face smeared with black, intense eyes staring out from a face as cold-looking as she'd ever seen, his arms extended slightly to the sides and his knees slightly bent as if ready to spring again. But he saw her, and he saw the gun, and he stopped.

"Don't move," she cried, her voice wavering. "Please, don't. I don't want to shoot you."

The man grinned, and the intense look vanished from his face. "That's really good, Andi. I sure don't want you to shoot me either. Not after all this."

She hesitated, staring. He knew who she was! She'd never seen this rugged face before, this somewhat older face than the man's she'd known as Grant. "Grant?" she asked, lowering the gun slightly. "Grant Kingsley?"

He straightened up, dropped the aggressive-looking stance. "Yes, I believe that is my name, Dr. Lawrence."

For a moment she didn't say anything, she just stared. Then, very slowly, she let the gun drop to her side. "Oh, my God, you did come for me, you did . . ."

He stepped forward toward her and she fell against him. "I came to rescue you but it looks to me like you were doing pretty well on your own."

She laid her head on his shoulder. "No, I wasn't . . . I wasn't even sure the gun could fire . . ."

He took it from her. "Safety's off." He snapped it back to the other position. Behind her back, he worked the slide. "Round chambered, too, it would've fired if you'd pulled the trigger. You were doing fine. How'd you get this, anyway?"

She gestured toward the lab. "There's a man in there, he saw me when I was trying to go into the hall, he chased me, I managed to hit him over the head with something—I took the gun from him." Pulling back a little, she studied his face, his eyes— not the face and eyes she'd been expecting when she'd flown to Los Angeles, but a nice face, a face full of character. He bore only the slightest resemblance to Colin. For this she was grateful.

Grant laughed. "You've been doing all right. Let's go take a look." He handed the gun back to her. She stared at it for a moment, not wanting it anymore; but then, with a small smile, she slipped it back into her pocket.

Together, they went to the lab and opened the door. To her absolute shock, the man she thought she'd so securely tied was free! Apparently having overheard them talking, he knew he was now facing a pair of opponents. He tried to bolt past them, knocking into her with his shoulder, headed for the outside door.

She'd never seen anyone react so fast as Grant did. Before the man could cover even half the distance, Grant was on him. He spun around, swung a fist; effortlessly Grant moved his head to avoid it, then landed a quick hard punch of his own. The man reeled back; Grant caught him, spun him around, put an arm around his neck, and pulled him up straight. The man struggled, but when he did, Grant simply tightened his grip. As the guard realized he was overmatched and quieted down, Andi watched Grant reach into the small backpack he was carrying and take out a roll of gray tape.

"I thought I'd tied him up well," she moaned as Grant taped the man's wrists. "And he was just waiting for me to come back . . . he would've taken me completely by surprise . . ."

"It isn't easy to tie someone securely with rope," Grant told her. "If it ever comes up again, duct tape does a better job." He looked at the man's uniform, the cut-off sleeves and pants legs. "What happened to him, anyway?"

"Well, I cut off his clothes with scissors and made strips to tie him. There wasn't any rope."

He grinned. "You Andis have a thing about cutting off pants, it seems."

"What?"

"Long story. You'll see, soon. You've been talking to Sue5, right?"

She brightened. "Yes. On the computer, over here."

"Good." He gagged their captive with a lightly applied strip of tape, sat him down on the couch, and went to the computer. Following him, she stood behind his shoulder. On the screen, Sue5 had repeatedly been asking why she wasn't responding.

"Hi, Sue," Grant typed in. "It's me, the Fish Man. Grant."

Sue went instantly, Andi noticed, on alert. "Fish Man? I don't know what you mean."

"Type in, 'the password is Nadine,' " Andi told him.

"Andi just said to tell you the password is Nadine. Talk to me now?"

"Grant! You got there! I knew you could do it! If I could I'd do a little war-dance down here!"

"Hold that off—I want to know where 'down here' is, because we're on our way. Tell me now or I'll start searching through this place, and that isn't going to help our chances of getting out of here clean. I've already left three guys tied up, a window out and a hole in a wall. They're going to know I'm here soon."

"Grant, please. You can't save me. Just take Andi and get out. Do whatever you have to to get this place closed down!"

"No," he typed back. "You've helped us, you've said you're a captive too, I'm not leaving you behind. Tell me where you are."

There was a very long pause. "I don't know exactly where I am, Grant. That's the truth."

"Close as you can say, then."

"I'm begging you not to come down here."

"I'm not listening."

Sue5 didn't answer for several seconds. "I have to get you out of here. If coming here will accomplish that, you'll have to come. Maybe you can do something for me anyway. I'm in one of the rooms on the second floor, right under you. I don't know which one."

"Let me ask her something," Andi said. Grant stood up, let her sit. "Sue, it's Andi. Can't you open the door a crack like I did and see the number? Or is it locked?"

"No. I don't know if it's locked. I can't get to it."

"Can you explain?"

"I'm not—" She paused for several seconds. "Is there any way I can convince you to forget about me? To just go, as quick as you can?"

Over Andi's shoulder, he watched the words appear. "Tell her there isn't." She entered the sentence.

"You can't take me out of here," Sue5 typed back. "You don't understand."

"Let me take it from here," Grant told Andi, and they switched positions again. "I don't know your situation, no. But I *will not* leave without you. I'll find you. If you can't walk out

I'll carry you. If I have to take Andi out and then come back in after you I will. Stop arguing with me, Sue."

There was a considerable pause before she came back. "Okay, Grant."

He grinned. "I don't know what you look like," he went on. "So you'll have to tell us it's you. You know what I look like, right? You've seen my web page?"

"Yes, I know what you both look like, and I have a video link on the door of my room. You'll know what I looked like when you get here, I'll put my picture up on the monitor screen now, it's one of the first things you'll see when you walk in the door. Right now, there's someone in that entryway—Albert Michaelson, Andi knows who he is. But please, please, don't come. Just go, get out."

"We're on our way to you as soon as we can figure out how to get there safely. Let Todd know what's happening. And be ready to go."

"Grant, I can't be ready. I wish you'd listen to me."

"I'm not leaving you. Just hang on, we're going to talk a minute, see what our options are. When we get ready to leave this room, we'll sign out here."

Swiveling the chair around, he turned back to Andi. "The way I came in is a little rough—how'd you get here?" He glanced at the gagged and bound man sitting on the couch. "Wait, we'd better talk back there."

They went to the lab and closed the door. Quickly, and as accurately as possible, she told him about the service shaft, how it fed from the basement to a passage under the sink. As she spoke she showed him, and he knelt to examine the passageway.

"You say there were other passages feeding off this too? On other floors?"

"Yes. Every floor, I think. The one below this, definitely. Several of them."

"This is the way, then. First we try to determine where these lab rooms are in relation to Sue's room." He stood up. "Let's ask her. Be careful you don't say anything out loud that'll let our guest know how we're going out."

"Got it." Together they went back to the computer, where Grant posed the question to Sue.

"There's a wet lab *in* my room," she answered. "Two of them, I think. One in the entryway and one in the section where

I am. As I said, Albert's in the entryway. He won't be a problem for you, Grant. He's unarmed and he's no fighter. Besides, he's asleep right now."

"Well," Grant typed back, "this may be a piece of cake."

"I don't think so."

"We're on our way, Sue. Hang in there. Closing down here." Rising, Grant took Andi back to the laboratory. "All right," he told her. "We want to mislead our friend out there, if that's possible, in case somebody finds him. So you're going into the hole first. I'll leave the door to this room standing open a little, make them think we out down the hall." He knelt, opened the doors in the cabinet. "We're going to need to put all this stuff back."

"Right." With her helping him, they moved the bottles and then the shelf out of the way. Kneeling, Andi went inside; she watched while Grant opened the door an inch and returned. He closed the doors, replaced the shelves, and she assisted him in replacing the bottles in their original positions.

"This way," Andi told him. Leading, she went down the passage to the platform overlooking the shaft, where she stood up. "They checked this," she said in a whisper as he joined her. "I saw the marks they left in the dust. But I was hiding in the basement then, and I guess they haven't looked here again."

"We'll be ready for them if they do," he said, sounding confident. "Let's go, it may take a while to figure out which room is Sue's."

"Okay." She watched as he swung out onto the ladder and, after quickly descending a few rungs, looked back up at her. Not nearly so swiftly she stepped out onto it as well; a moment later they were down a floor to the maze of corridors.

Andi pointed to one. "I think," she said, "that this one leads to the operating room where they took me when I arrived. It's shorter than the others, the room's not as far from here."

He nodded. "Part of the central group of rooms, I'd guess. Sue said right under us, so we need long tunnels. As long as the one we came out of."

"Left and right," she said succinctly. "And down this way—to the right—I could hear sounds like respirators, like patient rooms. An infirmary, maybe."

He grinned at her. "You should have been in recon," he told her. "Quiet from here," he went on as she flushed slightly at the obvious compliment. "I may have to check several rooms, may have to get some people under control. I'll go in first and you hang back."

"You're the one with the experience. Whatever you say."

He nodded, turned, dropped to his hands and knees, and started down the left tunnel. He moved to the far left room first, removed the obstacles, opened the louvered doors to a brightly lighted room; she saw him crouch, tense, and then vanish. A second later there was a thud and a groan, and a few seconds after that he returned. "Not here," he mouthed at her, signaling her to turn around. They checked the next room, which was empty, and the next. When there were none left down this passage, and they returned to the landing.

He frowned. "We go right, I guess. A patient room doesn't really sound right to me."

"But maybe those weren't respirators I was hearing."

"Could be." After moving down the right-hand passage, he scanned the rooms one at a time. Encountering no one, he wasn't required to go in very far. From the third he came out frowning.

He leaned close to her ear. "That is a patient room," he said in a very soft whisper. "There are monitors but they're dark. This doesn't make sense."

"All we can do is keep looking."

"Yes. Let's go ahead." Matching action to words, he went on to the next room. After taking a quick look, he slid back to Andi.

"Probably a go," he said. "Picture of a woman on a monitor, a man sleeping on a cot." She nodded; he returned to the exit, moved the apparently standard shelf, silently slipped through, and stood up. This time she didn't wait, she went after him; as she stood up she saw him looking down at a man sleeping on a cot, a man she recognized as Albert. On a large monitor mounted on the wall was a picture of a smiling young woman, a lovely girl with strawberry-blond hair.

"Albert," a female voice said from speakers mounted below the monitor. "I'd wake up. You have company, it's rude to sleep."

The man's eyes fluttered, then flew open as he saw Grant standing above him. He tried to scramble to his feet, but Grant caught his throat with one hand, controlling him.

"Don't . . . kill . . ." he gurgled.

"Don't plan to," Grant told him. "I'll even let go if you promise not to yell."

"O . . . kay . . . prom . . ."

Grant let him go; he rubbed at his throat and stared at them with his eyes still wide. There were glasses lying beside the cot. He picked them up and put them on.

"Who're you?" he demanded, peering at Grant owlishly. "What're you doing in here?" He looked at Andi. "Oh, you're . . ."

"That's who I am," Andi replied, succeeding in sounding more in control, that she felt—although having this Grant Kingsley beside her gave her a lot of confidence. "We've come for Sue, Albert—that is your name? Or do you know her as Nadine, like I do?"

"You've come for her? What're you going to do with her?"

"They've come to rescue me, Albert," the voice said from the speakers. "They've come to take me away from this hellhole you and Colin put me in."

Albert looked at the screen, then back at Grant and Andi. "You can't rescue her! Don't you know that? Do you know what you're talking about at all?" His head snapped around again. "Didn't you tell them, Sue? Didn't you?"

"No," the voice replied. "I didn't. They can, there is a way. You know that, Albert."

"No, I don't! What're you talking about?"

"Enough," Grant cut in. "Where is she?"

"In the other room," Sue said from the speaker. "Through that door. But Grant, don't go in there yet, please? Take just a minute for me . . ."

"I want to get you and Andi out of here, in one piece . . ."

"I know. But you don't understand. Does he, Albert?"

The man with the glasses looked glumly down at the floor. "No."

Grant and Andi both looked at the screen. "Okay, Sue," Grant said. "What is it?"

The face on the screen smiled charmingly. "This was me," she said. "This was what I looked like. Let me show you another one." The image changed; there was a picture of the same woman on a beach somewhere, dressed in a brief bikini. After remaining still for a moment, it animated, the woman walked about, waded into the surf. She looked happy and at peace with her world. Andi was beginning to have a sick feeling about this;

not something she could define yet, but something that was becoming uncomfortably strong.

"Was I pretty, Grant? Do you think so? Some people said so. I could never tell, not really. What do you think?"

"She's in love with you, Grant," Andi whispered.

"I'm sorry, Andi, I know you didn't mean me to hear that but I couldn't help it, the microphones I listen through are very sensitive. She's right, Grant. I am, I do love you. I wanted you and Andi to be together, I wanted you to be happy. I tried to help. I didn't want you to come here, please remember that."

"Sue," Grant said, "I think you're beautiful. I care what happens to you. You've helped us immensely, I couldn't've done this without you. I want to help you now, I want to get you out of here."

The screen image flipped back to the woman's face, and she closed her eyes softly. "And maybe you will. Albert, bring him in here now."

Albert stared. "No . . ."

"Yes, Albert," Grant said firmly. "Come with us." He pushed the man toward the door. With a trembling hand, Albert opened it; he stepped through, followed by Grant and then Andi.

They both froze in place just inside the door. It was a patient room, overly warm for comfort; on a specialized bed lay the nude body of a woman. She wasn't lying on a mattress at all, instead a thin film of some liquid swirled around her hips and shoulders. Her body was thin, gaunt, amazingly white, totally hairless. Her arms and legs both were elevated at thirty-degree angles; each wrist and each ankle disappeared into a metal sleeve mounted on a swivel. A thick black wire emerged from the other end of that sleeve, and was connected to a gray box beside her bed. Andi took in the colostomy tube, took in the permanent catheter in her urethra, saw the pumps they were connected to, saw the thick tube that pierced her stomach; her digestive and excretory functions were not her own.

Andi found her head hard to look at. Hairless, skull-like in its gauntness, it lay in the liquid as well. Into each eye socket thick metal tubes were inserted, a plaster seal holding them in place; her ears were missing, and other tubes were stuffed into the sides of her head. Over her mouth and nose was an oxygen mask into which was built a miniature microphone; wires connected all these devices to that gray box beside the bed.

"I'm not very pretty now, Grant, I know," she said, her voice audible as a harsh grating behind the mask but translating into a feminine contralto on the speakers. "I don't know exactly what I look like, I have no video link in here, but I'm very sure it isn't pretty." She laughed, bitterly, brokenly. "I didn't have a chance to put on my makeup, that's all . . ."

"My God, Sue," Grant whispered. "What happened to you? Some kind of accident?"

She laughed again. "Accident? Oh, Grant, oh . . . no, it wasn't an accident, it was quite deliberate. If Andi hadn't escaped, she'd look like this too right now. No, not quite so bad . . . we don't . . . last long. The human body isn't designed for immobility, we sag and rot inside. My friend Albert there hasn't found an answer for that yet. But he will, given time . . ."

"This is what they did in that surgery?" Andi demanded, her voice shrill. "This? They took you in there perfectly healthy and did this? That's not possible, that's inhuman!"

"But it's true. When I went into Dr. Singh's surgery I looked like the pictures you saw out there on that screen. I had hands, I had feet. I had eyes, and ears, and hair. They took them all away from me . . ."

Andi heard a small sound; tearing her eyes away from the horror she was seeing, she saw Albert edging toward the door, apparently planning to use their distraction to escape. "Grant!" she yelled.

Albert broke for the doorway at the sound of her voice; he didn't get through it. Whipping a dark-bladed knife from his pants, Grant pressed it, point first, against the man's throat.

"No," Grant said in a low, menacing tone. "The Navy trained me to kill people, I know a hundred ways. Up to now I've never killed anyone. It will not take much for you to become the first, not much at all. Understand?"

"Yes," Albert quavered. Then: "You owe me! God damn it, you owe me! Who do you think switched the sedatives around? Who's responsible for her getting away? Me! Me, that's who! She'd look just like Sue right now if it wasn't for me!"

Andi stared at the man's face; he was so terrified he was drooling. "You switched the sedatives?"

"Yes. Who else? Sooner or later they're going to figure that out, and if I'm not out of here by then I'll be in the shit for sure!"

"Did you know," Andi asked conversationally, "that I was hiding in your office when you and Colin were talking about that? I did understand, Albert. The reason I'm alive is because I faked being sedated. If I'd kept on fighting, I'd've gotten the second and third doses. And that would've killed me. Right? Isn't that what Colin was saying? Wasn't that the way it was set up?"

Albert's eyes were bigger than ever; he sagged in Grant's grip and he began to cry. "God damn it," he muttered. "Colin wouldn't listen! If you were found dead of an O.D., the police wouldn't ask questions about this place! You were a liability, that asshole Kingsley had figured out that—"

"I'd be very careful," Andi said mildly, "about referring to a man who has a knife at your throat as an asshole."

Albert sagged more. "Oh, shit," he breathed. "Oh shit, oh shit . . ."

"I just want to know," Grant snarled, his control obviously on edge, "why? Why would you do this, why?"

"Business," Sue answered. "Just business, nothing personal. Albert just wants to perfect his chips. Gonna make you a billionaire. You and Colin and Auan. All billionaires. So a few women get mutilated and die along the way, so what? You'll be billionaires."

"It wasn't like that!" Albert howled. "Once we got it perfected it wouldn't be like this!"

"Right," Sue commented. "That's why the market reports. Why us. Why we're the chosen subjects. Unattached young women just off a bad love affair. According to Colin's precious reports, the most likely candidates to sacrifice their bodies to a career in some nightmare of a future Auan believes in, a future where this could be all nicely legal."

"I don't believe in Auan's future!" Albert cried. "It's insane! I believe in this technology, its use for the handicapped, in—"

Sue broke into a peal of maniacal laughter; Andi shivered.

"What the fuck," Grant demanded, "are we talking about here? I don't understand a thing!"

"Some years ago," Sue said, calming down, "a Japanese company developed a chip that could convert the signal from a human neuron—a nerve cell—into a digital signal a computer could read. They did envision Albert's future—a use for the handicapped, a way to help them lead productive lives. They hooked up handless and armless people, those who'd lost limbs in accidents, to their chips. It worked, they could be trained to emulate a keyboard or a mouse.

"It worked too well. Not only could these people-chip combinations emulate a keyboard, they could go much faster than any person with hands, after only brief training. The Japanese saw a horror in their future, a world where people were paid huge bonuses to have their hands amputated for the sake of business productivity. They stopped developing the chip."

"And this company . . . " Grant put in.

"Picked it up and continued it. Perfected it. We are fully linked into the computer. We can run the equivalent of four keyboards at once. We see huge screens in these viewers that the muscles that used to move our eyes operate. We hear the computer's voice through implants in our ears. It's trained to our voices and adjusts as our voices deteriorate. We're powerhouses. With four hundred gigabytes of databases on line, all our nice RAID configured hot-swappable fast and wide Scuzzys, all our cutting-edge processor machines and our human ability to recognize patterns and sort out the crap from the meaningful, we can do the impossible, or what would be impossible any other way. We're processors. We're very good ones. The company has us on-line all the time, we do national defense work, we do police work, we track down hackers and blackmailers. We're good and they charge a fortune for our services. They pay us in glucose. And they let us live an artificial life on the Internet. They let us play in the chat rooms, on World's Chat, on Kymer, on the IRC channels."

Andi was stunned. "Why—why did they give you access to the chats? Didn't they know . . . ?"

"Oh, they don't like it. Never did. But they have to—they do it and they monitor us and they have us monitor each other. Because, Andi—because. If they don't, we're in sensory deprivation. Full and absolute sensory deprivation. You know what that means, don't you?"

"It means you'd go—insane—"

"Yes. Yes it does. And a lot of the early subjects did. They'd go insane and then they'd be useless and they'd have to be pink-slipped. We all get pink-slipped sooner or later."

"Pink-slipped?" Grant echoed.

"Yes . . . It's always ready. Above one of my arms you'll see a container of Nembutal, connected by a cath. You just turn it on, it's a mega-lethal dose, I'll be dead in minutes. Then they just take the body and throw it out with the other broken machinery. Real easy."

Grant's eyes dropped closed. "Oh, God . . ." he sighed.

"You know how you can rescue me, don't you, Grant? How you can save me? How you can take me away from here?"

"Sue . . ."

"Just turn it on. Just a twist of the knob. It's easy . . ."

"Sue, I can't do that . . ." Letting Albert go for a moment, overcome, he turned away. "There's got to be something . . . got to be something we can do . . ."

"No. Ask Albert. I'm ruined. Out of this rig I'm blind and deaf and totally crippled. My digestive system no longer functions, my lungs barely work. I have only a couple more years to live at the outside. I don't want to spend two years in some intensive care unit somewhere and I don't want to spend two more years here! Set me free, Grant. Turn the knob or use that knife you're holding against Albert's throat, I don't care, just set me free . . ."

Andi wiped at the tears already on her cheeks and started to move toward Grant, whose eyes were tightly closed. He was not, she realized, paying any attention to Albert.

Who took full advantage of his shock.

80

Torn, his emotions in turmoil, Grant found it impossible to look at the wreckage of what had once been a beautiful young woman. Emotions tumbled over each other like small stones in a flooded stream, bumping against each other, fragmenting; relief that this hadn't happened to Andi, terrible regret that it had happened to Sue, profound desire to release her from her suffering and a rigid unwillingness to accept that the only way was to end her life.

Awareness of his surroundings returned when something hit his wrist, hard; the knife he was holding fell to the floor. He looked down, saw a hand snatch it up. Then he realized Albert was holding it, pointing it at him.

"Okay," the man snarled. "Okay. Now things are a little different, aren't they?" He backed off, a grin on his face. "You two are up shit creek now, you know that? Up shit creek."

Grant glanced over at Andi; she was smiling slightly. "I don't think so, Albert," she said coolly. She drew the automatic from the pocket of her shorts, pointed it at him, and flipped off the safety. "I don't think anything has changed. Drop the knife, please. I don't want to shoot you." She shook her head. "I don't like guns. I didn't think it'd be possible for me to actually shoot anyone. Not before. But Albert, after what I've just seen, I think it'd be pretty easy right now."

Albert stared at her; then, with a sigh, he dropped the knife. "I know you could've handled that, Grant," she said, "but I was afraid Albert might not survive your handling."

"You might be right," he told her as he picked up the knife.

"And I have another question or two for Albert here."

"What is it?" Albert almost whined.

"That valve Sue was talking about. Is there any way you can put it under her control?"

His eyes flicked up. "No."

"He's lying," Sue said promptly from her speaker. "Just lying. I have all sorts of servo control abilities. I can feed myself, give myself water, clean myself up. All kinds of things. It isn't hard."

"I won't do it," Albert said. "She's too valuable, she's one of the best we have."

"How many do you have?" Grant asked, his voice ominously low.

"Fourteen," Sue5 answered. "Thirteen others, just like me."

"Fourteen!" Grant cried in a choked voice.

"Fourteen of us alive right now. I know the count; over the years there've been a total of twenty-seven in here, not counting the Thai village girls they started with. I understand there were some boys too, but men don't last as long as women. Twenty-seven American women Colin has seduced and dumped here, twenty-seven . . . Some have aged—we age fast—and been pink-slipped, a few haven't been able to adapt and they get pink-slipped too. A couple have died from accidents." She paused. "And you have big plans for expansion, don't you, Albert? There's so much money to be made . . . the government contracts . . ."

"And this place is being guarded by the Marines," Grant said with utter disgust in his voice. "By the Marines. How did this scam succeed, how is it the government doesn't know what's going on here?"

"You know better than that, Grant," Sue answered. "They do.

Some agency does. They've been here, they've seen. They don't like it, I guess—you can imagine the scandal if it comes out—but the benefits are so high . . . they look the other way. Grant, you know how that is. You of all people."

"Yes," he replied, his voice just a hiss. "Yes, I do. I know exactly how it is." He shook himself. "How long do you figure it'd take our friend here to give you control over that valve?"

"Fifteen minutes. No more."

He turned to Albert. "Get busy," he said harshly. "Right now. You have twenty minutes, I'll be generous, even though I need to get Andi out of here. If it isn't done by then I'll be upset with you, Albert. Very upset."

Albert looked like he was going to argue more, but studying the expression on Grant's face changed his mind. "I need some stuff from the other room," he said glumly.

"Let's go."

They moved to the other room; as Albert started working he explained that he was going to hook up a small servo motor to a control module, a motor which he'd then hook up to the lethal knob, the module to interface with the computer Sue controlled.

"I don't like doing this," Grant told Sue's image on the screen. "I don't. I want there to be some other answer."

"There isn't, Grant. This is the best way. This way you aren't responsible, and I may be able to help you two get out of here."

"I don't like leaving the others here, either. Even if I don't know them."

"Just get the word out, Grant, get the local cops in here. They'll all be pink-slipped and gone before that happens, but the nightmare'll be over for them."

Sitting down—and keeping a close eye on Albert as he worked—Grant shook his head again. "I've known," he said, "for a long time how the government can be. You said you knew the story, Sue. But this . . . this is beyond anything I could imagine."

Standing behind him, Andi put a hand on his shoulder. "This isn't something I know about, is it?"

He shook his head vigorously, laid one of his hands on hers. "No. Well, indirectly. It's what I always refused to talk about. Why I left the Navy."

"Can you tell me now?"

"Sure. Why not?" He sighed deeply. "You know my wife and

daughter were killed in a car crash. I was overseas at the time . . . it wasn't even that unusual, there wasn't anything mysterious about it. A drunk driver hit their car on the Beltway around Washington, where we lived then. He wasn't hurt; that happens a lot, I guess." Emotions started coming back, rolling over him; his voice grew flat. "At first, neither was Carol or the kids. But their car was spun sideways on the highway. There was a truck, a tractor-trailer. Not his fault, it was raining, he couldn't stop, he jackknifed trying. He hit the car broadside at fifty. His truck tore the car in half, ground it into scrap metal. Todd was thrown out and survived."

Andi's hand squeezed down on his shoulder. "God, Grant, that's horrible . . ."

"Yes . . . it was. I came back, I read all the reports. There wasn't much I could do except look after Todd, and that's what I did. But I wanted to see the drunk who'd caused it all brought to justice, I asked when his trial was going to be. I assumed he'd be charged with manslaughter."

Andi held his shoulder tighter. "And?"

He glanced around at her; there were tears standing in his eyes. "He hadn't been charged at all! With anything! Not even DUI!"

Her eyes widened. "What? Why not?"

"Because he was the son of the ambassador from Kuwait," Grant continued, his voice flat again. "His father had claimed diplomatic immunity. International relations. I went into a fury. I got a lawyer, I wanted to sue, at least. You want to know what happened?"

"I'm not sure . . ."

"I was called in by my superiors, I was told that my proposed lawsuit wasn't going anywhere. I was also told to drop it. It was an embarrassment to the Navy. An international incident. I was to let it go in the interests of national security. There was a veiled threat that if I didn't I'd be pushing paper in Norfolk."

"What did you do?"

"I don't know what I might've done. I was in a fury when I left the office. All I know is that I ran into the ambassador, his son, and one of the admirals in the hallway. None of them knew me. They were talking; they'd come to make sure there wasn't going to be an incident, and the admiral was assuring them that everything was being taken care of. The son was saying how stupid it was that they had to deal with this at all, just stupid, the death of 'one insignificant woman and her two brats.' "

"Oh, my God . . ."

"Andi, that phrase has stayed with me forever, sometimes late at night it echoes in my head. 'One insignificant woman and her two brats.' My family, my family I loved more than anything. I guess you can imagine. I went after him. Luckily for him, I went crazy, I forgot everything I knew—I did mean to kill him. I had him up against a wall, punching him over and over, until the MPs dragged me off." He stopped and stared at the busy Albert—who seemed to be ignoring his story. "I was thrown in the brig, of course. I expected a court-martial, something. Nothing happened, there were no charges. Again, nobody wanted an incident, it was embarrassing. My superior was pleased, he told me I was lucky. The ambassador, it seemed, felt his son deserved a few punches for his loud mouth."

"And then?"

"Nothing, Andi, nothing. The walls went up, the way they can in Washington. I had no place to turn. I resigned my commission, left the service; I felt it had betrayed me, I still feel that way. I left Washington and moved to the West Coast, I wanted to get far away, and I took a job as a commercial diver."

"What happened to that?"

He shook his head. "It was a disaster. Not the job, living in L.A., in the city. I felt I owed it to Todd to find him a mother, I didn't think he should grow up without one. As soon as I could—maybe two years after Carol's death—I tried to, I dated. Eventually I got involved. It turned out bad, your usual bad. Maybe I wasn't ready . . . Anyway, I wanted out. Away from people, away from the sea. I did know horses, I got a job as a wrangler on a small ranch and later I met Paula and she offered me a job at her ranch. So we moved there. And we've been there, ever since."

She put her arms lightly around his shoulders. "I'm sorry it's been so hard for you," she whispered. "So sorry."

He squeezed her hand. "You've had your own crosses to bear. We're two of a kind, Andi." He glared at Albert. "How's that coming?" he demanded. "It's been almost fifteen minutes!" Albert had now hooked the interface module up to a computer through a SCSI port and was entering various numbers on the screen; Grant, uncomfortable, realized he had no idea what the man was actually doing.

"It's coming right along, Grant," Sue said through her speaker. "He's programming it now, he's almost done."

"Good." He glanced at his watch. "Those Marines are supposed to check in soon, I'm going to have to take care of that or Mimi's going to have a serious problem."

"Mimi?"

"I'll tell you later. Albert?"

The engineer stood up. "Ready," he said. "I can hook it up now."

"Watch him, Grant," Sue cautioned. "You can't trust him. Tell me what he's doing at each step. Remember, I can't see myself."

"I will. Let's go." They trooped back into the other room, Grant and Andi both wincing at the sight of Sue in her bed. Using a small screwdriver, Albert removed the knob from the valve Sue had directed them to, connected it by a small sleeve to the motor shaft, then mounted the motor's base to the valve itself. The interface module he let hang free; he attached one end of a long black wire to it, dressed the wire around Sue's bed, then opened a panel on the gray box. At each stage Grant reported his activities.

"Watch him close here," Sue warned. "There're wires there he can pull out that'll bring EMTs and technicians scurrying up here. Don't let him. There should be free ports, several of them."

"Will you shut up, Sue?" Albert muttered.

"No," she responded cheerfully. "Not ever again."

With Grant watching closely, he connected the small round plug into a free hole inside the gray box; then he closed the door. Twice he glanced at Grant, an almost guilty expression on his face. Finally he stood up and moved away.

"I have activity on Port FC00 Hex," Sue announced. "Is that it, Albert?"

"That's it. It's in your hands, Sue."

"Do me a favor, will you, Grant?"

"Of course."

"Pinch the tubing above the valve so the solution can't flow while I check the valve."

"Got it." He folded the plastic tube over, held it tight. "Go ahead, Sue." The motor hummed; the valve turned a little.

"Is it moving?"

"Yes. Counterclockwise."

"Great! I've got control! I—shit!"

Grant turned to glare at Albert. "What is it, Sue?"

The valve spun back to the "off" position. "I do have control, but he programmed a message into the damn thing! He's sent an alert through the system! You're going to have company pretty quick, Grant, you and Andi better get out of here, now!"

81

Andi thought that Albert was a dead man, the way Grant looked when he turned to glare at him. Albert clearly didn't think so, he smirked. "Go," he said, waving a hand. "Just go. You have no chance now anyway!"

Grant smiled darkly. "Go, and leave you with Sue so you can disconnect the servo? I don't think so. I think we'll leave Sue in control of her own destiny." He grabbed Albert by the arm, so hard the engineer winced. "No, you're coming with us. And if you don't want to catch bullets you might tell us which way to go! First, which way is your security force going to be coming from?"

Albert struggled a little, but soon discovered that it was useless. "Up the stairs from the ground floor," he said. "Mostly from the left out this door."

"We're not going that way, then." He jerked his head at Andi. "Get your gun out, cover him. Stand well away from him. If he moves or turns shoot him in the ass or something."

She took the gun out again. "I'll do it," she answered.

Letting Albert go, Grant rushed to the door; taking a small tube of cement from his pack—Superglue—he poured a few drops into and around the lock and a few more into each hinge. "That'll slow them down," he said, taking Albert's arm again. "But it won't stop them. Down the hole, Andi."

She nodded, flipped the gun back to safe, put it in her pocket, and scrambled into the space under the workbench. An instant later, Albert was thrown in after her.

"Good-bye," Sue called from her speakers. "Good luck."

Andi bit her lip; by that time Grant was in the passageway too and closing the doors behind him. With Albert between them, they moved back down the tunnel to the landing.

"What's at the bottom?" Grant asked.

"Laundry room, air-conditioning, hospital supply," Andi answered crisply. "No outside doors that I know of. A hallway, I think. I didn't go out there."

"Albert?"

"I didn't even know about this shaft," he said slowly, peering down. "I swear. I do know the rooms she's talking about. There's an outer door just beyond the microassembly room."

"Microassembly?"

"Yes. Computer-controlled. Where we assemble components for the video and audio interfaces the recruits use."

"And where's this in relation to the laundry?"

"Across the hall. North end."

"Let's go. You first, Andi. When you get down, take out your gun and stand away from the exit, let's not give our guest any opportunities."

She nodded, and, with more confidence than before, swung onto the ladder and started down. It was amazing, she told herself as she climbed; she was all pumped up, far from tired now, doing things she couldn't've imagined herself doing two days ago, waving a gun around like she knew how to use it, feeling like a secret agent in a movie. A part of her felt guilty for the exhilaration she felt—especially considering Sue5's tragic plight. She knew, all too well, that without the other woman's efforts it could easily have been her lying mutilated in a bed like that. Feeling revulsion, feeling a fury at those who'd put Sue5 in that position—and trying to remind herself that things could still go disastrously wrong for them—she climbed down, opened the trap, pushed the ladder down, and descended to the floor. Once there, she drew the automatic yet again and stood away from Albert, covering him as he came down to the floor. Grant dropped down lightly beside him. Quickly, he looked around the room.

"That the hallway?" he said, pointing to a door across the room.

"Yes," Albert answered. "The exit's on the other side, past microassembly."

He reached into the backpack, brought out the roll of duct tape again. "Hands behind your back, Albert. It's not that I don't trust you, but, well, I don't trust you."

"Oh, no, don't . . ."

"Hands behind your back or I'll put them there, Albert."

With a grimace, he obeyed; Grant quickly taped his wrists. He looked down at his watch. "Now let's hold it for a minute, I have something I have to take care of." He walked away from them, and Andi watched him take a small radio from his backpack. It beeped; he spoke into it, giving a military-style code, then apologized abjectly to someone about something. Finally he put it away.

"Check-in for the Marines," he explained when he came back. He gestured toward the door. "Let's move." Pushing Albert along, he walked to the door, listened at it for a moment. "Seems clear," he whispered. He opened it, looked out, then motioned for Andi to follow.

Again, with Albert between them, they moved down the silent and brightly lit hallway to the right, Grant holding his automatic now as if it were an integral part of his hand. With glances to the rear, dragging the unresisting Albert along, he moved on to the corner and, dropping low, peeked around. Again he motioned them forward. As Andi rounded the corner she saw a stair at the end of a short hallway. All was quiet and peaceful. They moved toward it slowly, cautiously.

They were about halfway there when it burst open without warning. Men armed with rifles started running in.

Andi gasped; at first the men were not aware of them, but it was inevitable that they'd be seen. There was a shout; several guns were raised and pointed in their direction.

Grant's reaction was instantaneous. Covering Andi's body with his own he swung Albert in front of himself and started backing off. "No, no, don't shoot!" the engineer screamed. "It's me, don't shoot!"

The men hesitated; they knew well who Albert was. "Check the corner," he whispered to Andi. "Down low, like I did."

She followed his instructions; the corridor was still clear. As they continued to back off the armed men followed. At last they reached the room where the tunnel was, and here Grant stopped. With Albert last, he backed in, closed the door, and snapped it locked. Rapidly, he moved them back to the shaft access, where they could see both possible entries.

"Now what?" Andi asked.

"Now I don't know what. I don't want to get into a gun battle with those guys. Albert, where's the upper end of this shaft?"

"I don't know. I told you I didn't know anything about it, I didn't know it existed."

Grant pursed his lips. "Somebody will, but there's lots of ways to go from here. Andi, up the ladder; we're going back up to the room where you were hiding. You remember the way, don't you?"

She nodded and started up the ladder; Grant cut Albert's bonds and sent the engineer after her. Following, he pulled up the ladder and closed the hatch. The trip back to the third floor, to Albert's office, was accomplished without incident; the security man was where they'd left him. While Grant re-taped Albert's hands, Andi ran to the computer and began hitting the enter key repeatedly.

"Don't have pink-slipped yourself, Sue, please . . ."

She hadn't. "Yes?"

"Nadine."

"Andi! What're you doing back up there?"

"We ran into a patrol in the basement. They're after us. Any ideas?"

"There're going to be armed men all over this building in just a few minutes. It may be too late. You still have Albert with you?"

"Yes."

"Use him as a hostage, everybody knows him."

"We already did."

"If there's a way out, he can tell you about it. Force him if you have to."

She turned to Grant and began reporting on what Sue had just said. She hadn't yet finished when the door to Albert's office suddenly flew open.

"Albert!" a familiar voice cried. "What's—"

She looked up; standing just inside the slowly closing door was Colin. He was staring at the automatic Grant was pointing at him; his eyes moved slowly, taking in the whole room.

"Grant," Andi said, "meet the fake you." She stood up, felt for the gun in her pocket.

"Oh, Kingsley, of course," Colin said smoothly. "Very good, very good. I don't know how you got in here, but I surely didn't expect this much trouble from you. Very resourceful. How in the hell did you figure out your lady fair was in here, anyhow?"

"Sue5," Albert growled.

Colin glanced at him and took a step forward. "Oh, Susie-Q. I told you she was trouble, Albert. Told you we should've pink-slipped her a while back. No, she's one of the best. No, can't do without her." He looked back up at Grant; he was now far from the closed door. With a slight smile, Grant put his gun back in his pocket. "Hard to get loyal help nowadays," Colin continued. "You know how it is . . ."

"Yes," Grant said. "I've seen Sue5. In the flesh. What's left of it."

Colin made a face. "Oooh, nasty, I know . . . I try not to go down there at all, I leave that for guys like Albert, guys with strong stomachs." He slipped forward one more step; Grant didn't move.

"You put them there, as I understand it," Grant commented.

"Not me. I bring them here, deliver them to the gate. Dr. Singh puts them there. Dr. Singh and ol' Albert over there. I have nothing to do with that."

"Yes," Grant murmured, "I think you do. You know what's going to happen to them, but you deliver them anyhow. Women who think you're the man they're in love with. Women who—"

Colin laughed uproariously—and moved yet one step closer to Grant. "I am the man they're in love with! Hey, I have one fine old time with them before I deliver them." He looked at Andi; she winced physically, half-expecting what was coming next. "Like her. Man, you should've heard her moaning when I was fucking her. She gives a hell of a blowjob, too. Fucking great. Hot little mama, just couldn't wait to get back to the room, she about wore me out!"

"I am glad you enjoyed yourself," Grant said mildly. He waited, immobile as a statue, while Colin edged closer still.

"I did that, all right," Colin said, nodding. "But hell, man, it isn't personal. Just business. Everybody's got to take care of business." He grinned; then he suddenly lunged at Grant, his right hand flashing out, fingers extended, aiming for the other man's neck.

As Andi saw it, Grant's response was almost casual. He moved his head to the side, evading the blow; at the same time his left arm came up and over in a half-circle, his forearm catching Colin's arm above the elbow and knocking it to the side. Colin looked surprised. Then Grant's right hand smashed into his face.

He didn't get a chance to stagger back. Grant stayed with him, his right fist snapping forward and back with a smooth fast rhythm, over and over, right into Colin's mouth and nose. Andi saw the blood appear and then increase; Grant did not stop until Colin was against the wall, until his head was denting the sheet rock as the trip-hammer blows kept coming to his face. Stopping at last, Grant let him sag; he recovered, tried to throw a blow, Grant stepped back away from it. Struggling to his feet, Colin, who had some martial-arts training, threw a quick kick, a kick that never landed. Dodging it, Grant delivered a forearm blow to the side of Colin's head and a fist to the center of his chest, seemingly in the same movement.

His face red and puffy, his lips split, his nose smashed and bloody and his eyes bulging, Colin sat down against the wall, holding his chest, struggling to breathe. Grant stood over him, looking down. Eventually, Colin looked up at him.

"Who the fuck are you?" he asked.

"Just somebody taking care of business," Grant answered. "Somebody you pissed off."

Colin raised a hand defensively. "Okay, okay, you win. Christ." He touched his face. "Ah, shit, Jesus . . ." Again, he struggled to his feet. "Let's talk. We got a serious problem here."

"You do . . ."

"You do too. You want out of here in one piece." His eyes narrowed; he was having trouble speaking, his mouth was mangled. "You for sale, Kingsley? I can—" He stopped, shrugged, grimaced. "Guess not. Hero type. We're in a bind here." He threw up his hands, coughed, wiped blood from his nose. "Well, what can I do? Let you go, I guess. Both of you."

"Just like that?"

"Just like that. I have no choice. I'm not stupid. I know training when I see it. You could've killed me if you'd wanted to."

"I see. Just let us go. Just let us go back to Twenty-nine Palms or Los Angeles and start talking about what we've seen here, about what's going on here. Not too good for business, Colin."

"Business isn't worth my life."

"So. Let's say I buy this. How're you going to get us out?"

"I'll take you. Me and Albert, we'll take you to whichever gate—or whatever hole in the fence—you came in through."

Grant said nothing for a few seconds. "Andi," he said finally, "ask Sue if this Colin is enough of a big shot around here to actually do this, if he'll work as a hostage. Or he and Albert both."

"Okay." She hesitated, chewing her lip. "Grant, I want to tell you—"

He waved her off. "Not now. Later." She nodded meekly and moved to the computer again, wondering what he must think of her now, whether he was questioning his decision to come after her. Sitting down, she asked the question.

"She says they're two of the biggest cheeses around here," she reported a second later. "She doesn't think anyone will shoot at you if you have them in tow."

"I thought so. Ask her what she'd like me to do with them. Colin especially. Don't tell me, I'll look."

In spite of her mental pain, Andi smiled a little; Colin and Albert both blanched. Sue5's answer came in. Looking at it, Grant and Andi both scowled a little. "Well, I don't know why, but maybe we will," he said almost jovially. "Come on, gentlemen. Let's get up, we're headed downstairs."

"What'd Susie say?" Colin asked.

"I'll let you stew over that. Put your hands behind your back."

Colin looked like he might be thinking of trying to resist, but in the end he turned around and did as he was told. Grant pushed them both to the door and opened it; the hallway was deserted, they walked to the elevator unmolested, and rode it down to the basement.

When the elevator door opened, six rifles were pointed at them. "Cool it, guys," Colin croaked, holding his mouth. "Just wait, hold your positions."

"No," Grant said. He aimed his automatic at Albert's head. "Don't hold your positions. Clear this floor, now. Or this one's a dead man."

Colin turned to him. "You won't."

"I will. I have two hostages. These boys should know I mean business." He pointed to the nearest man. "You! Rifle on the floor, right here, right now."

Colin didn't look convinced, but he didn't look like he wanted to take a chance, either. "Do what he says," he ordered. "All of you, first floor. Wait there. Contact Auan and tell him what's going on here."

Still in the elevator, Colin and Albert in front of them, Grant and Andi waited until the men had left; then they stepped out cautiously. Grant picked up the rifle the man had left as he went by. Holding it, he stuffed the automatic into his pocket.

"Now what?" Colin asked.

"Now we go over there," Grant said. Prodding Colin, he shoved him to the room Sue had identified; on the door it said "Microassembly control." He opened it, gestured for them to go inside.

Colin and Albert, the color draining from their faces, stood still. "No," Colin quavered. "No, you don't know what you're doing here, you don't . . ."

"In," Grant said. "I don't know why Sue wanted us here, but we're going in." He shoved the men inside.

"Kingsley, listen to me!" Colin howled. "Throw the switch on the wall outside first! Kingsley, for God's sake!"

Confused, not understanding the reason for the man's panic, Andi followed him and Grant into the room—and stopped short.

It was an amazing place. A huge room, many tables, video cameras at several locations, four or five of which swiveled to look at them. From the ceiling hung four colossal mechanical arms, each on a swivel and the swivels on tracks. Near the door, a video screen sprang to life and Sue5's image appeared.

"Hi, Colin, lover," she whispered through the speakers. "Oh, you look like you've been having a hard time tonight, has the Fish Man been mean to you? You need some TLC, lover, I really think you do . . ."

As her voice faded, the nearest mechanical arm began moving. Fast and smooth, it came toward them, the jaws—a good three feet tall—spreading open, heading straight for Grant. Andi gasped, but the arm slowed as it reached him and gently nudged him aside. Then it slipped past her, headed for Colin. Colin shrieked and tried to duck away, but the arm's wrist swiveled and the jaws closed lightly around his waist. It lifted him off the floor.

Then the arm withdrew, and Colin shot by Grant and Andi so fast his body was bent into a bow. The arm swung around, another arm began to move, Colin was passed from one to the other; then the nearest two returned to a position in front of them, swinging back and forth idly.

"Kingsley! Stop her, man, for the love of God!" Colin was screaming. "Stop her, stop her, hit the switch!"

Grant started to move toward him, but the swinging arms moved to block his way. "No, Grant," Sue said. "He's mine, at last he's mine. You can't get to him; you're good, but I'm a lot better with these. I can block you and I don't even have to hurt you to do it." She giggled. "I can do things with these you can't imagine. My favorite toys. Colin knows . . . I handle microscopic gears with these big things, but I can form steel cases with them, too. I bet I could use them to take nerves right out of a human body, from one end to the other, without killing the person or damaging the nerve." Another arm moved, a little tongue of flame appeared at the end of a tube mounted to it, a flame that quickly turned blue. "Then I can use my little welding torch, you see . . ."

"Kingsley! Kingsley! You know what she's going to do! The switch outside, man! Throw the switch!"

Grant moved toward the keyboard; a video camera followed him. "You don't have to type," she told him. "Just speak normally, I can hear you."

"Sue," Grant said, his voice very calm, "don't torture him. You aren't like these people, you—"

She laughed hysterically. "Oh, oh, don't come down to their level? That old saw? Bullshit, Grant, bullshit. The world doesn't care what level you're at. Only if you win or lose. When I trusted this slime, I lost. Now I've won and he's lost, he and Albert both. That's all there is to it."

"Kingsley! The switch!"

Sue5's image smiled. "You know which switch he's talking about, don't you?"

"I think so. The big one right outside the door."

"That's it. It cuts the 440 volt power grid to these things. You aren't trying to get to it."

Grant shook his head. "I'll talk to you, I'll try to talk you out of this, but I won't take the decision away from you, I won't even try. Besides, I'm not sure I can, I'm not sure you can't stop me with one of those arms if you want to."

She didn't answer for a moment. "I can," she told him. "I can't say whether I would or wouldn't, Grant." The arm holding Colin rose, lifting him another few feet off the floor. "This," she went on, "is an evil man. I've never known a man so evil. He doesn't even think of it as evil, Grant, you know that? Because it's good for Colin. No matter what happens to a Nadine Berstrom or an Andi Lawrence or anyone else, if it's good for Colin, it's good. Not even Albert is this evil. Are you, Albert? You're a company man, you go along with the program, but you have a misgiving every now and then. Not you, Colin. Do you, lover?"

"How will it help if you torture him, Sue?" Grant persisted. "Isn't it—"

"The same? Good for Sue, to hell with anything else? We're big on the clichés today, aren't we, Fish Man?"

"It isn't good for us. We need Colin and Albert as hostages."

"I understand that." She laughed. "You don't know how much I was hoping you'd run into Colin. Hoping you'd kill him. But you haven't killed anybody in here yet, have you, Fish Man?" The arm holding Colin moved again, bringing him closer to one of the video cameras.

"I'm trying not to."

"I know. The honorable man. Everyone here is slime. They all know what's going on. They don't say anything, don't blow any whistles. Why not? Because they get paid very well. Here the janitors get rich."

"No, Sue, I can't believe that. The soldiers can't know—"

"They do. All of them."

"But—how could the management know that—?"

"No one would blow a whistle? They don't, really; everybody is watched, everybody watches everybody else. They're carefully selected, too. Colin's idea, right, sweetheart? Your ingenious little employment tests. Took them from Stanley Milgram, right?"

"I don't know what you're talking about . . . " Grant murmured.

"Stanley Milgram," Andi put in, "was a researcher who tested students who thought they were giving shocks—dangerous shocks—to other students. His conclusion was that a lot of people would inflict harm if an authority figure told them to, if they didn't feel responsible."

"That's right, Andi," Sue purred. "And these people, every SAF soldier, every God damn maid, has been given a pre-employment test like that. They're made to believe, for a while, that they've killed the person on the other side of the glass. It's very realistic because a Thai village girl was actually killed, electrocuted, to make the video they use. Some are bothered, they feel responsible; they aren't hired. Those that shrug and say, 'it isn't my fault, I was just doing what I was told,' those are hired. We're all good little Nazis here, aren't we, Colin?"

Grant looked at Andi. "I cannot believe," he muttered, "that a place like this exists. I just can't."

"Business is the new ideology," Sue commented. "Years ago it was political. Death camps, Gulags, radiation tests and nerve-gas tests on civilians and unsuspecting soldiers. That's over.

Now it's business." Her image on the screen smiled. "You know how, Grant. Was it national security that caused you to be treated the way you were? No. Oil. Oil dollars. Money. That's what it's all about. And that's what's going on here, too." As she spoke, Andi saw Grant's face become rigid, turn into a mask.

"Kingsley, the switch!" Colin shrieked. "The switch, Kingsley, you can make it, go for it!"

"I wish you'd brought some explosives," Sue mused. "Take this place down to the ground. No one here is an innocent." Her image closed its eyes momentarily. "Even Auan might be in the building, oh God, I wish I had him here right now . . ." Her eyes opened. "You don't want me to torture Colin. Okay. I love you, Fish Man. I'll compromise for you."

There was a hum; the jaws of the hand holding Colin closed around his midsection. He shrieked, piercingly; then his body fell from the hand in two pieces. Andi gasped, turned her head away for a moment from the twitching mess on the floor. Albert panicked; he ran to the door, stood at it screaming and jumping up and down, as if he could get it to open with his cries, with his desperation. Grant never moved, his expression never changed. When Andi looked back he was still watching blood drip from the now-idle arm.

"I'm sorry, Grant," Sue said. "I couldn't let him live. I just couldn't. You might not kill him, you know that. I'd like to do Albert too but I won't—as you say you need a hostage. I have what I wanted, I have everything I wanted. I'm sorry."

Grant looked at her image on the screen. "You didn't torture him," he said. "That's all I asked of you, Sue."

"You need to go now. Get Andi out of here."

"Yes."

"Can you spare just a moment? Just a moment before you go?"

"Yes, Sue, of course."

"Good . . . thank you, Grant. I'm activating the valve now." As she spoke, an EKG image appeared on the screen below her face.

"Oh, Sue . . ."

"No. It's what I want. Just stay with me, Grant, just stay with me until . . ." Her image smiled on the screen. "I can feel it already, it won't take long, not long at all . . ."

"Sue, I'm so sorry . . . I wish . . ."

"Nothing to be sorry for, Grant." Her heart rate started to

slow. "This is what I want, this is what all the recruits want. You and Andi . . . be happy with her, Grant. I wish it could've been me . . . I'm sorry, Andi, I can't help wishing that . . ."

Andi's eyes were full of tears; she came close to the screen. "Oh, Sue—Nadine—I understand, I do, you've been so wonderful to us, so wonderful . . ."

"We'll never forget you, Nadine," Grant said, his voice full of emotion. "Never."

"Oh . . . you used . . . my name . . . I heard you say . . . my name . . . I love . . . you, Grant . . ."

On the monitor, the image's eyes fell closed; an instant later, the EKG showed a flat line. Then, abruptly, the screen went dark.

82

Struggling with himself, Grant fought the choking feeling in his chest, fought the tears, and tried to keep his face impassive as he watched the screen blank. He looked at Albert; the temptation to walk over to him and use one of the killing techniques he'd been taught—techniques he'd practiced and knew well but had never used—was overpowering. No, he told himself, no. We need him to get out safely. You created problems for yourself by being irrational, you've come this far by planning, by thinking. He thought about the other women like Sue, thirteen of them, languishing in the same hell she had suffered, their only release the vial of Nembutal.

He blinked, resisted wiping his eyes; there'd be time to grieve for his friend later, too, the friend he, in his absorption with his own misery, had treated so casually. He moved to the door. "Let's go," he told Andi. He grabbed Albert's arm; the engineer had been leaning against the wall in relief after Sue5's death. He smelled, Grant noticed; apparently in his panic he'd soiled himself. "Get moving," he snarled.

"Where, Grant?" Andi asked. "Outside?"

"No. In a moment. Back to the service room first. There's something I want to do there."

She gave him a curious look, but didn't argue; Albert said nothing at all, and they trooped back into the service room. Leaving Andi and Albert near the door, Grant started disconnecting the oxygen tanks stored here, removing the hoses from them and leaving them turned on full-force. Two of them he did not disconnect, he lifted them—with effort—and put them on the ledges of the small windows high on the outside wall, stuffing a wadded piece of tape under them so they wouldn't easily roll back. He then opened the access shaft, leaving the door hanging.

Finally, he located the main gas line, the one-inch pipe that fed the dozens running up the access shaft. Taking a pair of cutting pliers from his pack, he nipped through the thick copper until he could hear and smell the gas escaping from it. Then, at a trot, he went back to Andi and Albert.

"Now we have to go," he told them. "And quickly."

"What'd you do?" Albert demanded.

"With luck," he said coolly, "you'll see." He shoved the engineer into the hallway, and they headed for the exit.

Outside the building was an armed camp, a scene from a war movie. There were men everywhere, a hundred rifles trained on the door; but, as Albert came out howling, no one fired. Keeping Andi behind him, her back to the wall to prevent someone from being tempted to try to pick her off, holding Albert out in front like a shield, he moved around the corner and down toward the gate.

"Tell someone to open that gate," he ordered Albert. "Do it now."

Albert didn't argue; he yelled an order, and a man ran to obey. Grant kept moving, wondering how long this was going to last; several of the men were talking on radios or cellulars, clearly getting commands from superiors, perhaps from this "Mr. Auan" he'd heard about. Passing by the windows of the service room, he saw the oxygen tanks he'd prepared; then he looked toward the cleft in the rocks, their immediate destination.

Followed all the way by soldiers and guards, they reached the end of the building. A quick dash brought them to the partial safety of the block building, then another brought them to the residence hall. The gate wasn't far now. Not far. His opponent was clearly indecisive, they did not want to let him and Andi escape but they hoped to rescue Albert.

They let them reach the gate, let them go through. Backing

up, Grant saw the soldiers—at least fifty of them—collect at the gate as they left the compound. In seconds the protective rock walls closed in on both sides of them. It cannot, Grant told himself, be this easy.

Grabbing Albert's shoulder, he placed the man's body as a barrier to the passage. "Here," he told Andi, "keep your gun on him. Stand flat against the rock. I have to check ahead, I smell an ambush. If he pulls something shoot him but don't kill him, if they think you have they'll be all over us."

"Understood," she answered, pointing her gun at Albert's knees.

Turning away, Grant studied the rock wall for a moment, then started climbing, picking his handholds carefully. Some seconds later he reached the top; scrambling over the sloping stone, he ran to the other side.

And saw that his fear was justified. There were a dozen or so men down there, their rifles trained on the opening of the cleft. This was as far as they were meant to get, Albert or no.

He took just a moment to study the situation. The soldiers, concealed among the rocks, had taken positions on both sides of the trail. With a plan in mind—something of a long shot— Grant moved along the ridge a short distance until he was behind the group on his left. Then, quietly, he descended behind the two nearest soldiers. Once on the desert floor he retrieved the fishing line from his pack, took out a stick of gum and started chewing it, and crawled rapidly forward on knees and elbows.

His target never saw him coming. Grant pounced, jerking a loop of fishing line around his throat and pulling it tight; as soon as he stopped moving, Grant stuffed the wad of chewing gum into the muzzle of the man's rifle. Chewing a fresh stick, he moved to the next one, taking him out in similar fashion.

Given time, he might've taken them all out this way, but he doubted the men back at the compound would give him that much time. After rendering the third man senseless, he took the superglue from his pack and cemented the man's finger to the trigger of his weapon. Then, after setting his victim's rifle on full automatic and flipping the safety off, he moved on. A fourth man got the same treatment. Then he retreated to a concealed position behind the two whose rifles he'd disabled.

Moments later, one of those first two recovered. Knowing he'd been attacked, he started yelling to his comrades, telling them that the enemy was among them. A few seconds after that, one of the men whose finger was glued to his weapon's trigger came to. As he moved his hand, the rifle went off, firing wildly.

Chaos erupted; the soldiers, panicked and assuming that Grant was attacking them from their midst, began shooting at anything that moved. Within seconds they were in a fire fight with each other across the trail. The man who'd first sounded the alarm tried firing his weapon—only to have it explode in his hands, pieces of the barrel curling back like the skin of a peeled banana.

Patiently, while the crackle of gunfire filled the night, Grant waited. Several of the men fell, shot by their comrades. Across the trail, the man commanding the squad was screaming orders to cease fire, and at last his men heard him; the shots slowed and ceased. The officer stood up from cover and looked over the battlefield.

Instinctively, but with precision, Grant fired at him and he fell. An answering shot came from the other side, instantly renewing the wild volleys from both sides.

Grant's weapon suddenly felt very heavy in his hands. "You're the first," he whispered. "The very first." Then, pushing it from his mind, he rolled over to the other side of the rock pile and peeked around it.

His enemy still had no idea where he was, again they were merely shooting at movement. Again a patient shadow, Grant changed positions, moving to a new spot behind a huge boulder. He'd been counting the number of men he'd seen go down. At the moment—if he'd counted right—he had only five left to deal with. Looking across the trail, he saw one of these clearly. Taking careful aim, he fired; the man fell.

As the fight went on, he tried only to think about eliminating this threat and getting back to Andi, who was still waiting in the cleft. The others, having seen several of their number fall, were even more panicky. On his side, another man regained consciousness and rashly stood up; someone from the far side, thinking he was Grant, shot him. The shooter, having exposed himself, was then taken down himself by a bullet from Grant's rifle.

Unable to see either of his remaining foes, Grant broke for new cover. This time he was seen, bullets pinged off the rocks around him. He felt a sharp burning sensation in the calf of his leg. He didn't even glance at it—the leg still worked. Looking out from new cover, he saw his attacker standing, perhaps thinking he'd gone down—his run-and-roll tactics gave that impression—and Grant took him down with one more bullet. The last man fled into the darkness. Letting him go, Grant cautiously stood up. No more shots were fired, and he hurried back to the cleft.

Nothing had changed. The men were still arrayed, waiting, expecting their comrades on the other side to take care of things. "They've started to come twice," Andi said breathlessly. "Twice! Albert's sent them back."

"Good boy, Albert," Grant said. "The way's clear now, I think." He leaned against the rock face, trying to steel himself for what he'd planned next. "One more thing here and we won't have to worry about them."

She looked at his leg. "You've been hit! You're bleeding!"

"I'm fine. Might've been a chip of rock. Don't worry about it." He shifted to a position where he could see the building where Sue had lived. The soldiers watched them carefully. Grant retreated into the rocks as far as possible without losing sight of the building.

"Move back," he told Andi. "Keep him in front of you."

"Grant, what're you going to do?" Andi demanded.

"What we both know I should do." He raised the rifle to his shoulder, and aimed carefully. It would take luck, he told himself; at this distance the bullet had to pass through the wire fence without hitting a strand. He squeezed the trigger—and watched a spark fly from the fence. Just as it did, he heard the sounds of rotors and glimpsed a helicopter rising from somewhere in the compound.

The soldiers started shouting; ignoring them, Grant aimed again and fired.

Maybe the bullet pierced the oxygen tank he'd left in the window, maybe it just glanced off of it. It didn't matter. It threw a spark, enough of a spark to ignite the mixture of methane and pure oxygen in the basement and up the access shaft, and that's all that was necessary. The entire building was converted into a blinding white fireball, the walls defined for an eerie instant by the bright light from inside the windows. Pieces of the building flew off, many straight up; one whole wall skidded outwards, still intact. The concussion was deafening, shocking; it blew down the fence, collapsed the residential building, and hurled the soldiers in the compound away like paper toys. Grant could not see what else it might've done, he was buffeted by a hot hurricane wind that came screaming through the cleft. Almost immediately there were several more huge explosions—the liquefied natural gas tanks had ruptured and ignited. A massive black and red cloud of fire and smoke rose from the ruin of the building; Grant turned away and sprinted back to where Andi and Albert waited.

"What'd you do!?" Andi squealed, her eyes enormous.

"I set the rest of them free, Andi. And, with any luck, ended this horror." Albert, pale as a ghost, said nothing; Grant herded them out of the cleft while he looked around for stragglers from the group he'd fought with out here. Turning back, he watched a pall of smoke and fire rising from the compound.

Out of this came the helicopter he'd seen take off. Itself buffeted by the wind and turbulence from the blast, it flew erratically for a moment, then stabilized. As soon as it did, twin searchlights came on under the nose, and it came toward the cleft, a huge and deadly night insect, looking for them.

"Shit!" Grant cried. "Go, the rocks ahead! Andi, stay close to Albert, real close!"

They moved as he said, at a near run; holding the rifle up, ready to fire, Grant came behind them. It took the chopper's pilot a moment to locate them, but before they could reach cover the bright lights exploded around them, bathing them in white starkness. Grant cursed; beyond these rocks were the horses, but the horses were a liability with that thing hovering overhead. He prayed it wasn't equipped with military weapons.

It swooped lower; the side door was open and a man with an automatic weapon started spraying bullets. They puffed into the desert floor, struck rocks and ricocheted away. Whoever was firing wasn't accustomed to shooting from an aircraft, he was firing wildly.

"Get to the rocks!" Grant cried. "Run!" He turned, fired shots at the helicopter; it pulled back and up. Andi was sprinting for the rocks, followed by Albert, who, with his hands still taped, was running clumsily. The pilot swung the aircraft around, cautious now of Grant and his rifle, and the man in the door spewed more bullets—a little less wildly this time, cutting a swath between Andi and Grant.

Where Albert was.

For one moment he froze, rigidly upright, quivering in the moonlight, as the bullets struck him; he managed a choked cry, very weak. Then he fell, blood gushing. Grant sped past him toward Andi, zig-zagging, seeking some sort of cover. He watched the chopper as he ran; it rose up to the crest of the outcropping, hovering there, facing toward the place where the horses were. Turning slightly, it moved toward them.

Catching up with Andi, he directed her toward a group of boulders, and both ran toward it. Firing on the run, he aimed for the helicopter's lights; one of them exploded in a shower of glass, went dark. It took him three shots to get the other one out, but it hardly helped; the bright moonlight still illuminated them, the pilot and the gunman would have to be blind not to see them.

He fired again, hit it again, but it had no visible effect. "That pilot's experienced, I can't see him at this angle and this rifle doesn't have the power to penetrate his floorboards at this distance . . . !" The chopper swung to the side, another volley of shots came at them, they jumped to their right, taking shelter behind a huge sandstone boulder, a rock that would offer scant protection if the chopper moved over them. Bullets struck the ground to the left, then to the right; the helicopter moved closer.

"He's got the range," Grant said flatly. He fired two more shots, again without effect. "We've run out of luck. All I can do from here is hope to hit his hydraulics or a rotor blade." He fired again, and again; each time the chopper pilot, wary, pulled up the nose. But as soon as Grant stopped he came on, hanging close to the crest of the rocky outcrop in case they ran for it, moving in for the kill.

Grant was still trying to decide what to do when he saw a slim figure, silhouetted against the bright sky, stand up suddenly among the rocks near the crest, close to the helicopter. He stared; the figure raised an AK-47-style rifle and began firing, one shot right after another, into the aircraft's cab.

"Mimi!" Grant yelled. "Not like that, get down!"

The door gunner fired back; Grant saw bullets hitting the rocks. Mimi bounced back, a small splash of dark liquid staining her middle. She didn't fall, she straightened up and continued firing.

Suddenly the helicopter veered away from the crest, off to the left, a hard banked turn. Grant could hear, over the sound of the engines, someone inside screaming.

But, as if a limp body were lying on the controls, the helicopter continued to bank and swing left and down. Seconds later the rotors hit the desert floor. The machine spun a half turn and started to come apart.

Grant looked back up at the ridge—just in time to see the slim figure with the rifle crumple.

"Shit!" he screamed. He turned to Andi. "Come on, hurry!" Together they ran on through the outcrop; Grant left her with the horses and scaled the rocks with as much speed as he could manage.

She was lying nestled in a shallow cavity, her hand on her abdomen. Looking up at him, she grinned and winced. "Looks like mission accomplished, sir," she said.

"Not quite." He unfastened her belt, opened her jeans, and examined the wound.

"Getting personal, are we?" she asked. "Shoulda done that sooner, Grant."

"Looks like a steel-jacket. I don't think it's too bad, not if we get you to a hospital quick . . ."

"Well, shit," she muttered. "You mean I don't get to play a classic death scene here?"

"I've had enough of those for one day, Mimi. Let's leave yours on the cutting-room floor." He picked her up in his arms; he had to go a longer way to get down carrying her, but eventually he reached Andi and the horses.

Andi stared at her. "Is she—"

"No, I isn't," Mimi answered. "Hi, me."

"What?"

"The other you," Grant explained. "Mimi Wang, actress. Hired to impersonate you. Come on, let's get out of here." He nodded toward Storm. "Untie him, we'll ride these guys out." Andi nodded, removed Storm's tether from the tree, and mounted him gracefully. Moving him close to Blue Fire, she helped Grant get Mimi up behind the saddle, after which Grant got on.

"Can you hold onto me?" he asked.

"Yeah. Shit, it hurts to get shot. Where's the other girl you were bringing out?"

"She didn't make it," Grant said, tight-lipped. He nudged Blue Fire's ribs; with Andi beside him they rode toward the pass where two tied-up and now very uncomfortable Marines were waiting for them.

83

Morning light streamed in through the windows, streaking the floor of the hospital waiting room with brightness. Andi, her eyes red and puffy from crying, sat in one of the institutional chairs beside Grant; she was curled slightly against the arm of the chair farthest from him. Stealing a glance, she saw that he hadn't moved. He was still sitting with his feet spread widely apart, his hands clasped in front of him. A plaid shirt had taken the place of the black pullover; he'd used water from the truck to wash away some of the black makeup he'd been wearing, but even so he looked liked he'd spent the night out in the desert, and Andi was more than aware that she didn't look much better. A nurse walked by, he looked up; it was not the doctor they were waiting for, the doctor that would let them know how Mimi was doing.

"It's a weird situation," he said quietly. "Complicated. There aren't rules you can apply to a situation like this one."

Andi forced herself to talk to him. "I don't know," she told him. "I don't know. The facts are the facts. I came here to meet you, another man met me and told me he was you and I didn't realize he wasn't. I didn't question it. I . . . went with him, I did whatever he wanted me to do. But I thought he was you, all along. Even after he dumped me at that place I thought he was you."

He nodded slowly. "None of that was your fault. You didn't have one reason to suspect he wasn't me."

"You suspected Mimi. You found out the truth."

"I was tipped off. I didn't believe it, but it made me pay attention to things I might've ignored. You didn't have that advantage, you had no reason to doubt him."

"I should have," she insisted. Fresh tears appeared in her eyes. "I don't know how, damn it! But I should have. He was just so . . . so . . . ."

"Charming? Sexy? That's what worries me, Andi."

She wiped at her eyes, looked back at him. "I don't understand. Why would that worry you? He's dead."

He leaned back and looked at her directly. "I don't," he said softly, "see how that matters." His eyes weren't wet but there was a distance there, a barrier, a shield. "It just isn't . . ." He hesitated. "It isn't your fault and it isn't mine, we were dragged into this." He shook his head and looked away. "It's been a long time for me, Andi. I don't think I have to explain it . . ."

She started to cry again. "Grant, it wasn't Colin I fell in love with! It was you! Do you think it matters to me that Colin was . . . that he was . . ." Unable to go on, not wanting to finish that thought, she sobbed bitterly for a few minutes. "There's another side to this too, you know." She nodded toward the closed doors to the emergency room. "There's Mimi. No, you weren't fooled by her. But she's quite a woman, she's beautiful, she's courageous, she's capable and exciting, she's clearly more than taken with you . . ."

He gave her a curious look. "I think," he told her, "that Mimi is 'taken' with me, as you put it, because she's been in Hollywood too long, it's been years since anyone treated her like a human being. She—"

Andi shook her head and kept right on shaking it. "No. You don't understand. She wouldn't've done what she did if she wasn't half in love with you already. No woman would. She insisted on trying to make things right, she risked her life and she almost lost it, she still could. No. In this case it's you who doesn't understand. You don't know how . . . how . . . truly special, that's a lame word but I can't think of another—you are." She squeezed her eyes tightly closed for an instant. "You came after me, you rescued me, you saved me . . . oh, Grant, oh damn . . ." She clenched her fists. "Why couldn't you have come sooner, while we were at the Hilton, before . . ."

"Like I said," he muttered, "it's complicated." As he spoke, the outer doors opened, and two local police officers walked in. They went to the nurses' station, Andi watched the woman point them out. The two officers came over to them.

"Let's see," one of the men said, looking down at a notepad. "Mr. Kingsley and Dr. Lawrence. You brought in Ms. Wang?"

"That's right," Grant said.

"Well, Ms. Wang has a gunshot wound," he said unnecessarily. "The hospital notified us. You want to tell us what happened?"

Grant shrugged. "Not much to tell. An accident." He ran through the story they'd composed on the drive in, that they'd been riding in the desert and that Grant had been instructing them on the use of a rifle, and that there'd been an accident, that Mimi'd gotten hit.

The officer frowned. "You were out shooting in the desert at night, Mr. Kingsley?"

"Yes, sir."

"Does that make sense?"

"No, sir. Not looking back at it it doesn't."

"Well. Assuming that Ms. Wang doesn't die—"

"She isn't going to."

"We hope not. Anyway, assuming that's her story too—"

"It will be."

"We'll see. It might not matter right now. You are Grant Kingsley, correct? You live in California, in Fillmore?"

"That's correct."

"Well, Mr. Kingsley, the fact is, you're wanted for questioning. I might have to take you in anyway." He looked over at Andi. "He's wanted for questioning," the officer went on, "in the possible kidnapping of one Dr. Andrea Lawrence of New York City. According to the report I have—what you told the nurse—you are Dr. Andrea Lawrence of New York City, is that right?"

"Yes," she answered. "It is."

"Can you prove it? You have some ID?"

She sighed; this had been discussed too. "No," she answered, "I don't. After the accident, we wanted to get Mimi here as quick as possible, and I didn't realize I'd left my purse. So I don't have an ID right now."

"I see . . ." The man looked suspicious.

"Officer," Andi went on, "I know what happened with that complaint. I know who made it, and why. I've already made some calls, it's been cleared up in New York." She paused, thinking about the calls they'd made on that cellular phone on the way back from the plant; Grant's calls to his son in Fillmore, to the owner of the ranch, his need to be assured that everything was all right there.

Everything was not all right there. No further lurkers, no more visits from the local deputies, but, at some point during the long night, Sue had said her good-byes to Todd before dropping off-line forever. Todd—who'd been up all night too, manning the computer, was more than distressed about it. He was crying on the phone, begging for reassurance Grant couldn't give him. The boy hadn't yet been told that his Net friend was dead. That was waiting for him when he got home, and it was, she knew, weighing heavily on his mind.

Her own calls to Vickie in New York hadn't been easy either. Her attempts at explanations were lame, which had annoyed Vickie considerably. Nevertheless, Vickie had promised to notify the police. Now, she looked up at the officer earnestly. "If you could just call . . ."

"That would have to be done from downtown, ma'am."

Grant pulled the cellular from his pocket. "Here," he said. "On my dime."

The officer didn't look too happy, but he did make the call; after talking with authorities in New York, he acknowledged that the request to take Grant in for questioning had been canceled. He gave the phone back to Grant.

"I want you to stay here," he said, "until I can talk with the shooting victim. Bad things happening around you, Kingsley."

"Yeah," Grant answered. "It's been a hell of a couple of days." The policemen stood staring at him for a few seconds, as if trying to read answers from his face, then moved away and sat down.

"So," Andi said when they'd gone.

He turned to look at her. "So?"

She bit her lip. "Maybe I should just go back to New York, maybe . . ."

His gaze was steady. "I think—" He stopped speaking as the doors opened and the doctor came out.

"Mr. Kingsley?" he asked.

Grant stood, went to him; Andi followed, and the two officers moved close to listen. "Yes?"

"You'll be happy to know that the surgery went just fine. Ms. Wang is awake and resting comfortably, she's going to be fine."

Grant smiled. "Wonderful . . . thank you, doctor. Can we see her?"

"We'd like to see her for a few minutes first," one of the policemen said.

The doctor glanced at him. "That'll be fine. She's tired, but in no danger. Not too long."

The policemen went to the recovery room; Grant and Andi

waited, standing near the door, until he came back less than ten minutes later.

"All right," the officer said. "She confirms your story, this one'll get listed as an accident. Mr. Kingsley, don't go shooting guns in the desert at night, all right?"

"I won't," Grant promised. "Never again." Nodding to the officers as they left, he turned and started back toward Mimi's room. Andi hesitated; he stopped and looked back. "Coming?" he asked.

"You want me to?"

"Yes." She joined him. Directed by a nurse, they made their way back to Mimi's room. Lying with her bed tipped up, she grinned at them when they came in.

"You two," she said, "are a mess, you know that? You're supposed to be perfectly groomed and looking gorgeous at this point, haven't you ever seen a movie?"

Grant smiled at her warmly, walked to her bedside. "How're you feeling?"

"My gut hurts," she said bluntly. "Getting shot isn't fun. I don't recommend it." She twisted her mouth. "And I bet I'm gonna have a scar, too. Not too good for the ol' career."

"If you need it," Grant told her, "I'll pay for whatever plastic surgery it takes. You saved our lives, Mimi."

"Aw, you'd've found some way out." She looked up at him, wide-eyed. "What'd you do to that place, anyway? You carry in a small nuke? That's what it looked like from where I was."

"Let's talk about that later. I'm just glad you're all right."

"That's what the Doc says." She lifted the sheet, peered down at the bandages covering her abdomen. "I don't think we'll worry about that little scar much, Grant. Think I'll keep it as a souvenir. I think maybe I'm done with the Hollywood star game."

"What'll you do?"

She shrugged. "What you do, more or less. Get a job at one of the ranches. Maybe as a riding instructor. Paula might know somebody who needs somebody."

"I'm quite sure," Grant told her with a smile, "that she does."

"They're gonna chase you out of here soon," Mimi told him. "Think you could slip me into the horse trailer? I don't mind riding there, it wasn't too bad."

"Not a chance. I'm going to drive up to Fillmore, take the

horses back, and then come back for you You can stay at the ranch—I'm speaking for Paula, but I'm sure it'll be okay—until you're on your feet again."

"Can't be too soon," she said. She reached out, touched his hand. "Now," she went on, "you go get some sleep. You hear me? Time you get back there you'll have driven that road four times in less than twenty-four hours."

He squeezed her hand; Andi couldn't watch it, the warmth and closeness between them. "I will. But I won't take forever getting back, either. Okay?"

She smiled. "Okay, Grant. Now go. That boy of yours needs to talk to you."

"Yes," he replied. "I know." He moved away from the bed; together, he and Andi left the room.

"She's something," Andi commented.

"Yes," Grant agreed. "She is."

Andi sighed deeply. "Look," she said, "I hate to ask you for anything else, but—can you buy me a plane ticket back to New York? From right here'll be fine, you can just leave me at the airport. I don't have anything, not a dime, no credit cards, no clothes, everything I had was in Colin's car and it probably got blown up."

"May have," he agreed. "And the answer is, yes, I could."

Her spirits sank even lower. She stared at the floor as they walked along. "Thank you, Grant. I'll send you the money to cover it when I get back, of course."

"I could," he repeated, "but I don't think that's what we should do."

She looked up. "You don't?"

"No. I think you should come back up to Fillmore with me. I may need some help with Todd, he's in for a bad shock when I tell him about Sue, I don't know how I'm going to do that. And besides . . ."

"Besides?"

"Besides." He stopped, gave her a long look. "We got off to a bad start. Let's not let it end there. I don't know what's going to happen with us, but let's get to know each other, Andi. Let's see where it goes."

She fought with her tears. "What about Mimi?"

"Mimi's a friend. Mimi'll stay a friend. Yours and mine."

"I don't know . . . she wants you, Grant, I can tell . . ."

"Well, we'll just have to see, won't we? You game?"

She smiled, wiped her eyes, and resisted her urge to throw her arms around him. Instead, she just touched his hand lightly. "Yes," she answered. "We'll see. Let's go, Grant. Let's go to Fillmore. Let's see."

EPILOGUE

With his hands in his pockets, Jack Delling stood on the hill above the remains of the IIC installation and whistled softly. "Somebody did a job on this place, a real job," he murmured aloud. Down below him, virtually nothing, save for a hole in the ground that once was a basement, remained of the main building, it was simply gone. Half of the residence hall nearby was crushed; the explosions of the liquefied natural gas tanks had leveled all but a small part of the long low building housing the "clean rooms" where integrated circuit chips were once manufactured. Cars, some burnt, some merely smashed, some flipped upside down, were scattered around the parking lot. Helicopters kept coming in and going out, removing the remains of bodies; it had taken some doing for Delling, on short notice, to get clearance for these helicopters to ferry the dead and wounded to a ship lying off Santa Catalina Island, a ship that, once loaded, would steam for Singapore. With any luck, no trace of the SAF would remain here by the time the county inspectors and the newspaper people got in here.

"What a fucking mess," Delling observed. He smiled a little.

"You'd better believe it is," a voice said from beside him. He turned, nodded to Colonel Wilson, the Marine who'd arranged for the perimeter defense. "One hell of a mess."

"Well, your boys weren't very alert," Delling commented. "Our guy, whoever he was, sure didn't have any trouble with them."

Wilson looked over the compound too. "Guy and girl," he corrected. "What the hell did he use, anyway? The two guys they took out on their way in swear he wasn't carrying anything big enough to do this."

Delling shrugged. "Who knows? Frankly, who cares? This sucked, anyway. You don't know, Wilson. If you're lucky you won't, ever. Let me tell you, this sucked."

Wilson regarded him steadily for a moment. "I don't like," he said coolly, "my Marines put in a situation like this. I wasn't told we'd be up against anything like this. We set a soft perimeter to keep civilians out, we weren't expecting a commando raid."

"Neither were we," Delling said succinctly. "Besides, it doesn't matter, does it? You don't have a single casualty. You haven't lost any equipment except for the ammo our commandos neglected to give back."

"I want them found and prosecuted, Delling. They assaulted two Marine M.P.s, and—"

"Forget it. Forget them. I have no leads as to who they might be, and frankly I'd rather pin a medal on them. I know, you don't get it. You won't, either."

Wilson was silent for a moment. "You'll get more of an argument," he said, "the next time you ask for something like this."

"Yeah, well, I wasn't the one asking, was I? I'm like you, Colonel. I get told what to do. I do my job. Sometimes it sucks, but I do it." The sound of another helicopter stopped their conversation; they both watched as it rose up over the rocky outcrop east of the facility, carrying the bodies found there.

"We didn't do it very well this time," Wilson noted. "Our job was to protect this place. It got blown to hell under our noses."

"You win some and you lose some. I'll catch hell for it, yes. I'll get assigned to a desk in D.C. doing shitwork because of it. I'll collect my check and I'll go home and get drunk. Doing shitwork sounds okay to me right now, Colonel, it really does."

"I don't understand you, Jack."

"I know."

The Colonel turned and walked away; Delling kept smiling as he watched the evacuation progress. But he wasn't allowed to stand there long; just minutes later, the pager on his belt beeped. He sighed and descended the hill slowly, down to the facility's garage, relatively undamaged and now a headquarters. He opened the door, went inside.

" 'Morning, Mr. Auan," he said to the gaunt man waiting for him. "I trust you're okay."

"Personally, yes," Auan replied. "I would like an update, Mr. Delling. What problems remain?"

Delling shrugged. "None, that I know of. Everything tying the Singapore government to this mess'll be gone in a couple of hours. In a way the commandos did us a favor by leveling the place, there's no way anything's going to come out about what was going on here—there's no evidence left."

"Have you any idea who the attacker was, or what his motivation was?"

"None. One of life's little mysteries." He grinned.

Auan nodded. "I do not fault you, Mr. Delling," he said.

Delling frowned. "No?"

"No. This could not have been foreseen." He shrugged. "The operation was very profitable; this is merely a setback. Our most significant losses are the deaths of Dr. Michaelson and Mr. Simmons. But the technology is well advanced, we can proceed without Dr. Michaelson's expertise. We will rebuild, of course."

"You will?" Delling was feeling a little sick. "Here?"

Auan smiled thinly. "No, not here. Too much attention will come to this place, not here."

"Yes, I agree," Delling told him, feeling relieved.

"Plans are already in motion," Auan went on, "for a new facility on an island off the South Carolina coast. We will move all our operations there and resume as soon as possible. There is a very high demand for our services, Mr. Delling!"

Delling closed his eyes for a moment. No, he told himself, no. You won't be asked to be in charge. Regardless, you'll be seen as having fucked up here. Shitwork, that's your future, shitwork.

"Our biggest loss," Auan was saying, "was Mr. Simmons. He will be difficult to replace."

"Yeah," Delling said, opening his eyes. "Your recruiter. Wasn't he training some understudies?"

"Yes. But—sadly—all were killed." He smiled his skull-face smile. "We do have, though, an assessment of someone Mr. Simmons believed could do the recruiting reasonably well."

Delling wasn't interested. He wanted to finish his job and get out of here, out of the desert, out of California. "Yes? Anyone I know?"

"Yes. Yourself, Mr. Delling."

He was speechless for a moment. Then—a common gesture for him—he pointed at his chest. "Me?"

"Yes, Mr. Delling, you." He shrugged. "Of course, you may not be interested, it would necessitate your leaving government service. But it would pay very well. And you know what the—shall we say, fringe benefits—of this position are."

He did. He'd talked to Simmons, more than once. Drank with him. Listened to the stories . . .

"Think about it, Mr. Delling," Auan urged. "You are our choice for the position."

No, he snarled at himself, tell him no, tell him you don't want to be part of anything like this, tell him to take his offer and shove it. He started to. He opened his mouth to speak the words.

They wouldn't quite come out.